# The Bronze and the Brimstone

**A HISTORY CAMP STORY**

**Book #2 of
The Verona Trilogy**

## Lory S. Kaufman

**fiction
studio
books**

The Fiction Studio
P.O. Box 4613
Stamford, CT 06907

Cover illustration by Karen Chandler
Cover graphics by Beth McMullen

ISBN-13: 978-1-936558-08-7

Visit our website at www.fictionstudiobooks.com

First Printing: July 2011

Printed in Canada

For my late father,
**Nathan David Kaufman**.
He taught me that taking a shower is
just as quick as a sponge bath at a sink.
It's odd how often I think about
this bit of advice.

# Acknowledgements

Never doubt the positive effect that Fear can have in getting things done. For years I was afraid of dying without achieving my dream of publishing a series of futuristic novels. It was Fear's relentless reminders that kept me seeking out the requisite skills as well as his harping at me to keep the words flowing. On the other hand, Fear must be counterbalanced with Hope. Without the positive effects of Hope cooling and warming my heart at the appropriate times, I would never have been able to stand the relentless reminders of my friend Fear.

Then there were the more flesh and blood influences whose help made my dream a reality. Once again, my daughter, Jessica Suzanne Kaufman, did the line-editing of this book, helping me keep the prose clear and sharp. And, of course, there's Lou Aronica, my editor and publisher. He's the guy whose talent and experience is helping the many authors of his Fiction Studio imprint navigate the crazy twenty-first century publishing business.

Other editors and readers who helped illuminate the typos and content include; fellow clansman Deborah Melman-Clement, the beautiful and brilliant Virginia Bartley, and hawk-eyed Connie Brobeck. As well, thanks to my pal Tom Taylor, author of *Brock's Agent*. Tom is always there to talk writing and marketing and give encouragement.

Finally, I'd like to give a thankful shout out (or maybe up) to a few of the late, great writers of the SF and dystopian genres whose legacies continue to inspire me. Giants like Robert Heinlein, Isaac Asimov, Stanisław Lem, William Golding, John Wyndham and Octavia Butler. Some influenced style, others content, and all imagination. They helped me realize I wanted – needed – to write.

To those
God-like emotions,
To the living and otherwise,
Many thanks.
Lory Kaufman
April 2011

# BOOK ONE

## The Savant

# Chapter 1

"Why don't I feel any pain?"

Hansum stopped pedaling the ancient wooden lathe and looked up from his work. He was making lenses for spectacles, the type used in what was historically called the Middle Ages. He put down the rasp and looked at his red, iron-oxide-stained hands, turning them over and inspecting both their fronts and backs. Doing repetitive manual labor for months had made his hands strong, but it also caused them to have a constant dull ache. But, curiously, not now.

"Why isn't there any pain?" he repeated, flexing his fingers.

Hansum was now eighteen years old, at least by the four-teenth-century calendar used in medieval Italy. He put his hand to his cheek and felt the rough stubble that now covered his lower face. This regular growth of facial hair was a new occurrence. It had surprised him when he caught his reflection in the rain barrel the other day. He peered at himself, finding it hard to believe that the serious, rugged face staring out at him had sported, not long ago, what his mother had called "boyish good looks." His face was now harder, like his hands.

Looking up from his calluses, Hansum swept back an errant strand of his golden-brown pompadour and gazed around the workshop. Though he had spent almost all of his working hours in this place over the last months, everything looked somehow odd. 'Things look more real than real,' he thought.

The workshop was the bottom part of a converted barn, a conversion he had helped with. Ripping out the old, rotten barn boards and replacing them with new heavy planking was hard, heavy work. Digging up the mud and manure floor, replacing it with gravel, then tamping it down, was even more grueling. This demanding work was what had changed him from a spoiled twenty-fourth-century teenager to a responsible young adult. But he was not of the twenty-fourth century anymore. He was trapped in the fourteenth century.

But now, months later, as Hansum gazed about the workshop, he felt comfortable and at ease surrounded by the tools of the early optics business. The room was crowded with several work tables. One was for fitting the finished lenses into bone-and-wire frames to create the spectacles — or discs-for-the-eyes, as they were called. Another table was to assemble the telescopes — or lookers, as they had been named.

Agistino della Cappa, the owner of the shop and Hansum's master, was grinding a lens on the other lathe. He was a big, burly man. When he walked, he lumbered much like a bear, and it always amazed Hansum how the Master's huge fingers could do such delicate work. A mass of hair, both on his head and face, made the older man look wild and unpredictable. But Hansum now knew him as a passionate, animated and fast-tempered man who was equally quick to forgive. Master della Cappa was very devoted to his family and his craft, characteristics the teen from the future had adopted as his own.

Hansum heard a noise and looked up. Fourteen-year-old Lincoln was climbing down the ladder from the barn's loft. He too had been kidnapped and brought back from the twenty-fourth century by a rogue History Camp counselor. The loft was where Lincoln and Hansum slept, curled up in the straw, wrapped only in a wool blanket. Back in the twenty-fourth century, they had their own bedrooms and slept on levitation mattresses. When Lincoln first arrived in the fourteenth century, he had been a slight, out-of-shape boy, sarcastic and confrontational, a prime candidate for "hard-time" History Camp. Now he practically ran Master della Cappa's shop and was boss to two little junior apprentices, nine-year-old Pippo and seven-year-old Benicio. Lincoln got off the ladder and corrected Pippo in where to stand when assisting Master della Cappa, so that glass shards didn't fly into the boy's eyes. Then he went and sat at one of the work tables. Hansum watched him open up the ledger folder, apparently about to make some notations in the Master's accounts. Lincoln looked up at Hansum and smiled. His chipped front tooth was still the only mar in his otherwise perfect set of teeth, very different from the atrocious dental hygiene of most people in Verona at that time. Hansum nodded and smiled back.

The shop door opened and Shamira slipped in waving a large sheet of parchment, covered in drawings. Also from the twenty-fourth century, she worked as the kitchen girl for Master della Cappa and his mentally ill wife, the Signora. Shamira was always sketching, and everyone was in awe of her talent. She had drawn the plans Pan had devised for an advanced lens-grinding lathe. This, along with the plans for the telescope (introduced one hundred and fifty years earlier in this new timeline), was what had given Master della Cappa's little shop such a high profile. It had also made him rich.

"I've finished the drawings for the cannon and saltpeter beds," Shamira announced happily.

"Shhh! Not so loud," Hansum warned, pointing to the Master. But he didn't look up.

"Oh, it's okay," Shamira said, coming over and showing him her work. Shamira was almost sixteen and looked completely Caucasian, an oddity in the twenty-fourth century. She had bright green eyes, and tiny wisps of her auburn hair stuck out from under her veil. The veil was tied under her long hair to keep it from falling forward while she worked in the kitchen or on her drawings. "You should familiarize yourself with these plans before you show them to Podesta della Scalla." Mastino della Scalla, the all-powerful Podesta of Verona and the region, had taken a special interest in these three teens.

"Let me see," Lincoln said.

Shamira went over to Lincoln and laid the drawings on the table in front of him.

A whirlwind of light shot out from the hem of Lincoln's cap. It turned into a small tornado and landed on the gravel floor, instantly turning into a tiny satyr. He was one meter high, with the hairy legs and the hooves of a goat. Atop this was the caricatured torso and head of a grotesque man. His ears were pointed, eyebrows bushy, and two golden, slit-pupiled goat eyes shone out. He had a purple butt and a long tail that flicked back and forth. But for all his grotesqueness, he had the most wonderful, happy smile. Hansum was surprised, but not because he was unfamiliar with this cartoon-like creature. This was Pan, a holographic, artificial intelligence. Pan's gelbrain, his organic computer matrix, lived in a small brass lamp, presently hidden in the hem of Lincoln's cap. Artificial intelligences were ubiquitous in the twenty-fourth century. Everybody had one. There was a law that they could be any shape but human, so Hansum was used to seeing cartoon entities come to life. What surprised Hansum was that Pan was showing himself where people from the fourteenth century could see him.

"Pan, what are you doing?" Hansum whispered urgently. "The Master . . ." but it was too late. Master della Cappa looked up and stared right at Pan. "Oh, oh," Hansum moaned. The Master would most likely think Pan was a demon from Hell. But to his surprise, the Master smiled at Pan and nodded. Pan smiled back and gave the big man a little salute. "What in the world is going on?" Hansum asked aloud. Lincoln and Shamira shrugged. Pan ignored him and ambled over to Pippo and Benicio. The satyr wiggled all ten of his stubby fingers, like he was going to tickle them. The two little boys giggled and ran behind the Master.

"What, this chasing game again?" the Master said in mock anger. "We have work to do!"

"What is going on?" Hansum said, exasperated.

"Hello, my son," a familiar voice said by the shop door. Hansum turned around. If he hadn't had reason to be shocked yet, he did now.

There, floating over the threshold of the shop, was Charlene, Hansum's personal A.I. nanny from the twenty-fourth century. She was a round yellow orb in the shape of a balloon, with a crayon-drawn face that Hansum had designed before he was three. They hadn't seen each other for months, since Hansum had left home. He had been spoiled and contrary then, a hard case, on his way to a two-week stay at an extreme version of History Camp in fourteenth-century Verona, Italy. It was hoped that his time there would scare him straight, allowing him to appreciate the perfected society that people in the twenty-fourth century lived in. That's what History Camps were supposed to do. But tragedy had stranded the three in the real fourteenth-century Verona and they expected never to see their families again. But here was Charlene, floating in front of him.

"How . . .?" Hansum began. Then he turned to the Master. He, along with the rest in the room, was staring at him benignly. Then, as one, everyone turned and went about their business.

"Others are waiting for you on the other side of this door," Charlene said.

"What?" Hansum said, as if in a daze.

"There are two people who really want to see you," she repeated, smiling. "Come."

Hansum took a tentative step, then looked around the room. Everybody was still going about their work. Hansum took several steps toward the open door, feeling like everything was moving in slow motion. It was bright outside, and he squinted as the sun glared off the mud puddles in the alley. As he stepped outside, he heard a distinct 'pop.'

"What the . . ."

As Hansum's front foot touched the mud of the alley, everything changed. The mud turned into long green grass, the alley to a meadow. Instead of the stale and fetid air of Verona in his nostrils, Hansum's next breath brought in clean ocean air. When he looked up and around, he was back in the community of his birthplace, on the banks of the New Hudson River, not far from the Atlantic Ocean, and in the twenty-fourth century. There was his dome-styled home, built from limestone blocks, sticking up, igloo-style, from the ground. There was also the familiar path down to the village's common gardens and grounds. Charlene was levitating quickly toward the house, calling into the open door.

"He's here."

"Hansum!" a woman's voice shouted as she ran out through the doorway.

"Son!" followed a man close behind.

"Mom? Dad?" Hansum said, with continued astonishment. They embraced with fervor, many happy tears pouring out the anxiety and worry of their separation. The next thing Hansum knew, he was sitting between his parents on a bench in the meadow, explaining why he had gone missing the last six months.

"After we disrupted the History Camp recreation of Verona, a time-travelling History Camp counselor named Arimus — he was from the thirty-first century — took us back to the real fourteenth century. But Arimus was killed and we were stuck there. We didn't know how to get home."

"The History Camp counsellor was killed?" his father asked, shocked.

"Brutally," Hansum said. "Murdered."

"But how have you survived?" his mother asked.

"It's been tough, very tough, but we're doing fine now. We're living with a lensmaker and his family. We were lucky to have snuck in a genie from here. His name is Pan."

"A genie? Lucky? How?" Father asked.

"With Pan's encyclopedic knowledge of technology from the future, we're introducing things earlier than they appeared in history before. It's making us rich. And safe."

"Aren't you going to introduce me to your family?" a gravely voice said.

The family looked up. There was Pan, the A.I. satyr, standing, arms on his hairy hips, smiling.

"Pan, how did you get here?" Hansum asked. "How can you be here without your lamp?"

"Oh, I have my ways, Young Master," Pan replied. "But go on with your story."

Hansum told his parents how the three teens finally accepted the fact that they were stuck in the past and had to make the most of it. Pan had shown them how to design an improved lathe and how to construct a crude telescope, which gained them the attention of the rich and powerful Mastino della Scalla, as well as nobles from a rival duchy, the House of Gonzaga. Hansum's parents sat rapt as he told them how the Gonzagas came and, not only stole a sample of the looker, but also kidnapped the Master's daughter, Guilietta.

"Guilietta. What a beautiful name," Hansum's mother said.

"Ah, speaking of beautiful," Pan said. Everyone looked up and there she was, all five feet of her, standing demurely in a flowing white dress, her deep auburn hair fluttering in the breeze. Guilietta's dark Cambrian eyes stood out in contrast to her fair, perfect skin.

"Guilietta!" Hansum shouted, getting up quickly and going to her side. He scooped her up in his arms and hugged her. "How did you . . . ?"

"Later," she whispered.

"Mother, Father, Charlene, this is Guilietta."

"And what else?" Pan asked, his impish grin beaming under his raised bushy eyebrows.

"What?" Hansum said. "Oh, right." He took Guilietta's hand and walked her over to his parents. "Guilietta and I are engaged."

Hansum was surprised at how easily his parents took the news. In the twenty-fourth century, where the average lifespan is one hundred and fifty years, most people didn't get married until their forties. Hansum's mother sat Guilietta down and held her hand as Hansum continued his story. He told how he was part of the mounted and armed search party, chasing after the Gonzaga prince, Feltrino, to retrieve the stolen telescope and save Guilietta. The parents were horror-struck at the brutality and killing their son had participated in and all the danger he was exposed to.

"You genies," Charlene was saying to Pan behind them. "I can't believe you gave people from the fourteenth century technological information from the future. Fixing the timeline has been a big mess for the Time Commission."

"At first I told Master Hansum we shouldn't do it," Pan said, "but he convinced me that it was a matter of survival. Shamira and I worked two long nights on those plans for advanced cannon and black powder. It really was the only thing to convince della Scalla."

"And how did this all work out for you, son?" Hansum's father asked.

"Oh, it worked out just . . ." Hansum began to say, and then he paused. He couldn't remember how it all came out in the end.

"And this whole adventure?" Hansum's mother asked. Her History Camp elder's lapel pin, an hourglass inside an eye, gleamed in the sunlight. "How did it work out for you? Do you get it now?"

"So, is everybody ready for repast?" Hansum's father interrupted. "Carmella has a wonderful meal ready for us."

"Carmella?" Hansum said. "I told you, Dad, her name is Shamira. They gave us all regional Italian names at History..."

"You are so beautiful, Guilietta," Hansum's mother said, now with tears in her eyes. She held Guilietta's face in her hands and kissed it. "My son loves you so much. I wish I could be around to see my grandchildren."

"Mother, what are you talking..."

"I said, a wonderful meal is ready," Hansum's father repeated. But his voice was much gruffer.

# Chapter 2

"Romero, wake up," the Master's voice shouted. "Romero, wake up!" Hansum opened his eyes. Master della Cappa's head was sticking out of the opening to the loft. He was scrubbed clean, his beard was trimmed, and not only did he have his new cap on, but also a wonderful jacket, vest and shirt. *"Buon giorno,* Romero," he said smiling. In the fourteenth century, Hansum was known as Romero Monticelli. "Everyone else is up and dressed. We're waiting on you to eat."

"Buon giorno, Master," Hansum yawned.

"How are your wounds?" Agistino enquired.

"Oh, much better," Hansum groaned, raising himself up. He still felt incredibly sore, and his body — especially his legs and butt — were still badly bruised from the hard riding and fighting the week before.

"Your new clothes are down in the shop. I didn't want to bring them up in the straw. Come, my son, the Podesta's carriage will be here soon."

It all came back to Hansum in a rush. Today was the day he was to visit the palace and complete a contract for a very large order of telescopes. Mastino della Scalla had shown them to his

Germanic allies and they had ordered fifteen hundred of them. Plus, Hansum told Podesta della Scalla that he could give him advanced information on cannons and black powder, again, information furnished by Pan. Shamira had worked on these drawings all week. It flashed in Hansum's mind that all of these happenings, along with his homesickness, were the genesis of his dream.

It wasn't only Hansum and the Master going to the palace. A letter had come earlier in the week from the Podesta's secretary, Baron Nicademo Da Pontremoli. In it, the Baron had written, "During an earlier visit to your shop, I was impressed with young Maruccio's talent for organization and his knowledge of letters. I would like to show him how to organize Master della Cappa's books, to run what will most certainly be a larger business concern."

"Zippy," Lincoln had said, his chest puffing out. Lincoln had been given the regional name Maruccio.

Shamira was also invited to view the Podesta's private art collection. Even the Podesta was impressed with her talent. Shamira had literally squealed when she heard this invitation.

"We must get a new dress for you," Guilietta exclaimed.

"Oh, can I, Master, can I?" Shamira asked, wide-eyed.

"Now I have two daughters to spoil and two daughters who will ruin me," Agistino laughed.

Hansum laughed even harder when he read out the end of the letter. "We shall send a carriage to bring you to the palace after first mass."

"A royal carriage?" the Signora screeched.

"Oh Papa, that's wonderful. Isn't that wonderful, Romero?" Guilietta said, looking at her secret fiancée from across the table.

That was four days earlier. When Hansum entered the house on the morning of the meeting, he was well scrubbed and had his new clothes on. His chausses, the balloon pants, were beige, and the braies, the leggings, were mustard-colored. He was also wearing a green jacket and a new cap. The cap was brown felt with leather piping along the edge. Bruno and Nuca Satore, the tailor couple across the street from them, had created a hidden pocket in the hatband. Hansum said it was for his lucky coin, the first he had earned, but actually, it was to hide Pan. Shamira had customized a small pinhole opening in the fabric for Pan to peek through. All the teens had been taking turns hiding Pan on them so that he could watch what was going on and help them when needed.

"Carmella, you have outdone yourself with your cooking again," the Master said to Shamira. Pan had been coaching her on medieval kitchen arts since they arrived. After all, she was supposed to be the kitchen girl. Shamira found cooking almost as creative as drawing, so she attacked it with fervor.

"You're welcome, Master. Grazie," Shamira said.

"And you don't even look like a kitchen girl in your new blue dress," Guilietta said. "You look beautiful."

"Grazie, Guil," Shamira said. "Come on, let's clean up the dishes before the Podesta's carriage arrives."

"Oh, no, dears," Guilietta's mother said. "Guilietta and I will do that when you've all gone."

The table went silent, all eyes falling upon the Signora. This was truly something new. The Signora hadn't done any work — housework or otherwise — in years. She was, Pan had explained, quite mentally ill. She saw visions of angels, had been totally irrational and demanding, and couldn't be counted on to do anything consistently. She had been a huge, blubbery woman, dirty and crazy, when the teens from the future first arrived. But since then, she had been taking the herbal tea which Arimus, the History Camp counselor from the future, had prescribed. This had cooled her brain considerably. And, since their family business was now doing so well, she was eating healthily and had a happy home environment. She was even going for long walks. Still, the household was happily surprised when she made the offer to clean.

As they all waited outside for the royal carriage to come and take the Master and three teens to the palace, Agistino was surprised by his wife again. She reached up and straightened his lapels, then patted him affectionately on the cheek.

"Never before did we supply royalty," she said. "Soon we'll have a carriage of our own."

"From your mouth to God's ears," Agistino answered. Then he surprised himself by doing something he hadn't done in years. He gave his wife a kiss.

When the royal carriage arrived, a crowd of neighbors gathered to witness the excitement. The carriage driver helped Agistino into the cab, as well as Lincoln, who was holding a large telescope and tripod, a gift for the Podesta. Shamira climbed up with her leather art portfolio under her arm. Hansum got in with the cardboard tube of plans for advanced cannon and black powder.

After waving goodbye to the Signora and Guilietta, everyone settled back for the ride to the palace. The Master sat back and closed his eyes, luxuriating in the experience.

⌛

"I had the strangest dream last night," Hansum said quietly to the two others. As the carriage trundled over the cobblestones, he whispered, "Guilietta, Pan and I were back home with my parents and Charlene. Everything was wonderful and we were all getting along. Then my mother asked me about History Camp and if I got it yet."

Hansum looked at Shamira and then Lincoln. Lincoln smiled a crooked smile and shrugged, like the answer was obvious.

"Well?" Shamira asked.

"Well, what?" Hansum asked.

"Do you?"

Hansum really didn't have to hesitate before answering.

"Oh, I do get it," Hansum said. "I mean, after what we've been through, what other lessons can life teach us?"

"Oh, many things," came the Master's voice. He had come out of his quiet reverie and was listening to what Hansum was saying.

"What's that, Master?" Hansum asked.

"My children, no matter how much a person experiences, there is always more to learn," he said gently. "Life always has surprises for you. And often, you will surprise yourself."

"But what more is there to learn?" Lincoln asked. "We've done pretty good."

"You've all done marvelously," the Master agreed. "But the more you achieve, the more life will ask of you. You will be tested and used by those above you and by those below. Oh, often I think life is learning to just keep a steady course, like a boat, and not get tipped over."

"But you are doing well, Master," Shamira said. "We all are."

"Yes, but the trick in life, I think, is not only to do well, but not to falter. Look outside this grand carriage and see all the people we're passing. Many have done well and some, no doubt, were riding in carriages at one time. Now they are walking again, or crawling. But enough preaching. Today we must focus only on what is in front of us. We must keep our wits about us and gird our loins for battle."

"Battle?" Hansum questioned. "We're going to do business that is mutually beneficial to us and the Podesta."

"Oh, make no mistake, business is battle and kindnesses are often feints meant to deceive."

"Oh, Master, you're being too cynical," Shamira said.

"Am I? Am I? Well, perhaps I am. We shall see. For now," he said, nestling back into the plush pillow-backed seat of the carriage, "I think I will enjoy the ride," and he closed his eyes again.

The teens looked at each other, astonished at the Master's uncharacteristic philosophizing. Then, as one, they all leaned out of the carriage window, looking at the people in the street. Hansum realized that he had become used to the look of fourteenth-century people. There were the haggard, looking like they were in a constant state of being beaten down. Then there were those with a fierce *joie-de-vivre*. As Hansum looked from one person to another, he tried to imagine which had experienced grand successes, only to come crashing down. And then, inexplicably, Hansum's memory jumped back to his old life in the future. He now realized, with clarity, how in his home time, it was always possible to become the best you could be. There was a social safety net and an educational infrastructure to help everybody bring out their potential. But here, those on top sucked as much as they could out of everyone below them, letting underlings rise only to a height which benefited the stronger. When the used became tired or sick, fell into trouble, or just stopped being of use, they were cast aside.

The teens, all dressed in their new best, continued to gawk. Hansum looked forward. He saw a familiar shape — familiar, but dressed in rags more foul than he had seen before. Suddenly, the ugly face at the top of the shape snapped toward Hansum, their eyes locking.

"Ugilino!" Hansum gasped.

"What?" Shamira and Lincoln exclaimed together, both turning to where Hansum was looking.

"Who?" the Master said, opening his eyes and leaning to the window.

As the wagon passed him, they all stared at Ugilino. He was staring back, gap-mouthed. His eyes darted among the four faces. His own face, with its broken and bulbous nose, its cracked and decayed teeth, was frozen in surprise. As he receded into the distance, they finally brought their heads back into the carriage.

"Old Ugilino don't look too good," Lincoln said, his eyebrows knit together.

"I feel awful," Shamira said. "Did you see the way he was dressed, and how he was standing in the middle of that garbage heap?"

"Is that where he gets his food now?" Hansum asked. "That's just not right."

"Right?" the Master said, looking sad. "Who can say what is right? I expected him to come home after we had that fight."

⧗

Ugilino stared at the royal carriage as it trundled down the road. A sinking feeling filled his empty stomach as the faces of his old family faded into the distance. He could still see the Podesta's crest on the back of the vehicle. It was the same coach that had brought the nobles to the house when they came to do business about the lookers. That was when he had lived with the Master and the others.

He had been doing so well, he thought, working as the Master's salesman, hawking the discs for the eyes in the streets. He remembered how he had shared the wonderful meals the kitchen girl,

Carmella, cooked, and how he had slept in his own dry stall in the barn, warm and comfortable in the straw, and even had his own clean blanket. His success had been so great that he even bought new clothes, including a jaunty green hat. Now all of that was gone. He had fallen from grace when he asked for Guilietta's hand in marriage and then got into a fight with Romero. He had even slapped Guilietta hard, and the Master kicked him out. Ugilino knew he could never be forgiven for that, so he didn't return. Now he was back living in the streets, grubbing through garbage heaps for food. Father Lurenzano let him sleep in his cell at the church whenever he wanted to, and he did feed him sometimes, but . . .

"Damn orphans!" Ugilino cursed. He always called the teens orphans. "Now they're riding in a fancy carriage and I'm . . ."

# Chapter 3

As the carriage neared the castle, Hansum adjusted his new cap, putting it on at a rakish angle.

"Can you still see properly, Pan?" Hansum mumbled, looking away from the Master.

*"Yes, Master Hansum. I can see just fine."* Whenever Pan wanted to speak to the teens, he projected a sonic beam into their ears, so only they could hear.

Captain Caesar welcomed them warmly to the palace. He shook Hansum's hand.

"You remember Master della Cappa, I'm sure," Hansum said to the officer. Captain Caesar smiled at the Master, the long scar from his temple to his jaw causing the smile to be crooked. He directed their attention to the roof. A soldier, with one of the telescopes from the Master's shop in his hand, waved. Hansum saw the Master puff up with pride.

The palace door burst open.

"There you are, Signori," a voice called. It was the Baron Nicademo Da Pontremoli, Podesta's personal secretary and cousin. He was a tall, slim man, with a long aquiline nose, long hands, and dark, fine clothing. Though he came across as aloof and haughty to people who didn't know him, he had kind eyes with friends. "The Podesta is entertaining the general and nobles from all over the district. They all wanted to meet the inventor of the looker." He was looking straight at Hansum.

As they walked quickly through the sumptuous palace halls with their marble floors, high ceilings and intricate woodwork, Nicademo said to Shamira, "Ah, Carmella, later when you are given a tour of the palace art collection, I have a surprise for you. A young artist from Florence is visiting. Would you like to meet him?"

"From Florence?"

"Apparently he has worked on many cathedrals."

"Oh, grazie, Baron Da Pontramoli. Grazie," Shamira said, exchanging an excited smile with Hansum.

When they entered the Podesta's planning room, they saw the backs of many nobles and military officers. Hansum, Agistino, Shamira and Lincoln stood behind the Baron, who cleared his throat to get the room's attention. Everyone turned and looked at the new arrivals. Hansum could feel all of their eyes falling on him.

A tall officer, an older man with a trim white beard and steely blue eyes, was holding a looker. When the Podesta turned, his mastiff-like face smiled broadly. He opened his arms and quickly walked toward the group, but it was only Hansum he hugged. A footman came in, carrying the tripod mounted with the large brass telescope.

"What's this? Another present?" the Podesta asked Hansum.

"A new looker, Excellency," Master della Cappa said. "It is mounted on a base to prevent shaking of the image."

Mastino looked surprised and then exuberant, still directing his attention to Hansum.

"Truly? It prevents the image from shaking?" He turned to the white-haired officer. "You see, General? My savant anticipates your need. Romero, this is General Chavelerio." The general nodded, but remained silent. Mastino continued effusively. "The general was just saying his officers comment that faraway images shake when holding the looker in the hand. But you have corrected this before we even told you. Come, come set it up." The footman put the tripod by the window. Hansum adjusted the legs and pointed the looker out the window. Mastino tried it. "*Magnifico*. The device is now so still now it's as if the steeple of San Zeno is right outside my window. I can even see the color of the work-man's hat on the roof."

"My Master is pleased," Hansum answered.

Agistino added, "The house of della Cappa is overjoyed its pa-tron is pleased with the new design, Excellency."

"This tripod is for your office, Excellency," Hansum continued, "where one can stand up straight when using it. My Master's plan is to have much shorter tripods made for resting on parapet walls or on the ground, when one is using the apparatus in situations of danger. Or they still can be used by hand, when appropriate."

Mastino paused, realizing he had been giving his attention to Hansum. 'If the savant wants to continue acting as if it was Agistino who was responsible for the lookers, why should I com-plain?' he thought. Mastino didn't make this concession out of po-liteness. He really didn't care who he insulted or stole ideas from.

"Signori," the Podesta announced to the other nobles in the room, "this is Master Agistino della Cappa, the master lensmak-er in whose little shop the wonderful looker was conceived. But like a woman's belly, where a *bambino* is conceived, your shop I think will soon swell, for you shall make for me thousands of this invention." Mastino saw Hansum smile gratefully as the Master accepted the praise. The nobles in the room politely clapped and nodded at the Master. Mastino continued.

"On the first day of my visit to our German neighbors, I showed our lookers to His Royal Highness, Karl of Luxembourg. He and his generals immediately requested a shipment of one thousand of them. The same happened with Ludwig of Wittelsbach, though I am sorry to say, they ordered only five hundred," he added as a joke. The room laughed. "Today, Master della Cappa comes to sign a contract for this commission, and for that I welcome him." More polite applause.

"And what about the cannon?" one of the nobles asked. "The original reason you went to the Germans was to observe their new cannon."

Mastino furrowed his brow, and put a finger to his lips. "We'll talk more of that in private, but yes, my new allies have agreed to share their secrets of a better cannon and black powder."

⏳

*"Now is the time to show the new plans,"* Pan whispered.

"Excellency," Hansum began, "you may remember I mentioned I would make some plans of what I knew about cannon and powder."

"Yes, Romero, I remember that well." Mastino looked at Hansum, his dark eyes full of anticipation. Hansum held up the cardboard tube.

"I have them here, Excellency. Would you care to view them?"

Pan watched the exchange closely, thinking how it would be hard for Hansum to say something else that could pique Mastino's interest more.

"Si, of course," Mastino said. "Anything you have to show me, of course I will look." He motioned to an open space on the large table.

Hansum strode over to the room's massive planning table and removed the dozen pieces of parchment Shamira and Pan had worked on. He took some of the objects on the table and placed them at the corners of the large drawings, then he looked at the Podesta and smiled. Mastino put on the bifocals Pan had designed and had Hansum show Master della Cappa how to make. Then the Podesta, along with the general and other nobles, stepped forward. The Podesta scanned the first page and caught his breath. He flipped a page, then another, and another. General Chavelerio exclaimed, "My God!" and the Podesta shot up a hand for quiet. Then he turned the sheet he was viewing and placed it face down, hiding all the other pages. There was an enigmatic look on the Podesta's face. He looked at each person in the room, stopping at Agistino.

"Are you aware of these drawings?"

The look on the Master lensmaker's face was one a man makes when he's afraid to give the wrong answer.

"I thought they were more drawings of the improved lathe, Excellency. I am sorry if my apprentice overstepped . . ."

Mastino's hand shot up again. He appeared deep in thought.

"Nicademo, take della Cappa and the other two into the other room," Mastino said. "Review with him the details for the order of lookers and — whatever else for the others. All of you," he said, addressing the nobles and military men, "leave me. I wish to speak with Signor Romero — alone."

After murmurs and looks from the exiting crowd, Hansum was left alone with Mastino. Alone, except for Pan. The Podesta stared at Hansum in the oddest of ways. Then, after a prolonged silence, he turned over the pages he had hidden from the others. He studied them at length, occasionally looking up at Hansum with a look of wonder and confusion. He stopped often and asked Hansum questions. After the answer, which Pan helped him with, Mastino looked even more confused. Finally, a good hour later, he sat down in a large armchair and stared into space. The implications of what he had just viewed seemed to be spinning around in his creative and devious mind. Mastino was not only shown new inventions, but also processes that should not have come about for another two and three hundred years. He got up, poured himself a large goblet of wine and took a swallow. And then he sat down again, wide-eyed.

"Romero, a cannon like a this has never been built," he finally said. "Cannon powder like this, never made. How do you know?"

*"Say it exactly as we rehearsed,"* Pan whispered into Hansum's ear. Pan had predicted they would be on shaky ground when they were asked where the ideas had come from. He had warned Hansum that they would have to say something concrete sounding, for giving imprecise answers to a man like Mastino wouldn't wash. Hansum would have to lie, but the lie they manufactured would have to be a big one.

"My Lord, the knowledge is not new. It is knowledge that has been known but not shared."

"Known? Known by whom?"

"Egypt, my Lord. The ancient knowledge of the priests of Egypt. Knowledge so powerful that it could explode the world. It was hidden there as the men of Odysseus were hidden under the belly of the Cyclops's sheep."

Pan cringed in his lamp. *"Young Master, no ad-libbing, pleeee-ase!"* Pan begged. *"Get back on script."*

"An uncle of mine was a merchant of spices and herbs. He was also something of a Greek scholar. Some years back, he found himself in northern Egypt by accident of a storm. He told me he came upon a library in the hands of illiterate thieves. They had plundered a secret monastery and taken the parchments as booty. They did not know what they had. My uncle brought the documents back to this land and translated them. They were the writings with which he taught me to read. This is how I know these things."

The Podesta was excited with anticipation. "And these documents now? And your uncle?"

"He is dead and they are burnt. Destroyed."

"Dead? Destroyed? How is this?"

"He died of a morbid growth in the brain, I am told. And when he knew he was soon to join God, he had the library destroyed by fire."

"But why?"

"He was a man of peace. It pained him to see how the world around him was always at odds with itself. He began to understand the power of the documents and why the ancients had cloistered the knowledge. As he became ill, and supposedly mad, he forbade me to continue my studies. Then one day I came to his home and found the library in ashes and him upon his deathbed. He mentioned something about Alexandria."

"The Library of Alexandria? You were reading texts from the Library of Alexander? Their value would have been beyond price."

"I do not know, my Lord. My uncle has been dead these two years. I only know the knowledge that is in my memory. Thank God I have a good memory. I look at a page of a book and it stays in my memory, like a painting. I don't even have to read the page when I look at it. I can read it *in* my memory."

"I have heard of this ability. A painted memory. Praise to the Lord for that."

A knock came at the Podesta's door. Nicademo leaned into the room. "Della Cappa and I have concluded our business. The boy is working with my clerk to learn double entry ledgers. The girl is still looking at art and talking with that other artist."

"I am not finished with Signor Romero," Mastino answered. "Send the lensmaker home with the others and say that Romero will follow. Then come back here. I want you to see this." When Nicademo returned, the Podesta showed him the drawings. He studied them intently for some time, and then looked up seriously.

"This black powder is an impossible formula," Nicademo said.

"How so?" the Podesta asked.

"The mixing of its elements. It shows the formula as seventy-five parts saltpeter, fourteen parts brimstone and eleven parts powder of charred coal. Our black powder, and even the Germans', is equal parts of the same three ingredients. And it is hard for us to obtain enough saltpeter for present use. This proposes we use over seven-fold more of it per portion?"

The Podesta turned to Hansum. "What say you to this, Romero? It is one thing to state you need such and such to do a great thing, but if that thing is not available, what is the point? For if horses were wishes, beggars would be riding."

"Just so, Excellency," Hansum answered. He reached into his new coat and took out one of the pamphlets Shamira had made. It had a ribbon around it, which Guilietta had given him. "Excellencies, here is the recipe with which you can make unlimited amounts of saltpeter quickly." Pan had explained how black powder was made from three substances: saltpeter, or potassium nitrate; brimstone, or sulfur; and carbon, in the form of charcoal. The key substance, saltpeter, originally came from cave scrapings of bat guano or from old, undisturbed stables, where the crystals formed naturally over long periods of time. Pan took information for mass production of it from an 1862 document, *Instructions for the Manufacture of Saltpeter*, by Joseph LeConte. It was written during what was known as the American Civil War. So, the knowledge that helped create the bloodiest of all civil wars in history was being offered to a warlord on a different continent some six hundred years earlier.

The Podesta took the pamphlet from Hansum, removed the ribbon and scanned it briefly. Then he smiled and then handed it to his secretary.

"Will this content you, Nicademo?"

All three studied the rest of the documents for some time. There were two production methods for the final powder. One showed a small-scale method, with mortar and pestle. This wasn't much different from what was done during their time, except for the percentage mixture. Then there was a large-scale method, showing the use of water wheels and a large machine called an incorporating mill. When they got to the final pages, they were looking at the new cannon design. Pan noted how the noblemen's pupils opened wider, their heart rates and breathing grew faster. They were working hard to remain calm in front of Hansum.

Nicademo said, "Excellency, while all of this is very interesting, some other matters need attention. May we speak privately and then continue with the young signor?"

The Podesta gave Hansum an apologetic look. "Would you mind, my boy? Go to the reception room and we will call you back as soon as we can."

*"Take off your hat and leave it here, so I can hear what they're talking about,"* Pan whispered to Hansum.

Hansum took off his cap with a flourish, as if he were being gallant, and put it on the table. "Of course, Excellency. I shall wait in the other room."

# Chapter 4

Pan's hairy eyebrows knit with worry as he listened to the conversation between Mastino and Nicademo.

"These designs for cannon, cousin, they are astounding," Nicademo began. "And if these powders are what they seem, pphht, down go the fortifications of the Gonzaga, down fall the turrets of Venice. Scattered are the knights of the Este."

"And from my conversations with Ludwig and Karl the other week, if we make an alliance with them and supply, nay, sell them these new cannon and powder, we will be the rulers of Europe in ten years."

"What of the boy? The savant?"

"Very strange. One looks in his eyes and sees something very different from what you would expect. I don't know what to make of it."

"I guess that's what being a savant is, seeing the world differently."

"Who knows what other miracles he will present us. We must keep him close. I shall entice him."

"He seems very devoted to his master."

"Yes. It is a sweet trait, but no matter. He must serve my needs. First thing, get della Cappa a new journeyman lensmaker from Florence. I want Romero with us immediately. He must oversee the production of this powder and cannon. But the old drunk will need help to make the lookers and we don't want him to fail."

"Can we not have the lookers made in Florence?"

"That will come soon enough. But let's give it a year, keeping this secret close. It will take that much time for samples of the lookers to get smuggled into Florence for copying. And besides," he laughed, "the Germans are paying us twice as much for the lookers as we're giving della Cappa."

"You're getting two hundred denarii for each of the fifteen hundred we've just ordered?"

"Si."

"But because of the bigger order, I just renegotiated a better price. We're now paying eighty-five."

"What a team we make, Nicademo. Such fun. Maybe young Romero will join our team."

"I'll leave that to you, cousin."

"Send Romero back in. I shall speak to him kindly. Let's see if I can net this fish."

"Si, Mastino. I'll write our Florentine ambassador today about a craftsman."

"Oh, and tell the others to come in when I've sent Romero off. They have much to prepare for. The continent can be ours."

⧗

"Romero, Romero," Pan heard the Podesta coo sweetly as Hansum re-entered the planning room, "I am sorry to make you wait. Come. Enough of plans for things. Let us sit and talk about plans for people."

"Si, Excellency. Ah, there's my cap. I left it on your table."

"Not to worry, my boy." Before Hansum could retrieve his hat, the Podesta put his arm around Hansum's shoulder and walked him over to a much smaller table with several comfortable chairs by it.

"But my cap, Signor."

"It's warm in here. You don't need it. Make yourself at home. Sit."

"As you wish, Excellency." Pan grimaced as Hansum sat down on a chair directly in his view. Hansum was staring right into his eyes, a look of subdued panic on his face. He was about to discuss important topics without the benefit of Pan's knowledge of the Podesta's scheme. Mastino came into view, sitting in a chair with his back to Pan. He saw Hansum look away from the hat and smile at the Podesta.

"Would you like some refreshment, Romero?" Mastino asked.

"Grazie, no, Excellency. There were some pears in a bowl in the other room. I had one."

"It's nice to have good food all the time, is it not? As an orphan, you must have seen some hungry times."

"Just for a short period, Excellency. And Master della Cappa feeds his apprentices as well as he feeds himself."

"Truly? Such kindness must inspire a great love from his workers."

"The Master is very strict. But he is also a very good man."

"And you are loyal to him. You love him."

"I owe him everything. He took me in."

"Just so. And you've repaid his kindness by showing him the invention of the lookers. And taken no credit for it. It will make your master a wealthy man."

Pan saw Hansum freeze. The teen obviously didn't know how to respond. Pan was equally frustrated. The imp clenched his holographic teeth. Mastino seemed to notice Hansum shifting nervously in his chair.

"Not to worry, dear boy. Not to worry. We respect your master as a fine craftsman, but it is you who is the savant, no?"

"I'm sorry, Excellency. You've used that word before, but I'm not really sure what it means."

"A savant. A *geniuso*. A person of great talent in some way. Mathematics, music, or a builder of churches. A sculptor or artist. Inventions," he said, pointing a finger at Hansum. "And every savant must have a patron. Romero, you are a savant, I am a patron. I come from a family of patrons. Over the years we have supported painters and builders and even writers. Was it not my Uncle Cangrande who supported the great Dante? Dante was so grateful he even mentioned my uncle in *The Divine Comedy*. I could be your patron."

"I have Master della Cappa," Hansum said.

The Podesta laughed. "No, Romero. You brought these plans to me. To me. Why? Because you knew Master della Cappa could do nothing with them. He didn't even know you were going to show them to me."

"I am sorry for my bad manners to Master della Cappa. I must have embarrassed him."

"Never be sorry for the things you must do, Romero. Things that must be done always help some and hurt others. The men who make these decisions must never waste their time being sorry. And I am happy you brought them to me."

"Then I'm glad too, Excellency," Hansum said tentatively. Pan was close to bursting out of his lamp, wanting to warn Hansum of this man's duplicity.

"Romero, tell me, do you trust me?"

Pan couldn't hold his place any longer. He must warn Hansum. Since the Podesta's back was to Hansum's cap, Pan chanced it and popped out, one-quarter size, onto the table. He pantomimed to Hansum, who was surprised to see him exposed, but tried to not stare.

"No need to act startled, Romero. It is an honest question. Do you trust me?"

"Excellency, you have been very kind to me and my master. Our whole household owes you a debt. How can I not trust you?"

"Si, your master's house has done well with my patronage. And it can do better. But can you be loyal to me, Romero? And only me?" Pan nodded up and down ferociously. Since he knew that Mastino was trying to play Hansum, the best thing to do was agree with everything he said.

Hansum looked over a bit too indiscreetly at Pan. Mastino turned to see what Hansum was looking at. Pan, sensing the Podesta's head turn, instantly popped out of sight. Mastino, obviously misconstruing Hansum's actions, stood up and went to the drawings.

"Don't be concerned about your drawings and inventions. Your loyalty will ensure your position and, I promise you, your wealth. Now, Romero, I ask you again. Can you be loyal only to me?"

Hansum paused and Pan grimaced, holding his holographic breath, waiting to hear the youth's response.

"You can count on me for my unmeasured loyalty, Excellency," Hansum said finally.

Pan collapsed in his lamp, relieved. Mastino broke out with an incredible smile. He rushed over to Hansum and pulled him up out of his chair. He hugged him, kissed him on both cheeks and shook him victoriously.

"That's my boy. That's my wonderful boy. Let us toast to our new position of patron and savant. Come." They walked over to a side table with wine decanters and goblets. Mastino poured two glasses. They drank and toasted. Mastino was animated, Hansum, quite reserved. The Podesta looked puzzled. Then he nodded, as if he knew what the problem was. He reached into a strongbox on the sideboard, pulling out two small pouches of coins. He thrust one at Hansum.

"A young man with a future must have spending money. Here, my boy, here. Spend it very unwisely." Hansum took the pouch, shook it a little and then untied the strings. It was full of denarii.

"I don't know what to say, Excellency," Hansum said.

"You have already said it, Romero. You are loyal to me and my city. But say more of the right things today, and you will receive these." Mastino undid the pull-strings of the second pouch and pushed it halfway across the table to Hansum. As he did, gold florins spilled out.

A long pause ensued. The only sound were the coins tinkling on the table.

"That's a lot of money, Excellency."

"Oh, just a start for the man who brought lookers, cannon and black powder to me. Have you ever held one of these, Romero?" He picked up a florin and pitched it to Hansum, who caught it in one hand.

"No, Excellency. Gold coins are not common from where I come from," he said ironically.

"Well, one lives with little and dies with nothing, eh? Life can be miserable. It's good to have lots of these to make us comfortable in our misery." Hansum smiled and nodded with a small laugh. Mastino continued. "Romero, I can make it so you will be very comfortable," he said more seriously.

"I understand that, Excellency. But what of the Master?"

"With one rear end, you can't be at two circuses. A man cannot serve two masters."

"I understand, Signor. It's just difficult to think of myself not in my master's house."

"Romero, look around you. You compare your master's house with this?" Pan held his breath, worried at the boy's answer.

"I said it was difficult, Excellency. Not impossible." Pan breathed another sigh of relief.

The Podesta laughed. Then he looked Hansum in the eye and smiled. The smile turned to a look of seriousness, to convey the importance of what he was about to utter.

"Romero, I have a daughter."

*"Holy Aphrodite!"* Pan shrieked to himself. *"This is a gambit I had not foreseen."*

"A daughter?" Hansum repeated.

"Si, Romero, a lovely girl. She even reads and has many interests, like you. She is intelligent and interesting. Her name is Beatrice."

"I see, Your Excellency."

The Podesta seemed to be searching Hansum's eyes for a response, obviously puzzled by the young man's low-key reactions. How often is an orphan offered the hand of a princess, his look seemed to be asking. Pan was aware how history would know Beatrice della Scalla as His Majesty George I's eighth grandmother, the twelfth grandmother of Louis the XVII, Prime Minister

Churchill's seventeenth grandmother, Lady Diana's eighteenth Grand Mama, and ancestor to many more notable kings and queens of the twenty-first and twenty-second centuries.

"Do you not understand what I am saying to you?" Mastino asked.

"I believe you are wishing to introduce me to your daughter, Excellency."

*"Say yes!"* Pan screamed in his lamp. *"Don't tell him about Guilietta! Don't tell him!"*

"That is correct, young man. I think you have promise. More promise than any young prince I have considered for her till now."

"You are very kind, Excellency. I don't know what to say."

A pause. "Say what is on your mind."

*"Don't tell him about Guilietta!"*

"It is good that this subject has come up. Master della Cappa said I couldn't proceed without your permission."

"And what would that be about, Romero?"

*"Not a word, fool!"*

"I have asked the Master for his daughter's hand in marriage. We are in love."

*"It's Pompei all over again!"* Pan cried, throwing his hands over his head.

Mastino della Scalla was silent for some moments. Then he smiled. But Pan could see it wasn't the same genuine smile of a minute ago. This was his business smile.

"I see," Mastino said.

"I'm more than flattered, though," Hansum said.

"I'm glad of that, at least."

"I'm sure your daughter's a wonderful girl."

"As I'm sure Mistress della Cappa is."

"Oh, she is wonderful, Excellency. A wonderful girl," he said, as if he were expecting his personal enthusiasm to be infectious.

Mastino smiled again. Pan sat in his lamp, his holographic head in his hands.

"Well," the Podesta said, clapping his hands, "it's time to get other work done. Ah, Romero, here's your cap."

"Si, of course," Hansum said, acting somewhat surprised that the meeting was being cut short. He took his cap.

"You're forgetting something," Mastino said. He went to the table they had been sitting at. "Don't forget your bag of denarii. And this one florin too. Keep it, Romero, and every time you look at its shiny surface, think of the full bag of them, and how that could be only one bag of many." Pan watched Mastino's face carefully as Hansum was ushered from the planning room. He was smiling sincerely at the boy, but there was that something else in his eyes. Mastino patted Hansum on the shoulder and repeated, "The first of many more," then he waved to a footman, whispered in his ear, and closed the door behind him.

Mastino stood by the door by himself now. The sincere smile faded. He was perplexed. Then he walked back to the planning table and studied the drawings of the watermill device that could manufacture unimaginable amounts of black powder per year. The study door opened again and Nicademo stuck his head in.

"Shall I call in the general and others?"

"In a moment, cousin. Look at this again. Who could have imagined such a thing? It's as if God spoke to him and gave him these secrets. And then he just gives it to us and I have to force money on him. It just falls into our laps."

"Well, it is a sign of great wisdom to profit from what God sends others," Nicademo said. "And what of your aim to make him one of us?"

"I offered him Beatrice."

"Really? So there's to be a wedding? He shall be cousin to me too? Mastino, why are you so sullen?"

"He turned me down. He said he was to marry the lensmaker's daughter."

"What? I shall have his head on a pike for such an insult to our family."

"If his severed head could tell us miracles such as this, I would let you. No, a father's wounded pride should not let me lose such a brilliant head as his."

"Cousin, let us proceed with these plans for cannon and powder and see where providence takes us. Brilliant young men are still young and often want to touch with their three hands what their two eyes see. But older, wiser heads must rule. I've sat with his master and, though an old drunk, he's no fool. A word about your wishes and he will make the youngsters comply. I'm sure of it."

"Always my wisest advisor, Nicademo. So many have died in my service and I missed not a wink of sleep. But a slight to my daughter and I'm . . . I'm . . ."

"A father."

# Chapter 5

Pan didn't give Hansum a moment's peace on the way home. He chastised the boy the whole way. And it was a long chastisement as Hansum had been left to walk. The Podesta, with a word to the servant, had cancelled Hansum's ride in the royal carriage.

*"Could you be more of a fool? Could you not think with your brain instead of your private parts? The Podesta was offering you his daughter!"*

"But he acted okay with it. He even said Guilietta was a wonderful girl."

*"You're still thinking with the wrong body part."*

"I'm not!" Hansum shouted, stopping in the middle of the Piazza Bra and stomping his foot. "Maybe with my heart, but not my . . ." Townsfolk were looking at him as if he were mad. He skulked off in silence.

Master della Cappa wasn't any more sympathetic. Pan watched Agistino's eyes go wide with horror as Hansum told him what had happened.

"From riches to the rack," Agistino gasped, putting a hand to his head. "From rapture to ruin!" Then his eyes went steely. "Romero, I rescind my approval for you to wed my daughter," he said sternly.

"But you can't do that!" Hansum said with equal force.

"I'm the master and I must make the decisions to keep this household alive."

"That's selfish, Master. What of Guilietta's and my feelings?"

"You think I do this for myself? The head of a household must do what is right for all. And right is what puts food in your mouth, a roof that doesn't leak over your head and coins here." He put his big, empty hand under Hansum's nose. Hansum took the pouch of coins the Podesta had given him and plunked it into the Master's palm.

"What's this?"

"A bag of denarii. The Podesta gave it to me. You keep it. I'll keep Guilietta."

"How dare you!" Now the Master really seemed angry. "My daughter for a bag of denarii?" He shoved the bag hard into Hansum's chest, letting it fall back down into the boy's tunic. "You not only insult me, but you miss the point."

"You want more? I'll get you gold. Plenty of gold."

"How?" Agistino shouted. "You have insulted the Podesta!" The Master slapped Hansum on the side of his head. Not hard, but hard enough to get his attention. His cap was knocked off. Hansum left it on the floor.

"No, Master," Hansum said. "The Podesta was fine with it. Besides, I am too valuable to him. I gave him inventions that will make him more powerful than ever."

"And when you are of no use to him anymore?"

"I have many more things to offer. You have no idea."

Just then Guilietta and Shamira came into the house. Both girls were smiling broadly.

"What is all the shouting?" Guilietta asked. "We can hear you from the street."

"How was the meeting at the palace?" Shamira enquired.

"This fool! The Podesta offered him Princess Beatrice's hand and he turned him down." Pan watched Guilietta's smile vanish.

"But Romero and I are to be married," she said, amazed.

"Master, I told you, the Podesta wasn't angry when I told him about Guilietta," Hansum insisted.

"He gave you his blessing?" Agistino asked.

"Si, well . . . no, not exactly, I guess."

"Are both of you fools?" Agistino asked. "What am I saying? Of course you are. The Podesta will be duplicitous on this matter, no matter what he said today. He will get what he wills in the end.

That is the way of the world. And if you have as much to offer as you say, you must be of his house. That is why he offers you this suit. He will not share you."

"I don't get it," Shamira said. "The Podesta would give his daughter to a man she never met?"

"Of course," shouted an exasperated Master. "Are you not of this world? That's what daughters are for."

"But you promised," Guilietta argued. "And I've already told Father Lurenzano."

"I told you to say nothing of this to anyone."

"He's a priest."

Agistino held up his big red finger. And when he did this, everyone knew he was finished talking.

"Not another word. Not another word from any of you. Daughter, you will go to the priest and tell him you spoke too early. Better yet, say nothing. Who remembers what a young girl prattles on about?"

"What's going on down there? What's all the shouting?" It was the Signora, up from her second afternoon nap.

"Can I get no peace?" the Master cried. "Go back to bed, wife."

"I don't want to sleep."

"I can't take it anymore," Agistino shouted. "I'm going to the shop. Carmella, come with me and bring your pen and paper. Da Pontremoli says I should do a contract with the bronze caster. You will write it up for me while I work. And no supper for anyone. We've wasted the day and no lenses have been made. We work late."

"Si, Master," Shamira said, rushing to a shelf and grabbing her portfolio.

"And you two, I tell you again," he said, glaring at his daughter and Hansum, "I rescind my approval of your marriage. It is not to be!"

Guilietta burst into tears and ran out the door, turning toward the city. A hatless Hansum followed and, although he heard the Master shouting at him to stop, he kept on. The Master grunted in disgust and stomped out of the house, turning toward the shop, Shamira close behind.

The Signora trundled down the rest of the steps and noticed Hansum's cap lying in the straw. She picked it up and flicked off the strands of straw sticking to it.

"Everybody is acting quite strange," she said, staring, unknowingly, right into Pan's eyes. "Maybe they should drink some of my tea."

⧗

"Guilietta, Guilietta, stop!" Hansum shouted as he chased his distraught lover. Guilietta slowed to a quick walk. Catching up to her and keeping pace, Hansum asked, "Why did you run away, Guilietta? Running away solves nothing."

"I could not stand it there," she said, furious. Hansum had never seen Guilietta angry.

"But where are you going, my love?"

"I don't know. Maybe I'll throw myself off the Navi Bridge."

"Guilietta, don't talk like that." Guilietta stopped quickly and faced Hansum. "Everything will be all right. It will all work out."

"How will they work out? You marry the Podesta's daughter and then my father gives me to some old butcher or miller?"

"I don't know. But I tell you, nothing will come out of you jumping off a bridge," he said.

"Fat lot you care! Being offered the Podesta's Beatrice."

"Guilietta, it wasn't my idea. And I do care, my love. If anything ever happened to you, I don't know what I would do. I'd jump off that bridge right behind you."

"You would?" she squeaked, her eyes welling up with more tears.

"Guilietta, I love you." The two embraced in the streets, then kissed. People passed, glancing at the two. Several little children laughed and danced around them, making kissing sounds.

Finally, Hansum said, "Come. Let's go home and talk to your father."

"No," Guilietta said. "I know my father." She took Hansum's hand and led him back in the direction they had come from. But at the first side street, Guilietta turned left, pulling Hansum with her.

"Where are we going?" Hansum asked. Guilietta didn't answer as she strode forth purposefully. "Guilietta, where are we going?"

"To see Father Lurenzano."

"Why?"

"To get married."

# Chapter 6

There was a knock on Father Lurenzano's cell door. For a man of just over thirty, he had more of his teeth left than most. He only had one which was dead and black, a front tooth. This good luck was probably because he was the youngest of three sons from a fairly well-off family. After his oldest brother inherited the family land and the other went to the army, he was given to the Church. But being from a moneyed home had given him a taste for some luxuries. The Father stopped what he was doing and shouted his reply.

"Why are you disturbing me? I'm in prayer."

"Visitors, Father," a monk replied through the door. "The lens-maker's daughter and a young man."

The priest already had a visitor in his room. The visitor looked back at the priest.

"Guilietta and Romero!" he croaked.

"Peace, Ugilino," the priest whispered. Then Lurenzano shouted to the monk on the other side of the door, "Have them wait in the rectory, Brother Sandino. Bring them to me at the bottom of the hour."

"Si, Father," the monk answered.

"Go for a walk," Father Lurenzano said to Ugilino.

"You're going to see them?"

"I minister to everyone who needs my guidance. Have I not helped you in your prayers and penance?"

Ugilino scowled. "I've been on my knees and suffered," he murmured.

When Ugilino left the priest's cell, he didn't go wander the streets. The cell next to Lurenzano's was unoccupied, so he quietly slipped into it and sat in the dark. He planned to go back in the hallway and eavesdrop on the conversation through the door. While sitting in the dark, Ugilino noticed a dull glow of light coming through a chink in the wall. He went over and saw a small opening. By pressing close to it, Ugilino could see and hear into Father Lurenzano's cell. The priest was straightening his robes and humming a chant. After some time, Ugilino heard a knock at Lurenzano's door.

"Enter, my children," the priest called. "Ah, lovely Guilietta and the handsome Romero. Welcome." Ugilino saw the two teenagers come in. They bowed and crossed themselves.

"Thank you for seeing us, Father," Guilietta said.

"My love for your family is great," the priest said. "I have helped your father in business and he has been good to me with alms, so how can I refuse his daughter? Is your visit about arrangements for the marriage between you and the fine Romero?"

Ugilino was shocked to hear that the priest knew of that.

"Si, Father. It is."

"It is a late hour to visit on such matters. Could it not wait till tomorrow, or when we can sit with the rest of your family? Making these arrangements gives joy to parents."

"My father does not know we are here," Guilietta said plainly.

"I see," Lurenzano said.

"Holy Father," Guilietta continued, "my father still approves of Romero and agrees to our marriage. But we can no longer wait till spring."

Ugilino gripped the bricks with his fingernails. To hear that the Master had agreed to Romero marrying Guilietta was another slap in his face.

"You can no longer wait till spring?" the priest asked. "Why is that?"

Guilietta paused and looked to the ground. "Because of our passions, Holy Father."

"Ah. So, you have broken God's law and fornicated before the holy union of marriage," Father Lurenzano surmised.

"Oh no, Father. We have prayed and found the strength to resist."

"What then is the problem, my children?"

"We cannot contain ourselves much longer," Guilietta said. "And I cannot bear the thought that my father would know I have sinned, even in my mind. I am his only child, and a female. My father thinks of me as virtuous and above the temptations of the world. I do not wish to burden him with my shame."

"But is your father not a worldly man who has known trouble and seen the weaknesses in men's souls?"

"Si, my father is worldly and experienced. He has sinned and with great effort is redeeming himself. It is therefore our wish not to add to his burden. If we could enter in the holy bonds of matrimony — secretly — then we can fulfill our desires. In the spring, when my father says we may publish our banns, we'll have another, more public, marriage."

The priest paused and looked thoughtful. "The young lady does all the talking. Do you have naught to add, Romero?"

"My care is for the Master too. Though I have earned my keep and know he loves me like the son I wish to be, I don't want to lose his trust."

"Such simple male honesty is a joy to hear. No womanly scheming. And what of your ardor? Will you burst into flames too if your passion is not quenched?"

"Father, I feel the same as Guilietta," Hansum answered.

An angry Ugilino banged his fist on the wall, but flesh pounding on thick stone caused no sound. The father sighed a little, then smiled.

"So it is with all females of our kind, as it was with the first mother, Eve, tempting man from righteousness."

"Righteous Father," Guilietta implored, acting desperate, "if we cannot persuade you to do this thing for us, as God is my witness, we shall find a place this very night . . ."

Ugilino couldn't believe his ears. The sweet, virginal Guilietta he had known since childhood was acting like a wanton.

"No, no, my child," the priest interrupted reassuringly. "All is well. All is well. We wouldn't want you fornicating in the alleys like common dogs and cats, would we? I see no harm in what you propose, just a little deception for thy father's own well-being. After all, a sin that's hidden is already half forgiven. Why, you are actually being true to the faith in your avoidance of what cannot be undone. As you said, you have already sinned in your hearts. And is not the heart of our beautiful Christianity forgiveness and salvation? And are you not creating your own salvation even before you are committing your sin? And is it not in scripture that the Lord truly helps those who help themselves?" As the priest spouted his fancy, convoluted phrases, Ugilino saw Hansum look very serious, like he really didn't like Father Lurenzano. At this moment, neither did Ugilino.

"All you say, good Father, cannot be denied," Guilietta replied. "Is it not true, my love?"

"Yeah, sure," Hansum answered flatly.

"Quite so," Father Lurenzano said. "Quite so. Now, for this act of compassion by the Church, you shall be in its debt."

"Si, we shall be in your debt, Father," Guilietta agreed.

"No, not my debt," the priest said, "the Church's. Can you pay the Church fees for this service?"

"Money?" Guilietta asked, surprised and now anxious.

"One must pay to Caesar what is Caesar's. Money is the coin of that realm, not prayers and devotions. The bricks of this church do not go up of their own accord."

"There's no problem on that account, Father," Hansum said. "What is the fee for your — excuse me, for the Church's services?"

"It is true what Master della Cappa says about you, Romero. You do have the makings of a master *and* a merchant." Hansum did not reply. He was just staring straight and strong into Father Lurenzano's eyes. "Two denarii," the priest finally said. Hansum reached into his tunic and pulled out the bag of coins the Podesta had given him. The priest's eyes bulged at the sight of the sack. Ugilino, upon seeing it, gasped loudly. The priest heard the sound and commented offhandedly, "Rats, I think. Romero, where did you get such a wonderful cache?"

Hansum paused before he spoke. "My Master has been very generous," he said. "I designed a new instrument for lenses, which Master della Cappa has sold to the Podesta. I am given a commission on each of these items he sells." Hot tears came to Ugilino's eyes.

"So, you see," Guilietta added to the fabrication, "my father wants my new husband to have the means to keep a wife." Tears ran down the ugly apprentice's face.

"A wise father and father-in-law." Lurenzano smiled, prettily. But Ugilino knew him better. He was probably angry that he hadn't asked for more money.

Ugilino had heard enough. He collapsed to the floor. He felt completely betrayed by everyone he knew. He was furious, furious at all the world. The Master had never given him that much money. And if it hadn't been for Ugilino stealing back the repossessed lathes and supplies when Master della Cappa went bankrupt, the Master wouldn't even be in business now. And when those orphans showed up and the Master saw they could learn to make lenses better than Ugilino, that's when his life started to fall apart. Now, here was that bastard orphan marrying Guilietta, not him. Ugilino wanted to lash out. How could he do it? A plan flashed in his mind. He would go back to the Master and tell him about Guilietta and Romero's deceit. Then he'd . . . well, that's as far as the plan went. Ugilino got up, ran into the hall and then out into the darkness of the Verona night. He wouldn't stop running until he was back at the della Cappas' house to tell what Guilietta and Romero were up to.

Father Lurenzano smiled, "Ah, such devoted young lovers. Stay here for a few minutes while I go arrange the chapel." Hansum took two denarii from his pouch and offered them to Father Lurenzano. The priest refused. "Pay later, when we are recording the union, my son. That's when it is proper." His real intention was to give himself time to think of a way to get more of what was in Hansum's pouch into his. "Wait in my chambers. I will be but a short while."

So, within the hour, Hansum and Guilietta were married by Father Lurenzano in the chapel at San Francesco al Corso. Several monks were in attendance as witnesses. While writing the details in the marriage ledger, Hansum took out the two denarii.

"Grazie, my son. Of course, there is also the chapel fee and we must pay a little extra for troubling the brothers to get out of their beds to witness. I've also told them to prepare the chambers next to mine, so you may consummate the union. They are even changing the blankets. And in the morning, you may break your fast with us. Only six denarii, total. For everything."

"Oh dear, that's a lot!" Guilietta said.

"We can't stay till the morning, Father," Hansum said. "We must get back to my Master's house."

"Okay. Five denarii, then."

So Hansum's purse was a little lighter and the priest was now satisfied. He walked them to their nuptial chambers and even gave them an extra oil lamp to brighten their room. They thanked him for the generous gesture. It did brighten the room and the newlyweds could see each other's wonderful, young bodies as they made love. The priest repaired to his darkened room and peered through the chink in the wall. He was so enthralled, he forgot completely about Ugilino.

# Chapter 7

As Hansum came down from the loft the next morning, he heard splashing in the water barrel. Then he saw him, stripped naked and scrubbing himself.

"Ugilino, you're back," Hansum said. Lincoln was right behind him.

"Hey, look what the cat dragged home!" Lincoln said.

"Romero, Maruccio," Ugilino said, in as sing-song a manner as he could. "*Buona mattina*. How are you, brothers?"

"We thought you ran away," Lincoln said, smiling.

"No, no, brother. We had a fight. What family doesn't, eh? I'm sorry I fight you, Romero. I try to be a good boy in the future."

"The Master knows you are here?" Hansum asked.

"Si, si. Last night. I come to the house, we talk, and then we went for a walk. A long walk and a long talk. After we eat, I go back to selling the discs for the eyes."

"Well, welcome back, old friend," Lincoln said. "Hey, let's get to the house. I'm starving."

"Yeah. Uh, welcome back, Ugilino," Hansum said warily. The tone in Ugilino's voice made Hansum suspicious. "We'll see you at the house."

"Grazie, Romero," Ugilino said. "I'll be there quick. Oh, and Romero," he added. "My congratulations for you and Guilietta." Hansum stopped in his tracks and stared. Ugilino looked back at him smugly, and then made a sewing motion across his lips. "See you at the house," he said, pulling his tunic over his head and turning his back to Hansum.

As the new bridegroom walked to the house, he had a nervous feeling in his stomach. When he and Lincoln entered, the Master and Signora were already at the table. The Master didn't acknowledge them. The boys took their places at the table and sat silently. The Signora smiled at Lincoln and Lincoln smiled back.

"Make that funny face, Maruccio," the Signora asked innocently.

Lincoln scrunched up his face, crossed his eyes and stuck out his tongue. The Signora laughed. Hansum sat very still. Shamira brought a large platter with a steaming loaf of bread on it.

"I've reheated the bread and put some spices on it," Shamira said. "Here's the olive oil."

"My favourite," Lincoln said. "Hey, where's Guil?"

The Master stared at Hansum. "She's still sleeping," he said stoically.

Hansum said nothing, but just sat looking across at the big man, who kept staring at him. Then, without removing his gaze, Agistino reached for the large loaf of bread and ripped off a piece. He looked like he was going to pass the loaf to Hansum, but slowly turned and handed it his wife.

The patter of light feet was heard hurrying down the steps.

"Here, let me cut the bread, Mama," Guilietta said. "It's better to cut it with the knife when you share."

"Si, I should have used a knife," her father said, not taking his gaze off Hansum. Then Agistino took the pitcher of oil and poured a generous amount on his plate, all the while not altering his gaze. Lincoln noticed the prolonged stare.

"Yikers," he said and made another funny face. The Signora giggled and blew out some of the little pieces of bread she was chewing.

The Master dragged bread through the oil and put the dripping morsel in his mouth. Oil stuck on his beard, but he didn't wipe it off. He just sat there, chewing and staring. Hansum continued to sit silently, blinking every few seconds.

"Buona mattina, Mama," Guilietta said nonchalantly, kissing the Signora on her cheek. She then cut up the bread and handed it around.

"You slept in this morning, daughter," the mother said. "Do you have the curse?"

"Mother!" Guilietta scolded.

"What's the curse?" Lincoln asked.

The door opened and in walked Ugilino. "Buona mattina, everyone."

"There's your answer," the Master said.

"Ugilino!" Guilietta exclaimed. Ugilino took off his hat and held it front of him.

"Signorina Guilietta, a thousand apologies for the other week. It won't happen again." Guilietta nodded.

"Look who showed up last night," the Master said in a voice that suggested innuendo. "We had the most interesting talk. Till late," he added looking at Hansum and his daughter in turn.

"You and Ugilino talked?" Hansum asked.

"Si. Si. Can't a man talk? Ugi had lots to tell me. Much to do with Father Lurenzano and San Francesco al Corso." Hansum looked over at Guilietta, and she back at him. Ugilino was still standing with his hat in his hands. "Well sit, Ugi, sit," the Master said. Ugilino went to the end of the bench and sat next to Lincoln. Everyone sat quietly, not moving. "Well? Eat."

Everyone ate in silence. Shamira brought a bowl of figs and finally a sound was heard. It was Ugilino, humming happily. When everyone looked at him, he was eating away with a big smile on his face and his eyes full of tears. He did not try to hide them.

When the food was finished, Hansum spoke seriously, like a man who would prefer to be anywhere but where he was at the moment.

"Well, then, I guess we should all get to work. There's lots to do."

"Si, everybody to work," the Master said. All rose from the table.

"I'm going to sit with Nuca while she sews," the Signora said. "It's a sight to see her fingers fly."

"I'll walk you over," Guilietta said, "and then go to the shop."

The house door opened again. It was the two young apprentices, Pippo and Benicio. Agistino pointed directly at Guilietta.

"Daughter, you stay here. You too, Romero. Carmella, take the Signora to the Satores'. Maruccio, take the boys to the shop. "

"Father, what is it you . . ."

"Just sit down, both of you. Ugilino, go with Maruccio and get yourself set up to sell discs for the eyes again."

"Si, Master," Ugilino beamed.

As everybody left, Agistino clicked the door shut. Then he turned around and looked at Hansum and Guilietta.

"What is it you wish to speak of, Father?" Guilietta asked. But Hansum reached across the table and put a hand on hers. She fell silent. He looked over at the Master and stood.

"Master, I am very sorry we deceived you."

"Romero!" Guilietta said, but Hansum spoke over her.

"Our plan was ill-considered and rash. We shouldn't have lied to your father. Our father."

Nobody said a word for some moments. Then Agistino sighed, walked over to the bench and sat down. He buried his face in his hand. Then he sighed deeply again and looked at the two.

"You have not only disobeyed and deceived me, you have put all that was possible for this family in jeopardy. Romero, if you were not the Podesta's favourite or if you had tried to carry on with your lie, I would have thrown you out on the street and worse. But you have stood up like a man and admitted your mistake."

"Master, I was wrong . . ."

"All men misstep. All men misjudge and fall back. But not all men have character. I see this in you and it is becoming."

"I will never lie to you again, Master. And as your family is my family now, I shall do what is right in the future, and not just what is my wish."

"How can I ask for more? But I have not accepted you into my family yet."

"Father, God has accepted us as family in holy matrimony."

"God may have, but I have not — yet. Romero, from this time onward, will you do what I deem right?"

"Si, Master."

"And you, daughter?"

"If I do, will you give this marriage your blessing?" Guilietta countered.

"No. No, not yet. Though I wish to. Like your husband, I must do what is right for the future. But fifteen years of being your father should have made me someone who has no need to ask you a thing more than once. But it seems still I must. Do you give me your promise of obedience, daughter?"

"I want to, Papa."

"Well, whether you swear or not, you must obey if you wish to stay. So, until the Podesta gives his unconditional approval of your union, you must not lie together."

"Papa!"

"Until the Podesta gives his approval, you must not be in the same room alone. Or stand together at church. Or touch."

"Papa," Guilietta scolded angrily, "next you will say we cannot even converse!"

"Oh, you may say 'good morning, Guilietta,' and 'good afternoon, Romero,' or 'isn't it a lovely day,' but that is it. For because of your young years, you know not what is at stake."

"I'm old enough to know what I want and to know that Romero is a fine man."

"Daughter, you will do my will and I will not repeat myself as to the why. I have already stated my case and it is only your lustful stubbornness which keeps you from accepting the wisdom of your elder. For there is the door," added the father without rancor. "If you wish to know what it is to make your way beyond its threshold, without the anchor of home and family, go ask our poor, stupid Ugilino. He is a learned man when it comes to the misery of the streets. The streets swallow up ignorant and unprotected souls. They beckon to all who will not be wise." At that very moment there was a heavy rapping at the front door. "See, the streets beckon."

Guilietta looked peeved at her father's wry comment and went to answer the door. She opened it and there, to her surprise, was a well-dressed coachman in the uniform of the Podesta.

"A letter for Signor Romero Monticelli, Signorina," he said. "I am to wait for him."

Guilietta took the letter and looked back at her father and new husband.

"So it begins," Agistino said, raising his eyebrows. Guilietta handed the note to Hansum, who read it quickly.

"It's from Baron Da Pontremoli. He writes that the Podesta wants me to go and meet with his generals and construction masters. I am to bring a change of clothes."

"And who is supposed to help me grind the lenses? We have the large order."

Referring back to the letter, Hansum added, "The Baron also says for me to assure you that a journeyman lensmaker has been found in Florence for you. He should be here this coming Sabbath."

"So quickly?" Agistino asked.

"Excuse me, Signor," the driver said. "My name is Grazzana. I am to drop off Signor Monticelli and then drive without stopping to Florence. The Podesta wants to assure you, Master della Cappa, he does not take your need for craftsmen lightly. The work you are doing for him is important. You see?" From a large coat pocket, Grazzana took out one of the brass lookers. "I use it every day, Signor. It is an important tool for me. As important as my sword."

"I'm glad," the Master grunted, then, "If you are to pick up this journeyman, you must know his name? I know all the lensmakers in Florence."

"I believe his name is Bembo Arturo, Signor."

"Bembo? He works for Frontinelli. A mean master, but a good shop. Bembo is a good man."

"But where are you taking Romero?" Guilietta asked. "Is it dangerous?"

"I'm sorry, Signorina. I'm not to tell where this meeting is to be held. It is a military secret."

"Romero, I'm frightened," she said, clinging to Hansum.

Agistino took her arm and pulled her away. "How many times have I told you to let my apprentices be, Guilietta? They are not your brothers to be treated so familiarly. She treats all the work-ers like family, Signor," he explained to Grazzana. Hansum saw the driver nod, with a look on his face like he was smelling some-thing rotten. "Romero," the Master continued, "go get your things and say your goodbyes to the others in the shop. Would you like something to eat, Signor?"

"Grazie, no, Signor. My orders are not to let the young signor out of my sight till I deliver him to the Podesta."

Hansum saw a look of anguish in Guilietta's eyes, but Agistino had her firmly by the arm. The newlyweds looked at each other longingly.

"Romero," the Master sternly said, "do not keep the Podesta waiting. Go! Go!" Guilietta struggled on her father's arm, and then gave up as Hansum left the house, Grazzana close behind.

"Fool of a girl!" Agistino scolded.

"Oh, my heart is going to break!" Guilietta sobbed.

"Did I not but some moments earlier say you must not show affection to each other."

"What was the harm?" Guilietta cried.

"The harm? The harm? That was the Podesta's man standing there."

"He's but a driver," she sobbed.

"A driver? The Podesta gave him a looker and he spoke of his sword. He's most likely a trusted military agent, doing errands in the guise of a driver. He is the eyes and the ears of the Podesta. I've always thought you a level-headed and sensible girl. But now you're like a cat in heat. Take care, girl. Take care."

Hansum's main objective in going to the shop, besides getting his possessions and saying good-bye to everyone, was to retrieve Pan. It was essential that the A.I. go with Hansum to wherever the Podesta had ordered him. Pan was hidden in Lincoln's liripipe today, tutoring him on the style of financial books that the Baron had shown him.

Hansum made a big show of hugging Lincoln, then Shamira and even the two small apprentices, who were confused at all the fuss. This gave Lincoln the time to take Pan out of his collar and put him in his palm. When the boys shook hands a final time, the transfer was made.

Grazzana followed Hansum up into the loft to get his change of clothes, though the driver said that the Podesta would probably outfit him much better than he has been in the past.

"After all, you will be working with the rich and powerful. The Podesta would not want you to reflect poorly on him. See how he outfits me."

"You've been working for the Podesta a long time?"

"Si, a long time. I'm a non-commissioned officer in his army, actually. A bastard son of one of his cousins. I can be trusted." As the two came down the ladder and exited the workshop, the others followed them. Grazzana put up a hand. "No long good-byes. The Podesta's waiting."

"Keep the place running smoothly, Maruccio," Hansum said. "Take care of everybody in the house, Carmella."

"There's no worries there, brother," Lincoln assured him.

"Keep safe," Shamira added with a pensive look.

At the street, the Master and Guilietta were standing at their open door. Agistino was behind his daughter, his hands on her shoulders. It looked like a sign of affection, but Hansum realized he was keeping Guilietta from bolting to him. Many residents were again milling around the fancy open carriage. They stopped gossiping and fell silent as Grazzana and Romero came around the corner from the shop. The Satores and Signora della Cappa looked out from the sewing room.

"When will . . ." Guilietta began, but Agistino spoke over her.

"Excuse me, Signor," Agistino asked. "When will Romero be returning?"

"A week, maybe a month, maybe more. I don't know."

"More than a month?" Guilietta said, hollow-eyed.

The Master nodded his thanks and tightened the grip on his daughter. Hansum could see Guilietta gently convulse and close her eyes.

"Go well, my son," Agistino said. "Do your best for the Podesta."

"Grazie, Master. I'll do my best, don't you worry. Goodbye, Guilietta. Keep well," he said, climbing into the open carriage. "Oh, one moment, Signor. One last thing." He got down and went over to the Master. He made sure he only looked briefly at Guilietta and then spoke directly to Agistino. "Hold this, Master," he said, taking out the bag of denarii and handing it to the big man. "This is to care for my wife," he said quietly.

Hansum no sooner got in than Grazzana whipped the horses and the carriage took off, bringing a quick end to the goodbyes.

# Chapter 8

Hansum travelled in the open carriage. With the wind in his face, he was sorry he wasn't wearing his old peasant cap. The new, more stylish, city hat just didn't keep his head warm. As they passed under the city gate and over the drawbridge, Hansum realized this was the first time he was outside the city since his arrival. Oddly enough, he also thought, he had probably been over this terrain before, but a thousand years in the future.

The road followed the Adige River valley, and the rolling hills they traversed were dotted with hovels. When Hansum asked how long the trip would be, he was told they would be there before mid-morning. He tried to ask a few more questions, like the name of the place and who else would be there, but he was told he'd find out when he arrived.

Hansum settled back and watched the landscape. He surreptitiously removed Pan's tiny lamp from his pouch and held it close to his ear.

"It's not all that different than in our time," he murmured to the A.I.

"Yes, this landscape is much the same as in the twenty-fourth century, though during the interim, it was much built up. But since humankind's twenty-first century decision to limit its population, the planet began to reclaim itself. It only took a few hundred years for the highways, rail lines and many cities to disappear back into a wild state."

Hansum looked around at the scenery as the carriage sped along the road.

"You know, Pan, I actually think the road is wider now than the paths in our time."

*"Yes, of course, Young Master. There's less need. First of all, there are more humans on the planet in the fourteenth century than in the twenty-fourth. Plus, the road system in our time is not required to support a society based on consumption and economic growth. A burgeoning road network is a sign of trade between cities, regions and continents and the fourteenth century was the beginning of massive continent-wide trading. In our time, the roads are little more than paths, used by people traveling between places for fun and exercise. Any transport of goods is done by levitation technology."*

After about an hour, they were passing freight wagons and ox carts loaded with old hay, dirt, garbage and buckets and barrels of filth. Much of it smelled amazingly foul. Soon they turned off the main road and wound their way up a less groomed track. The road ended at a heavy wooden gate, the only visible opening along a tall stone wall. A sign above the gates bore the della Scalla coat of arms and the place name, *Bella Flora*. Two soldiers manned the gate. They greeted Grazzana as an old friend and looked carefully at the passenger. Hansum smiled and said hello. The two guards took off their kettle helmets and bowed a little.

'They think I'm a somebody,' Hansum thought.

Passing through the gates, Hansum saw open fields lying in fallow, several stands of woods dotting rolling hills in the north and, as they came around a bend, a large two-storey manor house. It stood out against the ever-winding Adige River. They passed several more carts laden with dirty straw and such, and turned up a laneway to the manor. At the house, a soldier took hold of the horses and a butler came to receive them. Baron Da Pontremoli strode out of the house, all smiles.

"My young friend, Romero, how are you, dear boy?" He greeted him with an effusive handshake.

"Well, grazie, Baron. The countryside was very nice after being in the city all winter."

"Si, spring comes soon, eh?" Then to Grazzana seriously, "Was there any trouble along the way?"

"No, Excellency."

"Would you like to eat or freshen up, dear boy?" the Baron asked.

"I'm fine, grazie."

"Would you like to get right to work?"

"I actually don't know why I was sent for," Hansum replied.

Nicademo looked somewhat surprised. "Why, to put into practice the plans you gave us. Didn't you see all the carts coming along the road? Look," he said, pointing to the oxcarts trudging up the lane. Hansum looked, but the significance didn't register. "To make saltpeter, Romero. We're creating a saltpeter farm, as in your drawings. I thought you'd understand by what you observed." Hansum realized that, without Pan in his ear, he was totally ignorant of what was going on around him. He should have been tutored about the processes better, but was so busy making lookers and spectacles, he hadn't sat with Shamira and Pan while the plans were created. He needed to play for time.

"Perhaps I do need to freshen up a bit, Excellency. And maybe even rest. We worked in the shop almost the whole night, making lenses," he lied.

"Ah, well first, come present yourself to our host. He is with General Chavelerio and Master Calabreezi."

Hansum's heart beat heavily as he fathomed the depths of the situation he was entering. "As you wish, Excellency."

The manor house wasn't as grand as the palace, but it was substantial. A long, wide corridor stretched down the center of the building, with many rooms branching out from it. Servants and military men walked in and out of the rooms, all nodding in deference to the Baron and stealing glances at the newcomer.

Nicademo stopped partway down the hall and put his hand on the large, ornate latch of an oak door. As he opened it, there was the Podesta, leaning over another large table with many papers spread over it. But now, the papers being poured over were plans that Hansum had provided. Mastino turned and looked at Hansum. He was wearing his tortoiseshell bifocals. The Podesta smiled. There were two other men. One was the general whom Hansum had seen at the palace, the other was a man dressed in rough workman's clothes. He was a serious-looking, large, square-shaped man with callused hands.

"Ah, Romero, you've arrived!" the Podesta said effusively.

"At your service, Excellency."

"I was just reviewing your plans with General Chavelerio and Master Calabreezi."

Hansum, not knowing what else to do, let his naturally out-going personality take over. He smiled and walked boldly over to the general, putting out his hand. The general peered down at Hansum with his small squinting eyes, the irises the color of robin's eggs.

"Good afternoon, General," Hansum said. "We met the other day in Verona, but circumstances didn't allow for an introduction."

"Good afternoon," was all the general replied softly.

"He don't talk like a peasant," said Master Calabreezi, who looked and talked like a peasant himself.

"I had a travelled uncle who taught me some comportment, Master Calabreezi."

Master Calabreezi grunted, somewhat like Master della Cappa did when he was reserving judgement. Calabreezi had a short, squat build that bespoke a peasant childhood, where nutrition — or lack of it — didn't allow for growth to his optimal height.

"Master Calabreezi will supervise the casting of your wonder-ful cannon, my boy," Mastino said. "He has the largest bell foundry in all of southern Europe."

Hansum turned and stepped toward Calabreezi, but just as Hansum put his hand out, the old man turned his back and faced the drawings on the table.

"I have a question about your plans," the old master said gruffly. "It has to do with the saltpeter beds. Here," he said, point-ing to a detail on the drawing.

Hansum came over hesitantly. He looked at the drawing and really didn't understand what he was looking at. He knew gener-ally that it was a compost pile and that nutrients were broken down from its rotting contents. This was common biology that all twenty-fourth-century children came to understand by helping in their community's fruit and vegetable gardens. But he knew he must know more before talking with these men. He looked at the drawings for a few moments, like he was re-familiarizing himself with them, then yawned. Nicademo intervened.

"Signori, the young signor is fatigued. He did not get our summons till this morning and was up all night in the lens shop."

"If I could retire to my little space and rest till tomorrow," Hansum said, "I shall be able to answer all your questions and be of any service I can."

"This one question," Calabreezi insisted. "I watched the men building the first saltpeter bed today and it looks like they're doing it wrong."

Hansum acted as if he were about to speak, then feigned another yawn. "A thousand pardons, Master." Then he said, "Please, until tomorrow. Then I am yours."

The Podesta added cheerily, and his was the final word, no matter how he said it, "And I know you, Calabreezi. There's never just one question." The old master grunted.

"And I will need to speak to you tomorrow on the strategy of the cannon, Monticelli," the general added. "If these cannon and powder are so much more powerful, aiming will be a challenge."

*"These cannon can fire up to twenty-five hundred meters,"* Pan whispered. *"Ask him . . ."* and Pan whispered some more.

"General Chavelerio, it would be best if we chose gunnery officers who know trigonometry and are good with numbers," Hansum said, after looking like he was thinking hard. "They will need to calculate powder loads and quickly cipher trajectories. Do you have the like among your officers?" The general's eyebrows rose again, and he gave a single nod. Then Hansum created another large yawn. "Oh, please forgive me," Hansum continued. "We will add this to our future talks. Would you excuse me, Signori?" he said looking at the Podesta for permission. Mastino nodded, smiling a self-satisfied smile. Hansum bowed to each of the men and then looked at Nicademo to lead the way.

When Hansum was out of the room the three men looked at each other.

"So?" Mastino asked.

"I don't believe that boy came up with these advanced concepts," Calabreezi said.

"He doesn't claim to have," Mastino replied.

"Si, we know," the general said, then added with light sarcasm, "They are from his painted memory of ancient manuscripts."

"But I believe he is greatly improving the old knowledge," Mastino added quickly. "Like what he did with the looker. That shows great genius, does it not?"

"In all things we trust your judgement, Excellency," the general said in a placating manner, "but let us wait a few days to see what will be."

# Chapter 9

Hansum's "little space" was a room the size of the entire della Cappa house, including the upstairs. There was a large four-poster down-feather bed, quality linen sheets, soft wool blankets and big feather pillows. There were fine sitting chairs, a writing desk, a wash table, woven carpets on the floor and a fireplace that already had a good blaze going.

"Do you approve of your quarters, Romero?" the Baron asked. Hansum said nothing, but just stared at the opulent surroundings. His nights over the past months had been spent huddled in a blanket in a hay mound. "This all must seem strange and wonderful to you, Romero. Have you ever slept in such a grand bed as this?"

What could Hansum answer? Most people in the twenty-fourth century slept on reciprocal memory sponge, a semi-alive substance which conformed to the body, monitored vital signs and stress levels and could even record dreams on some levels. But Hansum preferred his levitation mattress and had even slept in the zero gravity of space during a vacation to the moon.

"Indeed, Excellency, I have never slept in a room such as this."

"Don't worry. It is my experience that people soon get used to luxury and take it for granted. You do look tired, Romero. Sleep now and I'll send for you an hour before supper."

"I am very tired, Signor. Do you think it possible for me not to join the others for supper, but just have a bowl in my room? I want to be very fresh for tomorrow."

"As you wish," the Baron answered, and then left.

*"Rotate around in a circle so I may scan the room for interlopers, Young Master,"* Pan whispered, then, *"All's clear."* Pop! Pan was standing in the middle of the room. "My scans can perceive any visual reconnaissance through holes, cracks, scrims in pictures, one-way mirrors, or acoustic stealth through listening tubes. Their technology would not be past that. So, you are tired?"

"No, Pan, not really. I said that because I'm going to need a crash course on everything before tomorrow. Both on what is in those drawings and answers to the things they could ask."

"But I will be at your ear, Young Master. Do not fear."

"Pan, I know you will. But I really want to be prepared. I want to understand what's going on, not just repeat what you say. All our futures depend on what happens here. Yours, mine, Shamira's, Lincoln's, and Guilietta and her parents'. I don't want to make any mistakes."

"You are now a serious man," the hologram said. "I shall no longer call you Young Master, but Master."

# BOOK TWO

# Exploding the World

# Chapter 1

It was still dark when Hansum heard a knock on his door. He opened his eyes and found it strange not to have straw crowding his vision or tickling his face. As he looked up from his pillow, Hansum saw the door open. A large brass oil lamp seemed to levitate into the room. It reminded him of Charlene, but it was followed by an arm, a shoulder, and then the rest of the butler.

"Buon giorno, Signor," the butler said. "My name is Duccio."

"Buon giorno, Duccio," Hansum yawned.

Duccio was followed by a footman carrying a pitcher of hot water, which was put on the wash stand. As the two turned to leave, the butler spoke.

"His Excellency invites you to meet him, General Chavelerio and Master Calabreezi in the planning room, Signor. I'll leave the footman outside your door to escort you."

"Grazie, Signor. Please close the door when you leave."

Hansum took his hat, with Pan in it, from under the pillow and quickly got up. Though the bed was warm and the morning cold, he did not hesitate to rise. Sleeping in a barn's loft had cured him of that. He placed his hat on the desk.

"You can come out now, Pan."

*"No, I can't,"* a small voice whispered. *"The footman is peeking through the keyhole."*

Hansum took a towel, walked over to the door and hung it on the latch. He heard a quick shuffling of feet on the other side of the door. Hansum turned and mouthed, "Now?" Pan popped out and onto the floor.

"So, Master Hansum, are you ready to beard the lions in their den?"

"Huh?"

"A term from the old Christian bible. It's a phrase used when going into a challenging situation."

"I see."

"And after last night's tutoring, do you feel properly prepared?"

"Still a bit nervous, but more ready than I was." They had reviewed all the subjects at hand. Four hours in the afternoon and then a few more after Hansum had eaten the supper brought by a servant on a silver tray. They brought wine, but Pan had Hansum order peppermint tea. The teen was nervous and it settled his stomach. The studying was intense, and Hansum studied harder than he ever did back home. Besides reviewing the drawings they provided the Podesta with, Pan hypothesised questions that could be asked. They spent a lot of time on the subject of making black powder, the biggest subjects being the large- scale farming of the saltpeter — or niter — and the design and construction of a gunpowder mill. This was to produce much larger quantities of the stuff than was possible at the time. As well as the static drawings, Pan also created life-like holographic animated projections. This way Hansum would really understand what he was looking at when he saw it for real. Hansum washed, dressed, put on his hat, took a deep breath and said to Pan, "Let's go and shave those damn lions, little guy."

"Beard, Master. Beard," Pan corrected.

Hansum smiled at the footman in the hall.

"After you, old boy," he said. The footman looked at him haughtily, turned and walked down the hall. Along the way they met the butler.

*"Give the butler three denarii,"* Pan whispered. *"Thank him for taking such good care of you and tell him to give one of the coins to the footman."* Hansum did so and got a fine reaction from both servants. *"Everybody spies on everybody here. You cannot hate them for it. It's their way of life. But in any conflict, you must build allies among your adversaries, especially among their staff. You never know when you will need small favours."*

Hansum was taken to the planning room. The Podesta, the general, Calabreezi and Nicademo were already there.

"Buon giorno, Romero," Nicademo said. "Did you sleep well?"

"Very well, grazie, Excellency."

*"Greet each one of the others by title and name,"* Pan whispered.

"Buon giorno, Signori, Podesta della Scalla. Thank you for the sumptuous quarters. General Chavelerio, good morning. Soon we shall talk of numbers for calculating trajectories of powerful cannon. And good day to you, Master Calabreezi. Today I hope I can answer all questions you have."

Master Calabreezi was still in his rough clothes and looked more out of place than Hansum. But his permanent scornful and serious face told all he didn't care.

"You're late," Calabreezi said gruffly. "None of my apprentices are ever late."

"I was not familiar with the house schedule, Master. I shall not be tardy again."

"My apprentices — late once, gone!" Calabreezi emphasised.

"But he is not one of your apprentices," the Podesta said cheerfully. "He is to be your equal. Your trusted and respected colleague."

Calabreezi snorted.

"Trust and respect are earned, Excellency," Hansum said diplomatically. "In time, I hope to pass that test with these gentlemen."

"Just so," the Podesta said. "So, how shall we start the day?"

Pan whispered to Hansum and he repeated, "Master Calabreezi had the question regarding the saltpeter farm yesterday. Perhaps we could start there."

Calabreezi grunted and walked over to the table. He pulled out one of the pages and pointed a thick finger to it.

"The question has to do with the building of the rot pile. The men are building the first pile in a way that I am not pleased with. It does not look like this drawing."

"If that is the case, we must go and observe the situation," Hansum said.

"As you suggest, Romero," the Podesta said. "Signori?" he said motioning to the door.

The sun was just coming up, but the peasants had been working for an hour. There was now a long line of carts backing up the road as far as they could see. The peasants were standing around, some laughing and joking, others sleeping in their carts on the old straw. One was urinating in the open. As the peasants noticed the Podesta, they stood with their hats in their hands. The man urinating tried to stop, but couldn't.

As they got to the front of the line of carts, Hansum saw that the first attempt at making a saltpeter bed was still in progress. He tried to see how it was similar to what Pan had shown him in the holographic creations, and could see that Master Calabreezi was right. It bore little resemblance to the plans. The foreman was yelling at the workers and the workers were arguing back. As they became aware of the Podesta, the quarrelling abruptly stopped. The foreman doffed his hat, but Mastino offered no greetings. He pointed at the half-formed pile and spoke to Hansum.

"What do you think, Signor Monticelli?"

"Allow me to inspect," Hansum said. Pan instructed him to walk around the pile, turn his head this way and that and kneel down so he could get a good look.

Hansum had learned that a saltpeter bed is essentially a compost pile, but with some methodology to its construction.

Apparentlly, Nicademo had taken the foreman into the planning room the day before and shown him the plans. Since he was illiterate, the Baron explained things to him verbally, once. Then he came out to the fields and began work with ten of his men and the jumbled up supplies in the long line of carts. A saltpeter bed was to be about fifteen feet long, six or seven feet wide and five or six feet high. Hansum saw that this first pile was about halfway constructed.

After walking slowly around the pile, Pan told Hansum to mash his boot into the ground to see how firmly the clay was packed. Then, *Stick your hand in the pile.* He had him look again down the long line of waiting carts. Hansum walked back to the Podesta and, on the way, was told what to say.

"Master Calabreezi is correct. The pile is not constructed properly. But before that, there may be a problem with the ground." He turned to the foreman. "The ground is soft by the edge of the pile.

I can move the soil with my foot. Is it the same underneath?" The Podesta looked at the foreman questioningly. The foreman nodded somewhat sheepishly. "The ground where the pile sits, and all around it, must be tamped down so it is impervious to accepting water. Otherwise, much of the goodness we require from the pile will soak into the earth. You must tamp down the ground till it is very hard. Then pour water on it to make sure it is solid. Then you must layer the pile with the required ingredients properly."

"Ingredients?" the foreman questioned. "It sounds like you're making a cake. We're working with rotten plants and merda."

All the peasants burst into raucous laughter.

"Silence!" the Podesta shouted. "Idiots." The Podesta berated the foreman. "Could you not follow the instructions? You must do it right. This is a very important."

"I'm sorry, Excellency," the foreman said contritely. "I've made many rot piles over my thirty-seven years. I cannot understand how this one should be different."

"Fool!" the Podesta yelled. The foreman shrank in shame. The general stood watching, motionless like a stone. Master Calabreezi shook his head and spat. Pan whispered in Hansum's ear.

*"Take the foreman under the tree by himself. Draw him a picture of how he should do it. Explain it simply, but fully."*

"With your permission, Excellency," Hansum said, "may I speak with your man alone? I shall detail to him what is needed and draw an appropriate diagram. Indeed, this is a rot pile, but with some special differences. Allow me to educate him."

"Go with him," the Podesta said gruffly.

Hansum walked over to the shade of a large ash tree and could see the Podesta and others watching closely. The foreman followed, hat still in hand. Hansum sat down on a pile of firewood and took out a small portfolio from his jacket. He bade the foreman sit next to him.

"What's your name?" Hansum asked.

"Jacopo, Signor."

"I'm Romero."

Hansum smiled and shook hands with Jacopo. Then he talked in an animated fashion, pointing at the long line of carts and then to a large open space. Pan had noted the inefficiencies of the situation and had Hansum explain the solution. The way things were, Jacopo was forced to pick items that came from the various carts and then fit them here and there into the saltpeter bed. This was taking a lot of time and caused the pile to become uneven. It also necessitated the carts to stand around all day. Instead, Hansum told Jacopo to pick his best man to inspect each cart. Then have the contents of each cart separated into six big piles. This way the carts could leave quickly and Jacopo could go directly to what he needed without hesitation.

"How should the piles be separated, Signor?"

Hansum took a blank page and a charcoal stick from his portfolio. Using the portfolio as a writing surface, he drew six little pictographs, each one representing a pile.

"In the first," Hansum said, "put the dark earth with all the gray and white flecks in it. This is where the saltpeter has already formed by sitting undisturbed." Jacopo said he and one of his men knew of this. They had collected saltpeter in the past. He even knew how to recognize it by taste. "Good," Hansum said, smiling. "The second pile will be any rotted manure or black earth that doesn't have the crystals formed yet. In the third pile, put old ground-up mortar and wood ashes. The fourth, old straw with young manure and leaves. Five, any other rotted material that needs further rotting: kitchen waste, fresh dung, scrapings from drains, rotten meat and skin. Then the final pile, the sixth, small twigs and branches." Hansum had drawn a pictograph for each. "Can you remember what these mean, Jacopo? Good."

Lower on the page, Hansum drew two rectangles, one, a top view and one a cross section of the beds. The top view showed how to lay out upside-down ceramic roof tiles at the bottom of the pile. These would act as drains to draw away any excess moisture. All the rows of drains would converge to a single spout, so that the excess urine and water could be recaptured and poured back on the pile.

When Hansum looked up, he saw the others were still watching closely. The Podesta, Baron and general looked somewhat confused by the way he was handling the foreman. Master Calabreezi was still scowling.

The second rectangle was the cross section of a finished pile. Hansum drew a series of horizontal lines in the rectangle, signifying layers. He stretched out his hand and indicated the distance between the tip of his thumb and little finger.

"Each layer is to be about this wide," he said. Then he redrew each pictograph, one in each layer, indicating where they go in the pile. "The first layer must be the dark un-nitrified earth. The second, ashes and crushed mortar. Then straw and manure. The next, animal and other waste. Finally, a layer of twigs and branches." Jacopo's face lit up as he now understood what must be done. Hansum added, "You do the layering four or five times, till the pile is six feet high, seven feet wide and fifteen feet long."

"I see, Signor. I see." Jacopo said. "But what of the first pile? The dark earth with the little specks in it already?"

"Smart," Hansum complimented. "You remembered that one, eh?"

"I do not read," Jacopo said. "I am not stupid."

"Indeed," Hansum said. "We will process this nitrified earth into saltpeter right away. But it took five to ten years to get this way in a barn or earth floor. Our saltpeter beds, properly made, can create it in only eight months."

"Oh, I understand now, Signor Romero," Jacopo said. "That is why this is so important. Is there more I must know?"

"Much," Hansum replied. "But it pertains to how the pile is to be worked over the next months. Let's first perfect the making of it. Then, when your men are trained, we shall do the next lesson. Do you agree?" Jacopo looked surprised at being asked his opinion.

"Si, Signor. This sounds sensible."

"Good," Hansum replied. "Let us show our lords the plan." When Hansum and Jacopo showed the plans, everybody nodded their heads in appreciation.

"You can follow this?" the Podesta asked his foreman.

"Si, Excellency."

Pan whispered something to Hansum. Hansum spoke.

"So, Jacopo, you are foreman here. How do you say we proceed?"

"Signor Romero, I suggest we start a new bed. I will have four of my men prepare the earth properly, as you have shown, with the drains, and have the others work to separate the carts into stacks. We should have the backup of carts cleared by midday and the base should be ready to build on then."

"Very well, Jacopo. Remember, I want to inspect the base first. Then I'll work with you to spread the first layers."

"Si, Signor Romero."

"All right then," the Podesta said. "To work."

Jacopo put on his cap and whistled loudly through his teeth to call his workers. "Over here. And listen." Hansum, the Podesta and the others walked back toward the manor. They could hear Jacopo say, "We must do this differently."

"How does one make a pile of merda different?" chided one of the more boisterous workers. Jacopo waved his paper with the plans on it proudly.

"Like this!"

# Chapter 2

Hansum and the others spent the rest of the morning in the planning room. The Baron took notes and Hansum scribbled any additional drawings. He wished he had Shamira to do them, but he didn't mention it. He was afraid the Podesta would have Shamira sent for, and it was important for Master della Cappa to retain the help he had in the shop.

Hansum described the process of converting the already nitrified earth into mounds of pure, white saltpeter. The group reviewed the booklet Shamira had illustrated showing the process. They saw how, within a year, the process would all be under one roof, with dedicated large vats and special drying racks. To make saltpeter now, to test their processes and first cannons, they would have to set up a makeshift conversion plant, using barrels and lots of manpower.

"Manpower is never a problem," Mastino said. "Let us proceed."

Hansum explained that after the hundreds of carts had their contents separated into piles, they would know approximately how much nitrified earth they had on hand. Then he told how they would use the barrels to make a water slurry —or ley — of the muck. The general found it fascinating when Hansum explained that the way to tell if the ley had adequate salts was to place a raw egg in it.

"When the egg floats, you know you have about a pound of salts to a gallon of liquid," Hansum said. "It floats as if it were in the Dead Sea." The general crossed himself. Then they would use large cauldrons to boil it down. "By a curious quirk of nature," Hansum explained, "when the water is heated up, common salts appear. But oddly, when the liquid is then cooled, raw saltpeter crystals form. These raw crystals are then stored and ready for final processing.

"The final part of the processing is the most exacting," Hansum said. To impress everyone with the potential, Pan had him explain how it would be when they had all the dedicated equipment. "We will have large boilers holding a hundred gallons of fresh water. As it is heated, it can dilute up to four thousand pounds of the crude saltpeter in it."

"We'll be working with lots this large?" the general asked.

"Most assuredly, Signor," Hansum said. "If we don't, what's the point?" Everybody smiled but Calabreezi. "As the water heats, some common salts will form again and we rake it away. But after that, we cool it quickly by adding sixty-five gallons of cool water. While this is done, we slowly add two gallons of fresh blood."

Master Calabreezi commented by snorting.

"Blood? Blood? Is this alchemy?" he asked acerbically.

"No, Master. This is not alchemy. The blood acts like a glue and gathers together any tiny bits of organic matter still in the mixture. It will rise to the top of the boiler as more scum. After this is removed, the remaining liquor will be very clear, very pure. It is then ladled onto large shallow cooling tables, which slope gently to the center. This is when the pure needle-like saltpeter crystals form. They are scooped up and rinsed several times. And there you will have it: Saltpeter, purer than in nature. But after drying, care must be taken. It is now very explosive and ready to be used in black powder."

Wine and dried fruits were brought in by the butler as re-freshments. Hansum ate, but didn't take wine, asking for more peppermint tea.

As for the other ingredients — charcoal, the carbon, and brim-stone, the sulfur — these were easier to get. Almost pure sulfur was available in Calabria, a short ride south. The Podesta had al-ready sent large wagons to fetch it. Charcoal was the easiest. They had many willow trees in the district and there was no shortage of peasants skilled in processing that.

"So, Romero, with all the ingredients assembled, we must build this?" Mastino pulled out the papers with the most detailed drawings on them. It was the incorporating mill. Its purpose was to grind together the saltpeter, charcoal and sulfur. Pan had ex-plained how experience taught the early black powder makers that it was necessary to grind the ingredients for many hours. From a modern, scientific understanding, the milling caused the saltpeter and sulfur to be forced into microscopic voids of the charcoal, bonding the elements together. Otherwise, over a short period of time, the ingredients would separate and end up fiz-zling and hissing instead of exploding. Of course, back then, no one knew what was happening on the molecular level. Like most discoveries, it was through trial and error, and over time, that processes were developed.

"The incorporating mill is run by water power, like a grain mill," Hansum explained. "As you can see, though, it is differ-ent from a grain mill, where the two grinding stones usually lie flat against each other. The incorporating mill's two large stone wheels run upright in an eight-foot-wide metal pan, pulverizing and mixing anything in their path."

"How many men does this replace?" the Podesta asked.

Hansum looked thoughtful, as if he were doing sums in his head. Pan whispered the answer.

"This device will produce as much finished powder in a day as one hundred men with mortars and pestles."

"My God!" Master Calabreezi said. Hansum noticed that even when the old man was impressed, he scowled.

"And how many men does it take to work the mill?" the Podesta asked.

"Over a full-day period, four — two in the day and two during the night. But once the saltpeter is in full production, say, in a year and we have, perhaps one hundred beds, we should be able to produce enough saltpeter to make sixteen thousand barrels of black powder a year."

"Sixteen thousand?" the general exclaimed incredulously. "That's more black powder than is produced in all of Europe in a year. Much more." The table fell silent, and then Master Calabreezi spoke.

"Tell me of the cannon, Signor, for this is my work to perform."

"Si, the cannon," the General added. "Tell us."

Hansum watched a contented smile come to the Podesta's face, obviously pleased that Hansum had convinced the general and Master Calabreezi of his authenticity. The young man watched Mastino sit back in his chair, beaming, vindicated for putting so much trust in a young peasant.

Hansum explained the cannon. Pan had described to him how cannon at this time were small, not mounted on wheels, used low-powered black powder, and shot out arrows, rocks and scrap metal. Cannon that could breach city or fortress walls were just being experimented with. Some of these were made of strips of iron bars, welded together and further strengthened by barrel strapping. For the most part, the greatest damage cannon did then was to scare the enemy with thunderous booms and flashing muzzles.

The cannon Pan chose was relatively small, a late sixteenth-century Dutch design, the Falcon. It was about six feet long, rested on its own wheeled carriage, weighed altogether some fifteen hundred pounds and fired iron balls that could just fit into the palm of a man's hand.

"What is its range?"

"Aimed level, it can do serious damage at about four hundred and fifty paces. On an angle, halfway between flat and upright, it will do damage at twenty-five hundred paces."

"Impossible," Master Calabreezi spat.

"Truly?" the Podesta asked.

"This is possible only because of the new powder, Excellency. Of course, the cannon must be very sound to withstand the explosions. But with Master Calabreezi's foundry skills, I don't think there will be a problem."

Master Calabreezi grunted, but not so grumpily.

"What I see of this design which is desirable," the general said, "is the cannon is attached on its own carriage. And with the large wheels, it can be moved by horses over rough ground. The battle can be taken to the enemy."

"But what damage can such a small piece of ordinance do?" Nicademo asked, looking up from his note taking. "Such a small sphere." Hansum opened his mouth to speak and waved his finger. This was giving time for Pan to coach him.

"An iron ball leaving the cannon's mouth at the speed of one league in the time it takes to count to five," Hansum said, "will do a lot of damage, Signori." There was silence while the men tried to imagine something moving that fast. Pan said there was no need to explain how mass times velocity increased the relative mass of an object. Newton would explain that several centuries in the future.

"At present, cannon can be fired two or three times per day," Mastino said. "How often may we use this design?"

"Oh, perhaps one hundred times in a day, Excellency. With a good crew, all day long."

"Imagine it, Mastino," the general said, excitement in his voice. "Sixteen thousand barrels of powder a year and cannons such as this. Walls like Verona's could be dust in a week. But long before that, the population would surrender."

"I'm thinking more of Brescia, Parma, Lucca, Florence and Venice," Mastino answered.

Chavelerio's bright blue eyes sparkled, and Hansum now understood these men's ambitions. Some years earlier, the Podesta and general had lost those cities to a powerful league, assembled from all the cities he had mentioned. Mastino wanted his cities back and he wanted revenge. With this new machine of war, all of the Italian peninsula — and perhaps more — could be theirs. The next hour was spent deciding what their next steps would be.

"I shall leave in the morning and go back to Verona," Master Calabreezi said enthusiastically. "I must give everything a great deal of thought. A cannon must take on a great deal more stress than a bell."

"If the bronze is pure and the dimensions true to the plans, there should not be any problem. I will endeavor to have the first samples of the black powder completed by the time you are ready," Hansum said. Then he turned to Mastino and asked something Pan had not coached him on. "Excellency, when may I go back to visit my family in Verona?"

"Family?" the general asked. "I thought you an orphan."

"My old master and friends are my family."

"Ah, I see, Signor."

The Podesta drummed his fingers and frowned.

*"Master, this is not an appropriate question. He knows who you really want to see."*

"When, Excellency?" Hansum repeated.

"When what?" he asked, a scowl on his face.

"When may I return to Verona?"

*"Oh dear."*

The Podesta thought for a few moments. "When you have your first barrels of saltpeter made," he finally said.

Pan thought for a few seconds and whispered into Hansum's ear. Hansum repeated it.

"That should be about ten days from now, Excellency." Hansum smiled widely at the prospect of being home again with Guilietta. "Master Calabreezi," Hansum continued, "during my stay in Verona, I should come visit your foundry. I have much to learn in that regard."

"Of course," Calabrezzi said. "We should be ready to pour the cannon by then."

"Then all works out just fine," Nicademo offered. "Do you really think we'll have a working cannon and the new powder in such a short time?"

"Perhaps," Hansum and Calabreezi said simultaneously. Then, for the first time, the old master smiled at Hansum. General Chavelerio added to the building enthusiasm.

"Now that I understand the scale of the industry we're to build, I must increase security. I shall bring in one hundred infantry, one hundred cavalry and extra draft horses. From them we shall train cannoneer teams. *Madonna Maria*, we have much to do."

"I should go see how the saltpeter bed is coming," Hansum said, now more anxious than ever to get things done. "I want the first saltpeter bed perfected by this evening. And tomorrow we'll take what nitrified earth we have and start processing it. We have a deadline to meet."

Hansum was in the field with Jacopo the rest of the day. With a few corrections, all was done properly. By mid-afternoon all the carts had been unloaded and Hansum and Pan were staring at mountains of rotting humus, high both in height and smell. There were also piles of ash, old mortar and twigs. Everything was now easily accessible to build the beds. Jacopo said he believed that about half of the farms ordered to bring the material had done so.

The smallest pile of the earth was the one with the saltpeter crystals already in it. It was thirty feet round and over six feet high. Pan calculated that it was enough to make about five thousand pounds of saltpeter, or about seventy-five hundred pounds of black powder. That would translate into about one hundred and fifty barrels or almost twenty-five hundred rounds for the cannon. When Hansum reported this to everyone at the evening meal, they all laughed joyously, even Master Calabreezi. Mastino came over to give Hansum a hug, but stopped. Still with a huge smile on his face, he held the younger man at arms length.

"My dear savant, this is your first time at my table, so I shall forgive you. But, please, in the future, come to it not smelling like an ill-kept stable." And then he laughed and had the butler put a sheet over Hansum's chair before he sat on it.

# Chapter 3

Shamira was standing in the larger upstairs bedroom with Guilietta and the Signora. She was brushing the old woman's hair while they all gossiped amiably and Guilietta repaired a stitch on the older woman's bonnet.

"I remember when my hair was long and wavy, just like yours, daughter," the mother said. "I was quite a beauty back then."

"You're still a beauty, Mama," Guilietta soothed.

"CARMELLA!" Lincoln's voice shouted from down stairs.

"Don't scream in the house, boy!" the women heard the Master scold. "Go up and announce her visitor." There was the sound of footsteps on the stairs. The women all looked at each other. A visitor for Shamira? Lincoln's head popped into the room.

"There's a guy downstairs for you. That art master we met at the palace the other week," Lincoln grinned and raised his eyebrows. The women all looked at each other, now with surprise and excitement.

"Who?" Shamira asked.

"You know, that stuck-up guy who called himself Master Starini. I think he's hot for you," he giggled.

"A suitor!" the Signora blurted, her bulk jiggling.

"Oh, Carmella, how exciting," Guilietta said.

"Starini?" Shamira repeated. "Oh, that dork? He showed me his portfolio. Not very talented. I don't know how *he* became a master."

"Is he handsome?" the Signora asked Lincoln.

"Why ya askin' me?" he asked, wrinkling his nose.

Guilietta quickly tiptoed out of the room. They could hear her padding down the stairs, then hurrying back.

"He's very tall and well dressed," she said, wide-eyed. Her mother looked at her expectantly. "And handsome."

The Signora grasped one of Carmella's arms and shook it excitedly.

"I guess I better go see what he wants," Shamira said flatly. But now she felt two hands on her arms, both the Signora's and Guilietta's.

"Carmella, not too fast," Guilietta said. "We must brush your hair and pinch your cheeks. And most important, make him wait."

"Si, si," the Signora agreed, hefting herself up from the side of the bed and pushing Shamira down in her place. "Make him wait."

"Maruccio, go tell Master Starini that Carmella will be down soon. Have Papa serve him wine and entertain him."

"What?" Lincoln said. "Why?"

Guilietta made shooing motions with her slim hands. "Just do it. Go. Now!"

"Oh, for Gai sakes," Lincoln grumbled, turning and leaving. "Women!"

By the time Shamira found herself walking down the stairs to the main room, her hair had been combed and pinned back tight, except for a few wisps that had been expertly pulled out by Guilietta, left to drift appealingly around her face. Plus, her cheeks had been pinched bright red by the Signora.

"Walk down slowly and stand tall," Guilietta whispered. "Don't look at him. Don't look at him!" she repeated.

"Oh, geesh!" Lincoln could be heard as the procession entered the room.

Herado Starini stood up from where he had been sitting with Master della Cappa. He smiled and bowed as the three women made their entrance.

"You remember Master Starini?" Master della Cappa said.

Shamira nodded. "Buona mattina, Master," Shamira said with little emotion.

Herado Starini bowed a second time. "It is very nice to see you again, Carmella. I hope you are not displeased that I come to call."

"A bit surprised, perhaps," Shamira answered.

"Oh, he is a handsome one," the Signora said too loudly.

"Hush, Mama."

"Master Starini," Shamira said, "this is Signora della Cappa, our Master's wife, and Guilietta, their daughter."

"Signora," Herado said bowing again. "Signorina." When he looked up at Guilietta, he looked at her longer than one would to be polite.

"Master Starini is still in Verona for extended discussions with the Podesta," Agistino said.

"Really? Your artwork? He liked it? I mean, congratulations."

"Yes, I am to speak to his Excellency directly. But I wanted to visit you first."

"Directly?" the Master said. "Podesta della Scalla is away from Verona."

"What? Oh well, yes, I knew that. I meant I will be waiting for his return, so I wanted to visit you."

"Hey, shouldn't we give these two some privacy?" Lincoln asked roguishly.

"Maruccio, don't talk foolishly," the Master scolded. "They must have a chaperone."

"Ladies, please sit," Herado said, bowing again and motioning to the table.

"Oh, he has such elegant manners," the Signora said, giggling and batting her eyes.

"Please, Mama," Guilietta scolded again.

The Master and Lincoln got up and went over to the side of the table with Master Starini. The women took one side of the bench and Shamira sat in the middle, feeling embarrassed by the attention. The men and women stared at each other silently for some moments.

"Would you care for more wine, Master Starini?" Agistino asked.

"Si, that would be very fine."

"Me too," Lincoln said.

"I'll get it," Shamira said, rising.

"You stay here," Guilietta ordered, a hand on Shamira's shoulder. "I'll see to it."

"But it's my job," Shamira complained.

"What is your job, Signorina?" Starini asked.

"To serve the wine. I *am* the kitchen girl," Shamira said.

"You are the kitchen girl? A kitchen girl? I thought you . . ." he said, seeming shocked.

"What, you presumed I was something more important than that? Is there something wrong with being a kitchen girl? I'm an orphan too," she said. "Do you have a problem with that?"

"Really? No, no, Signorina. It's just that . . ." Starini began defensively.

"What?" Shamira demanded.

"Here she blows," Lincoln said.

"No, nothing at all," the artist continued. "I am just surprised. You see, I am an orphan too. We have more in common than our talents."

"Well, there you have it," Agistino said. "We are all people of humble beginnings who have made our way in the world through our talents."

Guilietta came with the jug of wine and poured some into Herado Starini's glass. "Would you like more of your beverage, Papa?"

"No. Maruccio and I must get to the shop. You ladies stay with Master Starini and visit. Come when you are finished. Let's go, Signor Shop Manager."

"Ah, this is more fun, Master," Lincoln complained. "And how 'bout my wine?"

"Move your ass," the Master commanded.

"Okay, okay."

When it was only Herado and the women, they sat staring across the table.

"So, talk," the Signora said.

"I was very impressed with the drawings you showed me at the palace," Herado said. "You have a gift. Did you like mine?"

"I liked your colors, Master Starini."

"Ah, thank you."

As the conversation began, Guilietta looked down and sat very still, trying not to interfere. Her mother, with an open-mouthed smile, continued looking back and forth between the two.

"You mentioned, at the time," Shamira said, "that you've worked on many frescoes. I am fascinated by the process of painting on wet plaster. I've never seen it done. You said you specialize in them."

"What? Oh, yes, yes I did, of course. Yes, that, that is my specialty, frescoes."

"You could show her how it's done," the Signora blurted out.

"Mother!" Guilietta said in a loud whisper. "We are chaperones. Be silent."

"Oh, tosh!" the Signora said.

"Would you like that, Signorina Carmella, to see a fresco being created?"

"Yes, brushing pigments onto wet plaster, so the colors will be fast for hundreds of years, that would be fascinating to watch.

And to know all the pigments for creating the different colors and how to grind and mix them, that must have taken years to learn."

"Si, well that is my specialty, as you observe, the colors. I believe your draftsmanship is superior to mine. Perhaps you can do a design and I the execution." And then Herado smiled graciously at Shamira, locking his eyes with hers.

This took Shamira off guard. She had experienced enough now to know that, unlike the twenty-fourth century, the fourteenth was a male-dominated society. It was really something for a man here to give a woman credit for anything, especially to say she was better at something than him.

'Perhaps this Herado Starini isn't such a bad fellow,' Shamira thought, smiling warmly at him for the first time.

"You're very kind to say so, Master Starini. After all, I can only practice my drawing when I am not doing my kitchen duties."

"Signorina Carmella, if I have anything to do about it," Herado reached across the table and lightly touched Shamira's hand, "you will not be a kitchen girl for long."

Herado Starini's soft words and touch caused a warm flush to rush through Shamira's whole body.

"Oh look," the Signora cried, "Carmella's blushing!"

## Chapter 4

Lincoln couldn't believe the difference in Shamira when she and Guilietta brought Starini out to see the shop. She had this goofy grin pasted to her face and kept staring at Starini with puppy-dog eyes.

'Yikers,' he thought. 'She's fallen for the guy.'

Lincoln had been changing the lenses on the interchangeable dops so the Master and the new journeyman, Bembo, could shape and polish them. The Master got up and didn't even look perturbed that the workday was being interrupted. He welcomed Starini to his shop and patted Shamira on the cheek, smiling graciously the whole time. 'What is goin' on?' Lincoln thought. Starini looked interested in everything, especially the big stack of finished lookers in a crate.

Bembo, a big, happy, swarthy fellow with curly hair and an infectious smile, showed the visitor how his new lathe worked. He even let the artist sit and work the pedal. Everybody kept laughing and smiling and looking at Shamira with her happy smirk. 'What the heck happened in that kitchen?' Lincoln thought again. It got even worse when Shamira showed Starini how she set lenses in the lookers. The guy knelt down at eye-level with Shamira as she worked. Usually Shamira was all business and worked quickly. Now she kept giggling and staring up at him. She even burned the tip of her finger with hot mastic. Finally, when she finished, Starini put his hand on Shamira's, which made Guilietta gasp and everybody in the shop's eyes go wide.

"Such fine work you do," he complimented.

They let him try the looker out in the alley and he was amazed.

"Master della Cappa," Starini asked, "how much to purchase this fine instrument? It would be a boon for me to observe the birds and other animals, so I may draw them more perfectly for my art."

The Master looked seriously then. "I'm sorry, Master Starini. It is forbidden for me to sell lookers to anyone but the Podesta. He buys all I can make."

Starini looked disappointed, but quickly collected himself. "No matter," he said. "Perhaps in the future." Then he smiled broadly. "Well, thank you for your hospitality, Master della Cappa. I look forward to seeing you again, tomorrow."

"Eh? What?" Agistino asked.

"Yes, Master," Shamira said. "Master Starini is coming to supper tomorrow."

"He is?"

"Mama invited him, Papa," Guilietta chimed in. "Then he and Carmella can sit and draw together. And Master Starini is going to bring some plaster and show Carmella how frescoes are made."

"You are?" Master della Cappa asked.

"With your permission, Master," Starini said, "I will bring plaster and a few color pigments. We will build a small frame to pour the plaster in it, design an angel, and then paint it."

"This is all very quick," Agistino objected.

"It was Mama's suggestion," Guilietta said.

"I'm going to design the angel," Shamira added.

"And I shall execute it," Starini finished.

"Can I watch?" Lincoln asked.

"Me too," Ugilino said enthusiastically.

"Hmph!" the Master grunted. "Very quick, indeed. Oh, very well. Tomorrow then, Master Starini."

"Signorina Carmella," Master Starini said with a slight bow to a smiling Shamira, "it was such a pleasant first visit. I look forward to more." Starini took a step toward Shamira, reaching out with a hand to take hers.

"Hem, hem," Master della Cappa coughed.

Starini smiled again. "Till tomorrow, Signorina," he said, bowing again.

And then Lincoln saw something he thought he'd never see the independent and strong-minded Shamira do. She curtsied. She curtsied with that stupid grin still plastered on her face.

When Starini was out of the shop, Guilietta and Shamira grabbed each other's hands and hopped up and down, giggling.

"Okay you two, back to work!" the Master ordered, becoming his old self again.

Lincoln looked over at Bembo, who was taking the whole thing in with good humor.

"Women are nuts!" Lincoln said, tapping his temple.

"One day, you too will get the fever, little brother," Bembo said in his deep, friendly voice.

"If that day ever comes, pal," Lincoln said, "you can toss me out of the nearest bell tower!"

# Chapter 5

The initial saltpeter processing started out well and Hansum was getting used to being the center of attention. Mastino's good humor continued and he heaped praise upon his savant at every opportunity. But when it became apparent that they did not have nearly enough barrels, buckets and troughs to hold and process the ley they were to mix, Mastino's temperament changed instantly. He chastised Nicademo loudly in front of everybody.

"Fool," he shouted. "You should have anticipated the proper quantities of everything we needed!" He had brought in only ten old wine barrels. Hansum became concerned that the Baron might become angry with him now. Pan agreed. They didn't want to alienate someone who was supposed to be an ally. "How many barrels do we need to do this properly?" the Podesta screamed. "How many barrels?" He yelled this at no one in particular, but his eyes finally fell on Hansum. Pan calculated and whispered.

"About sixty to get us through the season, Excellency," Hansum said. "Maybe a few more for spares."

"Jacopo!" the Podesta screamed. "Get all the wagons and hitch up the horses. Go to all the vineyards within a day's ride and bring me a hundred barrels! Spill the wine if you have to, but bring me those barrels! Now!" Jacopo ran out of the barn and called his men. The Podesta continued to scream at Nicademo. "What else have you missed? What's next? What's next? You must think ahead properly!" When Nicademo had no answer, Mastino glared at Hansum. "What's next, geniuso? What's next?"

"We will have to boil down the ley, Excellency. When we have all our proper equipment next year, we will do it in a big brass boiler that holds two hundred and fifty gallons. And we will have several of them. Now we must do it in these large kitchen cauldrons."

"Do we have enough of these or will we come again to disaster?"

Hansum looked awkwardly at Nicademo. He didn't want this to reflect poorly on the Baron, who had been kind to him. But he had to tell the truth. Every word that came out of Hansum made him sound like he was in pain.

"Well, uh, Excellency, I do believe we will be short of boiling kettles. We only have four, which will mean we will be very slow. They hold only fifty gallons each. We need at least another twelve kettles this size."

Podesta della Scalla's eyes and nostrils flared as he heard these words. He whirled around on his heels and stomped out of the barn yelling, "Jacopo! Come here, come here, come here!" Jacopo was working feverishly with several other men, hitching up horses to several large wagons. "Cauldrons! I need cauldrons! Go to all the neighbors and bring cauldrons."

"Cauldrons, Excellency? From people's kitchens?"

"I don't care what room they're from! Bring me twelve large cauldrons by tonight! Large ones!"

"Si, Excellency," and he went back to work.

The Podesta walked angrily toward his horse. Hansum had come out of the barn and was struggling to keep up and talk at the same time.

"Excellency, please do not be angry with Baron Da Pontremoli." In between breaths Pan was coaching him on what to say. "The Baron could not know from the designs the quantity of containers and boilers that were required. Even I was not aware of the ancillary requirements."

The Podesta stopped quickly and looked at Hansum. He was clearly frustrated.

"Where does an orphan learn to talk like this? It just doesn't make sense."

"I don't know, Excellency. It's just the way I talk. But truly, do not be angry with the Baron."

"No man can make the excuse of ignorance when he is given great responsibility. And no leader can allow his officers and nobles the luxury of being forgiven too easily. It breeds more mistakes." And then the Podesta relaxed a bit and looked at Hansum again. He patted Hansum on the cheek and said, "Come. Walk with me, Signor Monticelli. Don't worry about Da Pontremoli. I scream at him all the time. Sometimes he deserves it, sometimes — I just need to scream. But he is my cousin, you know. He is family. One always forgives family after the business day is over." He was at his horse now. He untied it from its tether and got up in the saddle.

"Si, family is always forgiven," Hansum said.

"You can always trust family in the end, no matter what. Have you thought on this?"

"Si, in the end, your family is your family. I have thought of this a lot lately."

"Good," the Podesta said, pulling on his horse's reins. The stallion danced as he turned it around. "Think on it some more."

By that evening, Hansum was helping the men unload the one hundred empty wine barrels in the barn. Some weren't so empty. Several of the workmen were drunk, but Mastino's angrily-given orders had been completed. There were also a dozen more cauldrons being set up on flat rocks with a large space below them for a fire. Hansum stayed with the men, getting things set for the morning. The Podesta and Baron dined alone that night.

⧗

"Young Romero was quite concerned for you, cousin," Mastino said.

"He is a good boy," Nicademo said. "Did you villainize me well?"

"Well enough to make my point."

"And will he be ruled by you as concerns Beatrice?"

"I made my point, but he did not answer. What kind of man turns down a princess? He can have his lensmaker's daughter too, for all I care."

"Youths of today are intoxicated by the fantasies of romantic love. But were we not the same at that age? Did your heart not swell when certain damsels came around?"

"The only thing that swelled was between my legs. No, decisions made with your nether regions are not long-standing. They are only good for as long as one is not standing."

"The poor boy wants to be friends with his mate," Nicademo said, chuckling at his cousin's wit.

"Even when marriage leads to friendship, these are minor things when planning a dynasty. Marriages are best made by parents and princes."

"So, will you take my advice of the other week? Will you allow me to tell the lensmaker your mind?"

"No. I will do that myself, before Romero leaves for Verona."

"You will talk to him?" Nicademo said, surprised. "My Lord, how can he refuse?"

# Chapter 6

It took some work on Guilietta's part to make sure that Shamira and Master Starini had, at least, some privacy while making the small fresco.

"No, I will chaperone them alone, Mama," Guilietta had said after they all finished supper. Lincoln opened his mouth. "No, you may not watch either."

So Guilietta was the only chaperone, sitting by the shop door, sewing, while Herado sat next to Shamira at a worktable cleared of lensmaking supplies. On it instead were the fresco painting tools Master Starini had brought with him. Herado had prepared for this date by nailing together a frame and pouring plaster in it, then letting it harden.

"We must conceive a vision and draw it on paper," he said, smiling. "Then we shall transfer it to the plaster."

"But how do we do the transfer?" Shamira asked, excited. "And the plaster you brought is already dry and rough? How do we paint on . . ."

"Patience, dear Carmella, patience. Did your drawing masters not teach you discipline and how to hold your tongue? My first master had a very long stick for questioning apprentices."

"*My* teachers encouraged curiosity," she said, laughing. "And self expression." Guilietta stole a sideways glance at them and saw the two were continually grinning at each other. She was so happy to see the girl she considered her sister as happy as she was at having her Romero.

"So, before we draw," Herado said, "we must mix up some plaster and let it start to set." He took a bowl and mixed sand and lime with some water. "Be careful of your delicate hands. The lime can burn them."

"I'm pretty tough," Shamira teased.

As he stirred, he kept a contented eye on her. Then he put the bowl down and pointed to the paper.

"So, what shall it be? What we create here will be a present for your master."

Without hesitation, Shamira picked up a piece of charcoal and started drawing. Herado leaned close to her, watching her every stroke. Guilietta could see that, unlike when Shamira was putting lenses into the looker, she was very sure of herself. Her hand did not waver, not even when Herado was so close his arm pressed against hers.

"What a beautiful angel, Carmella," Herado said with awe. "It is more real than Master Giotto's, may he rest in peace. I watched him draw often."

"You knew Giotto?" Shamira said with equal awe.

"He died when I was a very young apprentice. He was my master's master. But your work, even as a simple line drawing, looks like it can fly off the page. I hope when I add the color, it will retain the same lightness. Look, Signorina Guilietta," Herado said, picking up the drawing.

"How pretty," Guilietta answered. "I've never seen an angel with a bow and arrow."

"It's Cupid," Shamira said. "The Greek god of love . . ." and then she stopped, mid-sentence, blushing a deep crimson.

They worked quite late making their small fresco. After completing the drawing, Herado had Shamira poke scores of tiny holes along its lines and then set it on the plaster base. He patted a bag of powdered charcoal on top of the drawing, so that the charcoal passed through the holes and marked an outline on the plaster. Then he took out a little pouch of brownish-red pigment and used a thin-tipped brush to mix water in with it.

"Carmella, can you redraw your Cupid with the sinopia? We will put a thin layer of plaster over it, so as to see the drawing below, and then apply the colored pigments and shadows while it is still wet."

After she recreated cupid on the plaster, Herado showed Shamira the different pouches of pigments he had brought and they worked together, discussing the color scheme and preparing the pigments. Then Master Starini took the bowl of setting plaster and used a small trowel to smooth a thin layer of it over the design, so you could just see the sinopia below. Then he mixed the pigments with water and, in an orderly fashion, put the watery colors onto the plaster.

"See how the plaster soaks up the color? Getting different effects, skin, shadows, clouds, is a matter of making some watery and some thicker," Starini explained. After the better part of an hour, a final outline was needed. "Here, Carmella, you do the fine work around the angel's hands and eyes. I do not want to ruin your work. My line is more clumsy than yours."

"But your colors are very beautiful, Herado . . . I mean Master Starini." Guilietta saw Shamira blush again.

"We will make a very good team, Carmella."

Several mornings later, Shamira heard the Master grumbling loudly downstairs.

"Why is the fire not on? Where's Carmella and Guilietta?"

"They are upstairs, preparing for Master Starini's arrival," the Signora was heard saying.

"He's coming to join us for church," the Master retorted. "What can they prepare upstairs?"

"They're preparing Carmella," the Signora said. "Now hush, husband. Maruccio, build up the fire."

"This Starini is coming too often," Shamira heard the Master say. "Supper the other day, church today. It is all too fast to be proper."

"They are in love, Agistino," the Signora's voice said. "You be nice to Master Starini."

Shamira's cheeks flushed hot red when she heard this, and she felt embarrassed. When she and Guilietta finally came downstairs, Shamira tried to act nonchalant. Guilietta had not only primped and preened her, but she was wearing the new dress the Satores had made for her trip to the palace.

"You look hot!" Lincoln teased.

"Hot? It's not hot in here," Ugilino said. "It's quite cool."

"Hush you two," Guilietta said. "Carmella, you sit down. I will prepare dinner."

The Signora came over and enthusiastically pinched Shamira's cheeks again.

"Ouch," Shamira cried.

While dinner was being prepared, Lincoln sat next to Shamira.

"Let me get this straight. You don't think Starini is a dork anymore?" he asked.

"Herado's kinda sweet, and says we make a good team."

There was a knock at the door. Shamira felt her face go hot again, when the Master opened the door and said, "Master Starini, please enter my home. See, see what we have hung above the door."

"Ah, the angel. The Cupid," Herado said. "This way, everybody who enters knows this is a house of love." Then he turned and bowed slowly toward Shamira. "Buon giorno, Signorina Carmella," he said very quietly.

Then the Master did something unexpected. He showed Herado to the table and allowed him to sit right next to Shamira. They both sat primly straight, and both ate very little. They looked at each other, smiling as everyone ate and talked. But Herado seemed a little more distant than the other day.

"Wait'll you see San Zeno, Herado," Lincoln said. "If you like frescoes, this place is full of them. But I like the carved dragons outside best."

"Oh, something has come up," the Master said. "I received a note from the palace saying they need a number of lookers ahead of plan. After services, I must return to work."

"Oh, so I'll have to come home too?" Shamira asked.

"No," the Master said jovially. "Guilietta is competent to do your job. Why don't you and Master Starini linger at the church and look at the artwork?"

At the church they met Father Lurenzano and introduced Starini.

"Well, perhaps you'll need my services soon for another . . ." Guilietta put her hands to her lips. Lurenzano smiled. "Ah, another secret."

After the services, when the Master, Guilietta and the Signora went home, Father Lurenzano asked Ugilino and Lincoln to help move some things down in San Zeno's crypt.

"Will we see the saint's bones?" was the last thing Shamira heard Lincoln ask as she was left alone with Herado.

They walked around the great cathedral, stopping and looking at the many wonderful frescoes, paintings, sculptures and mosaics. Shamira continued to be impressed with Herado's knowledge of the minerals and plants used to create different colors and the techniques of applying them. But she could see that Herado was still agitated about something.

"Herado, you look like you have something weighing on you," she said.

"Really? Do I look like that?" he said. "I am just nervous, I guess."

Shamira blushed, presuming that he was nervous about courting.

"I'm nervous too," she admitted. "But we must try to enjoy it. This is natural." And then she said something she thought she'd never say. "It's God's way."

Herado looked at Shamira for some seconds.

"Yes, it is God's way. God's will. And I will do everything in my life to take me toward painting great cathedrals." Herado seemed to relax, somewhat. "May I tell you what I have been thinking, Carmella? About a plan I want to show the Podesta?"

Shamira became excited. "Yes, please, Herado."

The artist became animated. "Come," he said, holding out his hand. Shamira took it and he led them up some steps and pointed at a still-bare spot on one of the ceiling's vaults. He stood tall on the steps and gestured upward. "Picture this, Carmella. Birds. Many birds, all the types of birds that live in Verona, flying high up on a ceiling of the church with angels, all circling the baby Jesus. And around the edges of this vision, scenes of the great buildings of Verona."

"This is a fabulous vision, Herado," Shamira said supportively.

"But the birds, they must look real. I must know how they look."

"Yes, you must make a study of birds. That by itself could be very interesting."

"Yes, a study of birds. I am glad we are of one mind on this."

"Well, in a large project, one must do lots of preparation. I would love to help you with this, Herado. Any way I can."

Herado smiled widely at this. "Anything?"

"Si. We can do it together, like we did the Cupid."

"Carmella," Herado began, then paused, looking deeply into Shamira's eyes. "May I make a proposal to you?"

A proposal? Shamira felt her heart flutter at the mention of the word.

"What, what is it, Herado?"

"Since you draw people so much better than I, you must draw the baby Jesus and the angels. I will do the birds, clouds, buildings and colors."

Shamira felt a lightness of being that she had never felt before, and she couldn't stop a broad smile from stretching itself right across her face.

"Si, Herado. Si. I would love to do this together."

"Oh, this is marvelous, Carmella. Such a monument to God this ceiling will be. Grazie."

"You're welcome, Herado. I said I would do anything."

"So, one more thing, a small thing, to help me with the birds. I truly need a looker, Carmella."

This stopped Shamira. "But the Master. You heard what he said about it, Herado. The Podesta has forbidden him to sell lookers to anyone but him."

"Oh, it's only one looker, Carmella," Herado said, still smiling. "Come, sweet lady, do not be argumentative with your man."

"I'm not being argumentative. I'm just reminding you of Master della Cappa's obligation. He is very loyal to the Podesta. He has helped our household greatly."

"Oh, what the Podesta doesn't know . . ."

"No, please, Herado. If we are to do business with the Podesta, we must be scrupulously honest. It would be wrong . . ."

"Do not tell me what is wrong or right," the young artist said seriously. "That is for the man to decide."

"What?"

"Important decisions are the man's prerogative. Do not presume to tell me what to do, please."

Shamira couldn't believe what she was hearing. "You want me to steal a looker and give it to you?"

"Not steal. Take. What is one looker?"

"You want me to take a looker and not tell Master della Cappa?"

"If we are to be together, you and I must keep our own plans. Don't you agree?" he asked, reaching out and touching Shamira's hand and smiling warmly.

"No, I'm sorry, Herado. I can't do that." Shamira watched as the smile vanished from his face.

"If we are to be a couple, you will do this if I tell you!" he said, his eyes now taking on a hard expression.

"Herado, this is unreasona . . ." Shamira suddenly felt her upper arm being grabbed.

"If we are to be husband and wife, you must obey me."

"Hey, we're getting a little ahead of ourselves here, aren't . . ." Shamira felt her other arm being grabbed and found Herado's face very near to hers.

"A wife supports her husband in everything he says." Shamira felt herself being pushed backwards.

"Herado, what are you doing? Stop, you're hurting me."

"You will get me a looker," he repeated, squeezing her arm harder and now shaking her. His voice echoed in the great hall.

"Herado, stop!" Shamira cried. "I'm going to fall."

"Do what I tell you," Herado cried into her face.

Shamira felt her foot slip on the marble step and she tumbled down several stairs to the floor.

"Ow, my ankle," Shamira's voice reverberated throughout the church.

"Hey, what's going on here?" Lincoln's voice cried as he came up from the lower church.  In a few moments, he was down by Shamira's side. "What happened? Are you okay?"

"Carmella tripped," Herado said, leaning down to help, but his words were cut short as Ugilino pulled him away from Shamira.

"That's not how it looked to me," Lincoln said. "Can you stand?"

"Yes, I think so," Shamira said, then, "ouch."

Herado's eyes went wide. "Oh my God, please forgive me. Carmella, please, please. I didn't mean . . ." Herado fell to his knees and clasped his hands together, but Ugilino was still holding him. "Please forgive me, sweet lady, please."

Shamira glared down at him. "I will not steal from my family!" she said tersely.

"I did not mean it that way. I would never . . ." But he didn't have the chance to finish his sentence.

"I'm going home," Shamira announced, turning and limping toward the church exit. Lincoln gave Herado a severe look and fell in beside her.

"Carmella," Herado cried. "Please, no, it was a mistake. Please." Herado followed Shamira, pleading with her. All the while Ugilino was by his side, scowling. They walked in silence, Herado, slogging along, his head hangdog. As they approached home, they could see, at a distance, the Master entering the house. But when they reached the door, Shamira walked right past and headed down the alley.

"I'm going to the shop," was all she said. When they got to the shop, Shamira entered and closed the door behind her.

Lincoln stood in front of the door, blocking Herado's way.

"Time to go home, Starini," he said.

"But I must say goodbye."

"You'll have to have the Master's permission to return now," Lincoln said. "Ugilino, you stay in front of the shop door. Come, Master Starini."

When Lincoln and Herado entered the house, the Master was on all fours by the fireplace.

"Damn!" Lincoln said.

The Master had the secret hiding place for his strongbox open. He had carefully chiseled out one of the hearthstones, so he could hide his strongbox in a hollow behind it. The box was open and coins, including many shiny gold ones, were showing. The Master spun his head around, sighing in relief when he saw it was only Lincoln. Lincoln then looked over at Herado. The artist's eyes bulged at the sight of the money. He stood there, frozen, till the Master closed the lid on the box.

"You're all back," Agistino said, smiling as he stood. "So, have you had a nice talk? Did you come up with some ideas for the Podesta? Where's Carmella?"

"Master della Cappa, we were having a nice chat. And then I said something, I'm afraid, that Carmella misunderstood. We had a small spat. Carmella, she went to the shop."

Master della Cappa looked serious for a few moments, then grinned. "A lover's spat?"

"Yes, yes that's it," Starini said.

"Carmella ended up falling down some steps and hurt her ankle," Lincoln said. "She's very angry."

Agistino's eyes snapped back at Herado. "Fell down stairs?"

"A difference of opinion, of who is the head of a house, you see, Master. I was simply exerting my manly prerogative."

"Manly . . ." Lincoln began to repeat, till Agistino held up his hand for silence.

"You chose the wrong woman to dominate. Our Carmella is a woman with a mind of her own."

"I. . ."

"Master Starini, you must leave — for now. It is the Sabbath and I insist my house be calm on these days."

"May I call again?"

"We'll see. I will talk with Carmella." Both Lincoln and Starini began to speak at the same time when the big hand went up again. "Good day to you, Master Starini."

# Chapter 7

Hansum found that being a leader, training men, always having to be positive, even when angry, was a fulfilling experience. But he found it difficult to relate to the peasants. Their world view was unfathomable to him. Their sense of time, or lack of it, confounded him. He wondered how the wonderful city of Verona, with all its cathedrals and huge walls, ever got built with workers like them. But at the end of the day, with perseverance and a strong hand, progress seemed to happen. Hansum noticed that the men especially liked it when he worked physically with them. He was mixing a large barrel of ley when he felt a hand on his shoulder.

"Oh, hello, Baron." The Baron did not smile.

"Come with me, Signor. I wish to speak with you." They walked under a large oak where they could speak privately. Nicademo wrinkled up his nose. "You still stink like a peasant."

"The men like it when I work with them, Excellency." Hansum rubbed his sore shoulder as he said this.

"It's good to be liked," Nicademo said flatly. Then, seeing Hansum favouring his shoulder, he slapped him hard on the back. Hansum winced with the pain. "But look around you, Signor. We have many, many men with strong backs who are used to slinging merda and only good for that one thing." Then he tapped Hansum five times on the forehead with his finger. And he did not tap lightly. "But this, this head, we have only one like it in all the land."

"What's the harm?" Hansum asked.

Nicademo looked at him seriously. Then he took a deep breath and sighed. Speaking more reasonably, he continued.

"Romero, the saltpeter is but one project. I have sat and made lists of all the projects, all the equipment, all the logistics of the men and materials to create the cannon our Podesta wants. In two years we aim to have one hundred and fifty cannon, ample ammunition, cannoneers, horses, stables, security for all this, security for all the supplies and supply routes." His eyelids fluttered as he ran all the things he was considering through his mind. It reminded Hansum of a light on an old museum computer, flashing while it calculated. "Romero, in the end, when you add up everyone, from the peasants in the fields to the cannon foundries, to the carpenters and wheelwrights, all the people in the mines from Cambria to Germany, we will have over two thousand strong backs making the cannon and ammunition and almost the same using them. And for all of this, we need you."

Hansum paused, truly taken aback.

"I didn't realize, Excellency. All this from a few ideas? I thought you were angry with me for the Podesta shouting at you the other day. "

"Oh no, Romero. Our lord has many cares. And all our cares are his cares. So, to be his whipping boy now and again is no great hardship. For I am family and secure within his confidence."

"So, you want me to stop working with the men physically and just oversee? Plus work more on planning with you? Is this what you are suggesting?"

"It is my suggestion, and the Podesta's. He too has observed your overzealousness to do physical work. We ascribe it to your past life as an apprentice. Do you think you can convert your mind to that of the bureaucrat, a planner? I assure you, you will be kept just as busy."

"Si, Excellency. And I want to say, I think you are right in everything you tell me. Grazie." Nicademo gave a little nod of appreciation.

"Are your men competent to keep themselves employed for the rest of the day?"

"Si, Signor."

"Then get yourself clean to the point where you stop smelling like a raw saltpeter bed and more like a gentleman. Many building masters are arriving to receive commissions to start building your great plan. And we will have a special guest."

For some reason, a foolish hope sprang up in Hansum's heart. His eyes widened as momentary hope excited his being. Could it be Guilietta coming to visit?

"Who, Excellency?"

"The Lady Beatrice."

*"Oh, oh,"* Pan whispered.

Hansum felt his face flush hot, and when he looked up, Nicademo was staring at him. The Baron pointed to his horse and a small carriage with the butler in it. "I've sent down some new clothes for you. Duccio will help you dress. Be in the meeting room within the hour. *Capisce?*"

Hansum told Jacopo he would be on his own till tomorrow. Then he asked that an exceptionally large cauldron of hot water have some cold water poured in it, to make it the proper temperature for a bath. The men were surprised when Hansum did not help them with the buckets. Then he stripped off all his clothes, except his hat, and got in the pot. He scrubbed and rubbed himself all over. Then he just lay there soaking for a few minutes. The men kept working at their jobs, but looked at him queerly. Most had never seen anyone in a hot bath before. Hansum called Duccio over and handed him his brown hat.

"Just hold it so I can see it. Don't play with it." Then he ducked in the water, rubbed his face, neck and hair as vigorously as he could for a good minute, getting off all the dirt and stink. "Cristo, that feels good," Hansum said, climbing out of the pot. Duccio handed him a towel and then an ivory comb.

"You look like a noble now, Signor," Duccio said. "A naked one, but a clean one." Hansum scampered through the chilly afternoon to the carriage and dressed. There was a basket with all new clothes in it, including a hat. He put on the new clothes, excluding the hat. "But your old one is filthy, Signor." Hansum brushed it off as best he could and put it on. Duccio then reached into the basket for one last thing, a piece of jewellery. It was a heavy silver chain with a large round pendant on it. "The Podesta insists you wear this with the new clothes. He said it is a gift."

Hansum looked at the pendant. On it was the della Scalla ladder in the middle, wider at the bottom than the top. On one side of the ladder was the image of a looker, sculpted in bas relief, on the other side, a cannon of the new design. Hansum didn't know what to think.

*"He made it especially for you, Master,"* Pan whispered. *"When you see the Podesta, you must make a great deal over this. But I am worried about all the new clothes, the medal and the daughter, all at once."*

"We must hurry, Signor," Duccio said. "The carriages of all the visitors have arrived. They are assembling in the meeting room as we speak."

"How do I look?" Hansum called to his men. Most of the workers made faces. One said he was so beautiful he wanted to kiss him.

As Hansum travelled back to the manor house, he flipped the pendant over and over in his hand, thinking of how to handle the upcoming situation. It was obvious the Podesta was making a move. It seemed to Hansum that his plan of making himself so important that Mastino would let him marry Guilietta was backfiring. The more he showed the Podesta what he had to offer, the more Mastino wanted him. He didn't know what to do, except try to emphasize that he would be loyal to Mastino, no matter whom he was married to.

# Chapter 8

After the incident with Starini at the church, Shamira tried working at the shop, but began crying and just couldn't stop. Guilietta took her to her room and sat with her while her friend wailed into the blankets. That night at supper, the table was quiet. Shamira sat, her eyes still red, picking at her food. Everyone seemed to eat slowly, showing an odd solidarity.

There was a knock at the door and Lincoln got up to answer it. It was a messenger with a note.

"It's from Starini," he announced, reading the outside.

Shamira jumped up and grabbed the note, then headed for the stairs.

"Read it here," Master della Cappa ordered.

"It's private," Shamira said.

"If we are family, there must be no secrets when it comes to these matters."

Shamira broke open the letter and read it quickly to herself. A small smile came to her lips, though only a small one.

"I'll read it," Lincoln said. Shamira handed the letter over reluctantly.

"My dear Carmella. It was a horrible mistake I made today when I asked you to take a looker without telling Master della Cappa . . . "

"What!" Agistino cried.

Lincoln put up a hand to let him continue.

" 'I see now how it sounded like I wanted you to steal it, and I can understand why you refused. Nothing could be further from the truth, dear lady. I meant only to borrow it, to make my study of Verona's birds. Then it would have been returned. I ascribe my ungentlemanly actions to the pressures I feel in finding a position as art master. I must admit, I am running out of funds, and it is these pressures which caused me to act in ways that usually do not reflect my character. If you would entreat your Master, whom I see loves you like a daughter, to allow me to call on you again, I promise my boorish behavior will never be repeated. With kind, pure thoughts, I remain, Herado Starini.' "

"Exquisite, sad words," the Signora said.

"It is a lovely missive," Guilietta added. "He seems sincere."

"I know the feelings he speaks of," the Master said. "Before a young man of ambition finds his place in the world, there can be frustrations. Those pressures cause problems, as we well know from our own experience."

"But he hurt me physically," Shamira said. "People who care for each other should never hit or hurt the other, no matter how frustrated they get. If my father ever hit my mother . . ."

"Carmella," Lincoln warned. She looked over and saw Lincoln slowly shaking his head.

"Perhaps you should give Master Starini another chance," the Master said. "He sounds truly repentant, and you two could make a fine team with your combined talents."

"But he really hurt me," Shamira repeated. She felt more tears running down her cheek again. The chubby hand of the Signora reached up and wiped them away.

"Let me make a suggestion, Carmella," the Master said gently. "Master Starini wants to borrow a looker to draw birds. I'm sure the Podesta wouldn't mind this one exception, since it will be returned to us and he is already in discussions with Herado. Why don't we fill a basket with some food and you two go out on a little walk around the city to draw together and have a picnic? He wants to draw scenes of Verona and also birds. And then you two could come back here and draw up this proposal and have supper with the family again. Let's say, day after tomorrow."

"But that's a work day, Master," Ugilino objected. "You're giving Carmella time off when we have the big order of lookers?"

"We can spare part of a day for one of my daughters."

"Who'll be their chaperone?" Ugilino asked again. "I'll do it."

"Like you say, it is a work day," the Master said. "I deem they can go on their own. And by what happens on your little outing," Master della Cappa added, "you will find if your Master Starini is properly endowed with the character he speaks of. What do you say to this, daughter Carmella?"

The table went silent, everyone staring at Shamira. She nodded once and then unrelenting hot tears flowed again. The Signora enfolded her in arms. Shamira had never felt more confused in her life.

Ugilino leaned over to Lincoln. "I don't think we will find that this Starini has adequate character for our Carmella," he prophesied.

# Chapter 9

Herado had been nervously walking the streets since spending one of his few remaining coins to send the apologetic note a few hours earlier. He felt he should get back to his room at the tavern, in case a reply arrived.

When he entered the tavern, it was noisy, as it always was, and he knew it would be another loud night. But at least he wasn't sleeping out in the fields or hiding in barns, like he had on most of his travels, searching out work as an artist. He ignored the calls from the bar girls as he walked up the steps to his room and grimaced as he lifted the latch to his quarters. Hopefully the landlord had found the rat which had bothered him the night before. The door creaked open and he stopped short.

"Good evening, Master Starini," said the figure reclining on his bed.

"Excellency," Starini gasped. Fear gripped him and he fell with his back against the now closed door. "What are you doing here?"

Feltrino Gonzaga propped himself on the elbow of his good arm. His left hand was still heavily wrapped in linens, a few spots of blood staining his bandages. He was a long, muscular fellow with cold eyes, which caused Herado to be nervous every time he was gazed upon by them.

Herado had first met Feltrino not long after he left Verona, having failed completely in impressing the Podesta della Scalla with his meager artistic talent. When he arrived in Mantua, he had gone to the palace to introduce himself and petition for an art commission. After waiting several days, he finally was allowed to speak with Feltrino's father, Luigi Gonzaga, the ruler of the Duchy of Mantua. He would speak to him while the old man ate dinner.

Feltrino happened to be at table as well, but he wasn't listening to the discussion about art. Starini found out later that Feltrino wasn't interested in such things. He was a soldier, currently healing from a serious wound. He had lost his thumb and barely escaped with his life in a sword fight against the most unlikely of opponents, a lowly apprentice. Just the other month, Feltrino had snuck into Verona on a mission to steal something called a looker, a new invention that brought faraway images close. It was of great military value, apparently. But he had failed and not only left behind the looker, but also his thumb.

Feltrino totally ignored Starini until he was telling his father how the Podesta Mastino della Scalla was impressed with his portfolio of designs, and that the only reason he wasn't employed there, at that very moment, was that della Scalla had many projects on the go and just didn't have any spare money at the time. The mention of della Scalla's name caused both Feltrino and Luigi to look up from their meals.

"You saw della Scalla? At his palace?" Luigi asked.

"Si. Podesta della Scalla was very kind to me and even showed me plans for buildings and cathedrals his masons were working on."

"You were in his planning room?" Feltrino asked, speaking for the first time.

"Si, Excellency. It was very impressive. Full of books and papers and maps and instruments of interesting design."

"Instruments?" Feltrino asked. "Was there an instrument which was a long tube and had crystals in it?"

"Si, Excellency. Such a marvel. I even looked through it. It made things a great distance away seem like you could touch them. He called it a looker."

Feltrino and his father stared at each other for some moments.

"Do you know anything more about this looker?" Feltrino asked.

"The day I was there, I met the master of the shop it was invented in and his artist who drew up the plans. It was very strange. The artist was a girl."

"You met the lensmaker, della Cappa?" Feltrino asked brusquely.

"Si, that's his name. Master della Cappa. A big bear of a man. And what was that artist's name? Ah, Carmella. Quite talented, for a girl."

"Father," Feltrino said, standing quickly, but Luigi put up a hand for silence. The older man turned and smiled at Herado.

"Master Starini," he oozed, "sit with us. I think we may have some work for you."

Not too many hours later, a deal was made. Herado was promised a commission, not only to create a fresco in Luigi Gonzaga's private family chapel, but also to work on a new church that was being built. It was a commission that could last the better part of his life. However there was one little task he had to perform first. He had to go back to Verona, reintroduce himself to the della Cappas and find a way to acquire a looker. It seemed an odd request at first, but Herado didn't want to refuse and put his commission in peril. But as he travelled back to Verona with Feltrino, something became very clear. He had made a bargain in which his payment was far higher than first realized.

"So, Starini," Feltrino said, smiling from his perch on the tavern bed, "where is it? We gave you money to stay in this wonderful place and it has been many days. Do you have the looker?"

"I have run into a problem, Excellency. I have befriended, and I must say, even beguiled the young female artist. But when I tried to purchase a looker from della Cappa, he said he couldn't because of an agreement with the Podesta. When I tried to force the girl to steal one, she balked and the family is disappointed with me. I sent a note of reconciliation only a few hours ago. Perhaps it will only take a little while longer . . ."

Herado heard a thunk against the door and was terrified to see Feltrino's long dagger stuck only inches away from his neck. Suddenly the Gonzaga prince was on his feet and standing eye to eye with him.

"Four days and no results?" Feltrino spit. "Why did you not just take one?"

"I am sorry, Excellency. I am an artist, not a thief." Herado felt Feltrino's strong good hand on his throat.

"Better to be a live thief than a dead artist," Feltrino said. "You saw what I did to that peasant on the way here, didn't you?"

The other day, when they came upon a fellow in the woods, Feltrino said he wanted to buy his food. When the fellow brought out some bread and cheese, which he said his wife had packed for him, Feltrino simply killed him and took it. That's when Herado really knew he was in trouble.

There was a knocking at their door. Feltrino took his good hand off of Herado's throat and put it on the latch.

"Master Starini," a young man's voice shouted, "it's Maruccio, from Master della Cappa's. I have a note for you."

Herado looked shocked, as if he had already been caught in his deception. Feltrino took his hand off the latch and smiled. Then he retrieved his knife from the door and leaned against the wall, pointing to Herado to open it. "Don't let him in," Feltrino mouthed.

Nervously, Herado took hold of the latch and opened the door a crack.

"Buon giorno, Maruccio," Herado whispered. "I'm sorry I cannot invite you in. I must share this room with another traveler. He is asleep." A note was thrust at him without a word. Herado took and unfolded it. His eyes lit up. "This is very good news." He looked back and smiled at Feltrino, who motioned with his knife to keep his attention on the hallway. "Maruccio, please convey to your Master and Carmella my deepest thanks and say I look forward to visiting again." Herado nodded and started to close the door, when he felt the door bang into his shoulder hard.

The boy name Maruccio had pushed on the door and brought his face very close to Herado's. Herado could see Feltrino's hand tighten on the knife, but the door wasn't forced open completely.

"I don't know why Carmella could possibly want to see you again, Starini, but let me tell you this: If you hurt her again, Ugilino and I will bury your ass."

"I give you my pledge, Maruccio. I will be good."

"We'll see," the boy said. Herado closed the door.

Feltrino relaxed, then smiled. He grabbed the letter from Herado's hand and read it. "A beautiful hand she has. Oh, and look, della Cappa will grant you the loan of a looker for the day. Perhaps this foolishness *will* work out."

"Si, si, I told you the plan would bear fruit and nobody will be harmed." Feltrino gave Herado that look which scared him so. "I will walk with Carmella to a quiet place in the city, far from her home but close to a city gate. When I have hold of the looker, I will excuse myself for a few minutes on some errand, then steal away to a gate and meet with you. Before she suspects anything, we will be away."

Feltrino looked impressed. "Very good, Master Starini. A grand plan."

"Grazie, Excellency. And then we can hurry back to Mantua and I can begin my creation of a fresco for your father."

"What? Oh that. Si." Feltrino laughed. "But one change to this plan of yours. Take this artist girl for a walk on the Verona wall."

"But how . . ."

"Take her to the San Zeno city gate. I have a man working at it. He will let you up. This way I will be there to ensure you do not fail to retrieve the looker."

"But she'll see you. They'll know I was working for you and where to find me."

Feltrino gave Herado that searing look again. "No they won't."

Herado gulped loudly, taking in what he just heard. "And then? Then we'll be off to Mantua for the artwork?"

"Si, Master Starini. Of course," Feltrino laughed. "You and your artwork."

Herado knew then and there that Feltrino would never allow him off the wall alive.

# Chapter 10

Hansum entered the planning room, clean from his bath, dressed in his new finery and still holding onto the medallion hanging around his neck. The room was full of the master tradesmen, there to receive commissions from the grand new project. But Hansum ignored them all. He spied out Mastino, steeled his resolve and walked toward him with purpose. As he got closer, he saw the Podesta stop speaking to a group the tradesmen and look intently at him.

"Be sincere, be sincere," Hansum repeated to himself. The tradesmen stepped aside, like they sensed this was a special moment. Only a step away from Mastino, Hansum stopped and looked at the noble as if he could find no words. The Podesta looked at Hansum as if he were a son, come home after a long time away. Hansum got down on one knee.

"Your Excellency, grazie. Grazie, grazie, grazie."

The Podesta took Hansum by the elbow and bid him rise. Mastino held Hansum's shoulders and kissed him on both cheeks.

"My boy," the Podesta said gently.

Hansum leaned into him and said quietly, "I swear before you now, I shall be loyal to you. All knowledge I have, all knowledge I acquire will be put to the service of you and your state. For as long as I live."

Mastino looked at Hansum as if he were in love.

"I am very moved by your gesture," Mastino answered, equally quietly. "Sincerely moved." Then more loudly, so all in the room could hear, "Signori, the project you have seen glimpses of was brought to me by this young savant, my savant, Signor Romero Monticelli."

Having seen the Podesta treat Hansum as a beloved son, everybody showed him great respect. They were very friendly to him during the social hour, when all drank and got to know each other. As time went on, Hansum was listening, his face now flush with wine, while an elderly gentleman, Master Zappatore, the canal builder, told a bawdy joke about a mermaid and a sailor. As Hansum laughed with the others, he looked up. The door to the room was ajar, and standing there, looking directly at him, was a young lady. She was taller than the average woman of the time, and stood straight and proud. She had clear eyes and a relaxed countenance. Hansum looked back at her and nodded slightly. She did not respond in kind, but stared pleasantly enough for another few moments before gently closing the door. Hansum thought for a second, then looked around the room for the Podesta. He too was looking at Hansum, watching his reaction.

After a while, the Podesta sent all the men out to cool their heels in the hall. They were to start individual meetings with each trade. Mastino, Hansum and Nicademo were to review with the masters their parts in the project.

"In two or three years," Mastino said, "everybody will start designing and making cannon similar to ours, so these months where we have an advantage, are precious. That is why, when we bring each tradesman in, we must have them put their mark or name on a vow of silence and also not tell them what the other trades are doing."

*"Black-box engineering,"* Pan said to Hansum. *"Every part made in secret."*

Hansum repeated the phrase and the Podesta smiled.

After signing their vow of silence, each trade master received a copy of the design part which concerned them. "Black-box engineering," the Podesta said to one of the tradesmen when he asked what his part was being attached to.

An afternoon of meetings had left Hansum very tired.

"See, I told you being a manager was just as hard as being a worker," the Baron laughed.

They went to the dining room where the trade masters were waiting for them. The long table was set with plates, goblets, candelabra, flowers, knives, spoons and a rare and new item, forks. All the trade masters were standing around the room, chatting. They fell silent as the Podesta, the Baron and Hansum entered. The Podesta went to his place at the head of the table and looked at the crowd. He smiled.

"It's time to dine and speak of more pleasant things than business," he said.

"What's more pleasant than business?" asked the old canal builder.

"Ladies, for one thing, Zappatore ," joked another master. "But not for you anymore, eh?" Everyone laughed.

"Duccio, please seat everyone," the Podesta said.

Hansum was seated directly to the Podesta's left. The Baron sat at the other end of the table and the butler then directed the trade masters to their seats. The more important and senior a trade master, the closer he sat to Mastino. The butler and footman pulled out chairs for the masters and most looked awkward perched upon a chair.

All seats were taken, except for the one to the Podesta's right. Mastino nodded at the butler, who pointed to three servers. They picked up pitchers of wine and started filling goblets. No one touched their glass. They all sat silently. A young man went for his goblet, but his father smacked his hand and gave him a look.

"Not till our host picks up his glass," the father chastised.

"It's been a mild winter," the Baron said, making some idle conversation.

"Si, si. Very good for everyone," replied one of the men.

"Not for the wheat," Zappatore said. "We tradesmen are happy when the snow does not fly, but next winter there could be empty bellies without snow on the fields the winter before."

"Always the optimist, Zappatore," the Podesta teased.

"Bricks without bread are much heavier, Excellency," the old man said.

The Podesta lifted his goblet. Now that he had touched his glass, everyone at the table was allowed to pick up theirs.

"May God grant success to our enterprises, Signori."

"Amen," the Baron said.

"Amen," replied the table.

The large double doors to the room opened. All eyes turned, and there, standing on the threshold, was the young lady Hansum had exchanged glances with. Da Pontramoli immediately put down his glass and stood up, Hansum and the others following suit. The young woman seemed to glide over to the remaining chair, which the footman pulled out for her.

"Signori, my daughter, Lady Beatrice."

There was a general murmur of greetings from around the table. The footman pushed in her chair, and as she sat, so did the table.

"My dear, my dear," said Master Zappatore, whose seat was next to hers, "the last time I saw you, you had two pigtails and were rowing a skiff. You were in a canal my men were working on for your papa. You splashed me and laughed, as I remember."

"You made a face and stuck out your tongue, Master Zappatore. I believe I was nine at the time."

"Such a good memory," the master answered. "That was almost seven years ago. You've grown into a gracious lady."

"Grazie, Master," Beatrice replied. "And please forgive me for splashing you."

Master Zappatore laughed.

"Introductions," the Podesta said, looking to the Baron. He went around the table, one by one, saying, "Well, you know Master Zappatore, the canal maker," and then he introduced each man in his turn. They were a collection of stone masons, millwrights, kettle makers, coopers, pipe fitters and more. The last one to stand was Hansum.

"An honor, Lady Beatrice," Hansum said.

"Master Monticelli," Beatrice replied.

"I am not a master yet, but I try to be of service in any way I can."

The Podesta looked back and forth at the two, obviously measuring what he saw. Then he clapped his hands, breaking the mood. "Duccio, let us dine. You may sit, Signor Monticelli."

Mastino leaned forward and touched Hansum's arm, then spoke in a whisper.

"Look at all these fellows staring at their eating implements. They haven't a clue," he chuckled. "Mine is one of the first tables to have that new piece upon it. The one with the tines, yes," he said, pointing to a two pronged fork with an ivory handle. Hansum saw that several men were staring at the things with confused expressions.

Hansum smiled as food was put on his plate: chunks of chicken, a large piece of lamb and mounds of steamed and spiced vegetables. He was hungry. He had eaten with his hands and only a spoon for months now. But as Mastino began to eat, Hansum absentmindedly took up the knife and fork, and started using them as he had done thousands of times before in his previous life. He looked up and was happily chewing away when he noticed everybody staring at him.

*"Be more awkward with the knife and fork, Master,"* Pan whispered. *"You are not supposed to have used them before."*

Even Lady Beatrice had stopped eating and was staring.

"What?" Hansum asked. "Am I using them wrong?"

"On the contrary, Signor," Beatrice said. "You could give the table lessons."

"It — just seemed obvious."

The men around the table found the new cutlery awkward, and most fell back to using their hands and a spoon. The one thing they didn't have a problem with was their goblets. Much wine was drunk and a great deal of joviality followed. Soon the lack of table manners didn't really seem so important.

"Excellency, where is Bernarius?" one of the masters asked. "I thought he was to be here."

"Yes, where is Master Bernarius?" another seconded.

"Master Bernarius?" Mastino questioned innocently.

"From Vicenza, Excellency," Nicademo said from the other end of the table. "His family makes wagons and wheels. Large ones for projects like we are planning."

"And he is where?" the Podesta asked. "Do you know?"

"I can't say," his secretary answered. "I suppose he is tied up somewhere?"

The butler came and whispered in the Podesta's ear.

"Excuse me, Signori," the Podesta said, standing up. "Please continue to dine. I hope not to be long. Daughter, please attend to our guests." And with that, he left.

The meal and conversations continued. Nicademo talked casually with several of the men at his end of the table. Old Master Zappatore continued to chat familiarly with Beatrice, though every once in a while, Hansum would catch her looking at him. Hansum, for his part, was content to sit at the table and eat quietly.

"You do not join in the conversation, Signor Monticelli," Beatrice finally said.

"Oh, I am sorry, Lady Beatrice. I was far away in thought. I was thinking of a problem I must solve for tomorrow," he fibbed.

"Ah, so the art of courtly conversation is not one of your savant gifts?"

"I'm sorry I am not better company for you."

"Oh no. You have very nice table manners."

"I think she's comparing him to us," Zappatore announced to everyone.

"I've never sat at a table like this, my Lady," said one of the men down the row. "I hope we are not too common for your company."

"Oh, gentlemen, if you are here, it is because of the high regard my father has for your talents. While courtiers may be witty in their conversations, I'm sure they would be witless when it came to making a structure that remained standing, a mill that milled or a canal that retained water."

"Still," Zappatore said, "it's an event for the likes of us to be at a table with one as elegantly attired as you, Lady Beatrice. We are most unworthy of your company."

"Nonsense, Signor. The cloth on one's body does not reveal the true content of one's character. That puts me in mind of a story," Beatrice thought out loud. "A true story, Signori, of the late and great writer, Dante."

"Who?" asked the uninhibited boor. By the majority of neutral faces, it was obvious that most of the table didn't know who Dante was either.

"Why, the great poet and writer, Dante Alighieri, one of the greatest talents of words the world has ever known. And my grand uncle, Cangrande, was his patron." Everybody knew who Cangrande was and gave an appreciative "Ah." "The story I shall relate is not a story that Dante wrote, but one that actually happened to him. I think it is well for you men of talent to hear it."

"She's gone from being told stories to telling them," Zappatore said.

"The great poet was travelling and given hospitality of a king I shall not mention, for it is to his shame that this happened, and he is long dead. As is the custom around kings' tables, the most notable guests are placed closest to the sovereign." Beatrice looked briefly at Hansum. "It should also be said that many men of artistic talent are not that keenly aware of the need to wear fine clothing. After all, they live in a world where beauty resides in their great minds." She glanced at Hansum again. "So, often it does not come to them to dress up on stately occasions. On this evening, the great poet came to the dining room in common clothes, dusty and even patched in a few places. He had just come from a wonderful walk in the king's woods, and had not even washed his hands. The king's butler — a man with his nose in the air, but never in a book — was ignorant of how great this guest was, so he seated Dante at the end of the table, in an inconspicuous place. Dante felt quite injured at the slight, but said nothing. He ate his meal and left before the festivities began. The very next morning, the author of *La Vita Nuova* left the castle without a word of complaint or good-bye. When the king found out what had happened, he was furious and sent messengers to retrieve his injured guest. That evening at supper, Dante came in elegant attire. He was seated right at the king's elbow. When the meal started, Dante astonished both king and court by nibbling a bit of food, then throwing some on his fine jacket. Then he sipped a bit of wine and then poured some onto his braies. The king asked him the reason for such strange actions. Dante replied, "Sire, though I am great, you honour me better when I am clothed in these fine fabrics. I therefore did not wish to deny the raiments their due of the food."

At this, several of the men around the table laughed heartily. Hansum laughed too. Beatrice was indeed as interesting as her father said. Hansum stood up, still chuckling.

"Excuse me, Lady Beatrice. I must retire for a short while."

"I hope not for the night," she said. "Your company is quite pleasant."

"I will be back. Hopefully you will have more witty stories," he said, giving a little bow as he left. He had drunk too much and needed his commode.

## Chapter 11

Hansum was making his way back to his room to use his commode, still smiling at the story Beatrice had told about Dante. He heard voices and an odd muffled sound coming from the planning room. The door was slightly ajar. He stopped and peeked in. A man was tied to a chair, his face bruised and swollen with rivulets of blood running helter-skelter across it. Grazzana was stuffing the poor fellow's mouth with cloth. The Podesta was also there.

"You have deceived me, Bernarius," Mastino said. "I am very disappointed. Your family has done much business with mine over the years, so it grieves me that you have been consorting with the Gonzaga family against me." He looked at Grazzana. "You don't think he knows anything more?"

Bernarius tried to protest, but all he could make were muffled sounds.

"I think he's told all, Excellency."

'So, this is what had become of Bernarius,' Hansum thought.

"It's lucky you came upon him, Grazzana."

"Without the looker, I couldn't have gotten close enough to identify them, Excellency," Grazzana said. "I recognized the Gonzaga from being across the battlefield from him at Bresca. He's feedin' the crows now," Grazzana added, patting Bernarius's shoulder.

Mastino clucked his tongue as if he were a schoolmaster admonishing a boy.

"A man cannot have two masters, Bernarius." Then he said coldly, "Those who deceive me pay the price. Take him to the fields." Bernarius made more sounds of protest and struggled against his inescapable bonds. The Podesta looked up at Grazzana, motioned with his head toward the window, then turned toward the door. Hansum hurried away.

⏳

Hansum stood shocked and speechless as he relieved himself into his commode. Pan popped onto the floor.

"The Podesta is a hard man," Pan said. "But I suppose he is a product of his time."

"I can't believe you're looking at it that way. He just ordered a man killed in cold blood," Hansum said.

"Yes, but what's a poor despot supposed to do," Pan replied, "when there are many strong families who would gladly kill him and take all *he* commands? It's how the world grew, I guess. Strong caveman leaders made strong tribes, then villages, then cities with armies."

"I was going to tell him the truth about Guilietta tonight, and ask his forgiveness for deceiving him. But after seeing that . . . damn!" There was a knock on the door.

"Signor Montecelli, are you about?" It was the butler.

"I'm using the commode, Duccio."

"The Podesta calls for you. The dinner is ending and all are dispersing." Hansum did not want to see the Podesta right then.

He didn't know how he would react after seeing him order some-one's death.

"Well, I shall stay in my room and see the Podesta in the morning."

"His Excellency told me specifically to bring you, Signor. I can-not refuse," Duccio called.

"A moment then."

"Just be careful and calm," Pan said, disappearing back into his lamp.

The dinner was breaking up as Hansum arrived back at the entrance to the dining room. Most of the trade masters were walking off to their rooms. The Podesta and Beatrice were alone in the dining room, except for Master Zappatore.

"You sent for me, Excellency?" Hansum said tentatively. Mastino didn't appear to be a man who had just ordered an-other's death.

"The dashing young signor reappears to grace the room with the beautiful signorina," Zappatore said.

"Master," Beatrice blushed.

"Good night, Master Zappatore," the Podesta said, smiling.

"Good night, Excellency. Sleep with the angels. Signorina. Signor." The old man made little bows, then put his hand on his back, to help him stand straight. He winked at Beatrice and Hansum, then tottered out of the room.

"Well children, did you have a good time this evening?" the Podesta asked.

"It was fun, Father," Beatrice said. "I like workmen. They are so honest."

"And you, Romero?"

"The food was excellent. I enjoyed it very much."

"That is all?" the Podesta enquired.

*"Refer to the Lady Beatrice, but not in too grandiose a fashion."*

"Lady Beatrice told a very funny story about Dante, Excellency. All in the room laughed."

"Truly? Such a hostess you are becoming, my dear. And did you two have a chance to talk? Young people should talk. Come. Let's sit. I'll be your chaperone." Nicademo stuck his head in the room.

"Excellency, may I have you out in the hall for a short while?"

"Excuse me, children. As you can see, my days are never over. There's always one more thing to execute. I'm sure I can leave you two unattended."

"Papa," acknowledged Beatrice, her eyes on Hansum.

"Excellency."

Beatrice smiled at Hansum. Hansum nodded, but was much more reserved. Finally Beatrice broke the silence.

"My father speaks highly of you, Signor. He says you are a great savant. I always have thought savants as old and wizened. You are quite pleasant to look at."

"I am continually complimented by your father's attentions. I fear he exaggerates."

*"She's given you a compliment, you ninny. You must compliment her back."*

"Withal, Lady Beatrice. I think this room more graced by your looks than mine."

"My father gave me one of your famous lookers. I have used it to spy on birds outside my window, and at people in the market. It's great fun."

"The fame goes to Master della Cappa. It comes from his shop."

"Modesty again. I am not used to such as this from the young men I know."

"Perhaps they have nothing to be modest about."

"Si, but most have nothing to boast about either. And yet they do. Perhaps they should choose to boast about their modesty as you do."

Hansum couldn't help but smile. She had skewered him well with that one. He was finding it hard not to appreciate Beatrice's wit and poise. Knowing what the Podesta had on his mind, he had hoped Beatrice would be plain and boring. But she wasn't.

"I'm sorry you think my modesty a boast," Hansum said, "but how can a person take credit for their talents? One is born with them, like a man who can run fast or who can lift great weights."

"So, if you are not responsible for all the wonderful ideas you bring my father, where do they come from?"

Sparring with words was something Hansum always enjoyed, and irony was his favourite device.

"A little voice in my ear, my Lady."

"Ah, you hear voices," Lady Beatrice said, taking a step forward. Her long, sweeping skirts made a swishing sound against the floor. She was now closer to Hansum. She looked at him out the side of her eyes. "Does your muse have physical form, or is she only a voice?"

Hansum continued the verbal jousting.

"I must admit *he's* not a beauty at all. What would you say if I told you he is half goat and half man?"

"I'd say he's the piper, Pan."

*"Master, stop jesting. It is a dangerous game you play. You must not say anything to encourage her. And stop flirting. You are a married man, after all!"*

This comment brought Hansum back to earth quickly. The look on Beatrice's face showed she expected him to continue the word play, but Hansum felt his face go cold.

"Your muse is Pan, Signor?"

A much sobered Hansum said, "I jest, Lady Beatrice. Forgive me."

"Not at all," the lady said. "It's fun." Continuing with her coquettish banter, Beatrice added, "To extrapolate upon your theory, your supposition presumes then, that compared to man, a bird must be a genius in that it can fly and we shall never be allowed to. We are ever chained to this earth till we fly with the angels. Or do you foresee in your savant mind a way and a day when man can join the doves and the hawks in the sky?"

"I fear, if man does learn to sit between wings and soar in the clouds," Hansum said in a subdued voice, "it would be as the hawk and not the dove."

"Do you really think it possible? What does your little voice say?"

*"Don't even conjecture on the future of flight,"* Pan warned. *"Not in the least."*

"Alas, Lady Beatrice, my little voice says not the least about flight."

Hansum had become so conservative in his tone of voice that it seemed Beatrice could do nothing but believe he was serious in what he said.

"So, you truly do give credit to God for your talents. Then I say, let us give the credit to God, who has put whatever talents you have in your humble frame. What do you say? Shall we give all credit to God?"

"I think you are making the joke now, Lady Beatrice."

"No, truly, this coming Sabbath. Come with me and Father to the local church. We shall all give thanks to God for your talents. Otherwise, if you are not humble enough in front of the Almighty, he may take your genius away."

"My lady, you are very kind, but I must not lead you on or be insincere."

"A prayer is not a promise of anything, Signor, except to God."

"But this trip to prayer is step toward a vow. And a vow is a promise." Hansum felt confused, and couldn't stop himself from rambling. "And a vow, whispered or shouted, said in secret or on a steeple top, is still a vow. I must not start a thing in hopes of a promise, which I intend not, and indeed, cannot fulfill. And I must fulfill the vows that I have thus far made to make myself worthy of that vow." Beatrice looked perplexed.

"Finally you say more than a short sentence and it is so complicated with vows that it might as well be full of ploughs and cows and sows, for all the sense it makes."

"Si, I'm sorry. Often the truth to one is a puzzle to others."

"Good evening, again, children," the Podesta said, re-entering the room. "There, I was not too long. How are you getting along?"

"Signor Montecelli is a complex man, Papa. Harder to fathom than any woman."

"Is that so? I have found him straightforward. Romero, are you having trouble finding words to say around a lady?"

"He's finding many words, Papa," Beatrice chided, "but very few make sense."

"I guess I *am* awkward around women, Excellency."

"Really? You didn't seem the type," Mastino said.

"Papa, I have invited Signor Monticelli to church with us this Sabbath."

"Excellent," Mastino replied.

They all stood around awkwardly for a few moments. Finally Hansum spoke.

"Excellency, with your permission," he said, "I would take my leave. There is much to do tomorrow and I would have myself well rested. Besides boiling down the ley, I will most likely need to make myself available to all the masters before they leave. I expect after studying the plans we gave them today, most will have questions."

"Well thought out, Signor," the Podesta said. "When I was your age, I would have rather stayed in the company of young women than go to bed early because of work."

"My inclinations are the same, Excellency. It's just the responsibilities you've given me are also an opportunity I must not shirk from." Mastino nodded slowly, then gave a small chuckle.

"Very good, Signor. Tomorrow's another day of hard work. But the Sabbath comes soon and after church we may loiter about the home and get to know each other better. What say you to that, children?"

"As you wish, Excellency," Hansum said.

"Will we see you at repast in the morning, Signor?" Beatrice asked.

Finally Pan whispered into Hansum's ear.

"I must be at the barn before daybreak. Perhaps tomorrow at supper," Hansum suggested.

"Ah, well, I'm to the city after repast and probably not home till late evening," Beatrice replied gently.

"Well then, children, you will see each other on the Sabbath," Mastino said. "I give you your leave, Romero. Rest well, so you may give your all in making machines my enemies cannot resist."

"Good night, Excellency. Good night, Lady Beatrice."

*"Bow, Master. Then leave quickly."*

⧗

The lady Beatrice nodded and curtsied, but said nothing as Hansum left.

"Daughter, he angered you with his lack of attention?"

"On the contrary, Father, he piqued my interest. I just could not seem too eager."

"Ah, stratagem. Of course. I see," the father said appreciatively.

"He's a very serious young man," Beatrice added. "But I sense a passion under his sober exterior."

"Si, I feel the same. That is why I like him."

"You actually like him, Father? That is high praise, indeed."

# Chapter 12

Hansum was up well before the sun and arrived at the barns a few minutes before Jacopo and his men. As the sleepy men arrived, yawning, stretching and scratching themselves, Hansum clapped his hands to get their attention.

"All right men, today is the most important day yet."

A few minutes later, coals from the day before were dug up and each of the fire pits crackled. Smoke and heat rose around the pots and the ley began to warm. By the time the sun was up, all the pots were boiling. Hansum leaned over each pot, allowing Pan to analyse the progress. Hansum's face became smudged and dirty.

"You should take off your hat, Signor," Jacopo said. "It's getting as black as your face."

The men skimmed off the organic scum, but suddenly there was a shout from one of them. Crystals were forming at the bottom of the pot.

"This is only the common salt, men. It's not what we're aiming for. But soon." Hansum showed them how to use the small wooden rake to scrape it out. When the salt stopped forming, he had them dampen the fires and pour water over the sides of the cauldrons to start the cooling. Within an hour, a different crystal appeared in the ley and sank to the bottom. These were whiter and more elongated. "There, men, there! Saltpeter," Hansum said victoriously. Even Hansum was amazed. It truly did seem like alchemy. "Quick, Jacopo, pass me the rake again."

"No, Signor. I overheard the Baron the other day. You are not to do the work." Jacopo leaned over the first cauldron where the magic crystals were forming. "Come, men. Come and learn." A dozen men crowded round and watched in awe as the crystals formed.

"They will do this for many hours," Hansum repeated on Pan's instruction. "But I wish to show these first results to the Podesta."

"Marco, hand me that bucket," Jacopo ordered. Jacopo raked out the first raw crystals and put them into the pail. He took a handful of the raw saltpeter in his hand and kissed it. His enthusiasm was infectious and soon all the men had the fever. They went from cauldron to cauldron, taking turns practicing with the rakes. Soon they had four buckets full of the raw saltpeter.

"Come with me," Hansum ordered two of the men. "Each carry two buckets. Jacopo, stay here with the others. Stir the pots slowly and rake out the crystals as they form. I won't return with the men. I have work up at the manor house, but I'll be back before evening. After these pots stop producing crystals, take the water and put it into barrels on the wagon. We'll dump the water back on the saltpeter beds later. Then fill the cauldrons with more ley and repeat this process. We'll be doing this for several days." For the first time, Hansum was not awkwardly polite about giving orders and gave them without Pan's prompting.

Hansum walked quickly to the manor house, the two labourers struggling to keep up. When they got to the house, the men stopped at the stairs, not daring to enter. The footman and another male servant took the buckets. They followed Hansum as he boldly strode down the halls to the planning room. Along the hall, many of the trade masters were standing around, talking. When they saw Hansum, they began asking questions about the different plans they received.

"Wait, Signori. I must show something to the Podesta."

Hansum opened the door to the planning room without knocking. The Podesta and Baron looked up from some papers on the table. Mastino looked at Hansum questioningly.

*"This calls for a dramatic gesture,"* Pan whispered. *"Spill a bucket onto the floor."*

Hansum tipped over one of the buckets with his foot and fifteen pounds of wet, raw saltpeter crystals spilled onto the floor. Like a wave roaring up a shore, the saltpeter swept toward the Podesta, the tongue of the wave licking his boot. Mastino reached down and picked up a handful. He smelled, then tasted it with his tongue, knowingly. A smile came to his lips.

"It's the real thing, Nikki." He looked at the servants. "Put those down and leave." When the three were alone in the room, Mastino stuck his hands into one of the buckets and let his fingers play through the crystals.

"You made all of this today?" the Baron asked.

"This is just the start, Excellency. Tonight we should have one thousand pounds of the crystal. By the time we process the first batch, we should have five thousand. They will need further refining, but that should reduce the quantity by only one part in five. And by the time we mix it all with the sulfur with the charcoal, we should have seven thousand pounds of finished black powder." Hansum spoke with excitement and without the need of Pan's coaching.

Mastino's eyes widened.

"Romero, I knew you could do it," he said. "Many doubted, but I knew. I took the chance." He then grabbed Hansum by the arms and cried, "Sixteen thousand barrels of black powder a year, you say? Sixteen thousand?" Then he kissed Hansum on both cheeks and laughed.

The door opened and Duccio stuck his head in.

"May I allow the first master in for his questions, Excellency?"

"In a moment, Duccio," the Podesta said. "Romero, here, sit at my desk to receive the questions. It is you they must talk to."

"But Excellency, this is your desk. I'm not dressed to . . ."

"Nonsense," the Podesta said. "Sit. There. Now, let's see how you look." Mastino and Nicademo stood back and laughed. "You look like a beggar on a throne. At least take off that ridiculous hat," the Podesta said. "It's filthy."

"No," Hansum replied curtly, surprising himself. "It's my lucky hat."

Hansum and Pan were busy for the next few hours answering questions. Hansum had learned that during this time in history, there was no such thing as a precise blueprint to be followed. Even great cathedrals were made from approximate plans. It was the expertise and experience of the builder, solving problems as they came up, which allowed the structure to rise. Therefore, the masters had many questions to make sure they understood their tasks properly.

By mid-afternoon, the meetings were finished and most of the masters had departed the estate. They would all be back within two or three weeks with supplies and parts to start assembling machinery or laying out buildings and canals. Within a month, Bella Flora would be a beehive of activity. When the last master left the planning room, Hansum put his hand to his stomach.

"Are you unwell?" the Baron asked.

"Just hungry, Excellency."

"Just like all savants," the Podesta said. "You forget to eat. Did you eat this morning? No?" And with that Mastino screamed for Duccio to prepare a meal.

# Chapter 13

Lincoln scowled at Herado Starini. After seeing him cause Shamira to fall down the marble steps at San Zeno, he didn't have much use for the fellow. And here he was again, having talked himself back for another date with a prettily-worded note. He was standing ramrod straight in the della Cappa kitchen with the whole household standing around. Shamira had her portfolio under her arm and a pained smile on her face, looking alternately down at the floor and up at Starini. Herado smiled at her, but looked nervous. Lincoln scowled even more when he saw Starini's gaze go toward the fireplace and land on the stone that hid the strongbox full of money. He watched him do this several times.

"Well, here you go then," Master della Cappa said. "Guilietta, give Master Starini the picnic basket to carry. And here, Signor, is a looker. Brand new. Just made yesterday. When you return it this afternoon, it will go back in the order for the Podesta."

"Grazie, Master della Cappa. I thank you for your generosity."

"It's nothing. We wish you well in your preparations for your plans to show the Podesta. Carmella is the one to help with that. Well, off with you both. The rest of us must get to our other work." Just as he and Shamira were walking out the door, Lincoln saw Herado do it again. He turned his head and stared for a brief moment at the base of the fireplace. "Enjoy, children," the Master called as the couple walked down the street. "All right, then," the

Master said, "the rest of us to work. Maruccio, I must go to the brass maker. I will be back in an hour."

"Master, I really don't know about this Starini. I saw him . . ."

"Hush, Maruccio. It will be all right. What's the worst that can happen?"

"But . . ."

"Enough already. I'm late."

"I'm going to take a nap," the Signora said.

As Lincoln, Guilietta, Bembo, Ugilino and the little apprentices walked down the lane to the workshop, Lincoln stopped.

"You guys go ahead. I'll be right back."

Lincoln walked back into the house. He could hear the Signora upstairs, humming happily to herself. Then he took the largest kitchen knife and got on his hands and knees by the fireplace. He removed the woodpile that hid the secret stone and fit the knife blade into an unseen crack. Soon he had the stone out. He reached in and pulled out the box. He replaced the stone and wood, then covered the chest with a cloth and carried it back to the shop.

Herado and Shamira walked in silence for a bit, then Herado screwed up his courage and turned to Shamira.

"Signorina Carmella, grazie, grazie for seeing me again. I went so crazy when I thought you would not. So crazy, I cried."

"You did? So did I, Herado."

And then, Herado leaned forward and kissed Carmella's hands. He looked up, and there she was, beaming at him. Herado sprang to his feet and motioned, with a smile, that they should continue walking.

They were halfway to the wall when he stopped and looked around.

"Ah, when we look back from here, Castelvecchio is at a good angle. Perhaps we can stop here and sketch?" he said, pointing to a broken bit of wall to sit upon.

"Okay, Herado," Shamira said, smiling.

They sat down on the large stones and took out their portfolios. Herado took out some paper, then searched around inside for something.

"Oh, merda. I believe I left my pouch of charcoals back at Master della Cappa's."

"You can borrow some of mine," Shamira offered.

"I'd prefer mine. My dear, I will be back in a very short time. Do you mind?"

"Well, charcoal is charcoal. I have some very fine . . ."

"I prefer mine," he said somewhat brusquely, then, "Forgive me. I have some special colored pastels too. We could both use them."

"All right, Herado. I'd like that. Hurry back."

Lincoln had been working for the better part of an hour when he looked up and saw Master della Cappa re-enter the work shop.

"Please come in, Captain Caesar," Agistino was saying jovially. "We will know the answer to your question in a few moments. Maruccio, come here. Maruccio is my shop manager. He knows everything here."

"Yes, I've heard the Baron mention how he is very clever." When Captain Caesar smiled, his long facial scar twisted and turned a bright red.

"Buon giorno, Captain. Yes, Master, what can I tell you?"

"As you know, the palace has need of one hundred lookers ahead of schedule. When will we have that many done?"

"Ah, we have seventy completed. One hundred can be delivered day after tomorrow," Lincoln said knowingly.

"No need to deliver. I will send a wagon," Captain Caesar replied. Just then, the captain's stomach growled loudly. He laughed. "Well, I must go. My stomach protests getting up so early and making rounds of all the gates. I haven't broken my fast yet."

"Well, come to the house, captain, please. We have some wonderful beef heart pie for that fretful stomach. Daughter, run ahead to the kitchen and prepare something. We will be right behind you."

"Si, Papa," Guilietta said, getting up from the workbench and hurrying out the door.

A few moments later, when the Master, Lincoln and the captain were walking up the alley, they heard a loud scream from the house.

"That's Guilietta!" the Master cried, and they ran.

As they rushed into the house, there was Guilietta, kneeling on the floor over her mother.

"My wife!" Agistino cried. "Is she . . ." But when he fell to his knees beside her, he saw the Signora was not unconscious, but had a gag tied over her mouth and her arms and legs were bound with cord. Guilietta was desperately trying to untie the knots, but without success. Lincoln rushed to the table and picked up the large kitchen knife. Captain Caesar drew his sword and went stealthily upstairs. Lincoln had the Signora's legs and arms free, and was cutting off her gag by the time the soldier returned.

"I suspect the Gonzaga," the captain said. "Were there any lookers in the house?"

Able to speak now, the Signora cried, "Starini, it was Master Starini. He tied me up and opened your hiding place, husband. Oh, we're robbed, we're poor again."

Agistino shot a glance over to the fireplace. The firewood was scattered and the hearthstone dislodged. "Thief! He robbed us. We trusted him and he's taken our gold!"

"No, Master. I moved the chest when you left," Maruccio said. "I never trusted him," and he thrust the knife angrily, blade first, deep into the wooden table. "I hid it in the loft."

But Master della Cappa's eyes were still wide with fear. "He has Carmella!"

Guilietta's hands shot to her mouth. "My sister!" she cried.

"At least he didn't get a looker," Captain Caesar said. "He may have been working as an agent for the Gonzagas."

"Oh, dear Cristo," the Master said. "That's why he made up all those excuses to get his hands on a looker. I allowed Carmella to take one with her on their picnic."

"You did what?" the captain shouted.

"We have to find Carmella before he hurts her," Guilietta said desperately.

"It may already be too late," Caesar said. "I must set up an alarm at the gates. You, boy, come with me. You can tell me what he looks like." They all ran outside, leaving the blubbering Signora in the house. Captain Caesar leapt onto his huge warhorse and thrust a massive arm down for Lincoln. He grasped it and felt himself being hoisted up behind the captain, like he was a bag of feathers. The captain spurred the beast and Lincoln felt himself lurch as the horse took off.

⧖

"My sister!" Guilietta repeated as she watched the horse disappear down the road. Her father stood beside her, gnashing his teeth. Guilietta looked back into the house, where her mother sat, hands covering her face. Beside her, embedded in the table, was the kitchen knife. She ran into the house, pulled the blade free and tore back out of the door, running down the street after Captain Caesar.

"Guilietta, stop!" she heard her father cry. But she kept on going.

⧖

Herado Starini was now desperate. He had been sure that if he brought Carmella to the wall that Feltrino would kill them both when he had the looker. His only option had been to get his hands on some money and run for his life, far away. Master della Cappa's gold could be his salvation. But the box was gone and the mother could identify him. Now he could either choose to run with no money or hope that Feltrino would keep his promise of the art commission.

"There you are, Herado," Shamira said pleasantly as he returned. She was sitting, sharpening her charcoal stick with a tiny knife she kept for the purpose. "I was beginning to think you'd been robbed."

"I'm sorry I took so long, my dear," Herado said, out of breath. "I could not get what I was looking for."

"Oh, that's too bad. Well, sit. Catch your breath. We can share my charcoal, poor though it is." She patted the stone next to her. Herado sat, hollow-eyed, trying to come to terms with his situation. "Here, look what I've done. Castelvecchio isn't very good from here, but I've drawn up some preliminary angels. What do you think?"

"What? Oh yes, very nice. Carmella, listen, I have a surprise for you, but we must hurry. I made arrangements for us to go up on the city wall, but we must get there before the guard changes. We can see the city better from there."

"Herado, that's a wonderful surprise. Guilietta says she and my friend Romero went up there. It was wonderful, she said, and romantic."

"Yes, yes, but we must hurry. Come, let us go." He grabbed some of her art supplies and shoved them in her portfolio.

"Herado, be careful. Don't bend the parchment."

"I am sorry. We must hurry."

"But I can't run, my ankle still hurts."

"Then walk as quickly as you can."

"Hello, Carmella," a voice called. It was the butcher who lived down the street from the della Cappas.

"Hello, Master Sanchetti," Shamira replied. "This is Master Starini."

"Yes, your Mistress told me yesterday you and a suitor would be out drawing today. Good day, Master Starini. How goes your drawing?"

"Fine, grazie. Carmella, we must hurry."

"I'm sorry, Master Sanchetti. We are going to draw from atop the city wall and must be there soon."

"Don't let me hold you up then. So very nice to meet you, Master. We will meet you soon, I . . ."

"Si, si. Soon. Come, Carmella."

By the time they got to the wall, Shamira's limp was more pronounced. Herado looked around desperately. There was only one guard on duty. He was a fellow with deep, hot eyes and full chainmail.

"You're for the wall?" the guard said in a low tone. Herado nodded. "Follow me."

The guard and Herado walked quickly up the dark, steep steps of the tower.

"Please slow down, Herado. My ankle. I need to rest," Shamira pleaded.

"We may rest all afternoon," Herado said. "It will be fine. You will see."

"Hey, I know if my own ankle will be fine or not, thank you. I'm resting here for a bit," Shamira said.

"Give me the portfolio. I will carry it. Come. Come, please, Carmella."

Shamira leaned against the wall, favoring her bad leg. The guard motioned in the direction they were to go, then left.

She finally looked up and tried to smile. "Wow, it really is nice. Let's find something to sit on and begin."

"No, I'm told the view is much better that way."

"Okay, okay. Give me a minute."

"Stop, stop!" Lincoln shouted into Captain Caesar's ear. "It's the butcher. Master Sanchetti, have you seen Carmella?"

"Si, si, I did. She was with that young Master. Starini. A rude fellow. I didn't like...."

"Did she say where they were going?" Lincoln interrupted.

"Si, she did. Atop the city wall."

# Chapter 14

As Lincoln and Captain Caesar galloped toward the wall, the captain pulled back the reins of his horse. He reached into a saddlebag, pulled out a looker and scanned the top of the wall.

"There, at afar, there. Your kitchen girl and the artist. They are walking."

"Well, what are we waiting for?" Lincoln demanded, kicking the horse with his own heels.

As they reached the gate tower, Captain Caesar grabbed Lincoln's arm and swung him off the horse. A single guard, with deep, hot eyes walked up to the captain.

"You," the captain shouted, "take your bow and sword and go up on the ramparts. There is a man and girl there. Block their way. I will go to the next gate and come at them from the other side. You, boy," he said to Lincoln. "You stay here. It could be dangerous." And then he tore off toward the next gate.

Lincoln watched as the guard grimaced, shaking his head as he picked up his weapons. He then entered the tower and disappeared up the stairs.

⏳

"Herado, why do we keep walking? There are so many beautiful views from up here."

"I am told the next tower, things are wonderful."

Along the wall there were small guard houses, to protect soldiers from the weather. As they came up to the next tower, a man stepped out from the small room.

"The view is especially nice here," he said, a sword in his hand.

"Feltrino!" Shamira gasped. "Herado, run!" She turned to flee, but Feltrino grasped her sleeve. She looked down to see a hand, minus a thumb, holding tightly to the fabric.

"Run, Herado. He means to steal the looker!" But Herado didn't move.

"So, finally you have accomplished your task, Starini," Feltrino said, smiling.

Herado stood silently, looking ashamed.

"Accomplished your . . . Herado, what is he saying?"

"I am sorry, Carmella," Herado said in an agonized whisper.

"You used me!" Shamira said angrily.

Feltrino laughed, "And well used too!"

"Excellency, we have the looker now," he said, pulling it out from the basket. "How do we escape here and get back to Mantua?"

"Eh? You go back to Mantua with me?" Feltrino said incredulously.

"Si, to paint your churches, as you and your father promised."

"What?" Shamira exclaimed. "That's why you wanted . . ."

"Shut up, girl!" Feltrino shouted, and he flicked his sabre at her. The flat of the blade hit her on the face. She fell to one knee. Starini went white. Feltrino calmly turned back to him. "I don't know if you deserve our patronage. You didn't do a very quiet job."

"But I'm not a soldier."

"I tell you what," Feltrino said. "Take my dagger. You kill the girl, and you will have your commission. Here, take it." Herado stared at the blade. "Come, be quick. She has but a small neck."

⧗

Lincoln stood at the bottom gate, pacing back and forth, when he saw a girl running toward him.

"Guilietta!" he said. "What are you doing here?" His eyes widened at the sight of the kitchen knife in her hand.

"Have you found Carmella?"

"Up on the wall with Starini. A guard is blocking their way from this side and the Captain went to go up from the next tower." Without another word, Guilietta was into the tower door and up the steps. "Wait, Guilietta. I was told to . . ." and then he took off after her.

Once up on the wall, Lincoln and Guilietta ran in Shamira's direction. The wall was curved at this point, following the bank of the Adige River. The quickly-moving waterway acted as a moat, giving extra protection to the wall and city.

"What are you supposed to do when . . ." They rounded a corner and stopped quickly, pulling back to let the curve of the wall conceal them. The soldier was standing by one of the many guardhouses along the perimeter. He was waving at somebody. The two teens stepped into the open just enough to see what the guard saw, then popped back, shocked.

"Starini and Carmella — with Feltrino!" Lincoln said. "It looks like the guard is working for him."

"Madonna mia!" a shocked Guilietta said. "What shall we do?"

"I don't know. Run and get help? Scream to distract them? Wait till the captain comes from the other side? I don't know."

Guilietta held the knife in front of her. "He has our sister. Let us at least get closer," and without waiting for Lincoln's comment, Guilietta crossed herself, then dashed forward as quickly and quietly as possible.

"Guil, wait," Lincoln whispered, but she was gone. "Madonna mia," he repeated, pursing his lips in resolve, and took off behind her. The sound of the river hid the sound of their movements, and soon they were hidden behind the guard room wall, not twenty steps from the armed guard. Lincoln and Guilietta looked at each other, wide-eyed. Guilietta held the knife up and Lincoln looked around for a weapon. He picked up a large rock.

⧗

A terrified Shamira looked up at an equally frightened Herado. His hand was shaking, but he still took the knife from Feltrino. Shamira looked up at him.

"Kill her, Excellency?" Herado asked. "Why? She is blameless."

"She is a witness. Come, I have this coil of rope. Do your business and we will escape down it together. The horses are in the trees not far from here." Herado stood, frozen with terror. "I won't stand here debating, Starini," Feltrino said. "Kill her!"

"I can't," Herado groaned pitifully.

"Fool," Feltrino said, raising his blade toward Shamira.

"No," Herado screamed, raising the dagger to attack Feltrino. But, without looking back, the Gonzaga prince brought the heavy pommel of his sword right into Herado's temple. The artist crumpled like a rag doll.

Shamira bit her lower lip and resolved that if she were to die, she would die fighting. She reached into her portfolio and grabbed her little sharpening knife. Feltrino looked down at her.

"So, you fancied this one? Now you can wed in Heaven. Him first," and he turned to stab the unconscious man.

Shamira pulled out her small blade and plunged it into Feltrino's thigh. As he screamed and turned on her, she immediately fell back onto her rump, grabbed the looker and executed a backroll, springing herself with her hands to her feet. Feltrino's blade flashed in front of her nose and she ran. Feltrino followed, but stopped short when the leg with the blade in it crumpled. Shamira ran with all her might, head down. She looked back and saw Feltrino pull out the blade, then look up and shout in her direction.

"Shoot her!"

Shamira turned and, to her continued horror, saw the guard, about a hundred paces from her, raise his bow.

Then, like a vision, two forms appeared behind the guard. It was Guilietta and Lincoln. They leaped on the soldier's back. The arrow let loose and screamed just an arm's length from Shamira's head. The man went down, with Lincoln smashing his fist with a rock in it onto the guard's helmet. The man threw Lincoln off and Shamira couldn't believe it when she saw Guilietta raise a knife blade high over her head. The man twisted and grabbed the knife, throwing Guilietta onto her back, and then grabbed for the blade with both his hands. Shamira ran at full tilt toward the fray, watching as Guiletta bit into the guard's hand with all her might and Lincoln flung himself back into the guard, forcing him to roll to the stone floor. It was a twisted and writhing pile of bodies that Shamira came upon, when the guard's boot came out and kicked her in the stomach. Shamira felt herself flying sideways, toward an open parapet, and then felt her head hit hard against the stone wall. A wave of pain rang out in her brain and she staggered in a daze to the floor.

"Help me, Excellency," she heard the guard scream through her fog. She slowly turned her head to see Feltrino throwing a rope over the side of the wall and climb down. Behind him, Herado Starini was staggering to his feet, trying to walk. Feltrino disappeared and Shamira had to close her eyes. She felt herself passing out, and then willed herself awake. She didn't know how long she had been unconscious. 'Seconds only,' she thought. 'Maybe a minute.'

"I'll kill you!" she heard a gruff voice scream. She opened her eyes and saw that the guard had regained his footing. He had Lincoln pushed between two parapets, his hands on the boy's throat. Lincoln's feet were lifting off the ground and he was about to be thrown off the high wall to certain death. Shamira strained to raise herself up and saw Guilietta, dirty and bleeding, pushing herself onto all fours.

"Carmella," she heard and turned her head. Herado Starini was staggering toward her. "Carmella," he repeated, and then a look of renewed terror gripped his face. Shamira turned to look at what he saw. It was Guilietta, both hands on the handle of her knife, the blade held high. Lincoln's feet were well off the ground now and Guilietta did not hesitate. The blade came down full force and plunged into the guard's back. The startled guard let go of Lincoln and shot backward. Guilietta retreated, pulling out the knife. The guard stood up to face his executioner, his mouth an open maw, questioning his now inescapable fate, and he fell dead to the ground.

"Carmella," Shamira heard again, and she turned to see Herado now, almost to her. "Forgive me, Carmella," he said, leaning down to her.

"MY SISTER!" came Guilietta's scream, and Guilietta flew over Shamira and crashed into Herado.

"No, Guilietta, no!" Shamira managed to say. She looked over and there was Guilietta, sitting atop of Herado, the bloody knife at his throat. "He saved my life, Guilietta."

"It was a mistake," Herado whimpered. "I didn't understand. I was tricked. Please forgive me. Please, please forgive me."

Guilietta, her dress bloodied and torn, stood and went to Shamira.

"Are you all right, sister?" she asked, the fierceness in her eyes still blazing.

"I hit my head. It hurts."

"A big bump, but no blood."

"You bastard!" they heard Lincoln scream. They looked, and there he was, with the guard's bow, shooting arrows after Feltrino. They were all going wild, and Feltrino was now hoisting himself out of the moat and hobbling over the fields. Soon he was too far to be reached. Now, in the distance, they could hear shouting and clanging from down the wall. It was Captain Caesar, coming with many soldiers.

"I'm sorry, Carmella. I'm sorry, I'm sorry," Herado continued to weep. "They promised me a church to paint, my own church. I didn't understand. I shall deserve my execution."

"Feltrino tricked him," Shamira said. "But Herado saved me." Shamira and Lincoln, both bruised and bloody, looked at each other, questioning what should be done. "Go, Herado," Shamira said. "Go quickly. Try to escape." The other teens remained silent.

"But . . ." Herado began.

"Go!"

Herado crept over to Shamira and grabbed the hem of her skirt, "Grazie, dear lady. Grazie."

"Go! Now!" Shamira ordered.

Herado struggled to his feet and hobbled as fast as he could. He slipped in the spreading pool of the dead guard's blood, then disappeared around the corner of the wall.

# Chapter 15

The mood was joyous all across the Bella Flora estate, for nobles and peasants alike. By the end of the first day of boiling down the ley, there was almost one thousand pounds of the raw saltpeter. Barrel upon barrel of the pebble-like crystals was lined up away from the barn and fires. Hansum had asked during his meal if he could give each of his men some cooked pork as a bonus for their hard work. The Podesta commented how strange and unnecessary something like this was, but humored his savant. After the meal, Hansum went back to oversee the men, and was surprised when, an hour later, the Podesta and Baron arrived at the barns to check on things. They laughed from their carriage when they saw Hansum sitting naked, up to his neck in one of the pots.

"Don't eat my savant," the Podesta called to the workers. "I bring you pork in exchange."

"That's the first time I've ever seen him laugh," said Jacopo, who was standing next to Hansum and holding his hat.

On the way back to the manor house, Mastino commented jovially, "You bathe more than anyone I have ever met. Very odd, since you smelled so badly the first time at my supper table."

"I was overly enthusiastic about my new work. But cleanliness is next to godliness," Hansum said, repeating what Pan prompted.

"Ah, speaking of the Lord, tomorrow at church," Mastino began, "it's only a village church, but we will take the local burgher's chairs. You will sit next to Lady Beatrice on the aisle."

"I must be honest with you, Excellency. All my new duties, position, these lodgings, all the responsibilities, they are very overwhelming. Please allow me a few months to complete the first plans. Then, then we shall see if I am worthy of whatever new challenges you have for me. I fear I'll be distracted from my work."

"What can I say to this?" the Podesta said in mock frustration to Nicademo. "Such a serious young man." Then Mastino laughed. "Okay, okay. Don't sit next to a beauty. Sit next to Nicademo if this will help your concentration." And then he broke out into an even larger laugh. "Come, let us to supper and an evening of relaxation. Then tomorrow we go pray to God for our salvation and to answer all our prayers."

So, Hansum was not required to sit next to Lady Beatrice at church the next day. They did travel in the same carriage and Hansum wore more new clothes that the Podesta had provided. When Hansum went to his room, he found a dozen new pieces — jackets, shirts, braies, chausses, hats, new boots — all fitting perfectly. In the coach, Beatrice and Hansum passed pleasantries, but she did not press him to talk. In the church, he sat on the aisle, next to Nicademo. Beatrice was on the far side of her father. Beatrice looked either straight ahead or down when she prayed, never to the side to catch a glimpse of Hansum.

Beatrice was quiet after church and at dinner too. The Podesta and Baron talked about many affairs of state. They talked mostly of rival cities, mentioning the house of Este and other families in the cities of Venice and Florence. They talked about the Azzone Visconti family of Milan, and the Papist Guelph Estes of Ferrara.

"Perhaps I should not be part of these political discussions, Excellency," Hansum said.

"Nonsense," Mastino said. "I want you to hear and understand what we nobles go through. Most people it is best to keep ignorant. We make our living from them not knowing how the world works. But you, I want you to understand everything. And after all, you were already involved in a conflict with the Gonzaga. Wasn't it you who cut off Feltrino Gonzaga's thumb with a sword?" he pantomimed. Then he laughed heartily. That was the only time Beatrice looked directly at Hansum and raised an eyebrow.

"It was a most terrifying time, Excellency. I fear I am better suited to what I am doing now."

"I suppose you are," Mastino said, continuing to chuckle.

"Excellency, would you excuse me?" Hansum said. "I should like to go to my room."

"To study and plan more, Romero?" the Baron asked. "You must not always work. It's bad for the disposition."

"Not to work, Excellency. To sleep. I am exhausted and it is going to be another long week."

"Si, si. Of course you're tired," Mastino replied, continuing to joke. "It's all those hot baths you take. Too many hot baths and then you're done. Did I tell you, my dear, how we found Signor Romero sitting in a cauldron of hot water yesterday, bathing before dinner?"

"Well father, that is why he smells so much better than the rest."

"Grazie, Lady Beatrice," Hansum said, getting up. "Now I'll say good afternoon and goodnight."

"Perhaps goodbye, Signor. I shall be leaving in the morning after repast."

"Oh? Travel safe then. Perhaps we shall see you soon."

"Perhaps," was all she said, keeping her eyes on his.

Hansum finally looked away, gave a slight bow to the Baron and Podesta, and left.

Pan wanted to talk when they got to the room, but Hansum fell right into bed and was asleep as his head hit the pillow.

Hansum slept right through the afternoon and all through the night. When he finally rose before sunup, he found a tray of food beside his bed and ate it voraciously. Before going to the fields, he went to the planning room to make a notation on one of the designs. He entered the room, and at the big table, looking at the papers, was Lady Beatrice. She was not in her day clothes, but wore a heavy cloak over her sleeping attire.

"I'm sorry. I didn't know anyone was here," Hansum said, turning away.

"Please don't go," Beatrice asked. Hansum turned around and looked at her. "I couldn't sleep," she said. "I was thinking about something my father said. How your plans are so powerful. I had to see for myself. I hope you don't mind."

"It's not for me to say, Lady Beatrice."

"My father says that with ideas like this, he could redraw the map of the world in a decade. And still, you act modestly."

"Lady Beatrice, I guess it's a matter of perspective. I find myself in a strange, strange world here. I could not begin to tell you the difference between the world I was in, not that many months ago, and now. Every morning I think to myself, when I open my eyes everything will be the way it was before. But then I look and I'm with the rulers of city states."

"My father told me you felt overwhelmed. I am sorry if I have added to your discomfort." Then Beatrice picked up a few of the original, now well-worn, plans and looked at them again. She moved her fingers over them. "All the things on these pages, they came out of your head?"

"Like I said, Lady Beatrice, it's more like they were whispered in my ear."

"Ah, your Pan again," she said, almost sounding sad. "But truly, Signor Monticelli, I hope one day, when you make other interesting plans, you will show them to me when the pages are not so well-worn."

"Perhaps. I cannot say, Lady Beatrice."

"Just so," Beatrice answered. "You have learned the lessons of my father and cousin well. Signor, the great Dante wrote a sentence I always believed, till now. He said, 'Your face shows the true colour of your heart.' But when I look at you, Signor, I honestly do not know what I see."

*"Say nothing,"* Pan warned. *"Do not engage in any more intimate banter."*

A long, awkward pause ensued. Beatrice broke the silence.

"Goodbye, Signor."

"Goodbye, Lady Beatrice."

# Chapter 16

Pan watched mostly silent over the next two days as Hansum directed the saltpeter operations. He was coming into his own and using Pan only as a resource, as a modern men would use computers or A.I.s. It didn't lessen his creativity or abilities, but allowed him to work faster and with more confidence. Pan was very proud of him. It took two more days for Jacopo and his men to process the ley and finish making the raw saltpeter crystals. Hansum checked on them several times a day. The rest of Monday and Tuesday was spent watching the saltpeter beds being built and overseeing a carpenter who was constructing the cooling table for the final crystals. As well, he had several more meetings with the Podesta and Baron. These were to sharpen up the estimates of the supplies needed during the following months.

The two nobles were continually impressed with how their savant was able to calculate numbers in his head. This was one of the few times Hansum still depended on Pan, but he stopped feeling embarrassed by the attention he was getting. He felt he was contributing and wasn't out of place. He was fully engaged, keeping alert, learning and, at night, asking Pan questions about things he didn't fully understand.

On that Tuesday, Hansum came with some important news for the Podesta and Baron.

"Excellencies, the balance of the raw saltpeter will be processed today. Tomorrow we start the final distillation."

"Good, Romero. Good." Mastino said happily. "Oh, Romero. I'm giving several receptions in Verona over the next months. Our German friends will be in attendance and I want to introduce you."

Hansum seemed to think a great deal on this. The Podesta and Baron looked at each other curiously. Finally Hansum spoke.

"Excellency. I am very flattered. May I comment?"

"Of course, Romero. What?"

"Perhaps it is better if I remain anonymous for now. Was it not you who urged me to keep our project secret?" Hansum didn't need Pan to tell him that Mastino's purpose in introducing Hansum in public was to nudge him closer to Beatrice.

"Will you at least join me at Santa Anastasia for mass on Sunday?" the Podesta asked.

"If you insist, Excellency. But I was looking forward to worshipping with my old master's family and the friends I was orphaned with. It's been some weeks since I've seen them. Of course, I'm to meet with you on Monday to inspect Master Calabreezi's progress with the cannon." Mastino seemed to consider what Hansum said for some time. He looked at Nicademo, who seemed somewhat nervous, as if he thought they were all about to see the Podesta's famous temper again. Mastino looked up and smiled.

"As you wish, Romero. Supper at the usual time?"

Wednesday morning, the saltpeter table was finished and the cauldrons heated up. The raw saltpeter was dissolved in the boiling water and the men removed the last of the common salts that precipitated to the bottom while it heated. The solution was now clear. Using large ladles, Hansum had the men scoop the liquid onto the drying table. It was a shallow, V-shaped affair, where the fluid cooled quickly. Hansum, Pan and the men then saw the first of the long, sharp, saltpeter crystals form. Everyone became excited. They raked the crystals out and put them on large canvas sheets to dry in the mild late-winter air. In the future, there would be special drying buildings for the saltpeter, but for now, this made do. The peasants were becoming excited by the events, and Hansum was too. But Pan cautioned him about something, and after Hansum listened, he motioned for the foreman.

"Jacopo, call the men to me." When all the men were assembled, Hansum took a small handful of the saltpeter and threw it into the fire. A flash of light and sparks flew while still in the air. The men jumped. "The substance we have created with our labors is very dangerous. We must draw up rules that each of us must follow when working with or storing the saltpeter. Does everyone understand?"

That night, Hansum brought a small pouch of the finished saltpeter to the Podesta. Hansum took a small pinch of it and walked over to the fireplace. He tossed the crystals into the flames and a burst of stars sparkled and popped. He had expected the Podesta to become excited, as he had been about the raw saltpeter. Mastino's response was cool.

*"Perhaps the Podesta's response is mild because he is so busy coordinating the massive amounts of assets the Baron spoke of,"* Pan suggested.

The noble smiled gently. "Are production quantities still as you estimated?"

"Si, Excellency. More, in fact. We shall have eleven hundred pounds of saltpeter by Saturday. More than predicted. The men will finish the four thousand pounds while we are gone."

"Good," the Podesta answered, still cool. "Next week, when we return, the charcoal and brimstone will already have arrived. We can make our first black powder then."

The door to the room opened and Nicademo entered. Hansum could see the shoulder of a man behind the Baron.

"The ambassador from . . ." Nicademo began to say when he saw Hansum. He closed the door somewhat to prevent the man from being seen. "Oh, Romero, I thought you were in the fields."

"Romero," the Podesta said, "please excuse us. Go out the other door, would you?"

The manor now took on a serious tone. The Podesta and Baron talked less at meals. Evenings ended earlier. There was no rudeness, but quiet politeness became the norm. There was an increase in the number of day visitors. Pan and Hansum viewed other well-dressed men who were not introduced and arrived in curtained carriages without crests. Many looked foreign and talked with accents. Also, many riders sped in and out of the estate with message pouches.

When Hansum came to dinner on Friday morning, he found that the Podesta was gone. He had left for Verona without saying goodbye. That night, after supper, the Baron asked Hansum if he wished to play scopa, a card game.

"It's a new thing to do. Wonderful entertainment. Have you ever played?"

"Scopa? No, Excellency."

"Well, you can learn. Duccio, bring us the cards and a bottle of Benedictine. A new drink to sip after meals."

"Excellency, you will spoil me to the good life and I will not wish to work in the fields again."

"Undoubtedly," the Baron answered. Scopa was played with a deck of forty hand-made playing cards. It didn't take long for Hansum to catch on, especially with Pan at his ear.

But, when Pan noticed Hansum acting a bit tipsy from the liquor, he warned the young man not to drink so much.

*"These nobles always have a reason for everything they do. Not that card, Master. See the drink really is going to your head. No! Not that card either!"*

Hansum twisted his hat sideways on his head. Now Pan's speech couldn't reach the boy's ear.

"Just take it off," the Baron said. "You look silly with it like that."

"It is to distract you from your concentration, Excellency," Hansum joked. "Besides, it's my lucky hat." A few discards later, Hansum put down some cards and won the hand.

Nicademo laughed lightly, sipped from his small glass, and then sighed.

"Romero, I think your lucky hat brought you more luck than you appreciate," he said.

*"Oh, oh. Here we go,"* Pan warned. *"Careful, Master."* But Hansum couldn't hear.

"Romero, I wish to give you advice that would allow me to call you cousin. Let me speak to you as a man to a man. Of your Guilietta."

"Guilietta?"

The noble put up a hand to silence Hansum. He took another sip of the Benedictine, put it down and continued. "Not as a cousin then, or as man to man. Let me speak to you as a father to a son. Romero, you need not lose your Guilietta by acceding to the Podesta's wishes."

"But how . . ." and Hansum stopped. The answer was obvious.

The Baron continued. "It is not uncommon — and perfectly acceptable — for all gentlemen of means to have a mistress or two. And to have children with those mistresses. I have two lovely bastard children whom I adore. From a distance, of course. Marriage is about family alliances and the control of lands or enterprise. In your case, ideas. Truth be told, while I like my wife, and we enjoy each other's confidence, I like one of my mistresses better. She is of peasant stock and not that bright or cultured, but she pleases me and I provide for her. A good arrangement for both of us, wouldn't you agree?"

"I just can't imagine thinking of Guilietta, or children I would have with her as, as . . ." Hansum hesitated, like he couldn't say the word.

"Illegitimate?"

"I guess," Hansum said. But Pan knew the word Hansum was thinking was the same word Nicademo had used to describe his own mistresses' children. Bastards.

Pan was tearing at his dreadlocks as he screamed in his lamp. *"Don't engage in this conversation. Say nothing!"*

But the cap was turned too far on Hansum's head for the sonic beam to reach the teen's ear.

Pan heard the Baron chuckle. It was if he were reading Hansum's mind.

"When you have money and power, my boy, this distinction is not so grave."

"I see," Hansum said.

"As for your luck," Nicademo continued, "do you not appreciate the unprecedented situation our master is providing for you? You, from humble origins, can one day be a prince. Oh, maybe not of Verona or of lands around here, Mastino has sons for that, after all. But as we expand our holdings, using your ideas, you and Beatrice could be rulers of your own territories. A prince, Romero. Think of it. Did you not understand this?"

"No, I didn't, Signor." He paused, feeling trapped. He looked down at his feet.

"Romero, look at me. I am giving you good news, not bad. You can have your Guilietta and wealth and position." Hansum looked up and gave Nicademo a weak smile. Nicademo added, "You just may not marry her." The smile dropped from Hansum's face.

"But why can't the Podesta just accept my loyalty? Why does he insist that I must be part of his family?"

"My son, he already has your loyalty and all you have to offer. This is taken for granted. He is your ruler. But what I think he desires most is the comfort that comes from knowing your future ideas will be part of the family's legacy, and perhaps that one of yours and Beatrice's children inherits that brain of yours. My cousin can be a generous man, Romero. He loves art and culture and strives to make his cities wonderful places. But he is a man of power. And when a man of power has made up his mind, you must not defy him. I am frankly quite surprised he's indulged you as much as he has."

*"Don't speak another word! Get out of the room! Get out!"* Pan cried.

Hansum sat in his chair gloomily. Nicademo pushed Hansum's liqueur glass towards him.

"Drink, my son. Drink."

Hansum took a gulp and the strong liquid burned all the way to his stomach. Heat radiated out and soon his head was hot. Hansum thought about what Nicademo had said. It would not be so unpleasant, he tried saying to himself. Immediately, he chastised himself for even attempting such thoughts. He felt horrible at the merest hint of betraying Guilietta. But also, if there was one thing he had learned in the fourteenth century, it was pragmatism. Flashing through his mind was the idea that, in the twenty-fourth century, where there was safety and security, muddled thinking was not deadly. But here . . . what was that phrase the Podesta had said the other week? 'If wishes were horses, beggars would be riding.' Hansum straightened his hat and looked at the Baron.

"Excellency, thank you for your candor. And thank you for being patient with my foolishness."

"Romero, is there anything else you wish to tell me? You look like a man who has more on his mind than is spoken."

Perhaps if Hansum hadn't straightened his hat, and Pan couldn't scream in his ear as he was doing now, maybe Hansum would have confessed about already being married to Guilietta. But Pan *was* shouting at him.

*"Fool! Not another word! Not one more emotion! Smile! Smile, you idiot. Never show weakness to these people! It will blow up in your face!"*

Hansum shook his head, as if clearing it, and stood up. He laughed and then clapped his hands.

"Please forgive me, Excellency. It's just the liquor and long days of work. I think I am overly tired. And you know how even wonderful things can seem bad when you are tired. I shall say good night. Thank you for the card game. I hope we may play again."

"Romero, are you sure there isn't anything else?"

"I really can't say there is," Hansum replied with as much sincerity as possible.

"Good night, Romero. Sleep well. We leave for Verona mid-afternoon."

A short while later, Hansum knew he was dreaming, even though it felt so very real. In the dream, he was simply lying in bed, looking up at the ceiling. There, hovering over him to his left, was Pan. To his right, translucent and ethereal, floated Arimus, the History Camp counselor from the thirty-first century. It was him who caused the three teens to be stranded back in the fourteenth century when he got himself killed.

"The nobles want me to marry Beatrice and still keep Guilietta as a mistress," Hansum said. He looked back and forth between the two images. "I don't know what to do." The apparition of Arimus spoke first.

"The advice that I gave you, was all advantages take.
The decisions for true happiness are easy to make.
Keep in mind that your life can be long and complex.
Just check the balances, and balance the checks."

Hansum had forgotten how Arimus always talked in verse. He furrowed his brow. Then the image of Pan spoke.

"Interesting advice from a person who got himself killed and eaten by wolves," Pan said with a smirk. Arimus just shrugged and grinned.

"Arimus, when you spoke in rhyme before," Hansum's dream self said, "I could understand what you meant. But this time, how does your advice help?"

"Advice makes sense easily, when it fits with our wants.
When decisions are hard, advice seems like taunts.
Those who are successful make decisions right and some wrong,

But they live with the results, and move on, for they're strong."

"Well, I have to admit, Master Hansum," Pan said, "that was pretty clear."

The next day, Hansum worked with the men, but knew he would have to leave before all the crude saltpeter had been processed. He gave strict orders about cleaning up afterward and about the careful storage of the saltpeter. Hansum also had a cauldron cleaned and filled with fresh water, so he could have one last bath. He wanted to be presentable when he saw Guilietta. As he sat in the hot water, his head was a cauldron of ideas and emotions, all stewing together.

# Chapter 17

At about the same time that Hansum was simmering in the pot, Mastino della Scalla was facing a plain wooden door. His man, Grazzana, knocked loudly upon it. When the door opened, the serious workman's countenance of Master Agistino della Cappa quickly turned to one of surprise.

"Excellency? Excellency?" was all Agistino could stammer, pulling off his hat.

"Master della Cappa," the Podesta said effusively, "forgive the unannounced intrusion. May I come in?"

"Why of course, Excellency. Of course," he said, opening the door wide.

Grazzana put up his hand and motioned for a moment's pause. Then he stepped in and looked around the back of the door.

"Who else is here?" Grazzana asked.

"Just my wife and daughter. They are sleeping upstairs."

Grazzana motioned that all was well and stepped outside.

"Forgive my man. He's just doing his job."

"Of course," Agistino said. "My old master said, 'never stop a worker when they are taking their job seriously.'"

"Just so," Mastino agreed. "Oh, one of the reasons for my visit, della Cappa. Here. I brought your next payment for the lookers."

He plunked a good-sized bag of coins into the Master's hand. It was heavy. "I know it's early, but everybody is very pleased with the lookers and I wanted to show my appreciation."

Mastino watched Agistino's eyes actually bulge and he smiled to see the craftsman half stagger to the table and put the bag down with a plunk. Della Cappa undid the pull strings and opened the pouch.

"It's gold!" Agistino whispered hoarsely. He became so overcome he had to sit. "Forgive me, Excellency," he said, actually short of breath. "I am overcome with . . ."

"Speak no more of it, della Cappa. May I join you in repose?"

"Oh, my manners, my manners. Of course." He tried to stand up, but the sight of all the gold still had him dizzy.

"Sit, my friend, sit. I'll make my own place." Mastino went to the opposite side of the table and pulled out the other bench. He smiled at the lensmaker as he sat. "So, Master della Cappa, let me tell you of how the world likes your lookers. It loves them. I am in hopes that later this month I may give to you an open-ended order to make lookers for years to come. And at that time, I may be able to give to you, by law, the authority to be the only maker of lookers in any land I command." He saw Agistino press a hand hard over his heart. "But in this hard world, there are pressures that even a podesta feels. Florence, because of its crystal guild, is petitioning me to cease production of lenses in my territory. They use it as a negotiation point on other matters of concern." Of course, this was a complete fabrication.

"This is good news and bad, Excellency. What can I say?"

"Oh, rulers of cities bluff and blow all the time. It's what nobles do best, eh? But it was you who brought this boon to me and I must be loyal, must I not? And, I understand while I was away, your family helped Captain Caesar foil another Gonzaga plot to steal a looker. So, do not worry. As long as you can provide, there will be no quarrel for a change from me. I have enough to worry about without wasting time fixing what's not broken."

"That's a good way to think, Excellency. My old master used to say that very same piece of wisdom."

"And how goes it with your house? Do you see any problem with supplying our needs into the future?"

"All is well and growing, Excellency. The journeyman you arranged is very good. The young apprentice, Maruccio, Romero's friend, is starting to grind lenses. We also have four new apprentices and a third lathe coming in a week. All this has required me to spend more time pondering the accounts, which is why I am here at the house."

"And now you have much more to account for, moving a debt to an asset," Mastino said, gesturing to the bag of gold.

"Si, Excellency. And all because of you."

"But because of your lookers," the Podesta added generously. Mastino saw Agistino stare at him with an odd look in his eyes. Then the tradesman said something that surprised him.

"We both know the lookers were Romero's invention, Excellency."

Now it was the Podesta's turn to say something he wasn't planning on saying, just yet.

"He cares very much for you and your family, Master della Cappa. He is very loyal to you." The two men sat looking at each other sincerely.

Then Agistino said, with more excitement in his voice, "Oh, my manners again, Excellency. May I offer you some wine? Some refreshment? I brought in some good stuff, just for when you and the Baron visit."

"Very kind. I would love some. It's been a very busy time lately. No time to rest and just enjoy a good glass of grape. And you?"

"Oh, the wine, she loves *me* too much, Excellency. Verjuice is my drink now," he said, getting up and bringing down two ceramic cups and two bottles from a shelf. He put one cup in front of the Podesta. The Podesta looked in and noticed how clean it was. Then Agistino poured the wine and verjuice.

"May your enterprises prosper all of Verona," Agistino toasted.

"And your enterprise with them," Mastino added. "Now, Master della Cappa, there is another bit of business we must speak of as fathers. Romero is an orphan, but as I have said, he cares for you and your family very much. So, as his old master, I come to you in council about his future."

"You honor me, Excellency."

"Though Romero is young, he has talents that are very rare. He has a potential that shows up even in tutored princes most seldom."

"I knew he had talent, but to such an extent, Excellency?" Agistino asked.

"I believe so, and others concur."

"Amazing. So, are you here to tell us that he is not coming back, Excellency? That you have need of him elsewhere?"

"Oh, no. He should be here tonight, in fact."

"That's good, Excellency. It will be good to see him."

"I know he misses you all. Now, I understand from him that, before he came away with me, he told you of my wishes for him and my daughter. And also of his refusal. He has a desire for union with your child."

"Guilietta," Agistino said, somewhat nervously. "I told him I would not give my consent without your blessing."

"Just so," the Podesta said. "That is why I am here."

"You are here to give it?"

"No. Alas, I am not."

There was an awkward silence. Mastino kept his face friendly. He watched Agistino nod slowly and with purpose. Finally, Agistino spoke.

"More wine, Excellency?"

"Grazie," the Podesta said. "It's quite good."

"To buy fine wines one must have money, Excellency. One could say, this wine is your wine."

"Da Pontremoli said you were a man one could talk to."

"I am only sorry that my house is giving you trouble in this matter, Excellency. My old master told me, when a person gives you payment for their services, you are supposed to lift their burdens and make their lives easier. Not harder."

"I like the sound of your old master."

"Excellency, we must be ruled by you. You are our prince, our benefactor. We owe you everything. When Romero returns I will tell him our minds. Consider the matter settled."

The Podesta nodded knowingly. "Grazie. And you know that Romero's apprenticeship has ended with you too, eh? He may treat you as his family, but will not be returning here to live."

Agistino nodded seriously again. Then the Podesta leaned forward in a very familiar way, relaxing in this hovel which reminded him of a barn on one of his poorer estates, not quite as good as the ones on his better estates. "I say to you, della Cappa, what type of world is this becoming, where husband and wife choose each other? Damn those troubadours and their songs of courtly love. Damn them to Hell."

As Mastino said this, there was a sound on the steps. Guilietta appeared, yawning, her hair tousled in a most comely way. When she saw the Podesta, she looked surprised for a moment. There was a large bruise on her temple from the fight, which she covered with her hair, then smiled warmly.

"Podesta della Scalla," Guilietta said, bowing her head and curtsying.

Mastino stared at the girl, for the first time realizing just how beautiful she was, even with the injury. She looked up and their eyes met, and he saw the two calm brown pools that had captured Hansum so, and he realized something. He nodded at her, and then turned to her father.

"So, della Cappa, we have an understanding?"

"Si," was all Agistino replied.

The Podesta then rose to exit the modest home. He stopped at the step and looked at Guilietta again. He reached up and moved her hair off the purple and black bruise.

"I heard how you used that knife on the wall," he said.

"I pray every day to Jesus for the man's soul, Excellency, but I had to save my family."

"You fight for what is yours," Mastino said plainly.

Guilietta stared into his eyes, nodded slowly, once, and then looked down.

During the carriage ride back to the palace, Mastino thought hard about Guilietta and resolved the proper strategy to deal with her.

# Chapter 18

A very excited Guilietta ran to the shop as soon as the Podesta left. When she told the others that Romero was returning that evening, Lincoln and Shamira were beyond excited. Shamira said they should run to the market and buy special foods.

"No, no, Carmella. You must go alone," Guilietta replied, shaking with happiness. "I must run to the Satores' and have them finish my new dress. Immediately! But at the market, get some salves from Signora Baroni to lessen my bruises."

"I can't wait to see the little guy," Lincoln blurted out.

Guilietta looked at him oddly, but quickly turned and ran out of the now crowded workshop. There were the two new lathes, the old one, several more work tables, two more apprentices, making four, and the new journeyman, Bembo Arturo. He was about the same height as Hansum, though quite a bit stockier. He had black, wavy hair, a dark complexion, bright brown eyes, bushy eyebrows that met in the middle and an infectious smile. Guilietta was so excited she bumped into one of the little boys.  Bembo, laughing in his deep, friendly voice, called after her.

"This Romero fellow must be a special one to make everyone jump up and down, run to the market and get new dresses." She gave a little laugh, then turned and continued running back to the house. As she did, she remembered something she overheard her father say when Bembo first arrived. He had said to her mother that if Hansum hadn't come into their lives, Bembo would have been perfect for Guilietta.

"But if the orphan hadn't shown up, we wouldn't have this fine life again," the Signora answered.

Not too many hours later, Guilietta was back in the house, sitting on the stairs and combing her hair. The mistress was at the kitchen table, helping shell peas. Lincoln was cutting other vegetables. Shamira was basting a goose that sat crackling in a roasting pan on the hearth grate.

The door latch clicked. Guilietta looked up to see a head with a worn brown hat appear. He looked up at her and smiled.

"Romero! Romero's here!" the Signora screamed joyously. She jumped up and clapped her hands. Lincoln and Shamira shouted joyously and ran for him. Guilietta got up from her seat on the stairs and shouted, "Romero!" Just then, Baron Da Pontremoli appeared in the doorframe, causing everyone to freeze.

"Please, all of you, don't stop your enthusiastic greetings on my account," Nicademo said. "Signor Monticelli, I will leave you to your family, but first, bring in the gifts," he said to someone behind him. A driver came in carrying a basket full of wrapped packages.

"Put them on the table, please," Hansum said.

Lincoln grabbed Hansum's sleeve. "Look at those fancy duds."

"Si, but he still always wears that hat," the Baron mused. "Please have him get a new one before we pick him up on Monday. Well, I will leave you to your evening. My family is expecting me."

"Grazie, Baron," Hansum said. "For everything."

"We shall see you on Monday, Romero. My best to your master." Guilietta felt the Baron's eyes fall upon her. She gave him a small smile. He nodded slightly, then turned and left.

The Signora clapped her hands and bounced again.

"Presents," she cried. "Presents!"

Guilietta watched Shamira and Lincoln hug Hansum.

"You look tired," Shamira said.

"I'm okay." Hansum replied. And the young bride saw her groom turn and meet her gaze. She felt his eyes moving up and down over her body, then into her eyes again. "Hello, Guilietta," he said. The room went quiet.

"Hello, Romero," she said quietly. He took a slow step toward the stairs, reaching out his hand, beckoning to her. She walked down the stairs, and then saw his eyes go big at the sight of the bruise.

"What . . ."

"We had a little excitement while you were gone," Lincoln said, and he quickly told the story.

"If I ever see that bastard, Feltrino, again," Hansum said, "I'll kill him."

"No, Romero, please," Guilietta said. "Please. You must not speak so. I must now live everyday with . . ."

The door burst open again and Guilietta watched her father, Ugilino, Bembo, and the four young apprentices enter.

"Romero!" the Master shouted jubilantly. He grasped Hansum in a huge bear hug, danced him off the ground and away from the stairs. He kissed him through his massive beard and twirled around the floor. "Everyone's together again. Everyone's together," he shouted.

"Hello, Master, hello," Hansum cried as he was carried to the center of the room.

"Presents," the Signora squealed again. "Romero's brought presents!"

"Truly?" Agistino asked, letting Hansum down.

"Si," he said, looking back at Guilietta for a second, then back to the Master. "Baron Da Pontremoli had the carriage come in the west gate and then he took me to a few shops. But, Master, first, this awful thing with Feltrino."

"Yes, yes, it was awful," Agistino said, "and we all survived." He looked hard at Guilietta. "Life will no doubt bring us more things we must bear. So . . ." he looked back at Hansum and smiled. "Enjoy these times that bring joy." But Hansum didn't smile back at the Master. Guilietta saw him look solemnly at her bruise, then into her eyes.

"Presents for everyone!" the Signora shouted again.

"Oh, I'm afraid I didn't know there would be so many people, Mistress," Hansum said, seeming to get back into a festive mood. "But perhaps a few can share."

"Ah, Romero, si. We have some new faces," the Master said. "This is Bembo, journeyman lens grinder from Florence."

Hansum shook hands with him. "Hello, Bembo. I hope Maruccio hasn't been too much of a bother," he joked.

"He's like a brother to me now," Bembo answered. "He doesn't even complain about my snoring anymore. Hello, Romero. Everyone is very excited to see you."

"Oh, the snoring. The horror, the horror!" Lincoln cried in mock complaint, covering his ears. Everyone laughed again.

"Hello, Ugilino," Hansum said, putting his hand out. "How are you doing?"

"Romero, I'm doing *fantastico*. We're making so many lookers that we haven't made that many discs for the eyes lately, but I'm keeping everyone with what they ask for. If you need something, I'm your man."

"Ugilino is doing a very good job," the Master added.

"Bueno, Ugilino. Bueno," Hansum said.

Guilietta walked into the crowd of people and stood by Hansum. Her lips moved to speak but her father put his arm enthusiastically around Hansum's shoulder and pulled him toward the table.

"So, let's see these presents and then we'll have wine and a meal. That goose smells good, Carmella. See, Romero, we bought a goose in honour of your return. We'll call the goose Little Romero!" He laughed and everybody joined in.

"Grazie, Master. But wine? You?"

"Me? No! But why should everybody else suffer because I'm an old drunk?"

"Romero, your friends couldn't even work in the shop after hearing you were on your way today," Bembo said.

"You knew I was coming?" Hansum asked. "How?" The Master looked somewhat guilty.

"The Podesta. He brought me payment for the last large order of lookers."

"He came here?" Hansum said suspiciously. "The Podesta? To make a payment on a debt?"

"Presents," the Signora squealed again. Hansum gave the Signora hers first. She opened up the wrapped package and took out three linen handkerchiefs with fine lace all around them. They were so soft that she kept rubbing them all over her face and making cooing sounds. Shamira was given a bundle of sketching paper and a box of coloured pastels for drawing. Lincoln was excited to see a new pair of boots, all shiny and of excellent quality, as well as three pair of new socks.

"Fantastico," he cried enthusiastically. "Warm, dry feet next winter!"

Agistino seemed truly touched by his gift. It was a solid brass oil lamp with a holy cross and an angel holding what looked like two lightning bolts. He laughed and cried at the same time when he saw it. He gave Hansum a huge hug and kisses on both cheeks again. For Ugilino there were socks as well. Being Ugilino, he sat on the floor and pulled off his boots to expose his scaly bare feet with long toenails. He put on the socks and declared they fit perfectly. Hansum had bought sweets for the two child apprentices he knew of. Since there were now more apprentices, Lincoln split them up. Hansum then brought out Guilietta's gift. It was a small bundle of royal blue cloth with a silver pin holding it together.

"The Baron helped me pick this one out," he said, handing it to her. "I hope you like it."

Guilietta sat down on the bench, put the package in her lap and undid the pin. As she unwrapped the cloth, there, shining up at her, was a delicate silver chain with an equally delicate filigree cross attached to it.

"Mercy me!" the Signora gasped, hands clenched to her bosom. "It's beautiful."

"Let me help you put it on," Shamira said.

Guilietta looked at Hansum with both a winsome and wondering face, passive as Shamira put the necklace on her. Hansum looked confused.

"Everyone has such wonderful gifts," the Signora said in a voice full of emotion. "It's just like before our troubles, Agistino. Better."

"Bembo," Ugilino shouted, "you don't get a gift."

"That's okay. We have just met," Bembo replied.

"No, no," Hansum said. "I brought extra things. Here. I want you to have this." He pulled a dusty bottle out of the basket and handed it to Bembo. "From the Podesta's own cellar. A new drink called Benedictine." And he made a very Italian gesture of kissing his fingers to illustrate its good taste. Bembo made modest pleadings that it wasn't necessary. "Please," Hansum said, "I insist."

"From the Podesta's cellar? Well, okay then," Bembo acceded. "We are all truly brothers now. Master, I am so happy to have joined this family," and a great chatter rose from everyone as the party started.

Shamira went back to basting the goose, laughing and talking as she did it. The little boys ran around the room, screaming and chewing on their sweets, Lincoln and Ugilino teasing them. The Signora clapped her hands and danced. The Master lorded benignly over all, his arm around Hansum's shoulder. Hansum was asked questions about where he had been and what he had done. Guilietta sat listening, a look of quiet concern on her face. Hansum told about living in the manor house with all the servants and butlers, all the fine big rooms, his own grand bedroom with the feather bed and pillows. He joked about having the men who worked for him fill up a big cauldron so he could take a heated baths, about riding in carriages, of dining with the Podesta and Baron, the general and builders of churches. Everybody was very impressed.

Finally Guilietta broke her silence and asked a question. It was so noisy and she spoke so quietly, Hansum had to ask her to please repeat what she said. When she repeated it, it sounded loud and rude, and more like a statement than a question.

"You are leaving on Monday."

"Just for the day. We have business in the city Monday to Wednesday. We go back to the Podesta's estate Wednesday afternoon. I can stay here till then."

"And you will live where after that?" she asked plainly.

Hansum opened his mouth to speak, but no answer came out. The Master intervened.

"One of the things the Podesta told me himself was that Hansum no longer works for the house of della Cappa. He is the Podesta's man now. Isn't that quite the honor, daughter?"

Guilietta felt like she wanted to throw up. Her father was looking like he expected her to agree with him, but she couldn't get any words out. Agistino looked about and repeated, "It's quite an honour."

"Romero doesn't live here anymore," Ugilino said, smiling.

"He lives with the Podesta," the Master said again.

"In the palace?" the Signora asked with an air of wonder. "And you will come and visit often with presents?"

"As often as I can, Mistress," Hansum said. "You are my family."

"And what of me?" Guilietta asked quietly. "What about us?"

"Not now, daughter," Agistino said softly. "We'll talk of this later."

"Did you get his blessing?" Guilietta asked again.

Just then Shamira took the goose off of the fire and was carrying the crackling pan to the table. "Your goose is cooked, Romero," she said, laughing.

"Did you get the Podesta's blessing?" Guilietta repeated, this time much louder. The room fell silent.

"Not now, daughter," Agistino said with authority. "I told you. We will talk on this later, when we are alone."

"I want to know now. Have you received the Podesta's blessing for us?"

"Everybody, leave us," the Master ordered. "Now!"

"But the goose?" the Signora complained.

"Carmella, take my wife to the workshop," Agistino said. "Keep her there. Bembo, Maruccio, Ugilino, take the young ones to their homes. It's getting dark."

"But the goose will be cold and greasy," the Signora complained again.

"Now, woman!"

"Come, Mistress," Shamira urged. "I'll take a leg off the goose to keep you busy."

The house that had been so gay and merry a few moments earlier now held a sombre air. Hansum went to sit by the passive Guilietta. The Master frowned. Hansum paused, but sat down anyway.

"You've been gone weeks," Guilietta said. "You come back with many presents, but not the one I want or need." She said all this looking straight ahead. It was only when she finished that she turned and looked at her young husband, her eyes now burning with emotion.

"I still want the Podesta's blessing, my love," Hansum said earnestly. "I am still working toward it. But it's become more complicated than we first thought. The nobles have tried to woo me with many things, but I have resisted, playing for time to convince the Podesta of my indispensability. Once this is accomplished, he will not be able to refuse me. It will take just more time is all, my love."

"Truly?" Guilietta asked, the sound of her voice showing she really wanted to believe him.

"If I'm lying, may I die on this spot."

"You do not lie, Romero," the Master interjected, "but your strategy has come to a close."

"Master?"

"The Podesta's visit, it was not just to pay for the lookers. There was another purpose."

"Papa?"

"The Podesta came to me, as father to father, to contract our houses together. He bound our contract for the lookers, and his protection from the Crystal Guild of Florence, to my forbidding your marriage."

"But Romero said . . ."

"And he did not lie, Guilietta. The Podesta and his nobles manipulate people as you do your ringlets of hair, making them do what you want to attract others. The Podesta himself told me of Romero's love and loyalty to our family, and to you. But the Podesta is the Podesta and his will must be done."

"He used me!" Hansum said, wide-eyed.

"Si, he used you, as all use everyone else, for their own comfort and in trade for comforts given back. Ever was it thus, but in youth it's disguised in the whimsy of love."

"You sound like Baron Da Pontremoli," Hansum said sadly. "He said much the same thing."

"And why shouldn't he? That is what all sane men with fortunes large and small have come to understand. That is why they are men of fortune. They think clearly."

"Old men who have lost heart and no longer love their wives say such things," Guilietta spat.

"Daughter, I'm talking reason. Soon I will end this talk with a decree. The Podesta has already made his and I have sworn to it. It is only the one true love, the love of a parent for his child, which gives me the patience to allow this conversation to continue. Be reasonable. Did you not see the wealth that Romero brought home in that basket? That was more than a year's wages for an apprentice."

Hansum frowned, making a face before he spoke.

"The Baron says that when he returns home from business, he brings his wife, mistresses and all his children gifts. Tokens of affection, he calls them. He said if I was to have means, I must do the same."

"His mistresses?" Guilietta repeated. "The Baron has a mistress and more than one? And children by all?"

"Apparently. He said that most men of means keep a wife and often . . ."

Pan had been quiet till this point. *"I wouldn't go there, Master."*

Guilietta looked long and hard at Hansum. "So, it was the Baron's idea to bring me this gift?"

"Si."

"It's a beautiful gift, daughter. A silver cross, so beautifully cast and polished."

"And did the baron also mention me as a mistress to a soon-to-be rich man?"

*"Don't say it, Master."*

"It was suggested, but I didn't agree to it. Even when they left me alone with Lady Beatrice, I remained polite, but aloof . . ."

"The Lady who?" Guilietta interjected.

"L . . . Lady Beatrice," Hansum said, now somewhat cautiously. "The Podesta's — daughter."

"And why was she there?" Guilietta asked.

"Because . . ." Hansum started, but then fell silent. Guilietta's piercing eyes became two hot saucers.

*"Oh, I give up, Master. You're on your own."*

"Let me understand this, husband. I am to understand that you did not directly broach the subject with the Podesta and that you were *very* busy, living grandly, taking baths, riding in carriages, being served at table every night, sleeping in a fine feather bed, and also, you were being courted by the Podesta's daughter, and that your new noble friends advise you to make me your whore mistress? Do I understand you correctly, husband?"

"It's not like that," Hansum shouted, raising his voice to Guilietta for the first time. "I was planning on telling him. And the night I was resolved to do so, I saw him order someone killed who had deceived him. We have deceived the Podesta and could receive the same fate."

"Oh that's a fine and likely story," Guilietta said haughtily.

"It's all true. And there's more. There's more."

"Enough!" Agistio shouted. "I am the father of this family. I am the lord, the law. Listen to you both, squabbling like children or worse, like an old married couple. The Podesta wants Romero and I have agreed." He made a gesture which signified finality. "Wisdom and tradition have decreed the disposition of his children's fate is the business of the father. It is sanctified as a rite. And the business of the child is to obey and honor."

"Your father's rite comes a little late, Papa, for we are already wed. You cannot lie when documents have been signed with the Holy Church, and which many monks were witness to."

"Heavier than your signed oath is the large bag of gold I now have," Agistino answered. "Father Lurenzano is an especially reasonable man with coins hovering above his palm. I will secure from him an annulment. No harm has been done, really. Just impetuous youth wanting to play house. You married without my permission, after all."

"Papa, please!" Guilietta said, starting to cry.

"I said silence and obedience. My mind is set and nothing either of you can say will dissuade me." The waterworks really began to flow from Guilietta. "You can cry your tears till they reach the bell tower of San Zeno. They will not wash away my resolve. I am hardened to them from long years of exposure."

"I must say something, Master."

"There's nothing to say, Romero. I have made my decision."

"But I am not your apprentice anymore. I don't need your protection from the weather or food from your table."

"You would talk to me so, after I have given you freely so much?"

"It was not free. There were conditions." Agistino took a step back, truly hurt. Hansum added, "But they were conditions from which I learned much and they were fair. Master, Father, friend, I honor you . . ."

"Honor me by refusing me?"

"I only disagree with you as it is fair for a man to disagree with another man. I tell you, you cannot imagine the things in my head.

I know they will convince the Podesta to give me my way eventually. Soon."

*"Master, you better run this by me first,"* Pan said, breaking his silence.

Hansum stood up straight and looked Agistino straight in the eye. "Master, I make you this promise. When I return from my next visit from the Podesta's estates, I shall have his consent to marry Guilietta."

Guilietta sprang up and flung her arms around Hansum.

"Oh, husband," she gushed.

*"What are you saying?"* Pan cried. *"This is all nonsense, based on nothing."*

"You will bring the roof down on this family!" Agistino charged angrily.

"Oh, grazie, my husband. Grazie, grazie."

"Calm yourself. Both of you." Hansum said. "My idea of becoming so important to the Podesta will bear fruit. You will see. It will just take a little more time. Within the month, I promise, he will consent to our request."

Agistino now stood quietly in the middle of the room.

"I have given the Podesta, our prince, my word. Now I must knowingly stand in front of him, knowing I am a liar. I am a leaf, hanging on a dying tree, waiting for the winds of fortune to blow me away. Still elevated above the rest of the world, but knowing that at any time, a wind will cast me to the ground to rot and become forgotten."

"Papa, don't be so dramatic. You must have faith my husband will do what he says."

"Si, Master, Father. Have faith and, above all, do not tell the Podesta what is transpiring. I have the means. Please keep your head in this matter."

"That's what I'm trying to do. Why don't I just slit my throat now?"

"You will see, Master," Hansum said. "I have learned from the nobles how to be patient and put a plan into effect."

"Si, Father. Be patient."

Without another word Agistino turned and trudged toward the door.

"Where are you going, Papa?"

"Going? To get the others. When the others come, be discreet. Around Bembo and Ugilino for sure. Carmella and Maruccio know of your predicament, I'm sure. And your mother, well, she is your mother."

Guilietta got up and ran to her father. She hugged and kissed him on the cheek.

"I'm sorry for causing these problems, Papa. Grazie for understanding."

"Understanding? I have none. Faith and familiar hopelessness is all that will get me through." And then he left.

# Chapter 19

At church the next morning, Hansum found it a bit odd to be back standing in the crowded nave with all the peasants and everyday citizens. He was used to sitting with the rich and royal in chairs. But this was okay, he thought. He could look across and catch a glimpse of Guilietta, laughing and smiling when the service wasn't being conducted. And when the Bishop spoke, she stood there as solemn and beautifully sculpted as the polychrome sculpture of Saint Catherine of Alexandria in the church of Santa Caterina al Chievo.

Mastino della Scalla motioned for his cousin to sit next to him after the church service ended at Santa Anastasia. The two caught up after being apart for some days. The Baron was shocked to hear about the Gonzagas' bold move to steal another looker. Nicademo told about what had transpired with Hansum after Mastino had left the estate, about the advice he had given him, the presents he helped him buy and his assessment of how he thought it would all work out in a month or two. Everyone would be satisfied in the end, he assured Mastino. The Podesta told Nicademo of his interactions with Agistino and how the lensmaker gave his word about not allowing the teens to wed.

"But we must have an insurance policy," Mastino added. Nicademo gave his cousin a curious look.

"Insurance?"

"Yes. Upon seeing the girl again, I worry about her allure — and her resolve. Have Devlena brought to me tomorrow night. We will want her services, I think."

Nicademo's eyes went wide. "Cousin, this cannot be necessary. These are not kingpins or royal personages who may inherit power. It's only a boy and a girl."

"Devlena is not for the boy, only the girl. Romero's mind — and what he has in it — makes him too valuable an asset to leave to providence."

"Devlena for the girl? Guilietta?" Mastino saw his cousin look into nothingness. It was a look which overcame the Baron every time Mastino gave an order that was distasteful. Without looking up, Nicademo added, "I told Romero he should keep Guilietta for his mistress." Then he met Mastino's eyes. "That way, all would be happy."

"To this I would have no objection. I suppose if Romero relents truly, and soon, this course can change. For now, this is my will." Nicademo sighed. "Take cheer, cousin. Devlena most probably can't get to the girl for a week or two."

Devlena sat relaxed and upright in the receiving room at the palace. She was a small and pleasant-looking woman, plump and round, both in body and face. She had two cherry-red cheeks and a cherry nose. She wore a wimple with a deep blue veil over it and a full-length habit, like a nun. It had large, billowing sleeves and deep pockets on the smock. Devlena was answering the Podesta's summons, coming to the palace after vespers. She had been waiting patiently for several hours.

When Podesta della Scalla finally came in, followed by a servant with a tray of food, he nodded to her as he sat at a table. The servant put down the tray and promptly left, closing the door behind him.

"Grazie for waiting," Mastino said. "My day has been long. I must eat while we confer." Devlena stood up slowly, her hands still folded in front of her.

"When my Prince summons, it is my pleasure to wait." As she walked, her head did not change height. It's was as if she floated across the room. She watched the Podesta pick up a knife and fork, think better of it, then tear off a leg of fowl. He took a bite of the meat and then a mouthful of wine from a silver chalice.

"I have need of your services," he finally said.

"Of course, of course," she cooed. "What prince doesn't need mine or one of my brethren's services from time to time? We keep the road to glory clear. Whom may I ease from your path this time?"

"This is what I require," he began, continuing to eat as he described her mission. All through the description, the look on the poisoner's face was light and pleasant.

"And the fee?" she asked at the end.

"The same as the last. Half now, half when it's done."

"The same amount?" she said, very satisfied. She thought, 'A prince's fee to dispatch an unarmed, unguarded, unsuspecting young girl? No armed guards to get past or a retinue of paranoid nobles to fool? Wonderful.'

"Do you need explanation?"

"Oh, Excellency, mine is not to ask for a reason. I am a soldier to be commanded. It is enough for me to know that, by accomplishing my task, I save many lives."

Mastino had the chalice to his lips, about to take more wine. But her comment made him smile. He put down the cup and chuckled.

"You save lives by your work? How does your work *save* lives?"

"Well, you are a great man of war, Excellency. In your schemes, you put the lives of many men against the lives of your enemy's men. Take out the one man and all his men are spared. I do not believe I boast when I say there have been times when my work has accomplished what armies could not do."

"Yes, it's true, it's true, dear lady. You and I have changed history together several times, have we not? And I assure you, my aim on this target may seem strange, but the future profit to my lands will be greater than one could imagine." And with that, he held out a purse of coins. Devlena's small, plump fingers grabbed the satchel.

"Oh, my trust in your judgement is total, Excellency. Total," she said, tucking the bag within a hidden seam of her robes.

"Keep me informed of your progress. I expect results within a month."

The poisoner nodded serenely.

"Good night, Excellency. Sleep with the angels."

⌛

As Mastino sat alone, wolfing down the rest of his meal, his mind went back to the events of the day.

When Hansum alighted from his cousin's carriage, very early that morning, Mastino had greeted the boy with open arms. After transferring to Mastino's much grander coach, the Podesta sat back and watched Hansum. The boy laid his head on the cushioned seatback and closed his eyes. He perceived a faint smile on the youth's face and wondered what had put it there. He saw Hansum hug himself and nestle into the seat, his face betraying some sweet, recent memory. 'Yes, the course I have chosen for this girl is the right one,' Mastino thought as he watched the sleeping youth sigh.

# Chapter 20

About an hour out of Verona, the roads became quite bumpy. Hansum awoke as he, Baron Da Pontramoli and Podesta della Scalla arrived at Master Calabreezi's bell foundry. Hidden off the road, in a wood, it lay by a fast-moving tributary of the Adige. A mill race had been constructed by the river's bank to run a waterwheel. Looking out the carriage window, Pan explained that the wheel was attached to four large bellows, two for each of the smelting kilns that were built into the side of a hill. The kilns rose out of the ground like giant brick bee hives and were half as tall again as a man. Wisps of white smoke wafted from their tops and large baskets of charcoal sat by the kilns, as well as half a dozen stone crucibles. Several tall wooden posts were set on either side of the area and a thick beam between the posts carried a heavy block and tackle at its center. Four men were digging at something below this rigging, with two others watching them, Master

Calabreezi and General Chavelerio. When they saw the carriage, they waved and walked toward it.

"He must be behind in his work," the Podesta said to Nicademo. "I thought the smelters would be in full bloom by this time of day." The Podesta was the first out of the carriage, not waiting for the driver to open the door.

"Good day, Excellency," Calabreezi called as he trundled over to him. The general saluted the Podesta and nodded at the Baron and Hansum.

"I believed the kilns would be at heat when we arrived," Mastino said. "I was expecting to see the first cannon poured. I say, Calabreezi, you look tired. And we didn't see you at church yesterday."

"I've slept little since I've seen you last," the old man admitted.

"Are you unwell?" the Baron asked.

"Just old," the master said. "But I must admit, young Signor," he said to Hansum, "I have begun to realize the scope of this plan of yours. I have set aside commissions for thirty bells and put all my men to work on this one project."

"Then I must ready myself for complaints from the priories," the Podesta joked. "But what of the first pouring of the cannon? You should have sent word if it is delayed. We have much else to do."

"Not behind, Excellency, ahead. We worked on the Sabbath and poured yesterday. My men are digging up the results now. Come."

As they walked to the hole, they could see the dull bronze finish of the cannon's muzzle sticking out of the ground. It was common when casting to bury the molds. This helped hold the shape and allow the molten metals to cool more slowly, to prevent cracking.

*"Walk around the hole so I can see what's been done,"* Pan ordered.

Hansum did so, looking intently at the emerging structure, allowing Pan to scan the results. The old master walked up to Hansum and put his hand on his shoulder.

"Young Signor, I have many things I wish to discuss with you."

Pan whispered in Hansum's ear. Hansum repeated it.

"I see you have poured the cannon with the chamber pre-formed. Very clever, Master Calabreezi. Does it still need to be cored?"

"I believe so, Signor," the old man said, his pleasure at Hansum's observation showing. He certainly seemed to have changed his opinion about him. "With sand casting, I could not ensure an even enough wall, so I left an extra finger's thickness all around the chamber. Now we need only to core out a minimum of metal."

Hansum seemed to think for a few seconds. "Very sensible," he repeated. "Perhaps when we've tested the cannon and de-termined final specifications, we can make a plaster mold of the form, to ensure exact shapes, like a sculpture. Since there are no undercuts, it would be much faster and more exact. After all, we are planning on making many identical copies."

"Brilliant, Signor," Calabreezi said. "I know just the master mold maker to call upon in Verona." Hansum then saw Calabreezi smile joyously at the Podesta, who laughed like he had just seen something absolutely remarkable. "Signor Monticelli," Calabreezi continued, "how goes it with the black powder? When will you be ready with that?"

"The saltpeter should be done by now. Over four thousand pounds."

The old master whistled in amazement. "You waste no time, Signor."

"We won't have the gunpowder mill ready till spring," Hansum added. "But the charcoal and brimstone will be delivered in the next few days. This is still correct, Excellency? We should be able to do some first tests of the powder, without the cannon, before this coming Sabbath."

"I may be ready before next Sabbath too," Calabreezi said en-thusiastically. "I tell you, Excellency, I have not been this excited about a project since I was younger than Signor Montecelli here."

"See, my boy, you inspire many people," Mastino said.

"A leader of men," General Chavelerio added.

*"Ignore the compliments, Master. Just ask Calabreezi how long the coring should take."*

"We've never drilled anything so deep that had to be so true, Signor Monticelli. Most likely today and tomorrow for the coring.

The rest of the week for polishing and then it must be mounted to its carriage. I could be there, with luck, before the Sabbath. Well, perhaps not. It's a long day's trek."

"Why polish at this stage?" the Podesta asked. "This is only for testing. That would save you over two days, no?"

"True, true. What say you, Signor?" Master Calabreezi asked Hansum. Hansum waited for instructions from Pan.

"It should be just fine. As to the projectiles, the plans do not call for brass, just iron. You can provide these in time?"

"Si, Signor. I was thinking ten pieces?"

Hansum looked thoughtful.

"Oh no, Signor," he finally said. "I believe we could use at least fifty projectiles. Once we have confirmed all is well with the piece, I'm sure the general will want to start training his men and do tests for range and accuracy. We will have enough powder."

"I'll put three men on casting the spheres," Calabreezi said. "To Hell with the bells," he laughed.

One of Calabreezi's workers called him over. They were ready for the winch. The workers secured heavy hemp ropes around the cannon and Master Calabreezi called on several more men. They hoisted the cannon into the air and it hung there, pieces of the sand and horse manure mold still stuck to its body. The men knocked off this excess and the dull gray-bronze form, over half a ton of potential lethality, swung before them.

"Well done, Calabreezi," the Podesta said. "The first of many. We shall begin making arrangements for more of the components for bronze from here to Germany."

"First things first," Calabreezi said. He went over to the cannon with a hammer and tapped lightly down the length of the cylinder. Pan explained that he was listening closely for sounds that would tell his trained ear if there were any cracks or voids in the casting. Deep, dull thuds of various tones emitted from the piece. "She's sound," he finally pronounced. "Though she doesn't sing like a bell."

"She may not sing, Signor," Hansum said, "but put three pounds of powder in her and she'll roar like a lion!" Everybody laughed heartily.

"You've gained quite a sense of humor, Romero," the Podesta said. "Your visit home has done you wonders." Hansum blushed.

They stayed and watched as Master Calabreezi had his men take the cannon over to a shed in a heavy cart. They manhandled it upright, setting it perfectly straight, using a string with a centered weight on it. Hansum had watched and helped back home when people were constructing the community's homes. They used laser levels and holoprojections to get things just right. But the work of these medieval men was almost as accurate, using no more than string, chalk, rope, their muscles and brains. The cannon was secured against any movement with many blocks of wood and much rope. The idea was that a very large, hand-turned screw drill with a steel tip would bore out the extra finger thickness of brass inside the cannon.

"Master Calabreezi, you have made it perfectly," Hansum said.

"Grazie, Signor."

"I see some changes that we can make when we go into full production, though," Hansum said. "In the coming weeks, when things quiet, perhaps we can get together and discuss at length some improvements to the process as a whole?"

"I would be delighted."

They finished their time at Calabreezi's by taking refreshment in his home. It was a modest place, with almost no furniture better than that of a peasant. His wife was a quiet, plump, though intelligent-looking, woman. She had one kitchen girl, but no other servants. Hansum thought, 'Obviously, not everyone strives for opulence.'

"Do you have in mind other designs of cannon, Signor?" Master Calabreezi asked.

Hansum decided this was the perfect time to put his plan into motion. He hadn't talked to Pan about this, because he knew what the hologram's answer would be. So, Hansum began what he saw as his subtle offensive.

"Si, Master Calabreezi. Si, this is a very general design. Easy to use, mobile. Both offensive and defensive. But, although I can envision many more designs for different purposes, we must first perfect our methodology with this first piece, solidify supply and manufacturing partnerships, train the men and more. Then in a year or two, we can branch out."

"You truly have thought this out, Romero," the Podesta said. "I had no idea you have plans for various other cannon."

*"Master, what are you doing? Stop this nonsense,"* Pan whispered. *"Immediately!"*

Hansum took off his hat and placed it in his cloak.

Mastino noticed the gesture. "Your lucky hat, Romero," he commented.

"Men make their own luck," Hansum answered.

"I suppose they do," Mastino said. "So, other cannon?"

"Si, Excellency. Larger balls for more force against walls. Mortars for short range over walls to create havoc inside fortifications. Cannon for ships. Small hand-held cannon for individual soldiers. They would expel a small missile more accurately than an arrow, and teaching a man to use them would be quick. No longer would you have to train archers from childhood."

"Hand-held cannon? Amazing," Master Calabreezi said. "I wish I were a young man. Oh, to see where this will all lead a score of years from now."

Perceiving that Hansum was up to something, the Podesta decided to probe. He looked at Hansum through veiled eyes.

"When did these ideas come to you? Were they part of the ancient documents?"

"Only vaguely," Hansum answered. "Their inspiration was only to inform me that it could be done. But I look forward to drawing up the plans for them in the future. Not now, but in the future."

The Podesta smiled his sincerest smile. Then, not waiting for the master's wife to pour more to drink, he picked up the wine pitcher and filled Hansum's cup himself, smiling brightly at the boy. 'In the future,' he thought. 'Of course. People always betray themselves with the small things they say. One just has to listen.'

Later, on their way to the wagon maker who was making the gun carriage, the Podesta continued his exploration of Hansum's intentions.

"Romero, I have known Calabreezi since I was a small boy," Mastino began. "Never in all that time have I seen him so excited. You have gained a great admirer. Do you like being admired?"

"Who does not like being appreciated, Excellency? I have great admiration for Master Calabreezi too. His work is superb. The bells he has cast will be around a thousand years from now."

"A thousand years? Perhaps. Churches and things like bells just show off that a patron has power and money. The cannon? They will redraw the map of the world."

"A philosophical difference, Signori?" the Baron offered. "Which lasts longer, great art and architecture or war and the memory of warriors? I fear that we will never know the answer to that debate, for who among us will be living a thousand years from now, eh?"

"Oh, this is more of your sophistry, Nicademo," the Podesta said lightheartedly. "War goes hand in hand with great monuments and art. I am interested in war for I am allowed to do it. And with the spoils of war in one hand, I can make great monuments to the glory of God and my family with the other. For I am like Romero. I like it when others admire me. But wait. I think Romero is one who wishes to stay behind the scenes and be the unseen hand behind history. I believe his motives are not so obvious."

Pan, hidden inside Hansum's coat, screamed his objections.

*"He's probing you, fool! He's setting you up! Baiting you! Can't you hear it in his tone? He knows your plan just by the way you set it up so amateurishly. You're so obvious to him!"* But Hansum couldn't hear.

"My needs and wants are not that great," Hansum said to the Podesta sincerely. "I just want to have a comfortable living and keep my family well."

"Si, I believe you tell me true, Romero. You have always been honest with me," he said. "Well, here we are at the wagon maker. Let's inspect the cannon carriage. If its measurements are correct, we'll have it sent to Calabreezi. We must keep very busy over the next few days. Say, Romero, you do look different without your cap."

Holographic steam sprouted out of Pan's ears. Hansum put on the cap so Pan could inspect the gun carriage with him. He left the hat on for the rest of the day, though when they weren't doing business, Pan took every opportunity to chastise Hansum and his dangerous plan.

# Chapter 21

The next morning, Devlena watched from an alley as a royal carriage approached what she had been told was the lensmaker's house. She saw a young man coming through the doorway. Then a young woman's hand appeared and took hold of his jacket. It pulled him up short, and then *she* appeared. Lovelier than the Podesta had described, her fresh, young face was surrounded by wavy brown hair that shone auburn in the early-morning sun. The girl kissed the embarrassed, but smiling, boy. There was laughing across the street, a man and a woman's strange laugh. Devlena looked over and saw two people in a large upstairs window, laughing and waving at the lovers.

"Such a thing for the streets," the man teased, wagging his finger jovially. The woman continued her honking laugh and clapped her hands happily.

The young man laughed too now, and the girl waved back.

"Good morning, Bruno. Good morning, Nuca," the boy called. "Okay, Guilietta, I must leave."

The young man got into the carriage and it sped away. The girl stood there, radiant and alive, bouncing on the balls of her feet, waving after the carriage. Then she turned happily and went back into the house.

"Such a beauty, such a beauty," Devlena clucked low to herself. Then, without guilt, she calculated the dosages of the potions necessary to cause what must look like one of the many natural deaths young women suffered.

Turning her head back to the house across the street, she noted the man and woman still at the window. But they were now sitting, heads down, working. After a minute, the man stood and put on a half-made coat. The woman held a sleeve to it, using her needle to baste on a few stitches. 'They're tailors,' Devlena thought, cocking her head and contemplating something. Her original idea was to just show up at the lensmaker's to buy discs for the eyes. But she knew it was always better to interact with her victims away from their immediate families. The man disappeared from the window, and then the door to the tailor's house opened. The man came onto the street and walked toward the city. Devlena smiled as an idea hatched. She waited to make sure the man wasn't coming right back, then reached under her arm, grabbed the fabric of her habit and yanked on it. She made a face as she heard stitches pop.

When Nuca opened the door, Devlena was greeted with a big toothless smile.

"Excuse me, Signora," Devlena said, "I'm told there is a tailor's house in the neighborhood. Can you direct me to it? I need my habit repaired." She lifted up an arm to expose the split seam.

Nuca squeaked an unintelligible sound and bobbed her head up and down.

"Here, 'ailor, here."

"I beg your pardon, dear? What was that you said?"

Nuca patted herself on the chest and smiled again. She had almost no teeth, her face was skinny and lined, but her eyes shone.

"Me ailor." Then she took Devlena's arm and pulled her into the house.

"Oh, this is the tailor's house and you're a tailor," Devlena said, laughing. "Such luck I'm having, well, except for having ripped my new habit."

"You 'un?" Nuca asked in her nasal squeal.

"Un? Un? Oh, nun? Am I a nun? Oh goodness, no dear. I'm not a nun, though I spent many years with them in cloister, when I was a small orphan. And I guess I just got used to this way of dress." She smiled when she spoke and gave an extra effort to the smile after finishing each statement.

She watched Nuca bob her head up and down again and thought that this woman must be a simpleton. She almost turned to walk out, till Nuca reached out and touched Devlena's sleeve. She pinched and rolled the fabric through her fingers expertly.

"Aulity," she said. "Aulity."

"What's that? Oh, quality. Yes. Yes, I like nice things."

"Ix?" Nuca asked, pointing to Devlena's sleeve. "Ix?"

"Fix this? My heavens, yes. How much?"

Nuca made a face. "Fee," she said. "Fee. Ooo itches."

"Free because it's only two stitches. Well, bless you, my love, you are very Christian indeed."

"Ake off."

Devlena took off her veil, but left her wimple on while removing her habit. She sat down on a bench by the table while Nuca put something on her nose and peered closely at the fabric. 'Those must be the things the lensmaker creates,' Devlena thought.

Nuca went to a table and rummaged through a canvas bag, pulling out a bobbin of blue thread, and then got to work.

"No 'un? What you do?"

"What do I do? Oh, I'm a herbalist, dear. I've worked for many nobles, even kings and queens. I keep everybody healthy."

"Good, good, healthy, healthy."

Devlena was amazed as she watched Nuca's dexterity with a thread and needle.

"Yes, kings and queens and all their families. They're people with ailments and boils and broken bones, the poor dears, just like us common folk. But who I like to help most is young women. To keep young women healthy and well, so they can have strong *bambinos* and not die birthing them. In my years, I've come to create a wonderful, powerful tea to help women. Some would call it my gift to our sex," she said.

Nuca finished the mending and looked up smiling. "Ixed," she said, handing back the habit.

"Why it's just perfect, dear. Just perfect, indeed. Grazie, Signora," and she pulled the habit over her head and replaced her veil. "Good as new, God bless you, dear." Nuca bobbed her head up and down, still smiling. "Say, I tell you what. If you won't accept money as payment, how about I give you a satchel of my special tea? I'd imagine you have a daughter — or even a granddaughter — who's of childbearing age."

For the first time since Devlena met Nuca, the mute stopped smiling. She pouted and looked sad. She put her hands out, like they were empty. "No *bambini*, no."

"Oh, poor dear. Tut, tut. Well, there you go, God's will and all."

There was a knock at the door. Nuca answered it.

"Gui, Gui," she cried happily. "In, in. Come in."

Guilietta entered the room with a dress over her arm.

"Buon giorno, Nuca. Could I get you to make another change on . . . Oh, I'm sorry. You have a customer. I'm bothering you."

Devlena couldn't believe her luck. She thought it would take days or weeks to befriend a neighbor and then meet Guilietta, seemingly by chance. But here her quarry had walked right into her clutches within minutes. Guilietta turned to leave, so Devlena jumped up and smiled, reaching out and taking the young woman's slim arm.

"Oh no, my darling, don't go," and she put on her most dazzling smile. "We were just talking. Having a wonderful talk, weren't we?" Nuca bobbed her head. "Come, dear. Join us. That would be all right, wouldn't it, Nuca?" Nuca smiled and bobbed her head again. "So now, I'm Devlena, my dear. You're Gui? Come and sit. Sit."

"Grazie, Signora. I'm Guilietta. You're sure I'm not interrupting?"

"Not at all, dear."

"Herb'ist. Make tea strong girls, strong bambini," Nuca croaked. Guilietta looked confused.

Devlena laughed jovially. "She saying I'm a herbalist. You see, I was just telling Nuca the thing I am most proud of. It's my mixture of herbs for young women, to keep them healthy for childbirth."

Nuca leaned over and hugged Guilietta, then patted the younger woman's belly.

"Beaut'ful bambini soon. Beaut'ful." Guilietta blushed furiously. Devlena laughed again.

"Are you with . . ."

"Oh no, Signora, no. I'm not even married."

"Omero, Omero," Nuca teased, wagging a finger at Guilietta.

"Don't gossip, Nuca," Guilietta scolded, but then she smiled impishly.

"Oh, so a suitor," Devlena said. "Omero?"

"Romero, Signora. His name is Romero."

"Ah. And he lives nearby?"

"Right now he's with . . ." Guilietta hesitated.

"Podesta, away with Podesta."

Devlena didn't need an explanation of this. She saw that Guilietta now sat very still, not wanting to elaborate. Devlena didn't know the reason and didn't care.

"Well, wherever and whoever he is, he's a lucky man to have such a beautiful young woman."

"And me, him, Signora," Guilietta answered, blushing again.

Nuca reached over again and hugged Guilietta fiercely.

"Lucky, lucky. Love, love," she said clearly. Then she looked at Devlena. "Give Gui tea? She like daughter."

"Oh, isn't this heartwarming," Devlena said. "Dear girl, I told sweet Nuca here I would give her some of my special mixture and she could give it to a daughter or grandchild. She was sad when she told me she didn't have any, but you can see how she feels about you. She wants me to give you the tea. Now, what do you think about that?"

Guilietta looked at Nuca, smiled, and then hugged her back.

"Well, I guess it would be good," Guilietta said. "I do get cramps sometimes and I'm a few days over my time and feel a bit bloated. That's why I wanted my dress taken out a little."

"Well, I don't have any herbs on me now," Devlena said, "but, how about I promise to come back in a day or two, to bring you a nice pouch of my herbal tea?"

"Signora, you are too kind. Oh, but I must get going," Guilietta said, standing. "Papa's waiting for me at the shop."

Devlena sprang to her feet and put out her hands, taking Guilietta's in hers. "I shall think of your beautiful face as I mix my very special herbs for you, dear heart."

"Grazie, again, Signora, grazie," Guilietta said, smiling back.

"God bless you, child."

# Chapter 22

By the time they had finished supper, Hansum had had enough of Pan haranguing him about the dangers of his plans.

"Master, may I speak with you alone," Hansum asked, as the girls cleared the table.

The two men went and stood on the front stoop. A bright crescent moon shone in the sky. Agistino looked at Hansum intently, and he back at him.

"Master, you know my plan regarding the Podesta. I must put it into action. But for that I need Carmella, who you know, draws my plans perfectly."

"But I need her in the shop."

"Carmella can split her time," Hansum replied. "She will work in the shop during the day and on the plans at night. But she must be left alone to work quietly." He felt like the Podesta when he talked definitively like this. "In fact, I shall make arrangements for her to go to an inn so there's no distraction. What I have in mind should only take her, say, three nights."

"All this extra cost. It is not nec . . ."

"I must bear it. I must have the plans and I know she will have distractions here."

*"Master, what have you got in mind? Speak to me first, please!"*

"Tomorrow the Baron's driver and I are going around the city to pick up a list of supplies for the estate. I shall pick up more parchment for Carmella."

*"Master! Please consult with me first."*

"Romero, I still don't like this idea," the Master said. "The little fish does not eat the big fish."

"I disagree," was all Hansum answered. Agistino opened the door to the house, somewhat angrily. As he stomped in, he bumped into Lincoln, who was coming out. Lincoln looked questioningly at Hansum, but no explanation was forthcoming.

"Where's Carmella?" Hansum asked Lincoln.

"Cleaning the dishes."

"And where's Bembo and Ugilino?"

"Bembo went to town to visit a friend. Ugilino's taken some discs for the eyes to the miller. The Master gave him permission to call on Serindella. The discs for the eyes are to help the Ugmeister make a good first impression, though for that it would be better if the miller was blind."

"Listen, we need a meeting with Pan. Get Sham and we'll go to the shop." Any discomfort Hansum may have felt about giving orders in the past had disappeared.

# Chapter 23

Secure in the shop against intrusion, Pan popped out onto a bench and started in on Hansum.

"Are you crazy, Master? Master della Cappa is right. This can't work."

"I can't let the Podesta separate Guilietta and me. And it will work."

"Master, I think you are beginning to believe your own press. Remember, you aren't really a savant and you really shouldn't be competing head to head with this man."

"I say it can work. We'll show him inventions that he must have and I'll say it will take five or ten years for me to oversee their development. I'll say I can't do it without Guilietta. I'll say I won't be able to concentrate if I don't have her as my wife. When he sees the things we can offer him, it won't seem such a big deal to him. You'll see."

"It sounds like a plan to me," Lincoln said.

"It would be beastly to make Hansum marry someone he doesn't want to," Shamira added.

"The way the Podesta will interpret Hansum proposal," Pan rebuffed, "is that he is being blackmailed, and worse, defied. The psychological profile I've created for him suggests he won't put up with it. Besides, what new and exciting inventions do you have in mind?"

"Well, like I said at the foundry, bigger and different cannon."

"That they could develop on their own, now that they have the powder and the idea of one successful cannon. You need things that are completely different. What ideas can *you* suggest?" the imp asked belligerently.

"I don't know," Hansum said. "That's your department."

"Oh, I see," Pan said, satisfied he was making his point. "You haven't a clue."

"Hey, it's your job to help us."

"Help you survive, not help you get into bigger and bigger messes."

"Come on, Pan," Hansum implored. "We need ideas."

Pan was unhappy being forced into this situation. He thought for a second, then spoke grudgingly.

"Well, if you are looking to drag out a learning curve to give you time, I would suggest electricity. And with that, batteries would be important. Also, simple motors and generators that could be combined with water power to produce electrical current. We could impress them, I suppose, with communications at first, but very crude. Maybe later, when the Podesta is bored, we could introduce artificial lights."

"I think all the Podesta wants is tools for war," Hansum said.

"Communications is key for battle," Pan explained. "We'll show him how to use simple electrical currents for things like telegraphs. Morse code."

"What's that?" Shamira asked.

"Oh, I saw that at a History Camp," Lincoln said. "It was way before implants or worldwide communications. People couldn't even speak over it. You had to send words letter by letter, with a code of little clicks."

"Absolutely correct, Young Master. But think how even this crude communication tool would give an enormous advantage to one army over another. Spies could say exactly what is happening in a city before an attack, and generals could give a change of orders to frontlines instantaneously."

"How would these codes be sent?" Shamira asked.

"Over copper wires that are wrapped in insulation."

"Right," Hansum said. "This way we would have to show him how to make wire in quantity. And he would have to make alli-ances with regions that have lots of copper mines. There are so many inventions and we could take years to dole them out. I'm telling you guys, this is a good plan."

"Yes, a plan always seems good at first," Pan warned. "But it's the details in which the devilish problems dwell."

"What else ya got?" Hansum asked impatiently, a bit of the Podesta's attitude showing.

"That's not enough?" Pan asked sarcastically. "Electricity in the fourteenth century is not enough?"

"I have to overwhelm him."

"How about flight?" Shamira suggested.

"Flight? Yes," Hansum said with excitement. "That's good. But what kind?"

"I remember at one History Camp, they had early hot air balloons," Lincoln said. "But we can make it more advanced."

"You know," Shamira said, "the thing I don't feel good about is we could cause a lot of suffering for the people who will come up against these technologies."

"I agree," Hansum said. "But look what he's doing to people anyway."

"Perhaps, Masters and Mistress, we will be able to have a positive effect in the long term," Pan suggested. "Electricity and flight have many avenues of development other than war. Perhaps their commercial potential will encourage trade, as opposed to conflict."

"Okay, we're all agreed," Hansum said. "Pan, I have to go back to the estate tomorrow afternoon. I'm going to leave you here to work with Shamira. In the next few days, you two draw up some general plans for electricity and an air balloon. Nothing too specific. I don't want them being able to do any of this without us."

"Yes, I suppose," Pan conceded. "Shamira could draw up the plans for a simple wet battery and . . . Wait a minute. When you go back to the estate, we're supposed to do the gunpowder experiments. You can't do that without me. It's much too dangerous."

"It's necessary. Tonight I will stay up all night and you will tutor me on what I must know for the gunpowder and cannon tests."

# Chapter 24

Hansum was up all night watching a complete and true-to-life projected animation of all the processes and experiments he was going to have to accomplish on his own. There were the proportions and techniques for grinding the ingredients of the black powder, the drying processes and the storage of finished product, the testing procedures for both powder and cannon, the making of fuses, charge sizes, forms for recording test data and much, much more. To impress upon Hansum the dangers of what could happen, Pan even surprised his pupil by having the holo-image cannon blow up and kill several men. Hansum had been getting sleepy, so this woke him with a start. The images of dismembered and bloody bodies made him angry.

"I'm sorry, Master," Pan said. "I thought it necessary to make an important point."

It was a long night. Hansum had been sleeping on the cot less than an hour when he awoke to the feeling of someone blowing lightly on his cheek. He crinkled his nose and stirred, but kept trying to sleep. Then he felt a soft kiss on his nose. He opened his eyes a little. There, her smiling eyes peering into his sleepy ones, was Guilietta. She was crouched down by the cot, looking at him with such love that he actually had to catch his breath.

"Good morning, my husband and my love," she whispered.

"Good morning, wife," and then he yawned and added, "my darling, my heart."

"Oh, you yawn when you call me darling and heart. You are bored with me already?" she teased.

"I was up all night," he said, leaning forward and kissing her lips. "Come. Cuddle with me before we must rise. It's cold down here."

She was climbing onto the cot when the stairs creaked. The Master came lumbering down the stairs.

"Why is the fire not on?" he called. "Where's Carmella? Carmella! Oh, it's you two. Why is the fire not on?" he said, looking serious. Hansum could tell that Agistino was still angry with him.

"I told her to sleep in, Master, since she will be working late tonight," Hansum said.

"Now you are master of this house?"

"I will start the fire and prepare repast, Papa," Guilietta said, getting up. Agistino frowned again.

Hansum saw Agistino sit at the table and look at his pile of study notes. He watched as the older man stared at all the sketches of cannon, the trajectory lines, the myriad numbers and point form safety notes. Page after page of things he couldn't read.

"It's all beyond me," he heard Agistino grumble. "I'm glad I'm not young. So much to know. So much to learn." Then the Master looked up at Hansum and said seriously, "I hope you're right about all this." Agistino crossed himself once, and again.

A while later, when everyone was eating, Ugilino burst into the house and excitedly told his news.

"The miller liked his discs for the eyes and Serindella smiled at me. They showed me the mill and were impressed that I could carry two bags of flour. I think they like me, Master," he said, "even the mother."

"We'll see," the Master replied, shuddering at some private thought. Hansum imagined Agistino was thinking, once again, how ugly Ugilino and Serindella's children would be.

A knock at the door announced that the Podesta's wagon was there to pick Hansum up. The driver handed him a message from the Baron. Master Calabreezi would have the cannon finished by tomorrow. General Chavelerio already had men there to transport it to the estate.

Hansum took his shopping list, kissed his wife and went to work. There were things to buy and things to be ordered for delivery later. First off, he went to an inn and paid in advance for a room. While inspecting it, he turned around so Pan could scan and detect any places where people could spy on them. Then he went about town to pick up what he would need for the creation and storage of the black powder.

At a cooper's, Hansum showed the drawing of the barrel he wanted for storing black powder. It was calculated to hold about forty pounds of the explosive. The barrel maker was stunned when Hansum told him how many he needed. "One hundred right away, one thousand by early summer, two thousand by fall, and the next year, ten to sixteen thousand." The man couldn't speak, and his wife, who happened to be in the shop at the time, fainted.

When they finished shopping, the wagon was full. There were large mortars and pestles, bags of rags for cannon wadding, large goose feathers, loosely-spun cord, heavy rope and more. One more stop and Hansum could rush back to the house to spend time with Guilietta before he had to leave. The wagon stopped in front of the palace and Hansum jumped out onto the cobblestones and trotted up the steps. Just as he reached for the door handle, the door swung opened and out walked a small, round woman in a blue nun's habit.

"Good day, Sister," he said as they passed. She nodded at him with a serene smile.

A servant showed Hansum to Nicademo's office. The Baron was sitting behind a big desk full of letters and accounts. He had several clerks about him, waiting on orders. The Baron looked deep in concentration, but when he saw Hansum, he smiled broadly.

"Romero, my boy, it's so good to see you."

"You too, Baron. How was the time with your family?"

"Wonderful, grazie. What there was of it. Your project has made us rather more busy. And your time at the della Cappas'? Did all enjoy their gifts?"

"Everybody loved them, Excellency. Loved them. Thank you for advising me."

"It was nothing, my boy. Nothing. And great news from Calabreezi, eh? Did you want to see the Podesta? He is very busy, but I know if you wait . . ."

"I came to see you, Signor. I have just finished my shopping and want to leave for Bella Flora as quickly as possible. I'm bringing you these notes. Here are accounts that need satisfying now, for the items I picked up this afternoon, and here is a list of items to be picked up by the end of the week."

Nicademo looked quickly and efficiently at the list, pursing his lips while he concentrated. Then he waved over a clerk. He pressed the papers into the young man's hand and stared at him as the youth read it. "You understand what has to be done? You've heard the young signor's instructions?" The young man nodded and took the paper to a small desk against the wall. He sat down and copied. "Anything else, my boy?" Nicademo asked.

"No, Excellency," Hansum answered. "I'll take the wagon to the della Cappas', say my goodbyes and be off to the estate. I want to arrive in time to get a good night's sleep. If we start grinding the powder first thing in the morning, we could be testing it by late Friday."

"Good man," the Baron said. "The Podesta and I should be there for Friday too. Perhaps we will see these first tests." And then he smiled at Hansum and slapped the table with both hands. "It's so good to see you, Romero. These are exciting times."

"Si, Excellency. We'll see you on Friday." Hansum put out his hand. The Baron shook it vigorously and then sat back, smiling in silence. Hansum turned around and walked back to the carriage. His only thought now was to get to Guilietta.

"Romero was just here," Nicademo said. "He leaving for Bella Flora this afternoon. He hopes to get the black powder tests started by Friday."

"Excellent," Mastino said. "He's a good boy. Conscientious. Oh, and Devlena was here as well," he added offhandedly. "She said she already made contact with the girl and is delivering her medicine this afternoon."

Nicademo stared at his cousin blankly, knowing the more he tried to hide the fact that he didn't like the idea of assassinating Guilietta, the more Mastino would see it. He also knew Mastino would ignore it.

"I thought it would be two weeks before she got to her," Nicademo said as evenly as possible.

"Fortune is smiling on us, I suppose," Mastino said lightly. "So, supper tonight? Our wives and all the children? That will be nice, eh? Some family time, since we shall be gone again soon."

"Si, very pleasant," Nicademo said, recovering his composure. "Is Beatrice coming to the estate this weekend?"

"No, why push the two together? We'll clear the way first," he said with some verve. "And I told Romero I wouldn't press him. Give him time to complete the first part of the project without distractions. There's time. See you at supper, cousin."

On the way home in the wagon, Hansum noticed the distinct blue habit of the nun he had seen at the palace. She was having an animated discussion with a man. He wasn't sure if they were arguing, as the nun had a serene smile on her face.

At home, he found there was food prepared for him. The others had already gone back to the shop, so only Guilietta and her mother were in the house. Guilietta had kept a nice plate of sausages, hare pie and squash for him. She sat him down at the table, put the plate purposefully in front of him and filled a goblet with the good wine her father kept for the Baron and Podesta.

"You both beam so when you're in the same room," the Signora said, clasping her hands to her bosom. "Well, I'm going upstairs to crochet. Maybe have a little nap."

Hansum ate with Guilietta by his side. She leaned against him, putting her hand on his arm and smiled contentedly as he ate. She daubed his chin with one of the fancy handkerchiefs he had brought the other day and they both giggled.

"I wish I had another night with you," he said when they finished.

"Me too," and she began to cry.

"What's this?" Hansum said. "Don't cry. I told you everything is going to work out. My plan is a good one."

"I know, husband. But I'm still afraid for you. For us."

"Oh, posh!" he exclaimed. "Come. Let's go say my goodbyes at the shop. Then I must be off."

Walking up the alley to the shop, they passed the wagon. Hansum told the driver to turn the vehicle around, as he'd only be a short time.

"It's not so grand as the others," Guilietta said. "It's only a wagon and the horses aren't even matched."

"It's only carrying me," Hansum laughed.

There was another emotional parting in the shop, during which Hansum took off his hat and handed it to Shamira.

"There's a loose thread inside. Could you please snip it. It's a bother."

*"Goodbye, Master,"* Pan said. *"Please, be very careful."*

Everyone came out to wave their goodbyes. Hansum sat in the wagon, waving back to them. The children and Ugilino ran and skipped after it, shouting all the way up the alley. When Hansum turned forward, he saw Nuca coming out of her house with someone. It was the nun in the blue habit. 'What an odd coincidence,' he thought. He waved at Nuca and she back at him. Nuca saw Guilietta and waved at her excitedly, showing off a small cloth satchel. Guilietta smiled, pleased, and then looked back to Hansum. As the carriage receded, she put up her hand and held it there, a sad, last goodbye.

# Chapter 25

A tiny Pan popped out onto the table at the inn as Shamira rolled out the large blank sheets of parchment. Lincoln latched the door and walked over to Pan.

"Hey, little guy, do you ever get tired of being cooped up in that little lamp of yours?" Lincoln asked.

"No," Pan answered. "Do you ever get tired of being stuck in your skin?" Lincoln thought for a moment.

"Actually, yes."

Pan clapped his tiny hands together. "Okay then, let's get this show on the road. We've got work to do." A wand materialized in his fist and he pointed it into the air. A holographic picture appeared. "Now, talented Mistress, these are not technical plans, as before. They are to be concept drawings, more illustrative than the blueprints we made of the lathes and cannon. There will be ten pages in total. They will show a hot-air flying machine, propelled by two electric motors and several large wet batteries. We will also illustrate a generator/motor itself, showing how one could use it as motor or a generator when combined with water power." He flashed an array of floating holographic pictures. "This is the telegraph. It's most likely the most practical invention to be made first."

Shamira sketched and had fun. Pan and Lincoln laughed with amazement at her talent. Shamira included pictures of clouds with lightening around the battery and motor. She drew Zephyr, the Wind God, blowing on the hot air balloon. She put Hansum and the Podesta in its basket. Mastino looked out over the front of the basket, a satisfied smirk on his face. Hansum stood next to him, one arm outstretched over the scene, showing the viewer that it was he who was bringing these wonders to the world. In the other hand, he held a telescope. Shamira even drew Hansum staring out at the viewer, like she had seen church artists do when they were showing some important person. She had Lincoln on the ground, holding a rope to the floating air vehicle. Shamira added trees, birds, snakes and people around the borders. Pan instructed her where to place the names of metals and chemicals, and to hint at things by adding a few sketchy cross sections, like copper wire wound around an armature of a motor, or mentioning copper and calamine on the drawing of the wet battery.

Lincoln said he found the most interesting part of the drawing was the battery.

"It's amazing to think, little guy, that this huge battery, which can hold a charge for only a couple of hours, was the great granddaddy of your energy supply. How long can yours last?"

"Indefinitely, Young Master."

"Wow," Lincoln replied in awe.

By the time Hansum's wagon reached Bella Flora, it was getting dark. He stopped at Jacopo's cottage and roused him and a few other men to come unload the supplies at the barn.

"All went well while I was away, Jacopo?"

"Si, Signor."

"How go the saltpeter beds?"

"I believe we have this many, Signor. He flashed all ten of his fingers twice."

When Hansum entered the dining room, he saw General Chavelerio having supper alone.

"Young Monticelli, so good to see you. Have you eaten?"

"No, General. Not yet."

"Well then, we dine together this night."

"This is fortuitous, General," Hansum said. "I would like to show you what I have in mind for the black powder and cannon tests. The cannon should be here by Friday and I am planning to have enough powder to make up to fifty firings with it."

"Wonderful. I am most anxious to try this new toy of yours." The general had been the quietest of all the important men Hansum met. But one on one, during supper, he opened up, telling war stories that both fascinated and horrified Hansum.

After they ate, Hansum showed the plans. There were graphs, expected trajectories and distances of the cannonball flights, and even a fill-in-the-blanks form to record the results of each firing. The general seemed most impressed with the procedures for loading and firing the cannon. Pan mostly used the 1652 edition of the *The Compleat Cannoniere* for this document.

"In these procedures, I've written that each gun must have an officer and eight men, plus two horses. Is this possible?"

"Absolutely."

"Good. Oh, and since we must measure the shots exactly, we must pace out a large distance and have men along it to find where the cannonballs land. Do you know of any place on the estate that is relatively flat, for about three thousand paces?"

"Yes, yes. Not perfectly flat, but as flat as you can get around here or on a battlefield. There's a very beautiful meadow with hills and trees around it. It opens up to the river valley."

"Excellent, General."

"I say, Monticelli, the captain I have chosen for this duty should see these plans. May I send for him?"

"Si, General. He is to do the firing of the cannon?"

"No. One of his lieutenants will do that. We have brought three lieutenants to learn. The captain will be responsible for training all and men on the cannon during the next year."

"Well, perhaps besides the captain, we can invite in all the officers and go over this tonight. We can plan together how we shall do the testing and give each their job."

"It's true what our Podesta says about you," the general said. "You are a man with a fire in him." He sent the footman to go get the officers.

"The men you picked are good with numbers and computation, as I asked?"

"Si," the general said. "Much better than me, I hope. I think war will be very different with this new weapon. Muscle will be irrelevant in front of the likes of these cannon. How the world is changing."

Hansum knew that the general wasn't the only one inept with numbers. Half a dozen officers came to the dining room. There was the captain, the three lieutenants who would train for the cannon and two more who would work security when it arrived. After being shown the plans and told what was to happen over the next few days, the officers had questions. Hansum was able to answer the procedural ones easily, but when they came to numbers, he had to fake it.

"So, gentlemen," General Chavelerio said, after seeing Hansum yawn a few times, "it's time for all to retire. No more wine. You and your men must all muster here at the house at sunrise. Dismissed."

All the young officers left in high spirits, each bowing and shaking hands with Hansum.

On the way to his room, Hansum thought how it was one thing to talk about cannons in the abstract, like it was a computer-simulated, school science project. But now he was about to do it for real, with living men, all of whom had killed in battle and looked forward to doing much more of it with the cannon. And here he was, all alone, without Pan, having to make important life and death decisions. But as he slipped into the bed, with the soft sheets and blankets, Hansum thought only of how it would be to be in a bed like this with his wife.

# Chapter 26

Early the next morning, Hansum joined General Chavelerio in his carriage for a ride to the barn. The young officers he'd met the previous evening were resplendent on their horses. They rode beside the carriage, all wearing their basilard helmets and armor. The enlisted men ran behind under their kettle helmets. All the metal banging on metal, the clomping of the horses and the noise of the wagons made a wonderful clatter. Some men carried poleaxes, others bows with a quiver of arrows on their backs. As Hansum looked at all the men and ancient weapons, he couldn't help but think how, in a few years, most of the bows, arrows and poleaxes would be replaced with crude rifles.

As they neared the barns, one of the peasant workmen shouted to the others, "It's Signor Monticelli. He's returned."

All the workers ran to the wagon, shouting their greetings. "It's been so boring without you, Signor," one of them cried over the clamor. As Hansum got down from the carriage, another of the workers chattered away at him, like a little boy.

"We did as much as we could with the merda piles, then Jacopo sent us back to the regular farm work. Making the exploding material is much more interesting."

"Don't call them 'merda piles,'" Jacopo said. "They're saltpeter beds."

"All right already," the peasant said. "But we missed you, Signor."

"Then let's get to work," Hansum said. "Jacopo, have you arranged everything?"

"Come and see, Signor."

The general and officers dismounted and everyone followed Hansum and Jacopo into the barn. Four of the soldiers were ordered outside to stand guard. The charcoal that had been collected locally and the sulfur from down south were stored in barrels. Only one barrel of the saltpeter had been brought down from its security shed in the fields.

"Now, we must mix these three ingredients together," Hansum said. "And they must be ground together for one full day." He showed the men one of the large stone mortars and heavy iron pestles. "After doing this job, you may be praying to be back doing regular farm work," he joked. All the men laughed. "These wooden bowls are for measuring the exact amounts of the three materials to make the black powder. Only myself and Jacopo are allowed to measure." When Jacopo finished measuring, Hansum took a fourth bowl and filled it with water. "You must put this much water in. This is a most important thing." He poured it on the pile of black, yellow and white contents in the mortar. "Mix it with your hands into a mud pile. It must be wet, so no sparks are made when you mix." A large ball of dark gray goop lay in the mortar. Hansum picked up a heavy steel pestle and began grinding the lump as he had seen himself do in Pan's holographic recreation. "Now you grind and grind and grind. Big round strokes like this." He waved over one of the workers and handed him the pestle. After watching and correcting the man, Hansum had Jacopo fill another mortar. Soon there were ten men grinding away. Each mortar only contained a little over what would be three pounds of black powder. Jacopo was also told that, after he was sure the men knew their jobs properly, he should conscript ten more people for a night shift. Making black powder in this fashion would continue till the incorporating mill was completed in the summer.

"General, the next hours will be tedious," Hansum said. "Your men will learn nothing more here. I suggest we go pace off the testing field."

With very little instruction, the officers seemed to take control of laying out the firing range. While they worked, the captain sat on his horse and spoke excitedly to Hansum and General Chavelerio. He had stayed up all night, reading and rereading the pamphlet on cannoneering. He saw how cannon could be used for softening up enemies.

"We can destroy their cavalry and infantry even before it attacks," he said.

"Captain Soranzo loves battle, Signor Monticelli," the General said. "And he hates Venice especially."

"Why?" Hansum asked innocently.

Captain Soranzo explained that he had lost a brother in Mastino's earlier campaigns and wanted revenge. "It's not so much they killed him, Signor. He was a soldier. But it's the way they did it. They captured him and flayed him to get information. Flayed him alive and didn't kill him clean."

Hansum became quiet. He realized how his life was now going to be consumed by making deadlier and deadlier killing machines for men like this.

"I think I must get back to the barn, General," Hansum said, a sick feeling in his stomach.

When Hansum dismounted the carriage near the barn, he heard singing and joking coming from it. 'Well, it is boring work, so it's good if they amuse themselves,' he thought. When he walked in, he saw that six of the men were away from their mortars. Jacopo wasn't there and this was not one of their break times. When the men saw him, they ran back to their places to work in silence again. When Hansum checked the mortars, he found most too dry. He became angry.

"Look what you're doing! It's all too dry," he yelled. "It could blow up. You're supposed to add water." The image of the holographic explosion burst into Hansum's mind. He was looking into the face of one of the men Pan had dismembered in the re-creation. He became very angry. "Do you want to die? This is dangerous work! Did you not hear what I said? Are you all stupid?" he screamed.

When everything was back to working properly, Hansum stationed a soldier inside the barn, with orders to call him if things got out of hand again. Then he went outside to calm down. The image of Pan's illustrative explosion, with all its blood and holographic guts, kept popping into his mind. When Jacopo returned and Hansum told him what he had found, the foreman vowed that everything was fine when he left. Hansum told him it wasn't his fault, but they were going to have to be more disciplined with the men. A second shift showed up before dusk, half were women. Hansum was now very terse in giving his instructions.

He found the women better workers. When the general came by, Hansum told him what happened and they posted one of the officers to oversee the night shift. Hansum went to the manor and had to listen to more of the general's grisly war stories over supper. That night he had a fretful sleep, dreaming about the barn exploding.

In the morning, he came down and saw the results, finally breathing a small sigh of relief. They had what would be their first forty pounds of gunpowder when dried. They put the doughy goop into a dozen large buckets and started the original shift back on a new batch.

It was time to dry and corn the powder. Hansum had decided how to handle this the previous night. He asked for the best two women bakers on the estate to be brought to him. He took them to a flat stone terrace behind the manor and had old bed linens spread out. He then instructed the women to push the pasty material through a coarse sieve, cutting the emerging tubules into seed-like balls. They were then spread on the sheets to air dry. He watched the women till he was satisfied they could continue on their own, and then gave them another task, black powder fuses. He had them braid some fifty arm lengths of soft cord. Then they made a muddy slurry of finely-ground black powder and soaked the cord in it. Hansum told the women that when it was perfectly dry, they should coil it very loosely. He left one of the soldiers with them to make sure nobody came near the terrace with a flame or coal.

When Hansum came back to the barn, he was once again angered by the noise from the first shift. These were the men who had done so well when making the saltpeter. Hansum could hear them arguing with Jacopo and the guard. Before he got to the barn, he saw another farm worker coming toward the barn, leading an old limping donkey. Hansum recognized him as Alfredo. He had worked with him the week earlier, but not seen him since returning. When Alfredo got close, Hansum saw that the man's hands, face and neck appeared to be burned.

"Alfredo, how did this happen to you?" Hansum asked. Alfredo looked down and didn't answer.

Just then, Jacopo came running out of the barn.

"Alfredo?" he shouted anxiously, "what are you doing here? I told you to stay home till you were better."

"I was told to take Gina to the field and put her out of her misery. Nobody wants her for the meat. She's too wormy. I'm to leave her back there for the buzzards."

"Well, you shouldn't be bothering the Signor. Get going."

Something seemed off to Hansum. "I still want to know how he hurt himself."

"Oh, he's just stupid, Signor. Go away, Alfredo . . ."

"How did it happen?" Hansum demanded, raising his voice. "And tell me the truth." Jacopo began to answer, but Hansum cut him off. "I want Alfredo to tell me."

"I'm very sorry, Signor. When you were gone, for a joke, a good joke, I took a bowlful of the saltpeter. To show my family how it sparkled in the hearth. I threw a handful in, but the sparks came out and hit the bowl of it my grandson was holding. It exploded."

"Your grandson! Your grandson is burned too!"

Alfredo hesitated, obviously feeling the pain his grandson must have felt. "Si, Signor," and he began to whimper.

Hansum flashed, "I left orders that nobody was to touch the saltpeter! I said it was to be guarded!"

"I was the guard, Signor," Alfredo said, now crying openly. "I didn't realize . . ."

"You didn't realize?" Hansum scolded, reminding himself of his own father and several school counsellors. "You didn't realize? But I told all of you. And you, Jacopo, you were supposed to make sure nothing went wrong." Hansum was shouting.

"Si, I know, Signor Monticelli . But it was only an accident," Jacopo said.

"It wasn't an accident," Hansum yelled without reservation. "An accident is something that can't be helped. Something unforseen." Again, the words of his father. "This was foreseen and warned against. And when I asked you if anything went wrong . . ."

"The fault is mine, Signor . . ." Alfredo continued, tears rolling down his cheeks.

"Shut your mouth, Alfredo!" These words seemed to fly out of Hansum by themselves. These weren't the words of his father. These were the Podesta's. "I want you to leave this area of the farm and never come back."

"But when I'm better I want to help again. It's such interesting work and I'm honored to . . ."

"I said leave," Hansum shouted. Other workers and soldiers came out of the barn to see what was happening. Hansum shouted, "What are you looking at? Get back to work!"

"But I'm supposed to take Gina to the back field, Signor," Alfredo said.

Hansum's eyes flashed with anger. Visions of the simulation Pan had shown him of an explosion invaded his mind again. How could he get through to these people?

"You leave Gina here, Alfredo. But you go and never come back here. You only do farm work now."

"But Signor . . ."

"I said leave!"

A soldier stepped forward and lowered his poleaxe between Alfredo and Hansum. Alfredo dropped the animal's reins and hobbled back to the other side of the property. Hansum motioned with his head for the soldier to take his position again and leave him with Jacopo.

"I'm sorry, Romero," Jacopo said. "The men don't realize how serious this work is. They are often like children."

"*They* don't realize? Jacopo, you lied to me. I asked you if everything was all right when I returned and you said yes. You are supposed to be my eyes and ears. My right arm. My trusted one. And you lied to me."

Jacopo fell to his knees and sobbed. "Please forgive me, Master Monticelli. Please forgive me, Master." And then he lay prostrate on the ground and grabbed Hansum's boots.

"Get up!" Hansum shouted, pushing him away with his foot. "Get up!" Hansum realized he couldn't fire Jacopo. In another situation he could have forgiven Alfredo too, but he had to make an example. "You get in there and make sure the men are working properly. Make sure their powder is not too dry or too wet. I'm not asking people to be unhappy, just careful. Look. Look!" he said, pointing at Alfredo, who was limping away across the field. "He could have been killed. His grandson could have been killed."

"It won't happen again, Master."

"Tie that animal up and go do what I told you! Then bring me two of the new empty barrels for the powder." Hansum took several steps away from Jacopo and turned his back on him. He signalled to the soldier to come again. "Bring a wagon and have Jacopo put the barrels on it when he comes back."

When the barrels were in the wagon, Hansum and the soldier rode back to the manor's terrace, where the women were just finishing up the powder. It was probably going to take several more hours for it to air-dry. In the future, a safe drying kiln would be built. As for the black powder fuses, the women had cleverly draped the fifty arm spans of the powder-drenched cord on the lower branches of a tree. With the breeze blowing through it, the fuse was dry already. Hansum took a sharp knife and carefully cut a piece the length of his outstretched arms. Then he walked well away from the terrace and had the footman bring him a burning

coal. He lit one end of the first cord and was pleased to see it ignite instantly. It hissed and fizzed, taking till the count of fifty to
consume the whole piece.

'Good,' he said to himself. 'At least that worked out.' Hansum
went into the house to have a nap till the powder was dry.

# Chapter 27

"Zippy," Lincoln said. "These drawings are really zippy, Sham!"

It only took two nights working at the inn for Shamira to
complete the plans. It was Thursday evening, just after midnight,
when she carefully rolled up the ten large pages and placed them
in a cardboard tube she had Lincoln make. Early the next day,
Lincoln went to the market with Shamira, then left her and ran
off to deliver the portfolio to the Podesta.

About a hundred paces away from the palace, Lincoln was
stopped by a soldier. The Podesta's carriage was at the front door
and trunks were being loaded onto it.

"You can't go closer," the soldier said. "The Podesta is coming
out. When he's left, you can go and deliver your package."

"But it's for him. He's supposed to get it before he goes."

"He'll get it when he returns. Don't be in such a hurry, little
man. You should join the army and learn patience."

"Believe me, he'll want this," Lincoln complained.

"You, boy!" a voice shouted from the palace door. It was the
Podesta himself. The soldier snapped to attention. "You are from
della Cappa's?"

"Si, Excellency!" Lincoln called. "I have something for you.
From Romero!"

"Bring it here."

"Told ya!" Lincoln laughed as he ran off.

Just as Lincoln got to the Podesta, Grazzana stepped forward
and put his hand on the boy's chest, keeping him a distance from
his master. Nicademo happened to walk out the door from the
palace at the same time.

"Maruccio," the Baron called in greeting, "what are you doing
here?"

"Romero said to bring these as soon as they were finished."

Nicademo held out his hand and took the paper tube. While he was untying the ribbon, the Podesta said, "Your friend Romero is a very clever fellow."

"Uh , si, Excellency."

"You look a clever fellow too. Are you?"

Lincoln shrugged and mugged a face. "Clever enough, I suppose."

Nicademo had the ten large sheets of paper out of the tube.

"They're more plans, Mastino."

"More cannon?"

"No. I don't know what they are. The writing says, 'Machine to Fly in the Air' and 'Device for Speaking Instantly from One City to Another.'"

"What? Let me see."

'That got 'em going,' Lincoln thought, turning to leave.

"You, boy, stay!" Mastino said. Grazzana's hand was suddenly holding onto the back of Lincoln's tunic. "What do you know of these?"

"I dunno. I watched them being drawn. Romero told me about them."

"Come with us." The Podesta quickly marched back into the palace. Nicademo followed, the loose rolls of parchment held to his chest. Lincoln followed with Grazzana still holding onto him. The Podesta didn't bother to go to the planning room, but ordered a footman to take a large vase off of a marble table in the foyer. Then he ordered all the servants to leave the entranceway.

"What's this mean?" the Podesta asked brusquely.

"Just what it says, Excellency," Lincoln said. "They are drawings for a flying machine. See? Men can travel in it. In the same way that smoke rises, a bag of hot air will rise into the air, if it's big enough and there's a constant source of heat."

"You can read too?" the Podesta asked. Lincoln nodded. "Did you help invent this?"

Lincoln thought for a bit and concluded that one savant was enough.

"No, Excellency. Like I said, Romero explained them to me and I watched while Carmella drew them from his sketches."

"What's this?" Nicademo asked, pointing to some propellers hanging off of the torpedo-shaped wicker basket under the balloon. "They look like windmills."

"No, Signor. The wind pushes a windmill's arms. These make their own wind and push the air bag and basket below it. The men inside direct it to wherever they want to go."

"And how are these arms moved?" Nicademo asked. "By men in the basket? By turning them with a crank?"

"No, electricity and motors. See?" And then he flipped some pages and pointed to several pictures. "Electricity is like lightening in a bottle. It has great energy, much more than people or animals. Different metals are put in a bottle between certain other metals. This produces and stores electricity. Also, you can make electrical energy from running rivers. They can run motors, like this windmill, and create their own wind. Many jobs can be done with electrical machinery such as this, apparently."

"Lightening made from metals and stored in bottles? The ability to use these engines and not animals? This is too fantastical," Nicademo said.

"You insisted his other claims were impossible," Mastino reminded. "And this. This Device for Speaking Instantly from One City to Another. What do you know of it?"

"Well, Excellency," Lincoln made a big deal of taking off his hood and scratching his head, like he was thinking. "Using electricity from the bottle, you can send little pulses through thin copper wires. At the other end of the wire, the pulses of electricity turn into the exact same clicking noises you produce at the beginning. If people at both ends know the clicking code, you can send messages."

"From city to city? Leagues away?" the Podesta asked. Lincoln nodded.

"And how long does the click take to get from one end of a league of wire to the other?" Nicademo asked.

"Instantly, Excellency. Whether it is a hundred paces or a hundred leagues. Instantly. That's what Romero told me."

"Are all the plans here?" the Podesta asked.

"I'm not sure," Lincoln said, playing his part. "Um, I think there are many things to invent and it could take years. Romero said many more ideas would come from the results of the first projects."

"Get in the coach, boy," the Podesta ordered.

"I'm supposed to meet Carmella on the way home, to help carry things from the market," Lincoln said with some panic. He didn't like the tone of the Podesta's voice. "The Master needs me to run his shop," he added earnestly.

"No, you're coming with us. You know too much of Romero's plans. It's not good for you to be unprotected. And Romero could use an assistant he trusts."

"But Master della Cappa needs me to work on the lathes, to make the lookers for you." Lincoln saw Mastino's eyes widen, the whites of his eyes making him look wild. Nicademo stepped forward and put a friendly hand on Lincoln's shoulder.

"Master della Cappa has a good journeyman now," the Baron said. "And you are more valuable to our Podesta working with Romero."

"But I've got to say goodbye. I need my clothes. I need to tell them what's going on."

The Podesta looked like he had endured enough. Lincoln felt Grazzana's strong hand move from his shoulder and take hold of his arm, ready to push him into the carriage.

"A suggestion, Excellency," Nicademo said, intervening. "Let us take young Maruccio to della Cappa's and allow him his goodbyes. Also, we'll inform Master della Cappa that we'll immediately arrange another journeyman for him."

"Si. Si. Of course," Mastino said grudgingly. "You go ahead, Nicademo. I will follow in another carriage. I just remembered some things I wanted to check on."

"We can come back to get you."

"No, go ahead. I'll be there when I'm there."

"Come Maruccio," the Baron urged kindly. "Into the carriage with you. Everything is going to be all right. A big adventure is about to begin for you."

"Another one?"

As the carriage drove away, the Podesta called Captain Caesar over.

"Bring me Devlena. Right away."

Devlena lived off the next square, so she was there within the hour.

"How goes your mission?" Mastino asked.

"Oh, splendidly, Excellency. I made contact with the girl three days ago and she started her medicine yesterday."

He stood staring very seriously at his poisoner. "How long?"

"Oh, it depends, Excellency. If she takes the quantity I pre-scribed, and keeps taking it as she begins to feel unwell, perhaps a week. But often, when they begin to fail, they cut back on the medicine. I had planned to go tomorrow or the day after to check on her progress. If she has cut down her consumption, I'll urge her on."

"So, a week or two?"

"I do not wish to give false hope, Excellency. My word is important to me. She's young and strong. I've seen them last a month. But I've never failed, Excellency. Never."

"I'll be gone a week," the Podesta said. "Report to me when I return."

"Travel well and God bless you, Excellency. God bless you."

"Keep driving. Don't stop!" Nicademo shouted to the driver, as he held Lincoln from jumping out of the carriage. They had just passed Shamira on the way back from the market, several hundred paces from home. Lincoln wanted to jump out and help her with the many shopping bags she was carrying, but the Baron wouldn't let him. They found only the Signora at the house, and the sight of the nobleman caused her to freeze with surprise and become mute. The Baron kept a hand on Lincoln's shoulder as they, along with Grazzana, walked quickly up the alley toward the workshop. When they entered the now crowded and busy shop, Master della Cappa hastily stood up and smiled at the Baron.

"What a wonderful surprise, Excellency," Agistino said. "Welcome. Do you have time for a glass together?"

"They're takin' me to work with Romero," Lincoln blurted out before Nicademo could speak.

Just then Shamira ran into the shop, breathless and eyes wide.

"But Excellency," Master della Cappa said, "if you take Maruccio, how will I keep production of the lookers up?"

"Not to worry, della Cappa," Nicademo soothed. "Not to worry. When I return, I shall make arrangements to smuggle another journeyman for you. You'll see, in the end it will be better."

"But that will take time, Excellency. I'm down another person today. My daughter is not feeling well."

It took a few moments for Nicademo to respond, knowing the reason for Guilietta's illness.

"Well then, till we get you new help, we must cut our expectations of delivery somewhat. Do not worry, my friend," Nicademo said, putting his hand on Agistino's shoulder. "It's all for the best. We would not do harm to our business together. It's too important. But from time to time, circumstances come up which require small adjustments. You understand." He smiled sincerely.

"Of course, Excellency. I understand perfectly," Agistino said, frowning.

Nicademo sent Grazzana into the loft with Lincoln to get his clothes. As he watched them come down, Guilietta came into the shop, looking pale and anxious. She had a hand on her stomach and was slightly stooped, very different from the radiant youth Nicademo saw the other week.

"My best regards to you, Signor," she said, curtsying in obvious discomfort. The Baron nodded, but said nothing. He watched her hug Lincoln and kiss him on the cheek. "Give Romero my love," he heard her whisper. All the little boys hugged Maruccio, and two cried, whining that they were losing their big brother.

"Who's going to teach us to read now?" one bawled.

"Hush. Don't worry," Shamira said. "I will continue the lessons."

'Such an odd, odd place,' Nicademo thought. 'Imagine a world where all workers can read. Impossible.'

# Chapter 28

Hansum had fallen asleep and was dreaming about himself and Guilietta. In the dream, they were again in the twenty-fourth century, but this time in Verona as tourists. Guilietta was up on the famous balcony and Hansum was speaking to her from the street, spouting silly things, love nothings. Arimus was there too, laughing along with them and speaking in his poetic verse.

> "You've made your decisions, for good or for ill.
> You're out in the world now, forcing your will.
> Bravo to you, though no guarantees are made.
> You've dealt your own cards,
> Now let's see how they're played."

Hansum felt his shoulder being shaken. When he opened his eyes and saw the butler's face over him, he sat up quickly.

"Is the black powder dry?" he asked.

"Apparently, Signor. And the Baron is back. He's on the terrace."

Hansum splashed some water on his face, used an ivory comb to smooth his hair, straightened his clothes and went outside. He saw the Baron, who turned and smiled. Nicademo made the grand gesture of spreading his arm out over the expanse of black powder lying on the terrace. He looked very pleased. Then Hansum saw Grazzana and someone short standing next to him. Lincoln!

"What are you doing here?" Hansum asked curtly.

"They said you couldn't live without me," Lincoln joked.

"Such a very funny fellow," the Baron laughed. "He kept me laughing the whole journey, with jokes and riddles and funny stories. One after the other."

"But why are you here? What about the Master and others?"

"Not to worry, Romero," Nicademo said. "I've never seen a house that is so worried about each other. I've worked it out with della Cappa. We'll get him a new journeyman soon. Everything is fine. Fine. And since this little man knows so much of your new inventions," he said, holding up the carrying tube for the plans, "we thought you could use a trusted assistant."

"Ah, well, I'm pleased then. Oh, forgive my manners, Excellency. So nice to see you." They bowed to each other.

"I see you've done very well, Romero," Nicademo said, referring to the black powder. "Everything went without incident?"

"I can't say that," Hansum replied. "We've had a bit of an episode. I'm taking care of it now. Come, I want to do this before the day is out." Hansum scooped up a handful of the now-granular black powder. "It seems dry enough." Lincoln kneeled right by him, so his hat was next to Hansum's ear.

*"Greetings Master Hansum,"* Pan's voice whispered in Hansum's ear. *"Hold up the powder so I may analyse it. Excellent. Excellent. Its moisture content is just over one percent higher than optimum, but otherwise, very good."*

"Signoras, you have done a wonderful job," Hansum said to his workers. "This is what I need you to do now." Hansum had them fill one of the barrels half full of sand. The rest was to be filled tightly with the black powder. "And make sure you use this measuring cup to fill the barrel. Level off each cup before pouring it in. I need to know exactly how many scoops of black powder are in the barrel." After the women filled the barrel with sand and measured in the black powder, Hansum secured the barrel's lid himself. The other barrel was half filled with the remaining explosive. The footman and driver put the barrels in the wagon and Hansum said, "Before we do our test, there's a little preparation first. Excellency, may I ask you to have the General and his men come down to the barn in an hour? We shall make the first test of the black powder then."

"Ah, wonderful," the Baron said. "I wouldn't want to miss it."

"Oh, I don't think anyone in this valley will do that," Hansum answered.

Hansum asked Grazzana to sit in the back of the wagon with the casks of powder and told the soldier to drive slowly. The soldier said he had experience with the explosive powder, so not to worry. Hansum thought, 'This stuff isn't what you're used to. This powder had six to seven times more saltpeter in it than any powder used before.' He walked behind with Lincoln to the barn, so they could talk privately. Lincoln caught Hansum up on what was happening at home.

"How's Guil?"

"Oh, fine," Lincoln said. "I mean, she's a little off, but Shamira says it's just women stuff."

"What do you mean?"

"I don't know. Women stuff. So, what's been going on here that's got your braies in a knot?" Hansum explained what was going on with his men and how he intended to remedy it.

*"Oh dear,"* Pan said, *"I'm not sure that I like this idea of yours."*

"I don't like it either," Hansum said. "But it's what needs doing."

When they got to the barn, all the men were working silently at their tasks. They barely looked up when Hansum entered with someone new.

"Have the two who give us the most problems come with me," Hansum said to Jacopo. "Have them bring a pick and shovel." The two biggest jokers followed after Hansum. When Lincoln tried to say hello to them, Hansum made a stern face. They proceeded in silence. Hansum told Grazzana to carefully hand the full cask of powder and sand to one of the men, telling the other worker to carry the tools. Hansum ordered two soldiers with poleaxes to go with them. One soldier was given the old donkey, Gina, to lead, the other told to follow fifty paces behind with a burning coal in a ceramic dish. Hansum carried a length of the black powder fuse two and a half arm lengths long, loosely looped over his shoulder. As he led everybody out into a large, open meadow, Lincoln looked over at him.

"You're getting to be quite the boss man," the younger teen commented.

Hansum didn't answer, but continued counting as he walked. At five hundred paces, he stopped.

"Put down the cask over there. Carefully, you fool, don't bang it. Now, both of you," he said to the two peasants, "dig. Dig a hole this high to put the cask in." He held his hand up to his just below his breastbone. The men did as they were told. While they were digging, Hansum and one of the soldiers used a poleaxe to carefully create a hole in the top of the barrel. When the hole was finished, he had the soldier put his poleaxe into it and carve a notch on it to mark the depth. Hansum had them carefully put the cask in the hole, not letting any dirt fall in with the powder. Then he stretched out the fuse and buried it deep into the cask's coarse granules. He had the men find over three dozen heavy round stones. Hansum carefully set them into the hole over the power barrel, making sure he didn't crimp or cover the fuse. When it was finished, a mound of boulders jutted above the ground.

"What are we doing this for, Signor?" one of the sweating peasants asked. Hansum ignored him.

"Put Gina over the pile and tether her to the rocks." There was no real need to tether the dying donkey, as she was lucky to be standing at this point. "Which one of you is the faster runner?" Hansum asked the soldiers. A long, lanky fellow with a scar emanating from his mouth nodded. Hansum then went over to the old nag, patted her on the muzzle and looked at the peasant who was wearing a tattered straw sunhat. He reached out and took the thing and replaced it on the bowed head of the donkey, using Gina's mane to secure it. He looked back at the worker. "Let's pretend this ass is you," Hansum said. Hansum walked toward the barn. "Come," was all he ordered. All but the scar-faced soldier followed.

By the time they got back to the barn, not only were the Baron, general and all the soldiers there, but the Podesta had arrived too. It was now a bright spring afternoon and the Podesta was even wearing his beautiful tortoiseshell discs for the eyes. Hansum told the workers to stand by the big oak. Then he went and greeted the Podesta and general, both of whom had inspected the quality of the half cask of powder. Both said how impressed they were.

"In the summer, when we have the incorporating mill, the quality will be much higher," Hansum said seriously. "More powerful. But this hand-ground stuff is good enough for testing the first cannon."

General Chavelerio was using his looker to peer out into the field. "Why do you have that old nag standing there?"

"Some of the men weren't taking the danger of the powder seriously enough. I am arranging to correct their thinking."

"Ah," the Podesta said. Then he put his hand on Hansum's cheek and looked deeply into his eyes. "Not so trusting now, eh? That's good, my son. That's very good."

"Si, Excellency." Then he took a step away and shouted, "Jacopo, bring out the rest of the men from the barn. Now!" When all the men were assembled, Hansum said, "Look over there. I want you to watch."

"Is that old Gina?" one of the workers asked.

"What's on her head?"

"It's Carlo's hat."

"The Signor said to pretend Gina's me," Carlo announced smugly.

Hansum borrowed one of the poleaxes and waved it with long sweeps three times. The soldier down in the field repeated the gesture with his poleaxe. Hansum confirmed the signal by repeating it a third time. Then the soldier could be seen kneeling down. After a few seconds, he got up and ran back up to the barn as fast as he could.

"Start counting out loud," Hansum said to Lincoln. Lincoln counted.

The officers and nobles took out their lookers, training them on Gina.

"Hey, that guy can really run," one of the workers joked.

"He looks like the flames of Hell are going to blow up his ass!" another laughed.

"Shut up and watch!" Hansum yelled.

When Lincoln got to sixty, people started to fidget. At the count of ninety, the soldier got back to them, out of breath and sweating hard. He leaned over on his poleaxe.

"What's supposed to happen?" a worker asked.

"I said shut your mouths and watch. Closely!"

"One hundred and twenty five, one hundred and twenty six," continued Lincoln.

"Watch for it," Hansum said loudly.

"On hundred and . . ."

A dark gray cloud of smoke appeared from the spot they were watching. The cloud obliterated Gina from sight. A split second later, a thunder clap so loud and overwhelming it deafened the entire group momentarily. A horrific secondary column of black smoke ejaculated up from the center of the first cloud. A huge apron of dirt blasted out all around ground zero. The whole thing took less than the time it took to count one. Many of the workers screamed involuntarily as the deep growl of a ground tremor reached the barn. The earth vibrated under everyone's feet, causing several workers to collapse in fear. And then the airborne shockwave hit them.

"Aaaeeeee!" one man screamed as he urinated in his pants.

"Look up," Hansum shouted.

A fountain of large round boulders and dirt flew high into the air. It continued on its trajectory for several moments till it reached its apogee and spread out.

"Mother of God," Carlo shouted, "those stones were heavy!"

Larger pieces of other things were seen tumbling through the crisp, blue air.

"Is that Gina?" another said.

"Bravo!" shouted many of the soldiers. "Bravo, bravo."

A succession of echoes from the explosion rumbled along the valley. Bits of stone and dirt began to fall on the crowd. Soldiers, who had been following the path of several of the larger missiles, rose an alarm.

"Signori, we best take cover," an officer shouted.

"Take cover."

"Take coooooover," went up the shouts of the battle-tested soldiers.

Men frantically ran under trees, under wagons, into the barn. The Baron and Podesta scrambled under the royal carriage with several soldiers.

Only the general stood his ground, hands on hips, laughing at the top of his voice. The last thing to hit the ground landed within ten feet of him. It was Gina's head. "Ha!" he guffawed, nodding with great pleasure.

Particles of dirt continued to sprinkle down from the sky for several long moments. Silence enveloped the area, a silence as loud as the noise of a few moments earlier. Slowly men crept out from their hiding places. People looked with astonishment at each other. Hansum was among the surprised. He hadn't expected the explosion to be this big. Catching Mastino's eye, he grimaced and was about to mouth an apology when the Podesta smiled.

Then his smile widened. Then he laughed. This caused many of the other men to join in the laughter. A soldier shouted.

"Look! In the tree!" He pointed to the large oak. "A strange fruit." Everybody looked, and there, caught up in the branches, were Gina's hindquarters, her tail blowing in the breeze. Everybody broke into a riot of hilarity. One of the officers applauded and shouted, "Bravo! Bravo, Signor Monticelli," and the others joined in like they had just witnessed a wonderful musical concert. "Bravo, bravo!"

The Podesta stood up on the running board of his carriage.

"Bravo, bravo, MASTER Monticelli." And everyone gave another rousing cheer for Hansum's promotion. "Come, Master," continued the Podesta loudly. "Let us go to the house and celebrate this great accomplishment."

"Grazie, Excellency," Hansum replied. "But with your permission, there's still work to be done. I must address my men. And also," he said, turning his attention to one of the young officers who, at the meeting last night, seemed the best with numbers, "we must measure the blast hole and record the results. We must build up records to be able to predict the explosions." The Podesta nodded. "Jacopo," Hansum called. "All the men. Here." Jacopo hurried the men into a group. A few wouldn't get off their knees. "It's okay, Jacopo. Leave them. Men," Hansum began, "so, do you fear it now? Do you understand why I said care must be taken, why there can be no foolishness?"

All the field workers now looked serious. A few were trembling. The one who had relieved himself stood stunned, a large dark circle at his crotch. The Podesta, the general, the Baron and all the soldiers listened in silence as Hansum spoke.

"It's good to be fearful," Hansum continued. "For the donkey could have been you," he said, pointing to Carlos. He paused, and then smiled. This oration was completely Hansum. He was feeling a confidence that only comes from accomplishment. "But more than fear, learn to have respect. Respect the power of what we are creating. Learn the rules we tell you and you will remain safe. And when word comes back of battles won by our gallant soldiers here, you will be happy. Then you can stand tall and be proud in your homes and villages, for it will be you who helped manufacture the means for our soldiers' victories. For then it will be them who will be feared by our enemies."

The crowd stood in silence. Then the Podesta applauded and others followed. Finally, Hansum motioned, with a simple flick of his wrist, for Jacopo to get the men back to work. As things calmed, Hansum called over an officer and told him to take a measuring stick and go to the blast crater. "We must gather all the information we can and learn from it." He looked up and saw the Podesta, Baron and general listening to him. Then he took Lincoln's arm and whispered to him. "You go too, so Pan can see the results firsthand."

Hansum stood with the nobles and general, alone with the elite of the region. They all looked at him with respect. Hansum actually felt, for the first time, that he deserved to be among them. Although Pan had been his teacher, he had taken care of this crisis on his own.

"Excellency! Excellency!" came a shout. They all looked toward the manor house. Coming quickly over a small rise was a carriage and horses. A chubby man was hanging out the carriage window, frantically waving his hands. It was Master Calabreezi. The usually stoic, grumpy man was as animated as a kitten.

"I tell you, Romero," the Podesta said confidentially, "over the past twenty years, Calabreezi has been an ill-natured pain in my ass. The only reason I kept him around is his genius. But since you've come along, he's like a puppy."

"Well," the general said, "it's said when you have an old dog, it's good to bring in a new pup before the old one dies. It gives the old dog life and teaches the new dog good manners."

"I think Romero's manners are fine," the Podesta joked.

"Si, but I can learn much from Master Calabreezi," Hansum said.

The Podesta put his hand on Hansum's shoulder and smiled. Calabreezi's wagon came screeching to a halt in the barnyard. They could now see, not too far behind him, a column of officers on horseback. Following them were two more horses pulling what looked to be a covered cart with stout wheels. Behind that was a wagonload of infantrymen. The door to the carriage flew open and Master Calabreezi was so anxious he half jumped, half fell to the ground. He sank to his knees and staggered to get up. Hansum and the nobles reached out to steady the old man, but he was so comical, they all laughed.

"Did I miss it? I missed it, didn't I? We could hear it from the road. And we saw the smoke and all the things rising in the sky. Oh, I wish I had been here."

"Si, it was quite a show," Mastino said, "but you are here now and we have plenty more powder to test the cannon."

"Excellent. Excellent. Tell me, my boy, how large a charge was that and what were the particulars of the setup?"

"Si, *Master* Monticelli," the Podesta corrected, "what were the particulars?"

"Ah, Master is it now? Of course, of course. Well done and congratulations, *Master* Monticelli," Calabreezi said. "But details, Signor! I must know details!"

As Hansum explained the setup of their black powder test, Calabreezi listened intently, like he was hearing the most important information in the world. "I've assigned an officer," Hansum went on, "who is measuring the crater and detailing the distances of the projectiles for analysis later."

"Well thought out, young, I mean, Master Monticelli. And fascinating. Fascinating."

"And he blew up an ass, a donkey," General Chavelerio added, laughing and pointing to Gina's poor head. Flies were already buzzing around it.

"Blew up an ass? What in Heaven for?" The Baron explained about the workers' foolery and the old master puffed up into his stoic old-poop act. "Now you know why I brook no nonsense from my men. No nonsense." The column of soldiers with the cannon arrived. "Well, here she is, Signori," Calabreezi said, childlike again. "Come and see. Come and see." The cannon was covered with a large tarpaulin. The only things visible were two large wheels and a heavy wooden axel. General Chavelerio walked over, just as an officer was pulling off the tarp, revealing the large, heavy object. He tapped it with his knuckles and then the pommel of his sword.

"Sounds solid enough," he said. "Quite a few bells in there, eh?"

"When can we try her?" Calabreezi asked. "Today? Right away?" When he asked, he looked at Hansum. Hansum had been well drilled by Pan on how the cannon's first tests should run. After all, they had just witnessed how dangerous the substance they were working with was. With only about four hours of daylight left, much still had to be done before safely firing the cannon. Hansum thought about it in silence. Everybody watched him thinking, familiar with his quiet pauses of concentration.

'The eight men working the cannon should practice their routine of setting up, loading, cleaning, reloading, aiming, and generally learning how to work as a team,' Hansum thought. 'Then they fire the cannon with only one pound of powder in it and with no cannonball. Then two pounds empty and then three. Lastly, fire the cannon three more times, with the same quantities of powder, but with a ball.' Hansum looked at the expectant faces of the others, thinking the prudent thing would be to leave it till tomorrow. But all the faces were so eager, and he wanted to keep the momentum rolling on his plan.

"General, can you have all your men assemble on the practice range after they finish taking the data by the crater? Say, in an hour? But the men who are going to be the first crew, have them join the cannon on the firing range now. Right away. They must practice their procedures without powder. If they accomplish their drills well enough, we can fire Gina today."

"Gina?" the general enquired.

"Well, we should name the cannon, shouldn't we? Let's name her Gina, in memory of the donkey."

## Chapter 29

Within an hour, the soldiers had the bronze Gina secured with heavy ropes to wooden stakes in the ground. There was slack in the ropes to take up the gun's recoil when fired. The men had done many dry runs loading, firing, cleaning and reloading. The captain, now familiar with procedures from seriously studying the pamphlet, worked his men hard. Several times he looked to Hansum to get his agreement on this point or that. Hansum nodded, but stood at a distance, respecting the chain of command.

The only thing not in the pamphlet was how they would ignite the powder. For safety reasons, they would use the black powder fuse, just in case the cannon exploded. Master Calabreezi insisted it wouldn't, but agreed it was a good precaution.

Hansum deemed the drills a success just as the rest of the soldiers and Lincoln arrived from gathering the statistics from the first blast.

"You may proceed with the first live test, Captain," Hansum said. The captain beamed. "Have the extra men spread out down the field every two hundred paces. Well off to the side of the range, of course." While this was being done, Lincoln came out to Hansum and extended his hand.

"We haven't had time for a proper greeting," he said and winked. A moment later, Hansum had Pan placed back in the hatband's secret pocket.

"We may now proceed, Signori," Hansum said. "Captain, have your men go through the drill again, this time with powder. Do the first ones very slowly. In the next week, we shall concentrate on speed. For now, it's the accuracy of the load and familiarity with procedure that's important. We must also be able to use the data to make an expanded training manual for other crews and officers."

Hansum saw Nicademo, the consummate bureaucrat, nod appreciatively and then whisper into the Podesta's ear. Mastino smiled broadly.

The first properly constituted cannon crew went through its paces. They measured off exactly one pound of black powder from the barrel and poured it into the scoop, which was attached to an eight-foot rod. They put the scoop in the cannon's mouth, pushed it to the breech and poured it out. Then they put rags around another wooden instrument, the rammer, and pushed home the powder to the end of the chamber. The cloth acted as a plug for the pressure of the expanding gases to push against. No ball was put into the cannon for these first shots. They put in a half arm-span of fuse, using a thin rod to push it into the black powder. Hansum inspected it carefully. Then everybody but one man went behind the rock outcropping. The soldier lit the fuse with a coal and ran to join the others.

"Okay Gina, sing us a pretty song," Master Calabreezi said.

BOOM! A wonderful explosion ensued, much smaller than the one set under Gina, the donkey, but a very satisfying one, nonetheless. The men came running around to see the results and were delighted that Gina, the cannon, was intact.

"Well done, Gina. Well done, Master Monticelli," Calabreezi said, grabbing Hansum's hand.

"Well done, Master Calabreezi," Hansum said, motioning to the cannon.

The second and third shots, done with progressively more powder, went well too. As they got louder, the men shouted, but the general quickly barked for order in the ranks. The first three shots with the cannonballs were just as Pan had predicted. The sound, with the cannonball in the breech, was much deeper and the recoil of the cannon more violent. The hot, expanding gas of the exploding powder caused the cannonball and cannon to be opposing forces. The cannon lurched backward and strained at the ropes. On the first shot, you could actually see the ball as it travelled its course. It went some three hundred paces. The two-pound charge sent the ball almost seven hundred paces, and you couldn't see the ball till it was over half way. The full three-pound charge sent the ball over one thousand paces. The men and the nobles were barely able to keep their demeanor when the ball smashed into the ground and sent up a large spray of dirt and rocks, still visible at the great distance. They used the remaining powder to perform three more tests. Two of those Hansum said he wanted to be exactly the same as the third shot, to check for consistency. They both landed within fifteen paces of the first shot. For the third and final shot, Hansum pointed at a tree that was about a foot in diameter and about one hundred and paces away.

"Your first target, Captain," he said. The captain pointed the target out to his subordinate and the lieutenant went to work directing his men to turn the wheels. The lieutenant sighted the gun, having all the men turning the wheels a little this way, then that, to fine-tune the aiming. Then the junior officer nodded to the captain, who had taken a place next to Hansum. Hansum whispered something in his ear. The captain looked surprised, then smiled.

"Stay by the cannon, men. Take your positions, as practiced!" The men stood at attention on either side of the cannon. Hansum motioned for the other observers to retire behind the rock for safety. The Podesta shook his head gently and smiled, putting his hands behind his back to watch out in the open. The others did the same. Lincoln was the only one wise enough to cover his ears. Hansum nodded to the captain, who pointed to the lieutenant. The man then lit a very short fuse.

# BOOK THREE

## The Stubborn Muse, Fortuna

# Chapter 1

Supper that night was a grand affair, and Pan worried about his boys. They were being allowed to make just a little too much merry with the wine and rowdiness. Hansum was at one end of the table, now at the Podesta's right hand, laughing and exchanging words with him like they were old friends. Calabreezi was on the Podesta's left, and even he had a somewhat contented look on his face, his cheeks red with a wine glow he confessed he hadn't allowed himself to enjoy in years. The middle of the table was flanked by officers, and at the other end, by the Baron, sat Lincoln, a large pastry in one hand and a goblet of wine in the other. He had tried to pour himself a full goblet of wine, but Nicademo, ever a dutiful father figure, made him fill his goblet half with water. Still, Lincoln became quite tipsy, and sat there, laughing along with Nicademo and all the other officers, pastry stuck to his lips. The captain's voice rose above the others.

"Master Monticelli tells me that tomorrow we shall have twice the powder to work with. We were supposed to have more today, but we used it to blow up the ass and put the peasants in their place." At that, he and the whole table roared with laughter.

"I still see that animal's head smiling up at you, my General," a lieutenant said. More gales of laughter.

"Here's to changing donkey heads into the heads of the Este!" General Chavelerio toasted.

"Hoorah!" shouted the table.

"Here's to the retaking of the Podesta's cities!" an officer called.

"Hoorah!"

"Here's to making our Podesta king!"

"Hoorah!"

"Emperor!" another cried, which brought on an even bigger cheer. The Podesta looked modest, but smiled.

"When can we use the cannon against an enemy?" a young officer asked enthusiastically.

"Patience," the general said. "It will be a year. Not this summer, but the next spring. How many cannon can you provide for us by then, Master Calabreezi?"

"The problem is the metals," Calabreezi said, becoming serious again. "We could provide a hundred\cannon by then, if we have the metals."

"Leave that to me, Signori," Mastino said. "To provide the raw materials is my work. However, let us not talk business tonight. All have worked hard. Ah, our meal is here. Talk among yourselves while we dine. Enjoy."

It was a wonderful banquet with everyone laughing and drinking. Nicademo told how Lincoln had been such a good storyteller on their way from Verona and bade him recount some of his jokes. He recalled one, and the officers burst into laughter. Pan watched nervously, seeing that Lincoln was becoming bleary-eyed. When Nicademo asked for another joke, Lincoln's body language told Pan he couldn't remember anymore. So Lincoln made a funny face and the inebriated officers all guffawed.

"Come, come, Maruccio," Nicademo urged, "tell the one about the monk and nun."

"Oh, that one. I'm sure everybody's heard that one," Lincoln said, feigning modesty. When everyone shouted for another joke, Lincoln got up and sauntered jauntily down to the other end of the table, pulling the hat with Pan in it off of Hansum's head. "There. Now you look better," Lincoln said to Hansum, and put the hat on his own head. Everyone laughed.

*"Young Master,"* Pan whispered to Lincoln, *"take care. You should remain sober and clear-headed. These are dangerous . . ."*

"Okay, then. The story of the monk and the nun," Lincoln said, seemingly to the crowd, but in actuality, telling Pan what was expected. Pan sighed, but then the old prankster couldn't resist complying.

*"Very well. A monk came upon a nun washing her habit in a stream. They were alone in a secluded glade . . ."*

Mastino was studying Hansum's profile as he watched the younger boy tell a joke. But the Podesta wasn't listening to the bawdy tale, he was looking at the smooth skin on Hansum's face. He marvelled how it looked so unblemished. There were no pockmarks, no blackheads, no scars from disease or mishap. He reached forward and touched the boy's arm. Hansum turned. Mastino smiled and bid him move closer. Hansum's eyes were shining from the wine and the day's excitement. Hansum leaned forward and ran his fingers through his hair. Thick tousles of hair fell around his face.

"All of this," the Podesta said, "is because of you."

"Oh no, Excellency," began Hansum, but the Podesta stopped him.

"And now there will be more, so much more." Mastino said this as he picked up the tube of drawings from beside him.

"You saw the new plans? What did you think?" Hansum asked.

"I was intrigued," Mastino said. "How long do you think all this will take?"

"Excellency," Hansum said, sweeping his arm around the room. "There's so much to do with what we have. It could be several years before we get to these new things."

"Well, I look forward to a long and wonderful life with you." Then Mastino leaned forward. He was very close to the younger man's face. "But tell me truly, Romero, why did you send me these plans now, if it will take such a long time?"

Hansum sat up straight, took a breath, and then leaned even closer to the Podesta.

"To show you, Excellency . . ." Hansum paused, the breath in him seemingly becoming lodged in his chest.

"It's okay, Romero," soothed Mastino, putting his hand on Hansum's arm. "Take your time, my son. You can tell me anything."

"To prove to you, Excellency, to prove to you that I have much to offer, and that you have nothing to fear in me being fickle toward you. To show you I have a life's work that would bind me to you, and . . ."

"And?"

"Excellency, some men are motivated by gold, some by power, some by putting together organizations and running them. I am not one of these men. Two things are important to me and two things only."

"And what are those?"

"One is inventing things. Imagining things in my mind and making them real." Hansum reached across the table and touched the cardboard tube. Mastino nodded and smiled. "The other..." continued Hansum, then he paused. Mastino furrowed his brow enquiringly. "The other is Guilietta."

There was a pause. Mastino sat back in his seat.

"Romero," he said, smiling. "are you negotiating with me?"

"Your Excellency," Hansum started, looking a mixture of serious and sad puppy dog, "she is my heart. I am your man and will remain your man. I will give you the things in those plans, and much more. I do not wish to be a prince or a king. Make me comfortable, allow me my interesting projects and give me the woman of my heart. With these, I will be content."

Mastino looked at Hansum, drummed his fingers, pondered, and then smiled.

"Romero. . . Master Monticelli," he corrected, "the other week you asked for time to get the first projects established before decisions were made on these other matters. I agreed. Let me suggest that we keep this understanding till, the Summer Solstice, say." Hansum looked at the Podesta seriously. "However," the nobleman added, "let me add that, as I get to know you better, I trust and love you more. And because of this, I truly have no objection to what you have proposed."

It took a second for what the Podesta had said to register.

"But, but what of your daughter? What of Beatrice?"

"Oh, there are many others for her. I had in mind a nice boy before I met you. Good family from Milan. But Romero, let us wait till we see what the solstice brings."

A smile came onto Hansum's face that Mastino could scarcely believe. A smile so bright, topped by such sparkling eyes, that the Podesta thought the naive boy was back.

"Grazie, Excellency. Grazie, Excellency." Hansum grabbed Mastino's hand and kissed it, keeping his head lowered in deference for many moments. "Grazie, Excellency," he said again, his voice so full of emotion it carried throughout the room. The room became quiet and Mastino looked up to see all the eyes from the table staring at them.

⧗

With Lincoln turning his gaze back to the head of the table, Pan was able to get Hansum and Mastino back into his view. He saw Mastino, with somewhat of an embarrassed look on his face, put his free hand on Hansum's bowed head and pat it.

"It's all right, Romero," the Podesta said. "It's all right. Get up. Get up, my boy."

"You will not regret it, Excellency," Hansum said, drunken tears of joy in his eyes. "Just you wait and see what the solstice brings."

Pan scowled in his lamp, wrinkles of worry adding themselves to his already severe face.

*"Oh, what did that boy say now? I hope it wasn't about Mistress Guilietta."*

## Chapter 2

"Mama, I feel faint. I can't get up. My stomach . . ." The Signora watched as a flash of pain streaked across Guilietta's face. As her daughter convulsed, motherly empathy caused the Signora to wince.

"Oh, my poor lamb," the Signora cried in a piteous tone, tears squirting from her pudgy eyes. She was on her knees by her daughter's bed, the sleeve of Guilietta's sweat-drenched nightshirt clenched in her hands.

"More med'cine," Nuca urged from the other side of the bed. "Make strong, better." She was in the della Cappa house much of the time now, helping the Signora with Guilietta. Shamira had to keep working in the shop, setting lenses along with the Master, Bembo and the little apprentices. As the girl's spasms seemed to ebb, Nuca helped the Signora sit Guilietta up and put the mug of "medicine" to her lips.

"It's so bitter," Guilietta said, coughing as she took a few sips. "I don't want anymore."

"Dev'ena said was bitter," Nuca reminded her. "But will help," The Signora watched as Nuca, crying herself, pressed the cup to her daughter's lips. "P'ease, Gui, for Omero."

Guilietta no sooner got the noxious concoction down, when she threw it all up. But with it came a thick, putrid, green bile. Nuca and the Signora screamed at this new occurrence.

"Get my husband," the Signora shouted. "Get help! Now!" Nuca ran out of the room. "Angel Michael," the panicked Signora cried, "please help my baby!" The stern and worried vision of the angel appeared to her on the ceiling. She hadn't seen him for some time. "Watch over her, sainted angel. Don't let her die, holy angel." Guilietta lay in the fouled bed, now oblivious to her mother's pleas and fantasies.

What seemed like the whole workshop ran into the tiny room. Even the little boys crowded the doorway to the bedroom, peeking between Ugilino and Bembo, the older journeyman holding them back. The Master and Shamira came to the bed.

"Cristo, she's a goner!" Ugilino uttered.

"Shut your mouth!" Bembo ordered, elbowing him hard.

"What shall we do, husband? What shall we do?" the Signora cried.

"We must remove her from this foulness," the distraught father said. "And call a physician. We must find a Jewish physician. They are the best. We can afford one now. Bembo, help me take her to my bed. Then we'll clean up."

Bembo picked up the limp Guilietta and some bile got on his clothes. Shamira went to wipe it from him.

"It is no matter," he said, manoeuvring himself and his burden out of the small room.

The Signora looked up at the ceiling abruptly.

"Water. The Angel Michael says to give her only water to drink. Lots of water."

"Shut up, woman," the Master started, but Shamira intervened.

"No, Master, that's a very good thing to do," and she ran downstairs to get the jug of boiled drinking water. She quickly returned, not only with the water, but with her satchel of paper. While Nuca and the Signora made Guilietta drink several cups, Shamira said to the Master, "We must get word to Romero. I will write him a letter. How can we get it to him?"

"Yes, the orphan boy will know what to do," the Signora said.

"Quiet, woman. Take the letter to the palace," the Master ordered. "Someone must be going to where they're working. But what can he do?"

"He'll want to know. I'll write a note and have Ugilino take it to the palace," she said, sitting on the edge of the bed, using the satchel as a writing surface.

"Dev'ena close by palace," Nuca said, helping Guilietta sip the water.

Shamira finished the note and turned to Ugilino. "Take this to the palace," she ordered him. "Make sure they know it's a matter of life and death and Romero must get it right away. Today, if possible. Tell them we will pay for a rider to take it. Master, give him a soldi."

"Hey, you can't tell us what to do," Ugilino protested.

"Shut up," the Master cried, taking a soldi out of his pouch. "Take this with the note and don't stop running till you've seen the herbalist and been to the palace."

Devlena was sitting in the small back room of her hovel, south of Signori Square. She had just put a mouse into a box, which was already occupied by a scorpion. She watched as the scorpion stabbed the mouse repeatedly with its barbed tail. The small creature writhed and squealed, then collapsed into silence. Next, she would dry the mouse till it was mummified, then grind it into a powder. This deadly poison was commissioned by a German prince for his older brother.

'Oh, how I wish all contracts could be as easy as that simple girl,' Devlena thought as she watched the convulsing mouse. Her memory slid back three days, when she watched Guilietta wave goodbye to that good-looking boy and then run right up to her, happily accepting the package from the mute tailor woman. The girl actually smiled and thanked Devlena for the herbs, and even kissed her on the cheek. Devlena sighed at the pleasant memory. They had gone back to the Satores' and Devlena had helped brew the first batch of deadly tea, and brought honey to mask the poison's harshness. She watched, relaxed and smiling, as Guilietta had downed the first draught.

Three days had passed since that first drink. Devlena was idly wondering how Guilietta was doing when she heard a frantic pounding at her front door. She put the top back on her scorpion's box.

"I'll be back in awhile, my darling," she said, then walked into her main room, which wasn't much bigger or less messy than the back one. She peered through a crack in the door and saw Ugilino, out of breath, his cracked teeth gritted. She didn't have her wimple or veil on. It usually covered her frightful tangle of white hair. "I'll be a minute," she called.

"Hurry!" he called back.

"All right, all right," she said. Thinking to herself that it was only a boy who was as horrible looking as herself, she unlocked the door and half smiled. "How is the young lady of the house?" She could see Ugilino's face staring at her unkempt countenance.

"She's not good. I think she's a goner but they sent me to get you. You gotta come quick."

"Well, if you will wait for me out here, I'll finish dressing and put something special together for the poor dear. Then I'll be right along with you," she smiled.

"No, I gotta go to the palace and take this letter the kitchen girl wrote. It's supposed to go to Romero, who's workin' with the Podesta."

"Oh, really? A note the kitchen girl wrote? Saying what is going on?"

"Yeah. Romero's a savant. Carmella and my mistress say he'll know what to do. They even gave me a soldi to pay to get it there quick."

"A whole soldi. Say, I know the captain of the guard at the palace. I could take the letter to him. He'll send a rider."

At the mention of Captain Caesar, Ugilino made a face.

"He don't like me."

"No? I tell you what, then. I'll go to the palace myself. You run back home and say I'm on my way. Run, mind you. Don't stop." And she put out her hand for the letter, which he handed her. She kept her hand out. "And the soldi," she said, smiling. "Now go. Go, go, go."

After she watched Ugilino run off, the first thing Devlena did was give the soldi a new home in her own purse. Then she opened the letter. It was just so many squiggles on paper to her. She ripped it in half and threw it in the fire. Then she hummed as she finished getting dressed. It was important for the world to see her as righteous.

Devlena was her angelic self again when the door of the della Cappa house opened. Shamira stood looking at her. Devlena smiled, but got a curious, penetrating look back. The poisoner could see there was something different about this one.

"You're the one who wrote the note?" Devlena asked.

"Si."

Devlena didn't like the look of the kitchen girl. Walking into the house, she found herself being stared at by the Master's, Bembo's and Nuca's fearful eyes. She smiled at them briefly.

"I must get to my patient," she said with some authority. "Everyone stay down here. I must examine her thoroughly and it's best that there's quiet. I can find my way." She stopped on the steps and turned. "I think it would be best if you all prayed." At this, everyone but Shamira got down on their knees and started doing their catechisms. Agistino turned to Shamira and motioned for her to pray too. As Devlena disappeared upstairs, she heard the girl speak.

"It will help more to boil water and wash sheets."

Signora della Cappa looked up as the curtain to Guilietta's room was pulled back and a woman in a blue nun's habit walked in. The woman seemed just as surprised to see her there. The nun smiled a disarming smile and spoke.

"I'm here to help your dear daughter." The Signora looked questioningly at the woman in blue. "Has she been awake at all?" The Signora stared at the woman in blue, shook her head once, and then looked up at the ceiling. The vision of Archangel Michael was staring at Devlena very suspiciously. The Signora snapped her head back at the woman.

"You're not a nun," the Signora said suddenly. Devlena had just opened one of Guilietta's eyes to check her pupil. While she was close to her face, she smelled her breath.

"What's that, dear? Oh no. I'm not," she answered, flashing her smile again. "Though I spent many years with them in cloister when I was a small orphaned child. I smell bile on her breath. When did she throw up last?" The Signora continued staring wide-eyed, not answering. She watched the woman feel Guilietta's arms, legs and stomach, like she was checking a temperature. "Oh, I see some of her medicine is brewed and waiting for her," the stranger said. "I think she needs it." The Signora looked up at the ceiling and the Archangel Michael's brows were knit with worry. Devlena sat on the side of the bed, lifted Guilietta's head into her lap and put the cup to her mouth. Guilietta barely woke up and took several minutes to drink it. All the while, Devlena sat there saying, "There, there," and hummed a lullaby. When the Signora looked up at the ceiling, the stoic angel had tears running down his cheeks. "That should do it," the woman in blue said, gently laying Guilietta's head back on the pillow. "A few more days of this and all will be just as ordered." And then she stood up and called downstairs. "Nuca, dear, come here, please." Nuca and Shamira came upstairs quickly.

"Gui get better?" Nuca asked.

"Si, si indeed," Devlena answered. "I believe she has just caught a malady of the stomach. Make sure she takes her medicine, though. I will leave this in your charge. Do not fail me or the child."

"Oh, no fail, Dev'ena. No fail," Nuca assured her.

"She's not a nun. She's not a nun," the Signora repeated.

"No, I explained that. You have enough herbs still? I brought you more. No charge."

"We still have some," Shamira said brusquely.

"Well, take this too," Devlena said, putting the package in Nuca's hands. "Brew up her evening draught now. Mix plenty of honey in it, and maybe some wine. Let it cool, since it's hard for her to drink hot liquids if she's sleepy. Tonight, give her double the amount."

On the way home, Devlena didn't smile. She thought of Guilietta's mad mother and the look in that kitchen girl's eye.

"Those two better not foul up this contract." She ground her teeth so hard she splintered the side of a rotting molar. She spit out the bloody bit of tooth and trudged home to her scorpion.

The Signora and her vision of the Archangel Michael sat by Guilietta all that day. The doting mother wouldn't even come downstairs for supper. Nuca brought the Signora her food and also the large ceramic chalice of the herbal mixture, honey and wine, which Guilietta was supposed to have when the sun went down. The Signora picked at her food, and then looked at Michael. He looked down at her. The Signora stared at Guilietta's medicine for the longest time, then at her daughter, then up at the angel, who was now looking at her very gravely. She looked at the draught of herbs again and noticed out the side of her eye that Michael had cocked his head enquiringly. The Signora picked up the draught and the angel raised his eyebrows. Trembling, the Signora shut her eyes tight and gulped down the foul beverage, wincing and coughing several times. When she completed the task, she looked up at Michael. The angel was smiling. He blessed her and radiated even more of his beautiful golden light than usual.

Nuca, Shamira and the Master came into the room a while later.

"It's time for Guilietta to have her medicine, Mistress," Shamira said.

The Signora looked up at her angel, who shook his head.

"She's already had it," the mother said, a quiver in her voice. "She woke and I helped her. She liked it."

"Oh, that's good," Shamira said. "Perhaps it *is* helping. We'll make more with the wine and honey again. It will be cool and sweet for her in the morning."

"But she's sleeping now?" Agistino asked gently. "He knelt by the bed and put one of her cold hands in his. "My only child," he whispered. "My heart."

The mother slept in the bigger bed with her daughter that night. Agistino stayed in Guilietta's room. In the morning, the Signora drank Guilietta's medicine before the others rose, saying again that she had administered it only a short time earlier. She performed this trick for the next several days. Archangel Michael told her to keep giving Guilietta a cup of water every time she awoke. The vision of the angel seemed very impressed with the Signora, and she watched him write her name in a large book.

# Chapter 3

Pan laughed out loud as he jumped out of his home in Hansum's hat and onto the boy's big feather bed at Bella Flora.

"Masters Hansum and Lincoln," the imp said as the two flopped down on the bed beside him, "you two seem to be having oodles of fun."

"Oodles?" Lincoln giggled. "That's a zippy word. Maybe I'll introduce that to my team too."

"Well, half the estate is saying 'zippy' now," Hansum smiled. "I've even heard the Podesta use it. It sounds funny mixed with Italian."

Pan was happy to see his boys settling into their new life and thriving. He had told them that when they got back to Verona and had a bit of time, they would start to create some antibiotics and medicines. These would be for the most common ailments they were likely to run into when their inoculation implants timed out.

Lincoln had become part of the cannon's testing team. Pan's tutoring on organization and critical thinking had made him on par with — or ahead of — a trained officer of the time. The captain had given him a chainmail balaclava and a kettle helmet to make him look like the other men.

"Not that it will save you if the cannon explodes," the captain said, talking easily about death.

"It won't explode," Lincoln assured him. "It would take a seven-pound charge before that happened."

"How do you know that?" the Captain asked.

"Um, Master Monticelli told me."

Lincoln was the primer on the firing team. Now that they felt the cannon was safe, they no longer used black powder fuses. Lincoln's job was to take the large flight feathers of geese and cut off the lower hollow tip to about the length of a man's little finger. He stretched open the top of this short, straw-like cylinder to form a lip and then made a slit in the thinner lower part. The hollow tube was filled with finely-ground black powder. The whole thing was then covered with horse glue and dipped in more black powder. When dry, this created a sealed unit that could be pushed into the cannon's touch hole. When the quill fuse was touched by a red-hot poker, it instantly ignited, sending a shower of sparks downward through the slit. A moment later, the black powder in the cannon would go off in a controlled explosion. Lincoln also had the honor and fun of lighting the fuse with the poker.

By midday on the Saturday, the cannon had been fired some twenty-five times. Careful records were kept of each shot. The Podesta, the general, Master Calabreezi and Hansum had watched the tests most of the morning. When they became convinced the cannon design was sound, they decided to get busy taking the project to its next level. Pan, in Hansum's now famous cap, listened proudly as his young master conversed with Master Calabreezi about the mass production method for the cannon. Pan was also listening to the Podesta and Baron down the table, discussing how they were going to acquire so much bronze and steel. This would mean expanding supply lines with their allies, the Germans. He also listened as the general and captain laid the groundwork to organize brigades of cannoneers. The goal was to have the first hundred cannon, over one thousand trained officers and men, five hundred support staff, two hundred and fifty horses, and more, within eighteen months.

Pan really began to like Master Calabreezi. He had listened as the senior master confided in Hansum that he had four grown and married daughters, all of whom he adored. But being around Hansum made him feel like he had the son he always wished for. The old man was reluctant to part from his protégé when he was reminded he had to leave for Verona after the morning dinner on Saturday. One of his grandchildren was being christened at Santa Anastasia, so he must attend. But he was pleased to agree to take a note from Hansum to Master della Cappa's home.

"Si, of course. I will stop on my way past Verona. And by the week after that, I should have the plaster casts ready for inspection. You must come and discuss with me any details that come up. You must promise me this."

"Of course, Master," Hansum said. "We have much to learn together." Pan was surprised and pleased to see how kind Hansum was to this adoring older mentor. Even at dinner, when Mastino pointed for him to take the seat on his right, Hansum insisted this was the place for Master Calabreezi. Mastino looked somewhat surprised, and when he asked Hansum about it in private later, Hansum said, "Excellency, I shall have many years to sit there. For now, it must be Master Calabreezi's honor."

But now Pan was watching as Hansum sat at his bedroom table, writing the letter to Guilietta and the family. Lincoln was already in a deep sleep on the bed. Pan read as Hansum wrote about what was happening on the estate, also mentioning, right at the beginning, what the Podesta had said about Hansum and Guilietta. He frowned.

"Do you think you should tell this, Master? Are you sure it's wise to raise hopes so?"

When Nuca entered the bedroom on Saturday morning, she found the Signora sitting on the side of Guilietta's bed, holding an empty cup. She thought to herself how the Signora looked very old now. She seemed unsteady and her eyes were bleary and unfocused. She thought it must be from staying up too late, nursing Guilietta. While worried for the old lady, she was also proud of her. Nuca smiled her nearly-toothless smile and bobbed her head. The Signora feebly tried to return the greeting.

"You give Gui her med'cine? Here food for you. Must eat." She smiled, sure that the Signora would not refuse the surprise that she had prepared. Nuca pulled off the cloth, and there, right under the Signora's nose, was the old woman's favourite, a big chunk of steaming pork.

But instead of showing delight, Signora della Cappa's eyes became more unfocused. She flushed, convulsing slightly, like she was about to hiccup. An instant later, she began to spew the same green vomit that Guilietta had a few days earlier. But Nuca did not become frantic like she did when Guilietta threw up the other day. Nuca smiled, reasoning that since Guilietta had thrown up a few days earlier and Signora Devlena had said it was a stomach ailment, this meant her mother had the same malady. Guilietta was getting better so, she reasoned, the Signora would too. She cleaned up the Signora and put her to bed in the other room.

## Chapter 4

Hansum spent more time working with the cannoneers after Master Calabreezi left. At supper, one of the lieutenants said that the cannon could be used against many men at once if it were stuffed with all sorts of debris, rocks, stone, slag, anything. Pan whispered a response into Hansum's ear. Hansum diplomatically repeated that the young officer had a fine idea, but experiments were needed to see if encapsulating the shot in different ways would cause it to be more contained and give the desired antipersonnel effect. Hansum paused and looked deep in thought again.

"To get a proper and predictable dispersal pattern, we must use as round a shot as possible. We shall use the same amount of spheres, first loose, then in a canvas bag, then in a hollow tin cylinder." After Hansum described this, one of the lieutenants voiced the opinion that this testing was becoming tedious and was unmanly. They weren't used to the scientific method, which, of course, wouldn't be invented for almost half a millennium. The Baron was the opposite. He was in awe of Hansum's methodical approach. In coming to Hansum's defense, Nicademo raised his voice.

"Lieutenant Raguso, you will not speak to Master Monticelli so!" he said vigorously.

This caused Mastino's eyebrows to rise. It was the first time he had ever heard his cousin get angry. The lieutenant still grumbled the opinion that the approach was unmanly.

"Cannon will be used to open up the walls into cities," Raguso argued. "It is still going to be the infantrymen and cavalry who will rush bravely through the breach and finish the job."

At that, the Podesta banged his hand on the table and the general hushed his men.

The next morning, they set up the testing ground. Peasants chopped long stakes from saplings and set up a five-pace-by-five-pace square with about one hundred of the saplings within it. Since this was an antipersonnel test, Pan suggested old armor, helmets, breastplates, chainmail and leather vests be hung up on the stakes throughout the target. Suddenly everyone became very interested in seeing the results of the smaller ammunition against men's protection.

⌛

"What the hell are they doing setting up all those poles, Captain?" Prince Feltrino asked this from his hiding place high on the hill above the valley.

"I don't know, my Lord," the Gonzaga captain replied. "But their new weapon is pointed toward it. We shall have to watch and see."

"Make sure the men stay hidden with the horses behind the ridge. We cannot risk being seen."

Prince Feltrino was there because a single spy of his father's had watched in astonishment, two days before, when they fired the first cannon shots. He then rode all night and excitedly told the prince about the power, precision and deadliness of a weapon that could fire a steel ball over a thousand paces. And when the spy told him of the savant and mentioned a name he had heard in the village, Feltrino felt his left hand throb where his thumb had been.

"Monticelli!" Feltrino growled under his breath.

They rode back that very same night and were in place before sunup to see the cannon being fired. Luckily, the stab wound the artist girl had inflicted on him was small and healing quickly. He rubbed it as he peered through the bushes of his hiding place.

"There's Podesta della Scalla himself," Feltrino whispered, "and General Chavelerio. And there's . . ." That damned apprentice! But he was now moving among the nobles and officers as if he were one of them. Feltrino bit his lower lip and the phantom itch where his thumb used to be throbbed and twitched more than ever.

He watched the tests all day, the cannon blasts echoing through the valley, and when he saw several trees blown in half, Feltrino was convinced. This weapon could tear his family's grip from the Duchy of Mantua. He rode again all that evening to tell his father of the terrible new weapon and, when there, pleaded with Luigi to allow him to act boldly. He brought the spy in and had him tell of what he learned from wandering around the village in the days before, about the saltpeter beds, the massive grinding of the black powders and about the first explosive tests. The peasants who had been there had even gossiped about the young savant, Romero, who had invented this wonder.

"Please Father, allow me to take men and steal their new weapon. The property is poorly guarded. They are spread over the vast estate. We could be gone before they know there's been an attack."

"Soon they must guard this marvel better," the captain added. "This is an opportunity we cannot put off."

"And we will steal this savant and bring him with us," Feltrino added, his eyes widening.

"And if he resists?" Luigi Gonzaga asked from his bed. They had awakened him in the night and he still had his night cap on.

"Then we kill him. If we cannot have his secrets, nobody should."

"I don't like killing savants," the father said. "It's a sin. Bring him alive, at all costs."

"And if he resists?"

"Then do what you must." Luigi dismissed the captain and spy, but bid his son stay. "This time, no revenge, no personal trophies, no distractions. If what you say about this weapon is half true, the fate of our duchy is at stake."

Prince Feltrino rode hard again the rest of the night with his captain and twenty men. Before dawn, the Gonzaga were well hidden among the trees with the sun behind them. Their captain had recently come into possession of one of the lookers, an irony which was not lost on Feltrino. It still bore the dent from the sword cut which had separated it from the hand of its previous owner. The officer and prince passed the glass back and forth. They cursed at what they saw. There were more guards today than before. They most probably would have to cancel the planned theft. Right in front of them was this new weapon, and just off to the side was its inventor, the young savant in the brown hat. The looker brought the young man's face almost as close as it had been when Feltrino had faced him, sword to sword. He was angry that, once again, it didn't look like he would best this opponent.

"Damn the fortunes of war!" Feltrino swore quietly.

# Chapter 5

Hansum smiled at the young officer who had contradicted him the night before. Lieutenant Raguso was on the firing range with his four calvary men and six infantry.

For the first test of the cannon as an antipersonnel weapon, it was primed with a full charge and had a few rags holding back the powder. Then they poured in round stones, picked from the banks of the Adige River. Iron would be used later, if this worked. More rags were put in to hold back the blow and build up pressure. Lincoln shouted off the information to the lieutenant working as a scribe.

"Thirty stones," Lincoln shouted in military fashion. "Loose fit. Two-hundred-and-fifty-pace range. Three-pound charge."

"Ready?" the lieutenant at the cannon shouted.

"Ready, Signor," Lincoln, the fuse man, cried in return. "Men to your positions." The five other gunners took their places on either side of the cannon, standing at attention.

"Fire," the lieutenant cried.

Lincoln touched the hot poker to the quill fuse and the cannon erupted, jumping backward and straining at the ropes that held it to the ground. Earth flew up in front and to the side of the target. Only seven of the stones hit within the area of the sapling posts.

"You were correct, Master Monticelli," Lieutenant Raguso admitted. He looked embarrassed.

"The testing is not yet finished," Hansum said. "My ideas might prove false as well."

They loaded the cannon again. This time, after the prime, they put in a loosely-sewn canvas bag that held the same amount of stones. This time, when they fired, there was a thwack as a bee-like hoard of stones attacked the target. Wood chips flew, helmets and old breastplates clanged and bonged as they were hit. They found eighteen of the thirty stones. Now they tried the shot encased in a tin cylinder. The lieutenant said to Hansum that this too must be a waste of his time. Hansum smiled, and then took special care, double-checking the hastily-soldered ends of the tube. The gunners loaded it and Hansum took a place by Raguso and smiled again.

"Never be afraid to fail when testing something. Better to learn now than in battle," he said.

The drill began. "Thirty stones in a tin canister," Lincoln shouted. "Two-hundred-and- fifty-pace range. Three-pound charge."

"Ready?" the lieutenant shouted.

"Ready, Signor," Lincoln shouted. "Men to your positions."

"Fire!"

The canister burst into one of the central stakes of the target area. There was a loud crack as it exploded. The stake snapped in half. Multiple cracks were heard as the round stones, compressed together with supersonic force, ricocheted out in every direction. Wooden stakes all around the first exploded outward, causing a void in the middle of the target. Clangs and pings rang out as holes appeared in the helmets and breastplates. Many of the ricocheting stones broke up into smaller missiles and many more of the staffs were shredded with the shrapnel.

"Yahoo!" Lincoln shouted.

"Order in on the line," the captain cried. All the men stood quietly at ease. "Okay then," he shouted after discipline had been restored, "let's hear it for Master Monticelli."

"Hoorah!" many of the men shouted. "Bravo!" shouted others, over and over. "Yahoo!"

Hansum shook hands with everyone in the crew and all the officers. They decided it was time to take a break and have something to eat. They would clean the cannon and have more tests later. The target must be reset. The captain ordered Raguso and his men to go back on patrol and told Hansum that he and the lieutenant taking notes were going back to the manor to report to the general. He asked if Hansum would join them.

"No, I'll stay here. I want to set the target up a little differently. I'll eat with the men." He also spoke to the Lieutenant Raguso. "Signor, this new weapon cannot ever replace bravery. The cannon will give our forces an advantage over our enemies, but in the end, I agree with you. We still must put our men on their holdings."

The lieutenant bowed gallantly to Hansum.

"Grazie, Master," he said. "You are a true gentleman. It is an honor to serve you. Now, if you will give me my leave, I must go back on patrol." He mustered his men and they all rode and marched away from the firing range.

# Chapter 6

Prince Feltrino became excited when he saw the column of riders and infantry trotting away. Then he saw the captain and two other riders heading back to the manor. That only left the cannon's eight-man crew, one officer, three infantrymen and the savant in the field. He and his captain fell back to the clearing over the hill. Feltrino quickly gave orders to his men.

"You nine with the Captain, capture the weapon and kill their men. You must not kill their horses. They must be quickly yoked up to the machine. You six take the savant's guard. You two, with me. We take the savant. You must not let anyone escape to warn the house. We need as many hours as possible to get ahead of them. But the savant must not be killed. He is to be taken prisoner.

If any of you kill him, you will die by my hand. Take rope to bind him."

⏳

"Okay, men, let's swab out the cannon and scrape the barrel," Lincoln ordered. "Then we can eat." Lincoln liked that his team didn't mind being told what to do by someone much younger than them.

*"You too are a natural leader,"* Pan had told him. Lincoln shrugged offhandedly, but felt very proud.

After cleaning out the heavy residue the black powder explosions left inside the chamber, Lincoln and three of the crew primed and reloaded another tin canister full of stones, making the cannon ready for when they resumed testing. For safety, they covered the touch hole with damp rag, so as not to ignite it by accident. Upon completing this task, Lincoln and his crew sat around the cannon, taking out food and bottles of watered-down wine from a basket. It was a glorious spring day. The Adige River valley was green and tranquil. With the cannon silent, the songbirds were singing again. Lincoln looked downrange and saw Hansum, the lieutenant, the two other men of his crew and the three guards resetting the target.

"Come and eat," Lincoln called.

"You go ahead," Hansum shouted back. "I want to finish this first."

"Hey, little one," Georgio, one of the gunners, said, "Bread and cheese. Catch."

They ate and passed a bottle of wine around, all drinking directly from it.

"So, little one," Daveed, another crew member said, "I heard Captain and Lieutenant say how you are good at telling funny stories. Tell us a funny story."

"Yes, a funny story," Caliveeta, a stocky older man with a grizzled beard and one tooth agreed.

"You wanna hear a funny story?" Lincoln said, taking a swig. He didn't have Pan with him, but he was starting to remember many of the jokes. "How about the one about the cuckold and the priest at confession?"

Just its description made the men roar with laughter. They roared even louder at the punch line. Lincoln told several more stories and the laughter became out of control. Lincoln got up and pantomimed his next joke, swinging his arms and stomping his feet. Tears came to his audience's eyes as they leaned back against the big round wheels of the cannon's carriage, the warm sun on their faces. The shining sun also gave the archer in the woods a clear target. He was only fifty paces away, with many other riders hiding behind him.

"So the bishop said to the nun," Lincoln said, ready to spring the punch line that had garnered the most laughs the other night, "I thought I recognized your naked arse sticking out from under the bed." But instead of laughter there was only a loud 'thunk' and a gasp. When Lincoln turned, he saw Georgio lying against the big wheel, a long arrow sticking out from where his eye had been. Blood streamed down his face. The other two men were running for their poleaxes.

"We're under attack!" Daveed and Caliveeta together screamed.

"We're under attack!" Lincoln screamed at Hansum. Lincoln saw Hansum turn, but then everything went black as an iron-tipped arrow punctured his helmet. As his consciousness ebbed into darkness, the last thing Lincoln was aware of was Hansum screaming his name in the distance. The voice then seemed farther away still, and everything went black.

# Chapter 7

It was late Saturday afternoon when Master Calabreezi's carriage stopped at the della Cappa house. His gruff countenance had truly been tempered by his association with Hansum and the new project. He was pleased to hand deliver a letter to the family which his young associate had such high regard for. Nuca answered the door, opening it halfway and peering around. She croaked at him that the master wasn't in. He was at his workshop around the back.

"Well then, I'll take Master Monticelli's letter there."

"Letter from Omero?" Nuca said to someone in the room. The door quickly opened fully. Shamira was standing there.

"Excuse us, Signor," Shamira said. "There's sickness in the house and we're being careful. You have a letter from Romero?"

"Si. Who are you? The kitchen girl?"

"Si Signor. May I have the letter?"

"Most certainly not. It's for Master della Cappa."

"Nuca, go fetch the Master. Quickly. Signor, are you a friend of Romero's?"

"I may hope so. My name's Calabreezi."

"Calabreezi?" Shamira repeated, surprised. "Master Calabreezi? The bronze caster? The inventor? Please Signor, come in. Can I give you some refreshment?" As he came in, Master Calabreezi smiled as Shamira continued. "Romero has told us all about you. He says he has learned so much from just being around you."

"He said that?" the old man asked, obviously very pleased.

"My name is Carmella."

"Ah, you're the artist, the draftsman. I have seen your work, young lady. You have talent. The Podesta himself has said I should meet you and perhaps . . ."

Master della Cappa came running into the house, Ugilino trailing close behind. Agistino looked haggard and exhausted.

"Ah, Master della Cappa. I am Master Calabreezi. Delighted to . . ."

"You have a letter from Romero? Why didn't he come himself?" Agistino said gruffly.

"Why, he's busy," Calabreezi answered, taken aback by Agistino's abruptness. He handed the letter over. Agistino broke the seal, looked at it for a few moments and handed it to Shamira.

"You read it."

Master Calabreezi, like everyone, was confounded about such a place. Kitchen girls who drew like artists and who can read and write.

" 'My dearest family. All is well here and I have wonderful news. I have broached the question of my betrothal to Guilietta with the Podesta. His Excellency has said he would give me a final answer by the Summer Solstice, but that he has no objection in principle. I believe he wants to see the success of our present projects, so that should be no impediment. We have just experienced a great success in our first tests. I am sure we shall have many more. Maruccio is well. It is good to have him here. Guilietta, please take extra good care of yourself. Eat and sleep well. Master, I will do you proud and I will look after our family's interests. Please give every courtesy to Master Calabreezi, who has been a good friend to me. Love to all, Romero."

"Romero and your daughter are to marry, Signor?" Master Calabreezi said. "I had no idea. My congratulations." Agistino began to tremble visibly and couldn't speak.

"Signor," Shamira intervened, "we sent a letter to Romero with important and troubling news. He does not mention it here."

"What is the news? May I ask?"

"Guilietta, the Master's daughter, the one Romero mentions in his letter. She has become very ill."

"Oh dear," Calabreezi said. "How is she? Has she been seen to? A physician?"

"We have the finest herbalist in Verona looking after her," the Master said solemnly.

"Good," Calabreezi answered. "But Romero received no letter. I'm sure of it. When was it sent?"

"Four days ago, Signor," Shamira said.

Agistino turned to Ugilino in a rage.

"I knew it was a mistake to give you the letter. And we paid a soldi for fast delivery!" He slapped Ugilino hard in the face.

"Master, I didn't fail. She promised she would take it to Captain Caesar. And she took the soldi to bribe him. I didn't keep it. May the devil take my soul if I'm lying."

"Who did you give it to, my boy?" Calabreezi asked.

"Signora Devlena, the herbalist."

"Devlena?" Calabreezi repeated, astonished.

"Si," Shamira said. "She is the one helping Guilietta."

Master Calabreezi was shocked. "Signora Devlena, who lives at the top of the Erbe?"

"Si," Ugilino said. "I swear on the baby Jesus that I put the letter in her hand. And the soldi too."

"I tell you," Agistino raged, "if she dies you'll not be marrying Serindella."

"Peace, Master, peace," Calabreezi said. "We must get to the bottom of this. What did Devlena prescribe for the signorina?"

"Herbs, Signor," Shamira said. "A mixture of herbs."

"Bring them to me." Shamira got the satchel of herbs from the shelf and gave them to Calabreezi. He opened the bag, smelled it, made a face, then put a pinch in his mouth. He spat it quickly on the floor. "Take me to her. Quickly."

They walked into the bedroom where Guilietta was resting. She looked pallid, but peaceful. Looking around the sick room, Master Calabreezi saw the wooden cup that had been used for the medicine. He picked it up and put it to his nose. He made the same face as he had when he tasted the herbs. "How long has the girl been taking this?"

Shamira thought. "Six days," she answered.

"Six!" exclaimed Calabreezi, shocked. "How many times a day?"

"Three," Shamira answered. "Sometimes four. Signora Devlena said it would strengthen her."

"Holy mother of Cristo." Master Calabreezi put his hand on the sleeping girl's forehead. Guilietta awoke with a bit of a start.

"It's okay, daughter. Be still," Agistino said. She smiled weakly and let Calabreezi put the back of his hand on her cheek, then her neck. He asked her to breathe on his face so he could smell her breath. Then he sat on the edge of the bed, confused.

"It's a malady of the stomach, is it not, Master?" Shamira asked. "The mistress has it too now. Nuca says she threw up bile this morning. She's in the other bed."

"The mistress? Her mother? Take me to her," Calabreezi said. He went to the other room and checked the Signora. When he pulled up her eyelid and she was unresponsive, he touched her forehead, neck, and then cheek. He smelled the Signora's breath, and recoiled from it. "She has been taking it too? I can smell it."

"No, no," Nuca began, flustered.

"What's the matter?" Shamira asked.

Calabreezi sat with a grave look on his face. He was in a very bad position. He knew what was going on. As a young man, when he gained the patronage of the first Cangrande, it had put him in the circle of many scholars, artists, mathematicians, natural philosophers, physicians and alchemists. From his time working closely with these experts, he had learned of botany and herbs, including poisons. He also knew who Devlena was and what she did for the Podesta. But he could not tell the lensmaker or anyone in this house the whole truth. And he could not let the Podesta know he knew what was happening. Why the Podesta wanted this simple girl murdered could not be seen to be his concern. He had survived these many years and had been allowed to create his many wonders by learning what was his business and what wasn't. These deals with the devil, these complicities by complacency, were the things that made good men of ability question if there really would be a place in Heaven for them. Master Calabreezi shook the old lady's arm.

"Signora, wake up. Please, wake up. I must ask you something." She was in such a stupor he finally had to slap her face lightly before she half opened her eyes. She looked at Calabreezi's stern face and gave a start.

"It's okay, Mistress," Shamira said gently. "This is a friend."

"Have you been drinking your daughter's medicine, Signora?" Calabreezi asked loudly. "Have you been drinking from this?" He showed her the cup.

The Signora's dilated pupils stared up at Calabreezi. She blinked several times and looked hard at something on the ceiling.

"Si, Signor," she said in a whispering croak "Three days, I think."

"Why, Signora?" he asked. She hesitated, as if she hadn't heard. "Why, Signora?"

"Michael. The angel. He said to do it. Save Guilietta."

"You drank our daughter's medicine because your crazy vision said to?" Agistino chastized.

The old woman looked at her husband and started to cry. "Si. I'm sorry, husband. Forgive me."

"No, Signora," Calabreezi corrected. "No, be not sorry. If your daughter had drunk it these past three days, she most certainly would be with the angels by now. The herbs have hemlock in it."

"Hemlock!" the Master cried.

"Hemlock?" Shamira asked.

"Poison!" Master Calabreezi explained. "Deadly poison. If the Signora had let Guilietta drink the poison, it would have killed her. And since she survived these past three days, she should be able to make a full recovery."

The terribleness of it all caused Agistino to sob. He fell to his knees by the bed.

"You've saved our daughter, wife. You've saved her." He hugged and kissed her.

"But will the Signora be okay?" Shamira asked.

"Give her vinegar to drink. This is to cause her to vomit two or three times more. Follow this with olive oil, to purge her bowels. Then keep feeding her warmed milk. I think the danger has passed for the girl. Make sure she drinks as much water as possible and eats well. Very well. Good food is the best medicine now. But first, Master della Cappa, and you too, Carmella, let us talk downstairs alone."

They sat at the table. As Master Calabreezi talked, Agistino got angrier and angrier. When Agistino asked why the herbalist nun would do such a thing, Master Calabreezi said he couldn't say why, but they must do nothing.

"If anyone asks — anyone —just say Guilietta is well."

"But we must denounce her to the authorities!" Agistino demanded. "We must tell the Baron and the Podest . . ." he stopped. His eyes went wide as the reality dawned on him.

Master Calabreezi put his large, callused hand on top of Master della Cappa's clenched fist.

"I cannot say another word. And none must know I was here today. All our futures ride upon on our agreed silence. I overstep my own family's confidence when I take your's into mine. I cannot say more," he emphasized slowly.

Agistino's mouth remained open, a gaping hole from which disbelief silently flew. The two men stared at each other for some time. Finally Agistino spoke very quietly.

"If we say nothing, act as if nothing has occurred, all will be well?"

The other master slowly nodded his head and repeated, "I cannot say more."

"We must send for Romero," Shamira said. "He must be here."

"But the danger has passed," Calabreezi said. "Romero is safe where he is. He is surrounded by soldiers and is important to the Podesta."

Shamira wanted to have Pan run a scan on the two poison victims.

"Romero really should be here," she repeated.

"Then write your letter," Master Calabreezi conceded, "but with no mention of me or the Podesta in it. Then send it thus." He said where to find a trustworthy private courier and told where he was to take it. Calabreezi then rose to leave. He went over to a still-shocked Agistino and extended his hand. The Master took it and looked into Calabreezi's intense eyes. "I shall always be Romero's friend," Calaabreezi said. "To survive among the nobles, he has much to learn. When he returns and we are working together, I shall tutor him in this art. I give you this pledge for as long as I live."

# Chapter 8

When Hansum saw the arrow plunge through Lincoln's helmet, then saw him fall to the ground, panic and terror consumed him.

"LINCOLN!" he cried, running toward him. The lieutenant grabbed Hansum's arm.

"No Signor, flee to the house. We will keep them busy while you escape."

Hansum looked up and saw the twenty knights on horses dashing out from the forest. Half went toward the cannon and the others came at a dead run toward his group. The horses were covered with armor and the men's bascinet helmets had their visors down. Some soldiers had swords, the others, poleaxes. The noise of the hooves on the ground, the men shouting, and the armor and weapon clanging all filled the air with a terrifying din.

"But my friend!" Hansum screamed.

"He's fallen, Signor. Save yourself!" the lieutenant shouted. He shoved Hansum in the direction of the house and pulled down his visor. "Form around me!" he called to the five men with him.

"You, go with the Signor," he said to one. "Protect him with your life." Hansum ran as fast as he could toward the woods that separated him from the manor house. Beside him ran the tall, lanky infantryman who had lit the fuse under Gina. He was running again, a look in his dark eyes that Hansum had never seen before. The long scar on his face, which spoke to the fact that he had been in these terrifying battles before, had turned deep red. Looking back as he ran, Hansum saw his protectors forming a line between him and the advancing horses. Three of the ten horses swung off to the right to go around them and were coming straight at him. The seven remaining horses barrelled toward the five standing soldiers.

"Shoulders together! On one knee! Brace!" the lieutenant shouted, pulling out his sword and stepping behind his line. "Shields!" All the men prepared themselves to take the charge. Their poleaxes were extended as far out as they could in an effort to spear their opponents. "Take the horses!" the lieutenant shouted, and they lowered their weapons slightly. The cavalry fell upon them. By standing so close together, only two of the seven mounted attackers were in killing proximity of the infantrymen. The horses ran into the poleaxes' pointed tips and luck was with the Podesta's men. Two spears found their way through the horses' armor. One horse reared up backward. The other tumbled forward over the defenders. The helmet came off its heavily armored knight, causing him to become an easy target for the lieutenant's sword. Luckily all five of the defenders survived the initial assault. They stood up and two attacked the second downed cavalryman. His helmet was still on. As he stumbled to his feet, they pummelled his covered head with the hammer side of their poleaxes. The pointed top of the helmet initially did its job and deflected most of the blows, but soon it caved, as did its inhabitant. Two of the defenders kept at killing him while the other three formed again in front of the lieutenant.

The remaining five attackers had swung their horses back around and, without hesitation, were charging again. It became a slashing, banging, cutting and spearing battle of attrition.

The fight for the cannon was not so grand. Only two men with poleaxes against eight men on horses and a bowman, not fifty paces away. Within a minute, all the cannoneers lay bleeding, dying or dead. When the attackers rode toward the cannon's horses, the animals bolted, breaking their leads. The mounted cavalry caught one horse quickly and had to chase the other.

More easily caught was Hansum. He was the most vulnerable. Feltrino rode ahead of him and blocked his way. The infantryman jumped in front of Hansum and slashed at the air to make Feltrino back his horse up. The brave defender then jumped back to confront the two other attackers. He swung his poleaxe at the closest one and it hit his shield. He pulled it back over his head to form another blow, but never delivered it. The other horseman was now behind him, slashing him on the back with his sword. Though the chainmail held, it threw him off balance and then the haunch of the attacker's horse ran into the poor man as he passed. He stumbled and the other rider's heavy sword came down and caught him on the top of his head. His helmet split and the man fell to his knees right in front of Hansum.

"*Perche*?" was all the man could say before blood and brains spurt out from his skull. He fell to the ground, dead.

Hansum screamed at the grisly sight. Feltrino got off his horse, sword in hand. Hansum looked to the infantryman's fallen poleaxe and leaned toward it. One of the prancing hooves of the horses came down on it, holding it fast. Feltrino looked at Hansum through his closed helmet. Then he sheathed his sword, lifted his visor and looked at Hansum.

"Feltrino!" Hansum gasped. Feltrino removed one of his gloves and held up the hand. It was short a thumb. But Feltrino didn't look angry or vengeful. He bowed slightly to Hansum.

"Master Monticelli," he said respectfully. "You are my prisoner, Signor."

Hansum didn't answer, but looked over at where the lieutenant and the infantrymen had formed their line. Only two of them were still on their feet: the lieutenant, who was bravely fighting two men, and one soldier who had dropped his poleaxe and was running away. Hansum watched as the fleeing soldier was overtaken and trampled by a pursuing rider. He flinched.

"Master Monticelli?" Feltrino called again. Hansum looked toward the cannon, where several of the enemy horses and soldiers were standing around, watching the other men coming back with the draft horses. "Master Monticelli!" Feltrino now shouted.

*"Answer him, Master,"* Pan whispered frantically. *"I believe he means to kidnap you, not kill you. Answer him quickly!"*

Hansum tried to speak, but couldn't. He looked at Feltrino and nodded.

"You are my prisoner, Signor," Feltrino repeated. "Tie his hands!"

One of the soldiers tied Hansum's hands in front of him, then pushed him in the direction they had come. As they passed in front of the target area of wooden stakes, Hansum looked down at the now-prone body of the lieutenant, whose dead, pulverized face stared up at the clear, cloudless sky.

"Why are you doing this?" Hansum screamed at Feltrino.

*"Do not resist,"* Pan said in Hansum's ear.

"My family controls the Duchy of Mantua," Feltrino said, like it should be perfectly obvious. "Scalliger is our mortal enemy. But do not fear. You will do well with us."

"But you've . . ."

"Charge!" came a far off cry.

"Excellency!" the Gonzaga captain shouted from the cannon. He was pointing furiously at something in the distance.

Scalliger forces were pouring over a hill in the distance. Hansum could see Lieutenant Raguso returning with his men. He and his five riders were coming at full gallop toward the fight. Behind him, his infantrymen were following on foot.

*"The horsemen will be here in two minutes,"* Pan said. *"The infantrymen, five."*

"Merda!" Feltrino cursed. "Call the men from the cannon to us. We must not be divided in the fight!"

Feltrino and his soldiers all screamed for their comrades to leave the cannon and rejoin the group. They were still twenty men to eleven and they only had to contend with six to begin with. The foot soldiers were still some time away.

*"He's alive!"* Pan said excitedly to Hansum. *"Lincoln's alive!"*

Hansum could see Lincoln getting up to his knees, the arrow still sticking from his helmet.

*"Look to the cannon, Master,"* Pan whispered. *"Now look to the target area. Yes, yes, this may work. I have a plan."* All the Gonzaga forces were now in a tight cluster. *"Turn off your language transplant, Master."*

"When della Scalla's men come through the trees," Feltrino shouted to his men, "attack as a force and stay as close as you can."

*"Call to Lincoln,"* Pan said. *"Tell him to light the cannon when you say."*

"What?" Hansum said in Earth Common.

*"Do it!"* Pan screamed.

Hansum put his tied hands to his forehead and touched the language node. Then he shouted, "Lincoln! Get ready to light the cannon! Get ready to light the cannon!"

*"Now run toward him. Fall to the ground when I say so."*

Hands tied, Hansum ran toward the cannon. Feltrino turned his horse and trotted after him. Lincoln staggered to the fire and picked up the red-hot poker.

Hansum tripped and fell on his face. His hat fell from his head, Pan with it.

*"Now!"* Pan screamed, but Hansum couldn't hear him. Left with no alternative, Pan popped out in the field, a Greek satyr for all the world to see. Feltrino's horse stopped over Hansum, Pan standing right in front of them. Feltrino peered at the apparition through his visor, then lifted it, his unbelieving eyes bulging at the vision. Pan, in an incredibly loud and echoing voice, shouted at Lincoln, "FIRE THE DAMN CANNON! Stay down, Master."

Lincoln put the poker to the touch hole, just as the Gonzaga Captain screamed at his forces. "Stay tight. Ready now. CHARGE!"

"BaBOOM!" exploded the cannon. The canister, filled with thirty smooth stones, whistled over Hansum, past Feltrino and landed squarely on the hindquarters of the captain's horse, just as it was tensing its muscles to charge into battle. The canister compressed and burst outward, the stone spheres colliding into one another and exploding in all directions. They tore through the muscle and bone of the captain's warhorse, then the captain. Many of the other stone balls tore through other horses and men. The stones broke and became razor sharp. The bones of the horses and men became missiles; flying bits of armor became scythes. Horses, terrorized by the pain of dying, jumped into and onto other horses and men. Fleeing horses tripped over the dying and the dead, further adding to their misery. It took all of three seconds, but where there had been a fighting force of twenty, now there was only five and their prince. Feltrino saw this and was aghast.

"Hey, tin man!" Pan shouted. "Get outta here!" He taunted the knight, hopping around like a demented demon, but purposefully moving away from Hansum, who was lying precariously close to the horse's feet. Feltrino spurred his horse and rode right over the projected image of Pan, trying to kill it. When he looked back to see if he had crushed the creature, Pan laughed and sneered. "Get outta here, tin man, get outta here!" Then he gave Feltrino the Italian salute.

Feltrino screamed to his men, "Retreat! The devil is among us!" and he galloped off the battlefield as fast as he could. His five men followed, one badly injured by bits of their captain's flying jawbone.

"Get your hat. Go to Lincoln. Quickly!" Pan shouted, disappearing before anyone else could see him. Panicked, Hansum scrambled to his feet, wriggled his wrists out of his bonds, put on his cap and ran to Lincoln. The poor fellow stood listlessly, his arms by his sides, eyes glazed, the arrow still sticking out from of his helmet. His face was covered with dirt, and blood gushed from his swollen mouth.

At that moment, Raguso and his horsemen thundered past them in pursuit of the fleeing Gonzaga. Hansum carefully took off Lincoln's helmet. When he saw that the arrow hadn't broken through the chainmail, he breathed a sigh of relief.

*"Have Lincoln open his eyes as wide as he can,"* Pan said. He scanned Lincoln. *"He has a light concussion. Master, take him and go to the manor house quickly. There could be a counterattack."*

"Come on, Lincoln," Hansum said. Lincoln just stood there, shell-shocked. "Come on. Pan says we have to get back to the house."

"I killed them," Lincoln said weakly. His lisp was gone with one of his front teeth. "I killed all those guys. Dead." He looked around him. The three cannoneers he had been eating, drinking and joking with were lying close by, horribly dead.

*"To the house, Master. Quickly!"*

Hansum grabbed Lincoln's arm and pulled him. As they worked their way up the rise, their own infantrymen rushed past.

"To the cannon," shouted one of the men. "I can see those bastards on the next hill."

Hansum stopped and turned. Sure enough, he could see the retreating Gonzaga riding like fury up the next hill. The infantrymen argued on what to do with the cannon.

*"Move, Master. Move, move,"* Pan shouted.

The infantrymen were still arguing about the cannon.

"Three pounds of powder, I tell you. That's what they put in," one of the untrained foot soldiers said.

"How much is that?"

"Uh, three scoops. The one with the long handle." One lifted the powder barrel and poured the corned granules into it. Powder spilled onto the ground as they stuffed three scoops of the powder down the cannon's mouth. "Ram it now," shouted a soldier and one of them stuffed in the swab. Two men picked up ammunition. One had a cannonball, the other a canister. "Put 'em both in," a soldier beamed.

"They're putting in too much," Lincoln said weakly as he was dragged along. "They put in over nine pounds of powder."

*"Keep moving, Master. Don't stop!"*

"Aim the damn thing," one of the soldiers said. The men grunted and groaned as they turned the heavy object toward the fleeing horsemen. They could see the Gonzaga riders almost to the crest of the hill.

"Too much," repeated Lincoln, but Hansum kept pulling him away from the battlefield. Lincoln finally pulled his arm free. "They're going to kill themselves," he screamed. He turned and waved his hands at the men. One man was on his haunches at the end of the cannon. He was lining up the shot, as the lieutenant had done. Another man was pouring powder freely over the touch hole. Another stood by the fire with the hot poker, ready to light the mess. "Stop!" Lincoln shouted. "You'll blow the thing!"

"Don't worry, little one, we'll blow those bastards to Hell!" a soldier shouted back.

"No, the cannon will explode!" But they couldn't — or wouldn't — listen.

"They're at the top of the hill," cried one of the untrained soldiers. "Fire it!"

"No!" Lincoln shouted as the red-hot poker was brought to the touch hole.

"Fire!" shouted several of the men with glee.

"NO!" Lincoln shouted again.

*"Fall to the ground!"* Pan screamed. *"Now!"*

Hansum tackled Lincoln and fell to the ground.

The powder in the touch hole sparked. "Those bast . . ." began one of the soldiers. KaBlaaBlaaBLAM, came a primary, then secondary, blast from the cannon. The overzealous and ignorant infantrymen had been behind and beside the cannon. They weren't in the proper or safe firing positions. But it wouldn't have mattered where they were. The cannon exploded out in all directions. Smoke, burning gases, shattered bronze, steel from the cannonball, rocks from the canister, wood hoops and cleats from the wheel all exploded, ripping, shredding and vaporizing everything in their path. What was left of men flew outward in chunks and bits. Fire fell into the open barrel of powder and it lit up like a Roman candle, sending sparks and more acrid smoke into the air. Hansum stayed on top of Lincoln, lying there, his face hidden. Debris fell all around them. A small chunk of burning bronze landed on Hansum's leg and burned through his braies. He pushed it off with his hand and ended up with a blistery welt on both his leg and palm.

Hansum heard the vibration of thundering horse hooves on the ground. He thought it could be the counterattack. He scrunched down harder on Lincoln, trying to make them melt into the ground. Then he heard the hooves come rumbling to a stop right over top of him. There was the quick sound of boots hitting the ground, then running toward him. Along with it was the sound of a sword scraping in the dirt. Hansum cringed as a hand grabbed his shoulder.

"Signor Monticelli, are you alive?" the voice shouted.

Hansum looked up and there was Grazzana, bending over him. Above him, still on their mounts were the general, Podesta and several other officers, all peering down at them. The Podesta looked up and cursed.

"Merda! Look at my cannon! It's ruined! My beautiful cannon!" Hansum, distressed beyond his wildest concept of what he thought possible, looked up at Mastino, disgusted at the lack of compassion he had for his men.

Hansum and Lincoln were helped to their feet. Smoke was still clearing away from the carnage of man and machine. The ground was a ring of charred black where the cannon had last sat intact. Blotches of red oozed from meat which had been men a few moments earlier. Gina, the bronze cannon, now looked much as her namesake. The largest part of her was some fifty feet away from where it had started, split open like a can made of tin sheet. The air was full with the smell of cooked flesh, burning bronze and brimstone.

"Ah, dear," General Chavelerio said to the air. "The fortunes of war, the fortunes of war."

# Chapter 9

When Devlena woke that Saturday morning, it was a bright, beautiful day. But this didn't cheer the poisoner. She was desperate for money and needed the contract on Guilietta completed. It had been six days since Guilietta had started taking the poison. When Devlena checked on the third day, the girl was well on the way out. But when she snuck into the della Cappas' neighborhood yesterday, asking discrete, leading questions about this person and that, no stories about a death had come up.

The poisoner fidgeted till late afternoon, distracting herself by grinding and regrinding the poor mummified bones of the scorpion-bit mouse, but it was no good. She had to know what was going on. Devising a plan, she borrowed the seven-year-old daughter of the neighborhood cobbler and walked with her to the della Cappas'. While they walked, she rehearsed the little child on what to say when she sent her to the family's door alone.

"Signora Devlena sends this little bit of chamomile tea for her patient. She should be better by now and this tea is just what she needs." Devlena had the girl repeat it back to her several times.

"That's a good girl. Do it properly and I'll buy you a fig after. And if you are asked if I am around, what do you say?"

"Signora Devlena is busy with patients at home. She sent me all by myself," the child answered.

"That's a good girl," the poisoner said.

They were walking in the middle of Bra Square when Devlena ran into the money lender, Ruben de Levi. She owed him some money and was overdue repaying it. She told him he'd be paid in a week.

"That's what you said last week, Signora. I'm losing patience. The only reason I lent to you is we both do business with the Podesta."

A carriage stopped by them and an elderly gentleman popped his head out.

"Ruben, my friend," the man in the carriage said, "I'm sorry to bother you on your Sabbath, but we must talk business as soon as possible."

Devlena watched the scowl on Ruben de Levi's face turn into a broad smile.

"Master Calabreezi, you are no bother to me, and the Sabbath is just ending," he said, looking to the setting sun. "I was just finished here. Come to my home and my wife will make us something. We can light the fire soon."

Devlena turned around to see who had saved her from the money lender's wrath. Her eyes met with those of Master Calabreezi. She knew him as a prominent maker of bells. Master Calabreezi looked shocked as their gazes met. He looked away quickly and accepted Signor de Levi's invitation.

"Si, we have much bronze to buy, Ruben. Much bronze."

By the time Devlena was in the della Cappas' neighborhood, she was in a state. She looked at the cobbler's child angrily.

"Remember what I said or they'll be trouble. Now smile." Devlena pushed the girl toward the della Cappas' door, then hid behind a tall pile of rattan baskets.

When the kitchen girl opened the door a crack, Devlena could barely hear the little girl recite her lines. As she held out the package of chamomile, the door tore open and the lensmaker stood there, fury showing in his face.

"Where's that bitch . . ." she heard him curse loudly. He stuck his head over the girl and looked up and down the street. The kitchen girl put her hand tenderly on the lensmaker's chest, said something to him, and then gently pushed him back into the house. The kitchen girl looked at the little girl and spoke, but Devlena couldn't hear her words.

⌛

Shamira looked down at the innocent little girl. "Where's Signora Devlena?" Shamira quietly asked.

"She's at home, but wants to know how the young lady Guilietta is. Here's some caminette tea for the girl to eat. It'll help, she says."

"I see," Shamira said, taking another discreet look up and down the street.

"How is she?" the little girl asked.

"Tell the Signora she is getting much better and that we won't need her services anymore. Can you remember that? She's not to come to this house. Do you understand?"

"Si," the girl said.

"Good night," Shamira said to the girl.

"Signora," the little girl said.

"Si?"

"Your camonbile."

Shamira took the package and closed the door. She went to Agistino, who was sitting on the bench with his head in his hands. She put a hand on his arm.

"Master della Cappa, remember what Master Callabreezi said. We must act as if nothing has happened."

"I know, I know. But what's a father and husband to do, Carmella?" He noticed the small package in Shamira's hand. "What's that?"

"Something Devlena sent."

Agistino grabbed the package and threw it in the fire.

Pan looked out at the results of the battle. It was now night and all the dead and injured from both sides were laid out on the front lawn of Bella Flora. Some were being treated by the maids, others questioned and tortured by Mastino's officers. Lieutenant Raguso and his men had been able to capture only one of the horsemen and three who were trying to escape on foot. They were hanging by their arms from an old oak and now being ignored. Feltrino had escaped back to Mantua.

"There's nothing more to be learned from the prisoners," General Chavelerio said to the Podesta and Baron, who were both standing at the top of the steps to the manor house. "They freely admit their prince's aim was to steal the cannon and savant."

Mastino was in an angry state.

"When I woke up this morning, I felt it only a matter of time before I was Emperor of all Europe, Asia and Africa. Now . . ."

Hansum sat with Lincoln lower down on the limestone steps. Pan had his senses tuned to hear as much of the Podesta's conversation as possible. Grazzana was inspecting Lincoln's mouth. His upper lip was very swollen and purple. When Lincoln had fallen unconscious, his face hit a pile of cannonballs. He knocked one of his front teeth clean out.

"It's stopped bleeding," Grazzana said.

"I was bleedin' like a stuck pig," Lincoln mumbled, holding his mouth.

"You are lucky you bled so much, little one," Grazzana counselled. "It made you look dead. If you just lay there with little blood, the Gonzagas would have speared you to make sure." Upon hearing this, Lincoln's grim face blanched even more. Grazzana added, "Hey, at least you won't whistle anymore when you talk."

But Lincoln didn't laugh. He cried.

"Georgio, Caliveeta, Daveed, my crew, my friends — they're all dead!" Lincoln cried openly, scrunching up his face into dirty rolls of skin. The grimace caused the black welt on his forehead to stretch and crack open again. A trickle of blood started down his face. "And I killed all those men with the cannon," he added, crossing himself involuntarily. Then he really wailed. "I killed them."

General Chavelerio spoke up loudly.

"What do you expect? This is the work of soldiers. To kill and to die."

"But I'm not a soldier!" Lincoln wailed. "I just liked playing with the cannon."

Nicademo sat down on the step by his favourite joke teller. "But you saved your friend, Romero, whose cannon will bring us glory. You are a hero."

"I'm a murderer!" Lincoln cried, and then buried his head in Hansum's arms. He sobbed and sobbed.

Nicademo shook his head and stood up to rejoin the brooding Podesta and general.

"This changes nothing," Mastino said quietly. Pan pricked up his ears. "That cannon was just a test. We can make more. Many more. In a few weeks, Calabreezi will have three more and then after that ten a month till we have a hundred. By winter we will have the powder mill and all this will be forgotten."

"And we'll have fifty more men here by midnight and a hundred more by midweek," the general added. "This will not be repeated, Excellency."

"And we still have Monticelli," Nicademo said. "That's the blessing here. Can you imagine if he were with Luigi right now? Or dead?"

"If he were with Luigi now, better . . ." Mastino looked to see if Hansum were watching, then drew his hand across his neck. An officer came up to Mastino.

"Excellency, a private messenger is here. He has a letter for Signor Monticelli."

"Give it to me," Mastino said quietly, gesturing to the officer to speak lower.

"He says his instructions are to put it only into the hands of Signor Monticelli, Excellency."

The angered Mastino marched over to the messenger. But Pan had overheard and told Hansum to follow him.

"The letter," demanded the Podesta of the messenger.

"Are you Monticelli?"

"I'm Monticelli," Hansum said quietly, appearing behind Mastino. The Podesta's eyes flashed at Hansum. Hansum reached

out and gently took the letter. "I'll read it here, Excellency." He unfolded the parchment. It was written in Earth Common. Hansum
translated. "Emergency. Come quickly. Guilietta very . . ." he
paused, shocked by the assault of one more hideous new fact. ". . .
very ill. Bring the little guy!"

"I'm to wait for a reply, Signor," the driver said.

"Tell them I'll be right there. No, wait, I'll ride with you,"
Hansum told him.

"I forbid it, Monticelli," Mastino ordered. "It's too dangerous
out there for you to travel."

"Then send soldiers with me. I must return tonight, Excellency.
You heard . . ."

"Nobody leaves this estate tonight, except you," he said to the
driver. "Leave. Now! While you can." Grazzana walked up to the
courier with his still-bloodied blade.  Nicademo whispered into
Mastino's ear for some moments, thinking nobody could hear. But
Pan could.

"Peace, cousin. If young Guilietta is so ill, she will expire soon,
as planned. Show compassion and it will deflect suspicion from
us. Besides, we must rush to Calabreezi and have a new cannon
made quicker than ever. Romero must be there." Mastino seemed
to soften.

"You are right, cousin. The first priority is to be with Calabreezi
and get the new cannon. We'll do that Monday. Messenger,"
Mastino called. "Hold! Tell Master della Cappa that Master
Monticelli will be there before daylight. General Chavelario, when
the new guard comes, have four of them turn around and escort
Master Monticelli and his friend back to Verona tonight. We will
go in the morning. Does this satisfy you, Romero?"

"Si, Excellency. Come on, Maruccio. Let's pack."

Back in their room, one of the maids brought Lincoln something for his pain. It was a small quantity of hemlock. Pan scanned
it and allowed Lincoln to only take a third. While they were waiting to leave, Lincoln lay down on top of Hansum's bed.

"When we get home, I'm going to fall into that straw pile and
sleep for days," Lincoln said. Then he passed out, staining the bed
sheets with his blood. Pan, sitting on the bed by Lincoln, watched

the worried Hansum pace and decided not to tell him what had passed between Nicademo and Mastino yet.

# Chapter 10

Hansum fell asleep only when the carriage left for Verona. It was well past midnight and he dreamed many frightening things, besides reliving the awful battle. In one dream, he was with a child, his child. They were playing in a meadow, which transformed into a busy cobblestone street. A fast-moving royal carriage appeared, heading straight toward the toddler. Hansum desperately reached out to save his boy, but somehow couldn't reach him. As the thundering hooves of the dream horses fell on the small victim, the boy turned his sad, childlike face toward Hansum. It turned into Guilietta, who mouthed the word *goodbye*. Hansum screamed and the thunder of the hooves and carriage wheels grew louder, buzzing in his ears. His body shook violently. The rumble of the dream turned into the noise of the Podesta's carriage going over the wooden drawbridge at Porta del Calzaro. Pan whispered in Hansum's ear loudly, and the teen woke with a start, relieved to be out of his nightmare.

*"We'll be home in a few minutes, Master. There's something important I must tell you."* Pan told Hansum what had transpired between the Baron and Podesta, and what he believed it meant, that they'd had Guilietta poisoned. Hansum got out of the carriage and ran toward the house as he was still being briefed.

His nightmare had turned real. The house door swung open even before he reached it, and Hansum quickly walked in, eyes wide, skin pale, worried sick at what he might find. He didn't say a word to anybody. Everybody just looked at him with weak, pained smiles. He rushed up the stairs, heading to Guilietta's room, when he passed the master bedroom and turned his head to peer inside. There, sitting up in her parents' bed, her hair combed, her hands neatly folded in her lap, was Guilietta. She smiled at him sweetly, and he ran to her, collapsing to his knees, his head falling into her lap. He wept openly.

"My darling, I'm fine. I'm fine, my love," Guilietta said as she lovingly soothed the top of his bowed head.

"The note . . . what I heard about the Podesta . . ." Hansum sobbed.

The Master and Shamira came in, closing the curtain behind them. They left the others downstairs to treat Lincoln's wounds.

"Just as you left, a woman came and gave Guilietta herbs," Shamira explained. "We thought it was medicinal, but it was poison. If Guil had taken it all week, she'd be dead now."

"And you found her out?"

"No, not till today. The Signora saved her."

"The Signora?"

"Si," Shamira continued. "She started taking the medicine when nobody was looking. We think Thursday. That saved Guilietta, but now the Signora is ill. She should start getting better, like Guilietta, in three days or so. Up and around in a week or two."

"My wife saved her," Agistino said, choking up again.

"Her and Saint Michael," Guilietta added with a smile.

"Well, I'll be," Hansum said.

"And your note, husband. Your blessed note. The Podesta has agreed to our marriage? Is that not true? I must hear it from your own lips."

"I do not know how sincere the Podesta is about that. I believe it was he who hired the poisoner."

Agistino ground his teeth. "We know. *Bastardo!*"

"Remember, Master," Shamira cautioned, "Master Calabreezi said we must act as if nothing happened. No matter what the Podesta says, we must act as if all is well."

"Master Calabreezi said that?" Hansum asked.

"Si. He cares for you greatly," Shamira continued. "But he acted quite frightened. He wouldn't say anything directly, but only implied things."

"I'm to see him on Monday. I'll talk more about this when we're alone. But his advice is good. And now that the first cannon is destroyed and we are at war with the Gonzaga, I'm more important than ever to della Scalla." That was the first time he had referred to Mastino by only his last name. "He must allow me what I ask now. But . . ."

"War?" Guilietta asked.

Hansum tried to explain what had happened earlier as simply and non-frighteningly as possible. He almost succeeded when there was a knock on the door frame and Lincoln came in. The wounds on his face and temple were now deep purple and black. His mouth was extremely swollen and the gap caused by his missing tooth stood out. Guilietta gasped when she saw him. Although Hansum tried to stop Lincoln, he continued Hansum's story. It just spewed out of him.

"They kidnapped Romero and had him tied up. But I shot the cannon over him and killed six of them and maimed four. So Romero got away and saved me."

"Stop!" Hansum said, but Lincoln's catharsis continued.

"Then the cannon blew up and killed five more of our guys. It was a bloody horror. A horror." Then he fell quiet. "I think I want to go to bed," he finally said.

"Si, it's late," Agistino pronounced. "Everybody to their beds."

It was well past daylight when the smells of cooking woke Hansum and Guilietta. They were cuddled in the Master and Signora's bed. They kissed and greeted each other. Shamira knocked on the door and brought some chamomile tea for Guilietta.

"I'll bring you up some chicken soup," Shamira said.

"I'll come down this morning," Guilietta smiled. "I feel much better."

"You should stay in bed," Shamira said.

"I'm much better. I'm not spotting now. See, my best medicine has come back to me."

"What's spotting?" Hansum asked.

The two girls giggled. "Women talk," Shamira said. "None of your business. Oh, I saw Signora Baroni back at the market. She sent herbs. I'll put them in your soup."

As Hansum helped her down the stairs, he saw that Guilietta's light, bouncing step was gone. He had to hold one of her arms and she the banister. Shamira brought a blanket for Guilietta to sit upon and wrap around her shoulders. Everyone else was already in the shop. Two solidiers were at the front door and two were by the shop.

Before Guilietta ate the chicken soup, Hansum looked at it closely, pretending to sniff it. But Pan was actually scanning the herbs. While Shamira was out taking food to Lincoln in the loft, the front door opened. In walked Nicademo. He looked at Hansum directly, with a grave face. Hansum rose, holding back an anger that quickly rose in his breast.

"Calabreezi's dead," the Baron said.

Hansum sat down again. "How?" he finally asked.

"He died at the Jew's, Signor de Levi's. The money lender."

"He was killed?"

"No. Just collapsed. Old age. De Levi's son is a fine physician. He's mine too, in fact. He was right there and couldn't help." Hansum sat back down, stunned. "My cousin is beside himself. The situation is desperate."

Hansum tapped his language node, and spoke quietly in Earth Common, making like he was crossing himself and saying a prayer under his breath.

"Can you talk me through the cannon casting, Pan?"

*"Yes,"* was the reply. *"Now is the time to sue for an understanding with the Podesta. But be very careful."*

Hansum clicked the node again.

"I can oversee the cannon production. Master Calabreezi and I discussed it thoroughly and he has good journeymen. All they need is leadership and to be shown the way to use the new molds."

Nicademo smiled. "I told the Podesta we could count on you," he said, taking a step forward.

Hansum stood again. "Keep seated here, my dear," he said to Guilietta. "And please be silent. I must talk with the Baron. Over there." Hansum got up and walked to Nicademo. He put his hand on the older man's shoulder, and then took it off. "Excuse my familiarity."

"No, no, it's all right, Romero. We are friends."

Hansum didn't reply to that.

"I can help. I want to help. And I will be loyal. But . . . Well, you know the situation." He whispered, "Lady Beatrice — and Guilietta. Can I get real assurances that my betrothal to Guilietta will not be interfered with? For if it is . . ." Now it was Nicademo who put his hand on Hansum's shoulder.

"My friend, let me sit with you and the lady. I have good news." Hansum gestured over to the bench. The Baron took his seat opposite Guilietta. "These sad situations often open up opportunities," he began. "But first, let us not deceive ourselves or each other. Let us talk openly. Now, let me say to the lady that I was very unhappy about how you were treated." He paused and looked sympathetically at Guilietta. Then he looked at Hansum. "Some would say that in the beginning the transaction between the Podesta and yourself was understandable. After all, you came from nothing, out of nowhere. But since then, Romero, you have proven yourself in so many ways. Your worth is much higher, your talents proven. In short, your negotiating power is greater. And as I said, in these days of change, where Calabreezi's death has caused a hole in the machinery of our enterprises, it opens up opportunities. For you, I hope. If you grasp it." Nicademo paused.

Hansum, now knowing how these people worked, understood that if he offered his help quickly, Nicademo would most probably lessen his offer. So Hansum just looked at the Baron blankly.

"Please go on, Excellency," Hansum said. "What is your good news?"

Nicademo took a deep breath and smiled.

"The Podesta has asked me to come here and say, without reservation, that he now trusts you totally and beyond any question. He therefore retracts any restrictions on your request to marry the fair Guilietta."

# Chapter 11

The Baron told Hansum that it was very important for him to attend Master Calabreezi's funeral mass at Santa Anastasia that afternoon. A carriage would pick him up mid-day, but till then, he could revel in the warm family feelings that now abounded in the della Cappa home. All were ecstatic with the news about the Podesta giving Hansum and Guilietta permission to wed. The news seemed to hasten the Signora's recovery. Everybody sat around her bed, laughing and talking at the same time. Hansum noticed the sweet and contented look on his addled mother-in-law's face as she looked up and saw her family chattering away.

The house was impressed when Hansum showed himself off in his new clothes. Guilietta was still weak, so when the carriage came for Hansum, he told her to stay on the bench.

"We'll all be going to church together again soon, my darling. For our official wedding."

Santa Anastasia was a sombre place that day. There were hundreds of people there to honor Master Calabreezi. Hansum cried to see his mentor on a bier in his family's private chapel. Men milled around the body, paying their respects. Hansum noticed that when the men looked at him, they talked in hushed tones, doffing their hats and bowing.

"What's this all about?" he asked Nicademo.

A faint smile came to the Baron's face. He motioned in a direction around some heavy church columns.

"They already know what you will learn in a few moments."

Hansum went where he was instructed. His eyes were still wet when he came upon the Podesta, sitting in a corner with several other nobles and Lady Beatrice. He bowed gravely to them.

"He was such an interesting man," Hansum said.

"You were one of the few who got through his hard exterior," Mastino said.

"It was my privilege."

Mastino motioned that the nobles standing by him should leave, except for Beatrice. When they were gone, he looked at Hansum directly.

"I understand you can oversee both the making of the cannon and the black powder."

"Si, Excellency. I foresee no problem."

"It's a lot of work and travel."

"I know, Excellency. But I have what I need now."

"Beatrice, my dear, I asked you to stay and say your greetings to Master Monticelli. But now I must speak with him alone."

"Of course, Father." Beatrice rose and looked directly at Hansum. "I understand congratulations are due to you in the matter of a betrothal, Signor."

"Si, Lady Beatrice. Grazie."

"It explains much as to the verse about vows, Signor. I wish you well."

"And I you, Lady Beatrice. I hope we may be friends."

"More than friends," Mastino interjected, "allies. For when I am gone, it will be those of your generation who will guard our much-expanded dominions for the next. Now, run along, dear." Mastino motioned for Hansum to sit next to him and spoke quietly. "There is much to be done to recover from our setback," the Podesta began. "In the morning, go to Calabreezi's and make immediate plans with his journeymen to remake the cannon. When this is started, run back to the south for the black powder."

Hansum paused as he listened to Pan.

"I agree, Excellency. Within the month we can be training three new groups of cannoneers. After that, if there are no major changes needed in the cannon's design, we can produce ten per month. By the fall, with God's grace, we will have the powder mill."

"With God's grace," repeated Mastino, crossing himself lazily.

"And within a year, we should have masters in place for both enterprises. This will allow me to oversee them, but not be mired in day-to-day details. Then I may concentrate on the new ideas you saw."

"I like the way you think, Romero. But don't let your youthful ambitions cause you to overstep yourself." He looked around to make sure nobody was listening to what he was about to say. "That was my downfall when I was a youth. Never forget that you have to drag all the dolts and fools, the ones who do the work, along with you. They will delay and ruin all the fine plans in that head of yours. Are you listening to what I say?" Hansum nodded. Mastino then reached in his cloak and took out several parchment scrolls.

"Here. A wedding present. Open them. A man in your position needs land and a household." The first scroll was the deed to the Calabreezi estate. Apparently it was five hundred acres with two hundred foundry workers, peasants and much produce and livestock. The second parchment was a promissory note for several thousand florins. Hansum was now a very wealthy man.

*"Don't make a big deal of it. Act grateful, but subdued. And repeat that you will be loyal."*

"I am overwhelmed, Excellency," Hansum said quietly. "Please forgive my lack of open enthusiasm. Today is not a time for me to bring attention to myself. Know, Excellency, that I shall strive to make myself worthy of your trust."

"Many people have said similar things to me, Romero, but you I truly believe. I'm also giving you Nicademo for the next year. You will need him. He will organize your house and affairs. Have your small friend, the one who cried after the battle, live at the Baron's elbow. I think he could be your administrator after some years. I'm also giving you Calabreezi's carriages and stable. You will need them to get around. Is all this too much to take in quickly?"

*"It's a lot, Excellency. But nothing I can't handle. Consider all you need accomplished."*

Hansum repeated this and Mastino sighed. He patted Hansum's hand and then dismissed him, pointing to Master Calabreezi's widow.

"I shall pay my respects, Excellency."

Later that day, Nicademo took Hansum to meet with Eli de Levi. Hansum deposited his promissory note with the money lender and discussed what the needs of the projects would be. Hansum was completely out of his depth with the financing, but Pan saw him through it. In the end, Pan had Hansum state that he didn't think money was his strong suit, and ask if de Levi would mind him coming for counsel once in a while. He had a lot to learn, he told them. Both Nicademo and Eli smiled broadly at this, congratulating the boy for not letting his new wealth swell his head.

"Shrunk it is more the truth," Hansum admitted. "I'm realizing how much I don't know."

"Realizing how little you know is the first sign of true wisdom," Eli said.

That evening, back at the della Cappas', Hansum told only Guilietta, her father, Shamira and Lincoln about their new fortune and lands. No need to brag to the others or get rumours going around the neighborhood.

"Why are you not excited, my darling?" Hansum asked Guilietta. "You are going to have your own home. An estate. Servants to boss around."

"I'm just feeling tired, husband. I think I will sleep a little. In the morning, when I wake and know all this is not a dream, then I will be excited."

"Master della Cappa, why are you crying?" Shamira asked.

"I'm so happy," Agistino croaked.

When Hansum put Guilietta to bed, Pan had him look closely into her eyes so he could scan her. Then he had her open her mouth wide, and even show him her fingernails. Pan looked for signs of complications from the poisoning.

"You sleep now, darling," Hansum said. "I must have a quick talk with Carmella and Maruccio." Bembo and Ugilino were out again that evening, so the teenagers were able to have a meeting with Pan in the workshop.

"I think it best if we all move to the new estate," Pan began. "Even the lensmaking facilities. In a bit over a month a great pandemic is going to reach Verona. It was known as the Black Death . . ." but before he could finish his sentence, his image wobbled. "Oh dear," he said.

"Pan, what's wrong?" Shamira asked.

"When the hat was dropped during battle, a small crack developed in my lamp. We shall have to be very careful with me from now on. We must reinforce my shell. I'm not impervious, remember."

Shamira took his lamp and inspected it with a lens.

"There's a tiny crack, barely perceptible," she said. "I'll use mastic and encase you in tin for now. But you're sure you're okay, Pan?"

"My gelbrain is still functioning perfectly. It's just the housing is rubbing against it slightly."

Then Hansum asked, "How about those scans of Guilietta? What did you see?"

"My scans show a low grade infection which could cause some problems if not treated immediately. We need some specific herbs and spores to make an antidote. But we must watch her carefully, for her immune system is very low. That's why it would be best if we isolate everyone at the estate."

"I can go see Signora Baroni at the market tomorrow morning, unless you think we shouldn't wait. I know where she lives," Shamira said.

"Now is best. Take down this list and then get the Master or Bembo to walk you."

"I can go," Lincoln said.

"No, you must sleep more," Pan ordered, "to recover from your injuries. And you will be going with Hansum in the morning. Let me add some herbs for Lincoln too."

"Hansum, you go be with Guil," Shamira said.

# Chapter 12

Late the next morning, Hansum and Lincoln arrived at the Calabreezi estate. It was a sombre place. Hansum could tell that, not only were the workers and peasants mourning the loss of the only master they had ever known, they were also understandably worried about their futures with the new young master. Adding to the tension was the fact that soldiers had surrounded the estate and officers were questioning everybody.

Hansum knew from being here the other week that Calabreezi had several long tables set up in a barn, where crews took their meals together. He had all the workers close to the house go to the tables and had women bring wine and food so they could have a long talk. Many workers were crowded around, including Calabreezi's four journeymen bell makers. Hansum started the meeting with a prayer, which Pan dictated to him. Then he made a fairly short speech about why they were getting back to work so soon after Calabreezi's passing. As wine was poured for all, he asked people to share remembrances of the old master. For a good hour, people cried and laughed as they recounted stories of the curmudgeonly man who had as pure a heart as the world would allow. When the question of the soldiers came up, Hansum told everyone there was some possibility of danger, and if anyone was afraid, they were free to go. They would be helped to find employment elsewhere.

Pan had Hansum end the meeting with another prayer, announcing that everyone was to have the rest of the day off.

Everyone except the four journeymen left. They sat around one table with Hansum, Lincoln, Nicademo and the officer who was to be in charge of security. Hansum personally poured more wine into everyone's cup.

"Signori," he began, "be not troubled by who will be the new master of this place. Be certain it will not be me. I know only of casting from a designer's point of view. Actual production is not my strength. As for yourselves, and the question of who's to be boss, for now I say, work as brothers. For over the next year we will aim to make one hundred of this first cannon design. But after that, and for years to come, we shall create many more designs and many more hundreds of these. We will need many more foundries. If you are deserving and loyal, each one of you will be a master with his own foundry. There is so much to be accomplished, so much to discover together. And when it's all said and done, so much to be gained, which will make our families and state more secure and prosperous." Hansum paused and looked at the four journeymen, their faces a mixture of tears and smiles. "So, Signori, I will be away much, and not able to always oversee things? What do you say to all this?"

Geraldo, the oldest journeyman, was almost thirty-five.

"Master, what you say gives much comfort." The other three nodded, one wiping his eyes of a great flow of tears. "However, even among equals, there comes a time when one voice must make a decision to break an impasse. Without a master, how can this be done?"

"A wise observation. Geraldo, you are the oldest. You will be master for the first three months, breaking any impasses that come up. Then, in the second quarter of the year, the next oldest will be master, and so on. This way all will learn a master's discipline."

"No," said the man who was crying hardest. "Not me. I cannot be a master. I'm not worthy."

"Why not?" Hansum asked. The man continued weeping into his hands, unable to speak.

"My older brother, Darmo, is a very good worker," another journeyman said, "very reliable. But I do not believe he has the temperament to be a master, Signor."

"Or the brains," Darmo said, finally able to get a few words out.

"Ah," Hansum said. "Well, this is the aim in life, is it not, to know one's limits and abilities? I congratulate you, Darmo, in being man enough to recognize yours. So, we shall have three rotating masters for the time. Does everybody agree?" The journeymen looked at each other, amazed that they were being consulted. "Well, if you are all to be masters," Hansum continued, "I must start treating you as such. What say you all?"

Geraldo lifted his goblet.

"In the memory of Master Calabreezi, I pledge to work in harmony with my fellows and to obey the decisions of whoever is master at the time."

Everybody lifted their glasses and drank to the toast, then crossed themselves.

"So, let us look at the plans that Master Calabreezi and I drew up," Hansum said. He pulled out a large scroll and smoothed it out on the table. Hansum described how it would be a heavy eight-piece plaster mold that would allow them to cast the cannon with its core already in place. "Tomorrow a master mold maker of intricate bronze statues will be here with his staff. He will work with you till it's completed. You are being given a week." They all studied the plans and had good questions. After a time, Hansum said, "That's enough for today. We must still mourn the passing of our master and friend. Geraldo, take the plans and study them. Think of every step of what we're to do and how we are going to organize so you may work smoothly with the mold maker. We shall see you all tomorrow at first light."

Hansum was invited by the Baron to stay at the main house, which was, after all, his now. But he declined.

"Signora Calabreezi may stay there as long as she needs. Maruccio and I will lodge at the guest house with you, if that is acceptable, Baron."

"Of course, Romero. Whatever you say. You are master here."

And then it really struck Hansum. He was the deeded owner of a large estate. He had gold deposited with the same banker as the ruler of the region. Servants were coming to him and asking about meals and foods and budgets. Nicademo interceded and put his hand on Lincoln's shoulder.

"Allow me to take Maruccio aside and counsel him on constructing a budget for your household, Romero."

"It would be an honor to have you do this for me, Signor. Give me a moment with him first." Alone with Lincoln, Hansum said, "It looks like things are turning around for us pretty quickly. Here, take Pan with you."

*"Take care,"* Pan whispered to both of them. *"Realize the competing forces that you are working within. The stubborn muse, Fortuna, changes sides often during this era."*

⧗

By the middle of the second day, Hansum became somewhat frustrated. It was taking time for the mold maker and journeymen to understand the plan's advanced casting processes, which actually came from the early eighteenth century. They wanted to alter them to be more like their current processes.

*"Patience, Master, patience,"* Pan counselled. *"These are talented men of another era. They will get it quickly enough."* Pan was right. By the end of the third day, the reusable molds were well under way. A sculptor even created a bas relief of the della Scalla dog motif, with the cannon's touch hole right in the middle of its open mouth. Below this image was inscribed the year 1348.

The plan was to make three of the cannons from the first mold, then test them at the now-fortified Bella Flora estate. Nicademo told Hansum that by the time they got back with the new weapons, there would be over two hundred and fifty soldiers patrolling the roads and land for twenty miles around. Just before supper, the Podesta showed up to inspect the progress for himself. He smiled radiantly at Hansum, hugged him repeatedly and lavished great praise on him in front of everybody. Spirits were very high at supper that night. They sat and toasted each other, speculating on what their bright futures would bring.

While Hansum was well into his cups, a guard came into the room and whispered in his ear. Hansum smiled widely.

"Of course. Bring her in," he said, beaming. "Carmella's here," he said to Lincoln.

They both got up from their chairs to greet Shamira, both smiling broadly from the wine. But she did not smile back. She grabbed Hansum's hands and whispered in his ear.

"Guilietta is very ill again. She has a high fever. We need Pan to diagnose her. Immediately."

Shocked, Hansum looked up, his face ashen.

"Signori, I must go back to Verona. My betrothed is not well. Excuse me."

The Podesta got up. He put a hand on Hansum's shoulder and looked into the shocked youth's eyes.

"But Romero, what can you do there? You are not a physician. And what about the cannon?"

Hansum gave Mastino a look that conveyed everything he was thinking: 'How dare you? It was you who caused this illness in the first place.' But this is not what Hansum said. He took a long breath.

"Everyone knows what they must do. They don't need me here."

The Podesta and Baron looked at each other with worried eyes. Hansum stared at them, daring either to say something. Then he turned and led the other two teens out into the night.

Pan popped out on the seat of the hired carriage as soon as they were off the estate and speeding down the bumpy road.

"What are her symptoms?" the hologram asked.

"Fever, sweating, pain in her belly, and below that. Bad pain."

They didn't talk much, as there was little to be said. But when they reached the northern city gates, there was a line of carriages and people waiting to get through. Hansum jumped out of the carriage and went to the lead guard.

"We've got to get into the city quickly. Someone in my family is sick."

"There are many sick people, Signor," he said, pointing at the line. People were sitting or lying on the road or hanging out of their carriage windows, groaning. Hansum took a step toward one of the people on the ground.

"Not that one, Signor," the guard warned. "He's dead."

*"It's happening a month earlier than the records indicate,"* Pan whispered to Hansum.

"What?"

*"The Black Death. The plague."*

Hansum reached into his pouch and gave the guard a florin.

"I must get in immediately." The guard looked at the gold coin and called to his men.

"Move those wagons aside. The Signor has urgent business in the city."

As the carriage window passed one house, they watched as two nuns and a priest carried a wrapped body out of the dwelling and placed it on an open wagon. The crying family was being comforted by another nun. They saw a similar scene, where a monk carried a child's body out of a house. A priest had to hold back the grieving parents from following it.

*"Historical records show the plague didn't show up in this area till May of 1348. The records must be wrong. It's showing up a month early."*

There were usually many people walking about the city at this time of evening. Today the streets were deserted, except for a few lonely souls who were stooped and ill-looking.

"But when we left a few days ago, everything was okay," Lincoln said.

"Just hours after that, people started getting sick," Shamira informed them. "Several people who I saw healthy in the market yesterday morning died this afternoon — Signora Spagnoli, for one."

"The butcher's wife?" Lincoln said, shocked. "She, she was so nice."

Pan made himself very small on the front seat, so as not to be seen from the outside.

"The bubonic plague was very virulent. Is virulent," he said, correcting his tense. "The writer Boccaccio wrote that people ate lunch with their friends on Earth and supper with their ancestors in paradise."

"Is this what Guilietta has?" Hansum asked, his eyes wide with fright.

"I don't know," Shamira said. "That's why I came and got you, so Pan can check her."

"How's everyone else at home?" Lincoln asked.

"So far, everybody's good," she answered.

"You all should stay healthy," Pan said, "if your inoculation implants are functioning."

"I just got mine updated before History Camp," Hansum said.

"I can't remember," Lincoln said.

"I'm pretty sure I got mine close to three years ago," Shamira said. "But it could be longer. I'm not sure."

"Well, the records show the first round of plague lasted three or four months in Verona before it burned out," Pan said. "Obviously the records are off, but chances are you all are safe for now. None of you have even gotten the sniffles or an infection from any of your injuries. Your immune systems must be strong. But the same can't be said about Guilietta or the Signora. We should definitely move the whole family out to the country immediately. Tomorrow. We'll quarantine the estate till things pass." The carriage pulled up to the house. Pan disappeared into Hansum's hat and the three teenagers got out of the carriage. Entering the front room, they saw only Ugilino and Bembo at the table. Bembo motioned that everybody else was upstairs. Hansum and Shamira started up the steps and Lincoln took a seat at the table.

"Lucky I'm ending up with Serindella, eh?" Ugilino said after Hansum. Hansum ignored him, but saw Bembo shove Ugilino so hard that he fell to the floor. Lincoln scowled at Ugilino, even baring his teeth. Ugilino saw the missing tooth and cut lip. "Eh, you look more and more like me," he said from the straw.

The Master, Signora and Nuca, along with Father Lurenzano, were in Guilietta's room. The priest had on his vestments. Hansum couldn't see Guilietta's face for the crowd.

"Oh my little lamb," the Signora cooed. "Your husband is here."

Hansum smiled and stepped forward, expecting to see Guilietta awake. He got down on his knees to be close to her face. But as he drew near, he realized that she was unconscious. Her face was gaunt and sweaty. Her hands, neatly folded over her slightly distended belly, continually shivered. Hansum touched her cheek and the side of her neck.

"She's burning up!" he exclaimed. "Why aren't you doing something for her fever?"

*"Pull back her eyelid and let me scan through her pupil,"* Pan whispered.

"She is very ill, my son," the priest said. "I have given her the last rites. We're letting her go now, to stop her suffering."

"Not yet," Hansum said with determination. He lifted one of Guilietta's eyelids and got very close to it. Pan scanned her. Hansum didn't care how odd it looked to the others.

"Perhaps some of you can leave," Shamira said.

"Don't give me orders, kitchen girl," Lurenzano barked.

"Father!" Hansum snapped. "All of you. Please leave me for a few minutes with my wife. Please." Everybody left Shamira and Hansum with Guilietta.

*"Pull down the cover. I want to scan her abdomen."* Hansum and Shamira exposed Guilietta's body. Hansum put his hand lightly on her belly and the unconscious Guilietta grimaced. *"As I feared,"* Pan whispered. *"She has a severe uterine infection, left over from the poisoning. Gently lift her arms. Shamira, you check her. Do you feel any lumps, no matter how small? There will be a thickening of the lymph nodes because of the infection, but we're looking for distinct roundish lumps. They may have a dark discolouration."*

"I can feel a thickness, but no lumps," Shamira said.

*"Now do the same thing on the inside of the groin. There are lymph nodes there too."*

"No," Shamira said, "but she's really hot."

"No lumps means she doesn't have the plague?" Hansum asked.

*"Hopefully,"* Pan answered.

"Tell us what to do, Pan. Quickly," Hansum begged.

*"We must get her core temperature down. Have Nuca and the Signora sponge-bathe her for half an hour with cool water. Make some willow bark tea and let it cool. Get as much of that in her as possible. But we all need to have a meeting immediately. I must dictate a more aggressive antibacterial recipe. Shamira must take the carriage and find Signora Baroni quickly. She has the skills and, with a bit more information, she should be able to prepare what we need."*

Hansum took quick, shallow breaths. Tears formed in his eyes. He bent close to Guilietta and lightly kissed her cheek, but she was so hot, he backed off. His large tears fell on the bed.

"We must hurry," Shamira said.

As the two came down the steps, Lincoln stood up from the table, ready for action. Hansum was looking fragile, so Shamira explained to Nuca and the Signora what Pan had instructed.

"My children," Father Lurenzano interrupted, "this is all unnecessary? I have seen it often. Let her lie in peace. God will soon release her from her agony."

"Father, please don't interfere," Hansum said, his eyes still wet from crying. "We know some things that can help."

"You can help? There is hope?" a tearful Signora asked.

"Hope?" Agistino said, sitting at the table, a goblet in his hand.

Hansum went over to Agistino. He could smell wine on the Master's breath.

"Master, this is no time to fall into old habits," Hansum said. "We need your strength."

"I tried to stop him," Lincoln said, "but he's been drinking all day, apparently."

"The Father told me it was okay," Agistino advised. "He gave me absolution."

"Absolution from drinking? No, Master, you mustn't. The family needs you strong."

"I am his spiritual guide now," Lurenzano pronounced. "In times like this, a bit of wine dulls the pain and lifts the spirit. It will also help ward off the sickness that is going around," he said, lifting a glass of his own. "I know these things."

"The sickness that is going around is caused by the bites of fleas off ship rats from the east. That and unsanitary, dirty cities and malnutrition. Wine will do nothing for it."

"Rats and fleas from the east?" the priest laughed. "A bit of dirt, dangerous? How incredible! The illness is caused by bad humors in the air, punishments from God. Some say the Jews are poisoning the wells."

"Oh, for Cristo's sake," Hansum scoffed.

"Don't take the Lord's name in vain!" Lurenzano blared.

"Master, please trust me on this," Hansum said. "We have no time to argue."

Agistino was bleary-eyed. He looked at Hansum, then at the goblet of wine in his hand.

"I don't know, my son."

"You must trust me, Master. Please."

"He must trust God," Father Lurenzano said. "We must all trust God. Guilietta is in His hands now."

Hansum became angry. He pointed a finger at the priest.

"You stay out of this, Father. This is my family. The Master is ill so I will say what is to be done." The priest's eyes glowered at Hansum, but he did not reply.

"Oh dear," the Signora said meekly.

"Nuca, Signora, do as I've asked," Hansum ordered. "Please. Bembo, go get buckets of very cold water from the fountain. Quickly. And don't leave Guilietta lying by herself too long. We'll be in the shop for but a short while, writing up some instructions for medicine. Let's go."

The teenagers ran through the alley. Their mission was clear and their time short. A storm was on its way. The wind was picking up and the workshop doors and shutters were rattling. In the workshop, Hansum sat down at a work table. He took his hat off and tossed it on the table. Pan's little brass lamp, reinforced with mastic and tin, fell out of its pouch. As it rolled on the wooden tabletop, a full-sized image of Pan tumbled out, rolling as the lamp did.

"Be careful, Master," the holographic imp cried, his image wobbling and going translucent.

"Oh my God! I'm sorry, Pan. I'm sorry," Hansum said, his voice breaking up. "I'm so scared."

"My shell is becoming more fragile," Pan said. "We must be cautious."

"I'm sorry, I'm sorry," Hansum sobbed.

"You cry and let it out," Shamira said. "Pan, dictate what we need."

"Yes, Mistress. Touch your translation node. This should be written in Earth Common, in case it falls into someone else's hands." Shamira wrote frantically.

# Chapter 13

Ugilino found it all very curious. He watched the goings-on with intense medieval fatalism. 'Perhaps, if Guilietta dies,' he thought, 'the orphans will leave. It could be better for me. And the way Romero and the Father were acting to each other, there's surely going to be trouble.'

"Drink, Agistino," he heard Lurenzano bid the Master. "Drink a little. Join me in a toast to God."

"I dunno," Agistino said. "Perhaps Romero is right."

"I'll have some," Ugilino said.

"Of course, Ugi. Help yourself," the priest said. "Bembo, do you want a cup?"

The stolid journeyman was sitting on the stairs. He had carried two large buckets of cool water from the fountain and was waiting to be called if the women needed more. Bembo shook his head and looked down at the steps. The father frowned. Ugilino poured himself a full cup of wine from the pitcher, and downed it in one go.

"So, this is what the nobles drink, eh? It's smooth, but no kick! Bah!"

"That Romero is a forceful young man," Father Lurenzano said to Agistino. "He is even telling you and me what to do."

"He's a good boy." Agistino said, crying. After every sentence he cried harder. "He loves my daughter. Really loves her. He brought us wealth. He's a big landowner now. My daughter could have been a noble. My grandchildren could have been princes and princesses."

"But he takes the Lord's name in vain. And here, Agistino, take some little bit of wine. That's what God gave it to us for. Si, Ugilino, you have some more too."

The world was a haze to Guilietta. She felt the cool cloths behind her head and neck. Hands were about her body, changing the cloths. She became aware that she was sucking on a wet cloth with a bittersweet taste. 'Willow tea and honey,' she thought. Then she became aware of voices. Familiar voices. Her eyes opened a crack and the dull light of the lamp-lit room opened up to her.

"I'm still alive," she whispered.

"Oh my little chicken," the Signora cried, kissing her. "You've not left us."

"Mama, Romero? Is Romero here?"

"Si, si. He's close by. Nuca, call for him. Quickly, dear."

Nuca leaned out of the small room and called down the steps. "Bembo. Send for Omero. Gui awake."

Ugilino was already up and going out the front door before Bembo was down the stairs.

"I'll tell him," Ugilino said. "I'm going to take a piss."

"Tell him first. Then piss," Bembo said sternly.

"Yeah, yeah," Ugilino answered belligerently. The drunken oaf trotted down the alley, almost crossing his legs, he had to go so badly. "Damn, it's starting to rain," he said out loud. The wind was now causing the shutters and door of the shop to clatter loudly. He reached for the door handle, but hesitated. His urge to relieve himself was so great, he couldn't wait. He took a few steps to the side, pulled his chausses down and urinated against the shop in front of a shuttered window. There was a thin crack between two pieces of wood. Light from the inside room was shining through. He squinted and leaned forward, resting his forehead against the planks. The light was brighter than an oil lamp could produce. His eyes focussed on what was inside the shop. At the worktable, Shamira was writing while Hansum and Lincoln looked on. And on the table was — a creature. Ugilino blinked and shook his head. His flow of urine stopped abruptly as he sucked in a fright-ened breath. Was it a dwarf, like he had seen at a carnival once? But it had pointed ears, was fawn-colored, with dwarfish arms and hands and it didn't have pants. And the legs and feet, they were hairy and — shaped like a goat's.

"The creature from Hell!' Ugilino gasped. The creature sud-denly turned and looked right at the window shutter where Ugilino stood. Two golden goat-slit eyes seemed to burn right into Ugilino's. The startled apprentice pulled away from the crack in the shutter and ran.

⧗

"Pan, what's wrong?" Shamira asked.

"I thought I detected something through a crack in the shutter. We'll have to fix my shell properly. My senses are becoming impaired with these temporary measures."

"What was it?" Lincoln asked.

"I don't know. Probably a bat. Here, let's finish these notes quickly."

⧗

Ugilino ran as fast as he could down the alley. That is, as fast as he could while he finished relieving himself. He was out of breath and stained with spots of urine as he fell back into the house.

"Master, Father," he gasped. "I've seen Satan! Satan! He's in the workshop!" The now-drunken priest and lensmaker looked up from the table, bleary-eyed and confused. "I mean it. And the orphans. I saw them in the workshop talking with a devil. He has yellow eyes and feet like a goat. He shines like a lamp. He's..." then he paused as he remembered. "It's the same creature from Hell."

"What are you talking about?" the priest scoffed.

"When they first came here, I had a dream, where a servant of Hell came to me and made me promise to change my ways. But it wasn't a dream. It was their way of stealing my rightful place. Damn those orphans!"

"Don't talk nonsense," Agistino said, slurring his words.

"Come, come quickly," Ugilino argued. "You'll see it's true."

The priest stood up and Ugilino could see his eyes sober somewhat. Agistino pushed himself from the table and spilled his goblet. When they were outside and the rain fell on them, Agistino cursed at Ugilino.

"Merda for brains! You drag me through the rain on some fantasy?"

"No Master, quickly. You will see. Hush. Don't alarm them," he said as they reached the workshop. "There. See the crack in the shutter? Look through that."

Agistino and Father Lurenzano peered through the crack at the same time. As the sliver of light reached their eyes, they both gasped. There on the table, just as Ugilino had described, was the image of a goat man. He was looking down at the teenagers, who were huddled in front of him. Shamira was writing and the two boys were leaning over something, working on some type of charm or talisman.

"They revere him," Lurenzano said. "They pray to him." Agistino and the priest pulled away from the wall. "They are servants of Lucifer!" Father Lurenzano decreed.

"Such evil in my own house!" Agistino gasped.

"See, I'm not merda for brains."

Just as a bolt of lightning lit the sky, Father Lurenzano threw open the shop door and bounded in, Agistino and Ugilino close behind him. The three stared menacingly at the room's occupants. Pan and the teenagers looked up.

"It's you!" Ugilino said to Pan.

⧗

"Si, dear Ugilino. It is I," Pan said, computing his best response to such a calamitous situation. Pan smiled at the other two men and bowed. "Welcome, Signori. Perhaps I should reveal myself to you in my true form."

"Devil!" Father Lurenzano shouted, holding up the large cross from his chest in front of the apparition. Agistino crossed himself.

"No, no, not a devil," Pan said lightly. "I am . . ." and with that, Pan transformed himself into a shimmering image of a beautiful man in white robes, with a close-cropped golden beard and lovely long limbs. He floated in the air, away from the table where both the teens and his cracked lamp were. "I am Aurelius, patron saint of orphans. I am here to give these children guidance and help."

"My orphans have a saint helping them?" Agistino said, crossing himself and falling to his knees.

"Ridiculous!" Father Lurenzano spat. "You're a liar. This is a devil's deception. I will not believe you."

"Si, you came to me as that ugly devil and made me do all sorts of awful things," Ugilino said.

"This is the devil who visited you before?" the astonished priest asked. "The one you spoke of?"

"Si, Father."

"And he made you do terrible things?" A fire and brimstone rage erupted from Lurenzano. "Demon, tempter, monster, fiend, ogre!" he cried. "You corrupted one of my flock!" Pan's image of Aurelius laughed.

"Corrupted him? Far less than you, I'd wager. Tell your confessor the terrible things I bid you do, Ugilino."

"He forbid me to sleep in the loft," he said accusingly. "He made me wash and keep myself clean. He made me . . ." and then even Ugilino seemed to realize how foolish this sounded. "Made me go to church every week . . ."

Father Lurenzano shouted a response at the top of his voice.

"The works of the devil are devious. He says and does things that sound sweet and righteous, but are designed to bring more souls to Hell in the end."

"Si! That's right!" Ugilino agreed.

"Your angelic appearance is made to confuse us," the priest proclaimed, "but we will not be deceived." He took an ominous step toward Pan.

"Tut tut, good father," Pan said. "I appeared as Pan for the children's comfort. Pan is a comical character of the Greeks. These fair orphans, who are from – Greece, gained solace at seeing something that reminded them of home, tis all."

"Liar!" Lurenzano shouted. "I'll exorcise you from this place. Be gone!" The priest ran right for the holographic image, waving his cross. Pan zipped through the air, again, away from his faulty lamp. The priest ran right through him and banged into a wall.

"Good father, did you hurt yourself?" Pan asked nicely.

"Don't show a care for me, demon! All true Christians will attack you and your minions."

"That's right, Father," Ugilino said, picking up the ax leaning by the fireplace. He held it up with two hands and stepped toward Pan.

Pan's image rose to the ceiling.

"Didn't my advice make you a better person?" Pan asked Ugilino.

"I'd rather be a murdering, filth-covered soldier in God's army, than a noble in the devil's," Ugilino answered. And with that, he charged Pan and swung the ax with all his might. It whooshed right though the hologram and came down on one of the new lathes, breaking the spindle frame in half.

"My lathe!" the Master screamed, jumping to his feet.

"Ugilino, stop!" the teenagers shouted. Pan zipped across the room to another corner, but Ugilino followed him. Father Lurenzano chanted and made signs of the cross. Ugilino, eyes filled with indignation, looked at the priest. Lurenzano nodded a benediction for Ugilino to continue and the ax was again swung through the image of the angel. It landed on a corner work table, breaking several lookers and spectacle frames. The Master screamed even louder, but Ugilino continued swinging at the retreating image. Many of the blows ended by breaking more lookers, lenses and spectacles. Grinding tools and supplies were strewn everywhere.

"Stop, fool!" Agistino cried again, but Ugilino continued tearing around with the sharp, heavy weapon. Pan's only thought was to stay away from the table with his lamp on it. He flew back to another corner and Ugilino followed, swinging a determined blow that whipped through the hologram and smashed into another new lathe.

"Not the lathes!" Agistino screamed. "That's our living!"

"Please, Ugilino," Shamira shouted. "Don't do this!"

"Stop, stop!" Hansum screamed, "We don't have time!"

Just then, the Signora waddled into the shop.

"What in the world is . . ." When she saw the image of the angel, she fell to her knees.

"It is the devil in an angel's form, Signora," the priest cried. "Do not be deceived."

"No, no," Hansum pleaded. "It's my guardian angel, just as he said. He's come to give us information to save Guilietta. It was him who told me all the things to make me look clever. Please, please, let him save my wife!"

"I am Aurileus, Signora della Cappa," Pan said.

"You know my name, angel?"

"Of course, my daughter. I am the patron saint of orphans. I left these children in your care and watched how you and your husband loved them so well. I've come to repay that debt by helping save your child."

"Don't believe him, Signora," the father shouted. "It is the devil!"

"We saw them with a vile-looking creature," Agistino said to his wife. "A little man, half goat and half I don't know what. They were speaking to it, praying to it. We cannot let these youths into our home again."

"But they brought us prosperity, husband. Food, work, love."

"All to seduce you with, Signora," Lurenzano argued.

"You're crazy!" Hansum screamed. "Guilietta has an infection and fever. We must cure the infection so she can heal. These are the instructions for Signora Baroni and a midwife," he said, waving the papers in front of the priest and master. "If they follow these..."

Father Lurenzano snatched the pages from Hansum. They were written in twenty-fourth-century Earth Common, in a script far different from the monastic writing.

"This must be some satanic hand," Lurenzano said. "I am an educated man. I've read over a score of books. This looks like nothing I have ever seen."

"No, no. It's just a different language." Hansum tried to grab the papers back but the priest pulled them away from him. Hansum, now panicking, began stammering. "I, I've got to get Signora Baroni. We ha, have to sa, save Guilietta."

"You will not step foot in the house of della Cappa again!" the priest pronounced with a flourish.

Hansum grabbed the priest's frock with two hands and shook him.

"You will NOT tell me what to do, priest. I have lands and men and money. If you delay me any longer, I shall go to the Podesta's palace and bring guards to take Guilietta to where she's ..."

Ugilino thwacked the flat of the ax blade against Hansum's back, causing him to lurch forward.

"You leave our priest alone, orphan! I don't care who you are."

Agistino grabbed Hansum by the shoulder. "You must not compound your wrong by harming a priest!"

"Wrong? Look what *he's* doing to Guilietta," Hansum cried. "He's letting her die!"

Lurenzano seemed emboldened by both Ugilino and Agistino's support. He came forward and pushed Hansum. "There's nothing to be done for the girl," Lurenzano shouted. "It's her time to die!"

"I CAN'T LET HER DIE!"

"Peace brothers," Pan, as the angel Aurelius said, spreading his arms and wings seraphim-like.

"Shut up, devil!" Ugilino shouted, swinging his ax again. It swung right though the hologram's face, the momentum causing it to fly out of Ugilino's hand. It sailed across the room and hit the leg of the table with Pan's lamp on it.

"My lamp!" Pan shouted. This brought all eyes to the object.

"It's his talisman!" Father Lurenzano shouted. "The beast lives in the talisman." Lincoln lunged for the table. The priest and Agistino did the same. The table toppled over and all its contents with it. The lamp, reinforced with mastic and copper, tumbled onto the unfinished floor.

"Please, peace brothers!" Pan cried desperately.

"Capture the talisman," Lurenzano screamed.

Ugilino picked up the ax again and raised it above where the lamp was. In desperation,  Pan flew his image right into Ugilino's face. Ugilino swung the ax repeatedly at the hologram, barely missing the others. Pan changed his image to bats and birds and dragons in an effort to scare off his attacker, succeeding only in causing the Signora to scream louder. Shamira ran around the table to get to the lamp. She was almost to it when Ugilino saw her. He literally growled as he turned to attack her. Pan watched in terror as Ugilino's ox-like shoulders raised and flexed. He twisted his body around, pulling his weapon high over his head.

"Not the girl!" Pan screamed.

"Shamira!" Hansum and Lincoln cried.

The Signora screamed and covered her eyes.

Shamira fell with the lamp in her hand, twisting her body to get away from the descending blade. She rolled away and the edge of the ax ripped through her wool sleeve, scraping her skin, and then burying itself in the floor. The lamp flew from her fingers and landed a short distance away. Pan could see Ugilino follow it with his eyes, like a hawk following a mouse that has eluded its sharp talons on the first attack. Ugilino lifted the ax again, and without raising it to full height, brought the blade on top of the already-fragile brass and mastic amalgam.

A pain-like cry came from Pan. His image broke into a million tiny cubes. The cubes buzzed around madly for a few moments, trying to reassemble themselves. The image of the angel momentarily changed back to Pan, floating in the air. A look of surprise and panic appeared on his face.

"I'm undone." he said. "Goodbye, beloved children."

Everyone froze. There was complete silence as they watched the image fade. All was quiet, except for the deep rumble of thunder outside. The now-translucent image floated to the ground, right over top of the crushed lamp. Pan looked up at Ugilino, his executioner. As everything went dark for Pan, he saw a spark rise through him and then a whoosh of wind expelled itself from the shallow hole. His final thought was, 'There go my power cells releasing their energy.'

"Pan!" Shamira cried. "You've murdered Pan!"

Lincoln rushed at Ugilino. "You idiot!" he screamed. Ugilino heaved the ax handle backward, driving the butt into Lincoln's guts. Lincoln stopped short, the wind knocked out of him. Then Ugilino swung the other end of the ax around and hit Lincoln's upper arm with the flat of the blade. There was the distinct crack of a breaking bone as Lincoln fell to the ground. Hansum now rushed Ugilino.

"You bastard! I'LL KILL . . ." and he was on him, despite Ugilino holding the weapon. They were down on the floor and Hansum was pummelling Ugilino in the face with all his might. Blood spurted out of the ugly apprentice's mouth and nose. His eye began to swell. The priest and Agistino grabbed Hansum by the arms and flung him away.

"I'm blind!" Ugilino screamed, writhing on the ground. "I'm blind! Romero blinded me!"

Lincoln tried to get up, but grabbed his now useless arm, screaming in agony. Shamira dropped to his side and held him. She watched Father Lurenzano pick up the ax and head for Hansum.

"NO!" she screamed as he raised it above his head.

"Enough!" Agistino said forcefully.

"We must kill all the demons," Lurenzano argued. "They will wreak destruction on us."

Agistino looked around his workshop. His lathes were splintered, his shop a shambles. His only descendant lay dying or already dead. He was once again drunk, and the boy who had brought him hope was lying under the threat of an ax.

"We are destroyed already. Enough." He pulled the ax out of the priest's hands and threw it into the corner. Then, like a man in a trance, he walked over to the Signora. He held out his hand to her. "Wife, we must sit by our child as she passes."

Still shaking with terror, the Signora took her husband's hand and rose to her feet, never taking her gaze away from Agistino's sad, sad eyes. They slowly walked out the door with some remnant of dignity. Hansum sprung to his feet.

"Master, I will go to Signora Baroni's and get the herbs to cure Guilietta. I will come back to the house . . ."

Agistino looked at Hansum dispassionately.

"You are no longer welcome in my house. You and the others may never pass through its door again." He continued walking.

"But Master, we can be a family again."

The Master stopped. "You brought worse than death to this house, Romero. You brought hope and then snatched it away. Come, Mathtilda." And they left.

Hansum watched as Father Lurenzano helped Ugilino toward the door.

"I can't see. Romero blinded me," Ugilino cried again.

"You're not blind," Lurenzano said gruffly. "You've just got blood in your eyes."

"Oh," Ugilino said as he was led out of the shop.

"The little guy," Lincoln groaned, holding his arm. "Check the little guy."

Hansum and Shamira rushed to where the ax had crushed Pan's lamp. They dug into the dirt and gravel and there it was. The small brass lamp lay cracked and almost flat, little bits of mastic and tin still sticking to it.

"He's gone!" Shamira said.

"Dead. Pan's dead," Hansum whispered. "We're alone, with no help."

"I can't move my arm," Lincoln moaned. "I think it's broken."

Hansum looked into nothingness. "Guilietta. How can I save Guilietta?"

"What are we going to do?" Shamira whispered.

Hansum steeled himself and straightened his spine.

"The hired carriage. It's still out front. Let's go to the palace and get soldiers. Help me with Lincoln. We'll take the carriage and then come back for Guil."

They helped Lincoln struggle to his feet, but his arm was so tender, the slightest move caused streaks of pain to shoot through it. Using precious time, they found a rag and used it to make a sling. Then they exited the shop and entered into the miserable rainy night. When they got to the street, they were shocked to find the carriage gone.

"Damn!" Hansum cursed. "I paid that bastard to wait." The three were standing in the rain, like drowning rats. Exasperated, Hansum turned and pounded on the door of the house. "Let us in. We must save Guilietta. Let us in!" The shutters of the second-floor window flew open and Father Lurenzano leaned out.

"Be gone, devils. I will see you hanged and burned."

"We must save Guilietta. Please, Father. I need those papers. Please!" The priest held out the papers with the herbal recipes. He ripped them in two. "NO!" Hansum screamed. "Please. Don't!" But the priest kept tearing at them. Then Father Lurenzano pulled back from the window and Ugilino appeared. He moved his hands quickly and something poured out from what he was carrying. A torrent of effluent came crashing down on Hansum.

"That's from us to you, devil orphans!" he screamed. Then he pulled the shutters closed.

Hansum let out a scream so visceral, it seemed to pour from the depths of his soul. Never before had panic and frustration exploded from him in such measure. Not even in the heat of battle, close to death, was he so angered and afraid at the same time. Finally he stopped. His hands and fists clenched.

"To the palace," he said with resolve. "Now!" He and Shamira flanked Lincoln and guided him along in the rain as fast as the boy's pain would allow. Hansum was going to tell Shamira that he would run ahead and send someone back for them, but when they passed the first house, he changed his mind. A woman was screaming at two men, apparently family. The men were removing the body of an elderly woman and placing it in the street.

"My sister, we can't," one of the men said. "We must get Mama's body out of the house." The corpse's face was contorted and covered with black spots, her arms and legs with large boil-like growths. One of the men covered the body with a sheet.

"She needs a Christian burial to go to Heaven," the woman cried.

"In the morning, wife," the second man said. Then the two men pulled and pushed the woman back inside their modest home.

As the teenagers fought against a driving wind and rain, they looked back at the grisly scene. Two dogs were already pulling the cover off of the body. Shamira turned to shoo them away, but Hansum stopped her.

"We've got to hurry," he said.

They passed many more houses with bodies in front of them. At one, the door was open and looters were tearing through the place, grabbing whatever they could. In other places, they could peer into the quiet darkness and see bloated bodies lying on the floor.

Even in his grief, Hansum saw that the only people helping the sick and dying were the clergy. He saw priests, nuns and monks, selflessly caring for and ministering to the sick and dying. 'At least most of the Church aren't like Lurenzano,' he thought bitterly.

The Bra Market was almost empty, except for a few suspicious souls. Hansum gave them sharp looks to keep them away. They passed Signora Baroni's house, and despite Hansum's persistent knocking, there was no answer. Hansum thought for a moment.

"Most of my money is back at the house. I have very little on me. Signor de Levi's is just around the corner. Let's go there so I can get more coins. I want as much as I can to bribe the guards."

But they received another shock. As they neared the money lender's home, with its high brick walls, small windows and heavy doors, the thick smell of a recently extinguished fire stung their noses. There were remnants of books and charred belongings strewn in the street.

"This is his house," Hansum said hoarsely. They were looking at where the door had been. Now there was only a black hole, the burnt maw of what must be the entrance to who-knows-what darker horrors inside. How many of Eli's family been killed and how many were scattered, Hansum could not guess. He found himself putting his hand to his temple, like he had in the past, to call out for help from his friends or family. He felt a bump. He must have received it during the melee back at the workshop. Hansum shivered. "Let's keep going," he said to the others. As they got near Signori Square, Hansum checked to confirm that he still had a little bribe money. He didn't know if the Podesta or Nicademo would have returned yet, and hoped that his reputation with the guards was strong enough to order them to do what he wanted. When he got to the palace, not only were the nobles absent, but Captain Caesar was gone too. He was overseeing the one gate left open to the city. There were only a few soldiers left at the palace. And even if there had been men to spare, he was told there were no carriages available. Not even a wagon and mule.

They were let into the palace and given a room. Hansum was now beside himself with anxiety. A valet provided them with dry clothes, but there was no physician to attend to Lincoln. They had all left the city. Shamira checked Lincoln, trying to assess whether his arm needed to be reset or whether it was just a crack. In the end, she bound it and gave him some boiled willow bark from the kitchen. Lincoln lay down on the soft bed and quickly fell asleep. Shamira lay on top of the covers and passed out. Only Hansum stayed awake, doing the only thing he could to help his wife. He got down on his knees and prayed.

# Chapter 14

Agistino was on his knees by Guilietta's bed, his huge hands caressing her wet hair, soaked by both sweat and the cold rags, used in a now vain attempt to keep her fever down. She had opened her eyes only briefly, to look at her father.

"Goodbye, Papa," she mouthed, then slipped back into a coma. The big man's body convulsed with grief, and he lay his head next to hers, his tears falling onto her hot cheek. Agistino felt a hand on his shoulder. Looking up, he saw Lurenzano.

"Come, my son. We must talk downstairs. You can do no more here." At the bottom of the stairs, the priest motioned for the Master to sit at the table. "Let us pray," he said.

"Should we go to the church?" Agistino asked, bleary-eyed.

"It's safer here," Lurenzano answered. "First though, let me fill your glass. That boy," Lurenzano started. "When we get our hands on him, we will burn him for witchcraft. Burn all three." Agistino didn't answer. He just sat there. "And you will come into question too, Agistino. I will do what I can to protect you, but this is witchcraft."

Agistino looked back at the priest. "I care nothing for myself, Father," he said. "My line is at an end."

"But your wife," Father Lurenzano added. "She is innocent, of course, but who will look after her if you are gone?" Lurenzano took another drink from his goblet. "No, we must find a way for the Church to protect you. We must find the means."

Agistino looked down into the depths of his wine, thinking about his wife. He could hear her crying and praying upstairs. Then he took a long pull of the beverage and banged the goblet on the table. He forced himself to his feet and walked to the fireplace. In front of the priest, he moved a pile of firewood and, taking a knife blade, worked the disguised piece of stone out from the wall. He reached into the hollow cavity and removed his strong-box. He put it down in front of the priest and opened it, then sat down listlessly. Lurenzano's eyes went wide with amazement as he saw the bulging bags of coins, much of them gold.

"Some of it is Romero's," Agistino said. "The rest, only the start of our new prosperity."

Father Lurenzano's eyes were so big, he could hardly speak.

"I say that Romero's fortune is yours now."

"But without my daughter, I have no heir. No future. What's the point?"

"With this, the Church can save you and sustain you, my son. The Lord has provided."

"But the money was earned with the devil's help."

"Like all things, my son, this can be used for good or for evil. We will use the devil's gains against him." Agistino didn't say a word. "Here, my son. Let me fill your glass. I shall tell you what I propose to save your soul."

But Agistino's only care now was for his wife.

Hansum awoke with someone shaking his shoulder. He had been up most of the night, finally falling into a fitful sleep on the floor. When he opened his eyes, he saw a servant kneeling over him. Standing above the servant was the Podesta. Hansum sat up quickly. He saw Shamira checking Lincoln's arm.

Hansum cleared his groggy mind and began his rehearsed speech.

"The city has gone mad, Excellency."

"The whole world," Mastino replied.

"There's dead in the streets. People are blaming evil spirits. A curse from God. The Jews. I went to Signor de Levi's house. It has been destroyed."

"Si," Mastino acknowledged. "I heard. De Levi is dead."

"Even my own has gone mad, Excellency. Guilietta's father has gotten some odd thought into his head, that I am to blame for his daughter's illness and that I have been in league with the devil."

"What?" the Podesta asked incredulously.

"When I wanted to get Guilietta proper care, Master della Cappa and a priest, Father Lurenzano, forbade me to come into the house. Guilietta is lying there, dying. Time is short. I came to get men and a carriage from the palace last night to take Guilietta away, but the guard was low and carriages unavailable."

"How is she now, my boy?"

"I don't know," Hansum said. "They even broke Maruccio's arm."

"You have my support in whatever you want to do, Romero."

There was a quick knock at the door and Nicademo walked in.

"Della Cappa is here with some priest. He says he must talk to you."

"A priest?" the Podesta asked.

"Father Lurenzano?" Hansum asked.

"Si, that's it. They're at the front door. What should I do?"

"He's the priest that caused the problem," Hansum said.

"I have enough to care for," Mastino said. "Romero, take three guards and my personal coach to fetch Guilietta. Bring her here or anywhere you want to treat her. Go, before those two get back home."

Part of Hansum told him to do just what Mastino had just told him, but another part wanted to heal the rift between himself and Agistino. When he had been confused in the past, Pan had been there to guide him. Now he must make the decision on his own.

"Excellency, Master della Cappa has some strange notion in his head about me. If you could use your influence to reason with him, I would be grateful. I'd like to get Guilietta with his blessing."

"When people's fears are in the way," Mastino advised, "it is often best to just ignore them and do your will. They come around when their stomachs tell them to."

Hansum paused again, weighing the options.

"I have trust in your abilities, Excellency. Please."

Mastino, who looked tired and haggard, smiled slightly, like he was pleased to receive such a compliment from his protégé. Then he shrugged and ordered Agistino and the priest to be brought to the receiving room. Mastino, Nicademo and Hansum entered the room from a back door and Mastino indicated they should all remain standing, as if to say that this was to be a quick audience. When Agistino and Father Lurenzano were brought in, they looked bedraggled. They had been drinking all night, were unkempt, dirty, and had just walked across the city in the rain. When the priest saw Hansum standing next to the Podesta, he became incensed.

"Excellency," Father Lurenzano began, "I have grave news of an evil that has invaded your city."

"We are well aware of the pestilence that has taken hold here, as well as in other parts of the peninsula."

"I do not speak of the sickness among the people, though what I refer to may have been responsible for it. I am here to denounce a servant of the devil who is now among us. In fact," Lurenzano said, outstretching an accusing finger at Hansum, "he stands next to you." With that, Agistino threw himself prostrate on the marble floor.

"I knew nothing about this, Excellency," he cried. "I thought I was doing a Christian duty by bringing orphans into my home. How was I to know my new fortune would be from inventions of the underworld?"

"Are you saying my young friend here is a servant of the devil?" Mastino asked lightly.

"Most assuredly, Excellency," the priest said, stepping forward. "I saw the demon myself." And then he described how they had snuck up on the workshop, peered through a crack in the shutters and saw the children bowing to this half-goat, half-man creature, who was giving them instructions from the underworld.

"What was this creature saying?" Nicademo asked, always a stickler for details.

"We could not hear that," the priest answered.

"Then how do you know it was giving instructions?"

Lurenzano opened his mouth, stumped for a moment. "It must have been," Lurenzano finally answered. "What else could it have been doing?"

"I fear my old master and the good father had been drinking, Excellency," Hansum stage whispered in the Podesta's ear.

Mastino took a step forward. He sniffed the air.

"You two smell like the inside of an old wine barrel. Perhaps it was this that stimulated your visions? Agistino, please get up, my friend." Agistino got up, helped by the Podesta himself. The lens-maker coughed and Mastino blanched at the smell. Regaining his composure he said, "Your future son-in-law begged me to see you, even though I am busy and said no. He loves you and honors you. And how do you repay him for all he has done for your house? You accuse him with such stories?"

"I saw it with my own eyes, Excellency. The Holy Father saw it too, as did my wife and my other apprentice."

"Ugilino," informed Hansum. "The uh..." and he made a circle with his finger around his face.

"The ugly one?" Mastino said. "That imbecile? And, I'm sorry to say, Master della Cappa, your wife is not one whose oath could be accepted in a court of law or that of the Church." Father Lurenzano stepped in.

"It's true we had been drinking, Excellency, but only a trifle before the incident. My poor Agistino's daughter is dying and he was distraught. I joined him in a few cups of solace. But after the incident, when we saw the creature and confronted it, the smell of brimstone was in the air. It made lightening flash right in the room. The creature transformed itself into angels and devils right in front of our eyes. And the girl called it Pan, servant of Lucifer. And he, the demon, called them his children when he was dying! After it was dead, we forbade the orphans to come into the home again. It was only then that we stayed up all night, afraid for our souls. That's when we prayed and drank more wine."

The Podesta looked again to Hansum, who shook his head slowly to refute the story. Mastino looked back at Agistino, ignoring the priest.

"Master della Cappa, for my sake and the sake of your family, good friend, forget this foolishness. Allow Romero back into your home quickly, so he can get help for your daughter. Let them marry and have a long life."

"But they are married," Father Lurenzano interjected.

There was an eerie silence. Hansum felt his stomach rise and his heart beat in his ears. He saw the Podesta's head slowly turn back to the priest.

"What?" he asked.

"They are married, Excellency. I married them myself, months ago." Hansum saw a look of surprise come onto the Podesta's face. Hansum then felt the noble's eyes snap onto his own. He felt his own face flush and a dizziness came upon him which almost made him faint. "You did not know of this, Excellency?" Lurenzano went on, the sound of his voice showing he knew he had just hit upon something to cause trouble. "They came to me months ago, begging for the Church's holy blessing so they could fornicate."

Mastino walked up to Hansum. Hansum's was so dizzy, he had to fight to keep himself standing.

"Is this true, Romero?" he whispered in Hansum's ear. "You betrayed my trust and lied so blatantly?"

"My Lord, Excellency," Hansum started, his voice faltering. "I'm sorry. It was not my intention." He stared at Mastino, his ashen face begging.

A knock came at the room's door. An assistant of Nicademo's entered and whispered in his ear. Nicademo then whispered the message to the Podesta. Mastino's look of hurt transformed to a seriousness of another kind.

"You two must leave," he said to Agistino and Father Lurenzano.

"But the heretic, Excellency," Father Lurenzano said. "You must arrest him or give me authorization for the church to do so. We must cleanse his soul."

"Leave," Mastino repeated to Agistino and the priest. "You," he said to Hansum, "stay."

Father Lurenzano left under protest and with a guard's hand on his shoulder. Agistino trudged out quietly. Hansum and Agistino's eyes met for a moment and Hansum mouthed, "Forgive me," but he was brought back to reality by the Podesta's hard stare. He repeated, out loud, "Forgive me," to the Podesta, who, after a few seconds of burning a hole in the boy with his eyes, spoke.

"I am very disappointed, Romero. Very disappointed. We shall talk of this later. But right now we have things to take care of, you and I both."

"Excellency, the carriage and the men you promised . . . I must get Guilietta and see to her. Then I'll come right back."

"You must deal with this first and then you can go. Journeymen from the bell foundry are here. They are having trouble making the cannon." With a quick wave, he motioned to Nicademo to bring the men in.

"But we've no time for this, Excellency," Hansum begged.

The butler brought in Geraldo and Darmo, two of the journey-men. They appeared overwhelmed by the fine surroundings, but smiled broadly when they saw Hansum.

"Master Monticelli," Darmo beamed.

"It is good to see you well," Geraldo said.

"What is it?" the Podesta asked curtly.

"It's the molds, Excellency," Geraldo said. "The big molds for the cannon. They are cracking with the heat of the bronze. Falling apart, exploding even. If we are to have a cannon made by the time you said we must . . . I thought it important to ask you what to do. I've come all this way."

Hansum was having a hard time focusing.

"What of the master mold maker? What does he say?" Hansum finally asked.

"He left the estate the same night you did, Master. Late in the night, after you. He got word his family was sick. We went to his home before coming here." Hansum sat silently. Nicademo spoke up.

"What did he say of the problem?"

"Nothing, Excellency," Geraldo said, looking down. "He is dead of the sickness."

"Mother of God!" the Podesta said.

"Dead?" Hansum repeated slowly.

"Si, Master," Geraldo said. "That's why we came here."

"Well?" Mastino asked. "What say you, Master Monticelli?" No answer. "Signor? Are you listening?"

"I'm sorry," Hansum said. "I'm distracted. Forgive . . ."

"His betrothed, his wife is deathly ill," Nicademo explained.

Hansum slowly sat down at a small table, despondent. He put a hand to his head.

"We are very sorry to hear that," Geraldo said. "Perhaps we should leave and . . ."

"No!" Mastino barked. "You explain to Master Monticelli what the problem is and he shall give you your answer. We must make the new cannon without delay."

Hansum knew that everybody was used to him always know-ing what to do and expressing himself eloquently. Mastino waved Geraldo over to Hansum.

"Tell him again. Tell Master Monticelli what the problem is."

Geraldo walked up to Hansum, Darmo silent by his side, and repeated how the molds were cracking with the heat. He described all the procedures that Hansum had gone over with them at length, neglecting one thing. Hansum didn't catch the mistake. The heavy plaster cast still had too much moisture in it. A day in the sun or a heated room would cure the plaster and the problem.

"I'm sorry, Geraldo," Hansum said, truly trying to control himself. "I don't know."

Mastino took a step back and stared intently at Hansum.

"But these are your processes, Romero," the Podesta said, frustrated. "You invented them. How can you not know?"

"I'm sorry, Excellency," Hansum said, feeling like he wanted to throw up. "I really don't know," and then he broke down and wept, his head buried in his arms.

"You two better leave," Nicademo advised. "The footman will show you to the stables. Sleep there tonight. Perhaps in the morning, Master Monticelli will be his old self."

"Yes, Excellency," Geraldo said.

Darmo turned as he exited and said, "We are sorry your wife is not well, Master. I will pray for her recovery." Hansum looked up weakly. Through his tears, the last thing he saw of the men was Darmo scratching under his arm and wincing.

Mastino and Nicademo stared at Hansum's tear-streaked face.

"Perhaps he has lost his inspiration?" Nicademo suggested.

But Mastino could hold his frustration no longer.

"This is most strange, Romero. Ludicrous," he said with force. "One day you are a savant, the next you say you don't know anything and don't know why. And now, when things are bleak and I need strong and trustworthy men about me, fools and priests come to my door and tell me you are communing with Hell? And tears? We have no time for tears! Why are you doing this to me?"

"I'm not doing anything on purpose, Excellency," Hansum said, wiping the wet off of his face with his sleeve.

"Well, why would those two say such things? What cause could they have?"

"I don't know, Excellency. They were drunk."

"And why can you not remember anything?"

Hansum played for time. He had to say something to keep as much of this man's confidence as possible. Guilietta's life depended on it. He looked up, praying for inspiration.

"I was in a fight with them," he said. "They struck me on the head with an ax. Look at my face. Feel my temple. It's swollen. Perhaps my memory is damaged?"

"Damaged? For good?" Mastino asked.

"I think these things are usually temporary. Excellency, please, let me fetch Guilietta. Then your best physician can examine us both."

Nicademo went over and put his hand on Hansum's temple, confirming the swelling.

"It could be possible, Excellency," Nicademo said. "I've seen temporary memory loss from war wounds to the head."

"Please let me go and get Guilietta, Excellency. I know you are disappointed in me. I lied to you. But that was early in our association. Trust has grown since then, you said it yourself. Oh please, please, I beg you. Don't make Guilietta pay for my mistake."

Mastino, eyes still flashing, pulled Nicademo aside. He whispered something and then, without looking at Hansum, left the room. Hansum jumped to his feet.

"Excellency!" But Nicademo stopped him.

"The Podesta has ordered that you be kept in your room with the others. A physician will attend to you as soon as one gets back to the palace."

"But Guilietta?"

"I'm sorry, Romero. It's impossible. Tomorrow, perhaps."

"Tomorrow? No! No! She needs help now!" Hansum ran out of the room. Two guards stopped him and, under Nicademo's orders, dragged him screaming back to the bedroom. Shamira watched in shock as a loudly protesting Hansum was manhandled into the room and the door closed behind him.

⧖

Sometime later, Mastino exited the planning room where he had just finished a long and stressful meeting with city officials. They had to determine which actions to take regarding the sickness gripping the region. On his way to his quarters, he came upon Nicademo.

"You look pale, cousin," Nicademo said.

"This pestilence is more perplexing than war. The enemy is unseen. I've ordered that any house with the sickness is to be shut up with its inhabitants. The only time the doors may be opened is in the morning to collect the dead. If everyone in the house dies, it's to be torched to cleanse the disease with fire."

"What shall we do about Romero?" Nicademo asked.

"Have you seen him these past hours?"

"Not long ago. He still insists he must get to Guilietta. It's his only thought."

"Can't he see what I'm dealing with? Many, many people are dying. And I don't know if I want her brought here. She may have the sickness."

"True," Nicademo said. "What of his memory loss?"

"We'll have the physician look at him and if he recovers, fine."

"Well, it must be that."

"The only other reason would be if he's planning on giving the knowledge to another power. It can't be that devil nonsense. No, we must keep him close."

"I know you feel of him like a son. Let's see what the morning brings."

Mastino looked at his cousin. Hearing Nicademo's sentimental words clarified his own true motives, and they weren't sentimental. No matter how angry or disappointed he was with Hansum, he still needed the youth to give him cannons, the powder, and even the flying machines and communication devices. His future depended on it.

# Chapter 15

Hansum, Shamira and Lincoln sat forlornly with two guards still outside the door. Lincoln's pain wasn't too bad, as long as he stayed still. There was no swelling or infection, so his inoculation implant must still be working. However, the new wound Shamira received from Ugilino's ax was another matter. The scrape was becoming irritated and red. It was weeping and showed the first signs of festering.

Hansum was familiar with one of the soldiers guarding the room. He had opened the door several times, asking when he could see the Podesta.

"Whenever his Excellency gets here," he was told.

"Please, I must get to my wife. She is so ill."

"Signor, I cannot let you. It would mean my life. And the sickness is out there. It's better you stay here."

The other soldier added, "I heard that doctors are refusing to see the sick, mothers and fathers are abandoning their children, lawyers refusing to write wills. No, Signor, even if we could give you leave, I would tell you not to do it." As an officer passed, they closed the door on Hansum again.

It was becoming dusk. None of the teenagers had eaten since early morning and no food seemed to be forthcoming. Lincoln and Shamira were lying on top of the covers on the bed, either dozing or looking into space. Hansum sat on the floor in a corner, hugging his knees, his head bowed and eyes closed. He was worried about Guilietta. He wanted to be near her, to commune with her. He imagined being able to touch his temple, as he had done in his previous life, and talk to her. He allowed himself this fantasy.

"My darling, I am ever here for you," Hansum said quietly, as if he were using his implant. "I am your slave, your devoted."

"Romero. My Romero. Where are you, my Romero? I hear your voice. I see you in my mind, like a window to another place. Is this a dream? Is this Heaven?" Hansum opened his eyes in surprise. It was just like the semi-telepathic experiences he'd had back home. But this was impossible. "Where have you gone, my love?" Guilietta's voice asked in his head again. "You've disappeared. Please come back to me." Dream or hallucination, it didn't matter. Hansum closed his eyes again and drew up his knees tight to his chest.

"I'm here, my love. Don't be afraid."

"I can see you again. Oh, thanks be to God, I can see you again."

"And I you, my love. How are you, dearest?"

"I was in pain, husband, but now I am calm. And you?"

"The Podesta is not allowing me to leave the palace. I am okay, but worried for you, my darling." And then tears poured from Hansum's eyes. "Oh, Guilietta, I miss you so much."

"Oh, my poor darling," Guilietta's voice soothed. "To be alone, without each other at this painful time, me without you and you without me. Be brave, my Romero, like I know you are." The image of Guilietta smiled in Hansum's mind. Hansum smiled too, thinking of the dream's irony. The dream had questioned whether he was a dream. "Father says — they all say — you are devils."

"No, my love. We are not. I am only a man. Just a man. A man who loves you."

"And I love you, Romero. But why do they say such things?"

"Because they see we are different. And they are right in that. But I am not a devil."

"Then what are you?"

"I am a man, Guilietta. I am a man from a different time. From the future. Why God has sent me here, I don't know. How to get back? It's a mystery. I will clear up this fear everyone has of me, and we shall be together soon, my beautiful Guilietta."

"I fear not, husband. I fear not. I am dying." Hansum didn't like this daydream anymore. He pulled his knees even closer and wept openly. "Come to me, my darling," Guilietta's voice said. "Hold me while I go to God." Hansum heard a low male voice in the background of the dream. It sounded like the Master.

"She's talking to herself," Agistino's voice said. "What's she saying?"

"Maybe Gui see St. Peter," a voice sounding like Nuca's said.

"He's right on the ceiling with Michael," the Signora's voice wept. Then Hansum saw Guillietta wince in pain. "Oh, my baby," shrieked the Signora's voice, and there was the sound of someone collapsing.

"Help take the mistress to her bed," the man's voice said frantically. "Then send Ugilino for Father Lurenzano. He's gone back to his church."

"Come to me, my darling," Guilietta's voice whispered desperately. "One last kiss before I meet Jesus. I am content that your voice is the last thing I'll hear."

"No, Guilietta. You're not dying. You mustn't die!"

"I am done, my love, but I am happy."

"You mustn't die, Guilietta. I love you. I need you. I've always loved you. Before we met, I loved the idea of you. I need more of you."

"We had the time on the wall, with the moon and cool breeze showing us we were alive," Guilietta said.

"I want that time again," Hansum wept. "You cannot go. I've not had enough."

"Who's to say what's enough? Not those who say it," and then there was silence.

⏳

Devlena was again sneaking around in the della Cappas' neighbourhood. Desperate for money, she was elated when she got word Guilietta was ill again. She snuck the long way around the city, avoiding the people she owed money to and the dead and dying that now littered the street.

"How much longer is that girl going to hang on, damn it?" Devlena muttered. "I need my final payment."

A cry emanated from high in one of the houses. The shutters of the della Cappas' second-storey window flew open. The Signora burst through the opening, screaming at the top of her lungs.

"She's dead, she's dead, my daughter's dead!" spewed her shrill cry.

Devlena saw the old woman collapse in the window frame. The poisoner smiled. Hands came out of the window and pulled her back. Then Devlena saw Nuca running across the road with her husband.

"It is done," Devlena whispered to herself. "I may claim my fee."

Devlena saw Nuca stop at the della Cappas' door and, as she pushed at the latch, the tailor looked up. Their eyes met. A look of rage erupted onto Nuca's face. She pointed at Devlena and shrieked as loudly as her burned vocal chords would allow.

"Pois'ner! Murd'rer!"

Devlena turned and ran back toward the palace. Half filled with the fear of being caught and elated at the success of her commission, she shrieked with glee as she ran, pushing and shoving herself by anyone who happened to be in her path. She did not stop till she got to Piazza Bra, and then took an especially run-down rat's nest of an alley the rest of the way. 'I'll claim my reward,' she thought, 'and be off to Germany.' Her newfound bliss was such that she could have been walking in a beautiful meadow, not past crying children, lamenting husbands, wives and dead bodies being gnawed at by dogs and rats.

But as she came to Signori Square, she saw a crowd converging. She gleaned from the squabbling of the people around her that the city gates had been closed because of the pestilence. Desperate to leave, they were going to protest *en masse*. They could not know that there were just as many people outside the city who were desperate to get in. Devlena assessed that this crowd could quickly turn into a mob and decided it was not a good time to go to the palace. She slunk back home to pack some belongings and then hide out in the city till morning.

# Chapter 16

"Guilietta, NO!" Hansum shouted as he shot up from the floor.

"It's okay," Shamira said. "It's just a bad dream."

"No, no, it wasn't! I've got to get to her!" Hansum opened the door again. Frantically he begged the guards, trying to give them the coins he had left in his pouch. Shamira came and took him gently by the shoulders.

"It was just a dream. She's okay. Come back in."

"No. Feel my forehead. Maybe they didn't remove the implants. Maybe . . ."

There were shouts from down the hall. Among the many voices they could hear the Podesta's.

"Guards. All guards! To the front door!"

"Into the piazza."

"Call the horse guard too!"

"There's a mob!"

"Hurry!"

They heard the guards outside their door running down the hall. Shamira tried the handle of their door and it opened. Nobody was there. Hansum quickly looked outside.

"There's another way out of the back of the palace, through the kitchen," he said. "You stay here with Lincoln."

"No way," Lincoln retorted, getting off of the bed. "I'm not stayin' here. You'll need help. But Shamira, she should stay. Her inoculation implant has obviously stopped working. With the plague out there, she shouldn't leave."

"He's right," Hansum agreed. "The Baron likes you. You can assure them I'll be back tomorrow or even tonight."

"But Lincoln should stay too," Shamira said. "His arm."

"No!" Lincoln countered. "Hansum will need help with Guil. At least I have one good arm and two good eyes to watch his back. Come on. This confusion will cover us."

The halls were empty of guards. As they passed through the kitchen, Hansum picked up a large, ugly knife. In a few minutes they were back on the plague-filled streets.

The streets and markets were less congested than the front of the palace. The rain had stopped and Lincoln's pain had settled down, so he could walk at a good pace. People, sick with the plague, were now being quarantined in their homes. There were children in the streets, but, where they had often run about in joyful packs, now most had wary and hungry looks. Hansum made sure the kitchen knife was visible in his belt.

It was getting dark and soldiers with torches were stopping people. If they didn't have a good story, or looked too ill to make it to their home, they put them in carts to be locked up in the bowels of the Arena, as the jails were full. They were also rounding up healthy-looking men and youths, conscripting them as laborers to dig mass graves. The boys ducked out of the way to avoid the soldiers.

Soon they were close to home. All looked quiet. Only a few dead were lying about and all the houses were dark. They took refuge in a tight space between two houses, not a hundred paces from the della Cappas'.

"What do we do now?" Lincoln asked.

"I don't know." Hansum's dream seemed to be losing its power. Maybe Guilietta was still alive. "I guess we better just knock on the door and hope the priest isn't there. Maybe the Master will listen to reason now."

The della Cappas' front door opened. People walked out. It was Nuca and her husband Bruno, followed by Bembo. Nuca dabbed at her eyes and Bruno put his arm around her. They crossed the street and went into their house.

"Maybe we should talk to them first?" Lincoln suggested. "Find out what's going on? They're not nuts like the others."

Before Hansum could answer, the door opened again and a face peered out. It was Father Lurenzano. He looked up and down the street, and then signalled for someone to follow. Ugilino came out, holding a heavy box. Father Lurenzano hastily covered it with a cloth, then scolded Ugilino and called him a fool. Then they walked quickly down the street.

"That's the Master's money box," Lincoln said.

"Come on," Hansum ordered.

The door to the house was unbolted. It was dark, except for a very dim oil lamp on the table. It was the brass lamp with the angel holding the lightning bolts, the one Hansum had brought as a gift. The light blazed up as the open door let in a gust of air. It revealed Agistino, passed out, face-down on the table. There were half a dozen empty wine jugs strewn about and several cups on their sides. The Master's breathing was labored and his face was covered by his dishevelled hair.

"You stay here," Hansum told Lincoln. He took a second ceramic lamp and lit it. Then Hansum quietly climbed the stairs. At the top, he could hear the Signora snoring in her bed, her breathing mixed with occasional whimpers. He came to Guilietta's room. The curtain was pulled closed and the room dark. He put his hand on the curtain, hesitated, then slowly pulled it back. He took a half step in. Light from Hansum's lamp cast long shadows. He saw the bed, but couldn't see Guilietta's face or hair. Hope rose quickly in his chest and fell just as fast. There was a lump under the cover. Pain stretched over his face. The lump took on a recognizable shape. And it was so still. So terribly still. "Guil," Hansum said as he approached the bed. "Guil?" Hansum fell to his knees. The pained look on his face morphed into unprotected, vulnerable sorrow. He put the lamp down on the side table and reached out to touch the form's shoulder. It moved slightly, but was inert. Hansum took the end of the cover and pulled it down slowly. Dark auburn hair appeared. Hansum froze. He closed his eyes and took a slow breath, pulling the sheet down further. His breath was heavy as he gathered the courage to reopen his eyes. When he did open them, he saw nothing. He had to force the image of what was before him to make the trip from his eyes to his brain. Hansum's face contorted into a mask of twisted rubber. He couldn't move. Breath could neither enter nor exit his frozen lungs. After some moments, the need to breathe broke through his paralysis. A labored cry finally emitted from between his clenched teeth.

"Guiiiiiil. Oh . . . my . . . Guil."

Thoughts flashed through the young widower's mind of how, in the time he was born, people could be revived minutes or even hours after they died. But these useless truths were quickly washed away by the hot tears that burst from his eyes. Hansum's head fell forward onto Guilietta's shoulder and he cried freely. Great sobs erupted from him as he cried her name over and over again. When he picked his head up and awkwardly kissed her cheek, his tears fell onto her unresponsive face. He put his hand on her forehead and caressed her hair. "I'm sorry, Guilietta. I'm sorry." And then he broke completely.

A hand was on Hansum's shoulder. Hansum looked up and there was Lincoln.

"I'm sorry, man," Lincoln said softly. "I'm really . . ." The sound of crashing furniture came from downstairs, followed by the guttural sounds of a creature in mortal pain. "The Master," Lincoln said. "Hey, man, we've gotta go. We can't help here any . . ." but before he could finish the sentence, they heard screaming.

"ROBBERS!" the Master's hoarse voice shouted. "THIEVES!"

Lincoln ran out of Guilietta's death room and down the stairs. Hansum found his knees glued to the floor, unable to leave. Torn, he leaned one way, then the other, unable to take his eyes off of the beautiful, still face.

"DEVILS!" Agistino's booming voice cried. "You ruin our lives then steal what's left!"

"Master, we didn't steal," Lincoln cried. "We just saw Ugilino and Father Lurenzano running down the street with the strong . . ."

"LIAR! I'll kill you. I'll kill . . ." and then there was a crash of furniture.

"Master, the lamp!" Lincoln's voice shouted. "Hansum, help! Help! Quickly!"

Hansum was up on his feet and running down the darkened stairs. Suddenly light illuminated the way in front of him. The straw on the floor was on fire. The table was turned over and the Master was lying face-down on the ground, Lincoln kneeling by him.

"He just grabbed at his arm and collapsed," Lincoln said.

Hansum, consumed with grief for Guilietta, tears still streaming down his face, ran to Agistino. He tried to pick him up and drag him to safety. But Agistino was so large and limp, he couldn't be budged. Lincoln tried to smother the blazing hay with his one arm and an old coat, but it was spreading too rapidly. Hansum continued to struggle with Agistino. Lincoln went to the door and shouted to the neighbors for help. Another shrill scream came from upstairs. Hansum looked up and there was the Signora on the stairs, watching him standing over the prone, slack-jawed body of her husband. Hansum and Lincoln's forms were flickering in the bright flashes of the fire.

"DEVILS," she screamed. "DEVILS! You've killed my whole family!" And she ran back up the stairs.

"Mistress, no!" Lincoln shouted. "The Master's alive. Come downstairs."

"Help, Michael," she cried. "Take me to Heaven to be with my beloved daughter and husband." Lincoln was about to follow her, when several neighbors rushed in. It was the butcher, his burly sons and several others. They could hear the Signora screaming. "They've killed my husband! Devils!"

"It's them!" shouted one of the butcher's boys.

"Mistress, come down here," Lincoln shouted again. "Help us, Signor Spagnoli," Lincoln begged. "She's afraid of us. Send your sons to get her. Quickly!"

The fire was now taking hold of the dry wooden structure's walls. Flames climbed upward.

"Seize them!" the butcher cried. "A soldier told me the Podesta put out a reward for them."

"Save the Mistress and Master," Hansum shouted, but nobody would listen. The men grabbed Hansum and Lincoln and dragged them onto the street.

Mathtilda della Cappa, tears streaming from her eyes, was praying on her knees by the still, ashen face of her daughter. The fire had now caught hold of the floor rafters to the second storey. Smoke and flame licked out through the cracks in the floor and into the bed chamber. Wispy clouds of smoke curled around Guilietta's beautiful white face and delicate hands. The Signora saw her daughter disappear within the cloudlike form. Mathtilda thought of Heaven.

"Save me, Archangel Michael," she prayed, and felt the flames caressing her gown. The fabric lit with a poof. But she didn't move. She stayed kneeling by Guilietta's bed. Grasping her dead daughter's hands in hers, she sobbed, "Take me, take me to your bosom, Michael, so I may be with my beloved daughter and husband. Oh, Agistino, I'm coming." She took a deep breath to repeat her exultation and paralyzing smoke entered her lungs.

Hansum was screaming at the top of his lungs.

"He's still alive, listen to me, the Master's still alive!" But Hansum was being held by three men. "And the Signora! She's upstairs!"

"Don't believe them," the butcher said. "They're trying to trick us. The priest said they're in league with the devil."

"It's not true," Lincoln shouted. "Please. Save them."

One of the butcher's sons kneeled down at the door of the house and peered under the smoke.

"It's true, Father. I can see Master della Cappa breathing."

At the next moment, flames exploded out the second-floor window and the thatched roof caught fire. The open window and rising heat caused a wind tunnel of flame to roar through the structure.

"Save them!" Hansum screamed again. "GUILIETTA!"

The butcher and neighbors let go of Hansum and ran to the house.

"Stay low to avoid the fumes," the butcher shouted. But now the whole doorway was filled with billows of black, acrid smoke. The men lay on the ground, making a human chain to extract Agistino, but then they heard the floor rafters crack. The butcher quickly commanded them back. "It's too dangerous!" he screamed.

"Seize them!" shouted a voice up the road. It was Father Lurenzano, coming back to the house with Ugilino. "Devil worshippers! Thieves! Seize them!" The priest and Ugilino ran toward the group. Now stunned and confused by the situation, the butcher just stood there. But Hansum acted. Having heard the Podesta had a reward out for them, he reasoned he no longer had his support. Nothing good could come from waiting. He ran at the man holding Lincoln and crashed into him, making him let go of his friend. Then he grabbed Lincoln's good arm and ran toward the city.

"Quick! They'll kill us!" Hansum shouted.

As they ran, Hansum's only fear was Ugilino. He knew there was no way he could outrun the strong oaf. But when he looked back, he saw Ugilino stop, tearing at his hair and screaming.

"MY MASTER?" The butcher slowly shook his head, gesturing to the inferno. Ugilino shrieked and shook his fists to the sky. "MY FAMILY! MY HOME!" Then he turned to Hansum and Lincoln, who were almost to the end of the road by the old city wall. "I'LL KILL YOU, YOU BASTARDS! I'LL KILL YOU!" And with that, all the men, the priest and Ugilino took off after Hansum and Lincoln.

## Chapter 17

The next day found Podesta Mastino della Scalla in a foul mood. He was in another conference with city officials on the details of what to do about the plague. Meanwhile, plans for his future glories were in a shambles. His savant had run away and he had no word of what was happening at his new centers of industry. He was confined to sitting around a table with two dozen officials who, in the true fashion of regional politicians everywhere, were arguing. There were the various guild leaders, leading merchants, several bishops, nobles who ran different departments of the city and region, a notable physician and the captain of the guard. One person would say something sensible, but it would be undermined by someone who would lose some advantage in trade or influence. This had been going on for some time when Nicademo came into the room. He tapped his cousin on the shoulder. Mastino turned his head.

"The girl, Guilietta, is dead. Devlena is here for final payment." The Podesta looked at the Baron. He neither gloated nor looked sad. He just looked back at Nicademo as if he were being told it was morning or evening or some other mundane thing.

"Pay her," was all he said and turned back to the meeting. The Baron touched his cousin's shoulder again and Mastino turned, this time annoyed.

"She says she's been undone and must leave the city. She requests extra payment."

"That's her problem," Mastino said and turned away with finality.

Mastino went back to listening to the self-serving and opportunistic arguments. His eyes glazed over as his mind wandered to his own lost opportunities.

A few minutes later, Nicademo was back with more news.

"Romero and the boy, Maruccio, were spotted last night." This got Mastino's attention. "They were seen running from a fire and are accused of starting it. Della Cappa, his family, his house, the shop too, were burned to the ground. The two boys are also accused of stealing Agistino's strongbox of gold." Mastino looked surprised.

"Agistino? His crazy wife? Dead?" Mastino asked. Nicademo nodded. "Leave us!" Mastino shouted at the arguing officials. "Come back in an hour." When they left, Mastino said, "It's all falling apart, Nicademo. All of it. Do they know where Romero is now?"

"No."

"Do you think he did it? The fire?"

"Why would he? No. Apparently a son of the local butcher said that when they held Romero back, he begged them to save the lensmaker. Della Cappa was lying on the floor of his house. The flames prevented them from getting to him."

"That crazy priest and he were so drunk, *they* probably started the fire," Mastino said. Then, frustrated, he made a fist and pounded the table. "Why did Romero do this to me? I didn't make the rules of the world."

"You think the stories are true? He made a pact with the devil?" Nicademo asked. Mastino gave his cousin a look of disdain.

"Devils and angels? As children we decided it was all puffery. No. I don't believe it. But the cannons, the cannons, Nicademo," Mastino said, a vein in his neck bulging. "We need Romero for the cannons. We must find him, console him as the prodigal son. You've put out the reward for him to be brought safely to us?"

"Si, Mastino. Last night. I had it circulated by word in his neighborhood."

There was a knock on the door. It was one of Nicademo's assistant's again.

"An urgent letter, Excellency." Nicademo took the parchment. It had a thick wax seal affixed to it.

"It's from the Bishop of Mantua," he said, breaking it open.

"Luigi's territory?"

"Si," Nicademo said. He scanned the letter, and then swallowed. "You better read this for yourself."

Mastino read the letter and looked up. His mouth went agape. Then he read an excerpt out loud.

"When Feltrino, son of Luigi, left the field of battle at Bella Flora, it was because he was confronted with a devilish apparition he could not kill. It was half man and half goat." Mastino looked up with surprise and amazement.

"That's just how the lensmaker and priest described it," Nicademo said.

Mastino continued reading. "Feltrino, son of Luigi, has sworn with me, the Bishop of Mantua, that these and other facts of devilish warfare are true. Be informed, Mastino II della Scalla, that as Bishop of Mantua, it is my duty to pass on this information of apparent pacts with Lucifer. I shall inform not only Our Holy Roman Emperor, but also your allies, Karl of Luxembourg and Ludwig of Wittelsbach, as well as all Church officials in *Europa*."

"Perhaps, perhaps they were in league with the devil."

"It, it doesn't matter," Mastino gasped. "We must distance ourselves from these accusations. These stories can be serious, true or not."

"What must we do then?"

"I think..." Mastino said, and then he paused. "I think we must abandon the orphans. If they are found, we must jail them and hand them over to the Church. Put out a new order." Neither man said anything, both realizing the import and scope of what they had just decided. Then, in an effort to salvage whatever he could, Mastino added, "Nicademo, all of Romero's plans, they are at the Calabreezi and Bella Flora estates. Go to both yourself and re-trieve everything. Immediately. Then go to Mantua. Gossip from one bishop can be more damaging than an army — or a poisoner. And when you are at Bella Flora, cousin, go into my chambers and bring back my discs for the eyes. I left them there."

Nicademo slowly nodded. The two didn't say another word to each other. Nicademo looked at his cousin sadly, and then he slowly walked out of the room for the last time.

Sitting in his carriage, Nicademo thought about Hansum. He thought back over the past months. He recalled the fine feelings he had when in proximity to the boy, and how he had wished he had a son like him. He leaned against the side of the carriage, gaz-ing into space. He thought about how Romero and the beautiful Guilietta made such a handsome couple when they sat across the table from him at Agistino's house.

"Ashes, ashes, everything is ashes," he said to himself. Then Nicademo closed his eyes, trying to banish these powerful visions from his mind. He decided to nap, but he felt a strong discomfort under his arm and scratched.

Now rich with gold, Father Lurenzano had decided he was best protected if Hansum and Lincoln were dead. As he ran with the neighbors and Ugilino after the teens, he shouted, "I believe they robbed brother Agistino. Their pockets are probably full of gold." Then, out of breath, he stopped and called, "A reward of five florins if they're captured! Dead or alive!" And then he winced with the pain of running, but the wince turned into a sardonic smile as he stopped and thought.

Turning, he made his way back to the burning house, and then, protecting himself from the flames, made his way up the alley to the shop. The place was deserted and dark, lit only by the raging fire across the lane. It was as he had left it, the floor strewn with supplies, broken lookers and spectacles. Lurenzano squinted into the flickering darkness, looking for the spot on the floor. He saw it and walked forward carefully. There was the depression where Ugilino had crushed the demon's talisman. He crept up to it slowly, holding his breath with fear. Within the gravel, a glint of brass sparkled up at him. He knelt down and peered more closely. Nothing. Dare he touch it? He put a dirty hand forward, letting one of his long cracked fingernails scrape against the brass.

CRACKLE! A small spark and then an arch of electricity buzzed. Father Lurenzano fell on his backside and scampered toward the door.

"Master?" a small, weak voice said. "Please, help me, Master." Lurenzano looked around and saw a small glow coming from the shallow hole. "What's happening to me, Master? Where am I? I'm scared," the voice said.

The voice was so pitiful, the priest felt his fears ebb. Then he found himself crawling back to the creature.

"Are you there, Master?" the voice said with a bit of hope. "I can hear you. Please come to me, Master."

Father Lurenzano was now over the hole again. It was no longer dark, but had a dull glow emanating from it. In the glow was a small face, ugly, but not malevolent. It was the creature he had seen earlier, but only the head and much smaller. It floated in the hole, over the brass talisman, looking up at him with innocent eyes.

"Are you my master?" it asked.

"Know you not who I am?" Father Lurenzano asked. The small face looked confused and worried.

"No, I don't," it finally said. "Master, I'm scared."

The light in the room increased. Father Lurenzano looked up through the opening to the loft. The fire from the house had jumped to the thatched roof of the barn. It was now ablaze.

"There's a fire, Master," Pan said calmly. "From what I can perceive, it will spread and consume this room in about seven minutes. However, you will be overcome with smoke in about four. You must leave, Master."

"How do you know this?" the priest asked.

The image hesitated. "I don't know. I think I know many things, but I don't know how. Why is that, Master? Was I injured?" Father Lurenzano was thinking hard and quickly. He looked around. There was a long machete-like blade in the corner. He got it and returned to stand over Pan. The holographic face looked up like a trusting child at him . "What are you doing, Master? You must get to safety. Are you going to kill me? Put me out of my misery?" The Father now looked extremely confused. Was this another devilish trick? He held the blade over Pan. "If you are about to kill me, Master, do it quickly. And I thank and forgive you. It will save me the unpleasant experience of being burned and boiled while conscious." Lurenzano raised the machete. "Goodbye, Master,"

The priest stuck the end of the flat metal blade into the gravel beside the vision, pushing it under what remained of the brass lamp. He loosened and lifted a bed of gravel and dirt under the charm. Father Lurenzano then looked around. He spied, and then reached for, a small wooden box. He put it by the machete and gently let the gravel and lamp slide into it. The hovering face looked down at itself being moved. "Master, you're saving me. Thank you. But hurry. We must go now." Lurenzano gingerly picked up the box and walked to the open door.

"You will do my bidding," Lurenzano said to himself.

"Of course I will. You are my master. I live to serve you."

"You will do my bidding," Father Lurenzano said again, smiling as he walked into the night.

## Chapter 18

Lincoln had to run through the pain of his broken arm. Finally they hid in a darkened, unlocked house. After bolting the door, they looked around in the dim light. A family of open-mouthed cadavers lay on the floor and rough beds. The house was a shambles from being ransacked. A pounding could be heard on all the doors of the street as their pursuers searched the neighborhood. Finally, there was a pounding on the door the boys were behind.

"Let us in," shouted the voice of Signor Spagnoli. "We're looking for murderers."

Hansum and Lincoln looked at each other. Then Lincoln turned around and half covered his mouth. In a high, pitiful voice, he cried out, "Save me. Save me, I'm dying. My children are all dead. Save me."

There was silence on the other side of the door, then a shuffle of footsteps as the butcher left. Hansum and Lincoln stayed in the death house for a good hour, trying not to look at the corpses. Hansum soon wept without any apparent ability to stop. Lincoln put his good arm around his friend's shoulder and they sat in silence.

⧗

When Hansum could finally stop weeping and all was quiet outside, the boys snuck out of the house and slunk from one darkened street to the next, heading to the northwest part of the city. They would find a hiding place and then figure out their next move. They came to some fields lying in fallow and ventured into the middle of one. They crept into a dilapidated shack, and there, on the cold ground, amid rotted wood, abandoned rats nests and old spider webs, they tried to get some sleep. Hansum slept fitfully, an image of Guilietta's burning body haunting his dreams.

As the sun rose, the boys looked out from where they hid. A heavy morning dew covered the ground. From their rat's-nest view, they looked out at the cityscape and city walls. Few chimneys puffed with smoke and no one was about on the street.

"We should have brought Shamira with us," Lincoln said.

"We didn't know the Podesta would put out a reward for us. I thought he was our . . ."

"Friend?" Lincoln finished. "He was never that."

There was a rumbling in the distance. Soon they heard the clattering of metal tools and shouted orders. Half a dozen ox carts piled with bodies, followed by men at arms and about twenty-five civilians with shovels and picks came into view. The two watched in silence, expecting the convoy to head for the city gate. A soldier pointed to the field where Hansum and Lincoln were hiding, and the column turned into their field. The wagons and men stopped about a hundred paces from the decaying shack and the conscripted citizens were ordered to dig. Hansum didn't recognize any of the soldiers, but he recognized a few of the townspeople. Most weren't laborers, but craftsmen or merchants from the market.

"Look, there's Bruno," Hansum said, pointing to the tailor.

After half an hour of digging, they started dumping bodies into the first hole. There were men and women of all ages, clothed and naked bodies, partially-eaten ones, pregnant women, babies, limp bodies and ones in rigor. Several of the carts were full of brush and wood. While some men moved on to start another pit, others piled the flammable material over the hole, creating a high mound. One of the soldiers took a torch and lit a fire. It soon turned into a bright, hot blaze which the boys could feel from where they lay.

"Maybe we should go talk to Bruno," Hansum said, "to see if we can find out anything from him."

"What'll he know?" Lincoln asked.

"I don't know, but we need information. I'd say let's run from the city, but we can't leave Shamira."

"Okay. But I'd better go myself. A guard may recognize you. Nobody really knows me and they probably won't make me help because of my arm."

"Yeah, you're right."

Lincoln crawled out of their hiding place when nobody was looking and walked nonchalantly over to the group. As the odor of burning flesh filled the air, most covered their faces and some became sick. Soldiers and workers noticed Lincoln approaching and stared menacingly at him. Lincoln put up his good hand and smiled. He thumped on his chest lightly, as a way to say he was healthy and strong, except for his arm. Then he pointed to Bruno, who was looking the other way, indicating his reason for being there. Lincoln tapped Bruno on the shoulder, and when the tailor turned, he looked surprised. Then Bruno looked around to see if anyone was close enough to hear them talk. He took Lincoln by the shoulder and walked away from the crowd.

"Thanks to God you are alive," Bruno said when they were out of earshot.

"How is your family? How's Nuca?"

Bruno crossed himself. "Si, si. We're alive, at least." Then he shook his head slowly and his eyes took on much pain. "Such tragedy. The della Cappas, such wonderful neighbors. So beautiful a young lady." He crossed himself again, then flailed his arms. "All gone. Poof." Then he asked. "And Romero? Carmella? Where are they? Are they . . ."

"You don't believe we're witches, do you?" Lincoln asked.

"Of course not," Bruno said quickly. "Not us. But some of our neighbors, the guard, and the Church are after you. That priest wants to burn you at the stake. Where are the others?"

"Romero's over in that shed. Carmella is still at the palace. We don't know how she is."

"You must all leave the city, without delay. You must get out."

"We have to figure a way to get Carmella. We can't leave without her."

Bruno became very serious. "Take me to him. Right away. We must speak."

The two of them walked nonchalantly to where Hansum was. Bruno and Hansum's eyes met. They looked at the pile of burning bodies. Black, greasy smoke rose from the burning flesh. The soldiers seemed occupied, so Hansum took a chance and came out of his hovel. Bruno hugged him and kissed him on both cheeks. And then, with two mournful eyes, he peered at the young widower.

"We're all so sorry to hear about Guilietta and her family, Romero. And this foolishness that has befallen you . . ."

"I don't know what to do, Bruno," Hansum said weakly.

"You must flee, my boy. Flee for your lives. Insanity has gripped the city." The blaze had become so bright and hot, you could hear the fat of the bodies crackling. Workers were backing away from the pile and everyone was becoming more and more agitated. Bruno looked at the two and said, "I must get back. Being seen with you is dangerous."

Bruno was walking back to the mass grave when Hansum noticed an officer riding up on a horse. He was surveying the ugliness when his eyes locked onto Hansum. Standing up on his stirrups, he shouted,

"It's him! The savant! Arrest them! There's a reward!"

Hansum saw many heads turn toward Lincoln and himself. The two teenagers stared down the mob.

"We can't make it together," Lincoln said. "Not with my arm. Go by yourself. Quickly!"

"Shut up!" Hansum said. "Start running!"

The townspeople turned into a mob. The officer on horseback could not go around the group and the flaming mass grave was in his way. He spurred his horse through the crowd. Most cleared out of his way, but the broad chest of the trotting warhorse knocked others aside. For Lincoln and Hansum's part, they were limping across the field with no hope of getting away. Hansum saw a large hole in the ground and ran around it. He saw Lincoln turn to look at the horse, who was closing in on him.

"Lincoln, the . . ." he shouted, but it was too late. Lincoln disappeared, swallowed up by the void. Hansum stopped quickly and turned back. He fell to the ground and peered down into what was an old well. "Lincoln!" he shouted.

The officer stopped his horse and stood quietly, looking down at the two. Lincoln was about a dozen feet down, lying on some rotten planks. The mob descended upon Hansum, grabbing his arms and hair.

"Hold!" the officer shouted. "Let him go! Now! Whatever the Podesta wants this man for, he is still a gentleman and will be treated as such." The officer motioned to the other soldiers, who came around and surrounded Hansum, pushing the townsmen aside.

Hansum leaned back over the well. "Are you all right?" he asked Lincoln.

"I dunno," Lincoln said. "I can't move my legs. But I don't hurt."

"His back is broken," whispered one of the soldiers.

"Do you have a rope?" Hansum asked the officer. "I'll go down and get him."

"Those planks are rotten," the officer said. "It won't hold you both."

One of the mob spoke up. "I know this old well. Under the wood is an old spring. Very deep. You don't want to fall down there."

Just then, the wood under Lincoln creaked.

"Hansum, you better hurry," Lincoln warned.

"Rope!" commanded the officer. One of the mob ran back to the wagons.

"We'll get you out in a minute. Hold on, buddy," Hansum said.

"I can't feel my legs," he repeated. "What a damned way to . . ." and there was another creak from the wood.

"Hurry!" Hansum shouted again. He saw Lincoln struggle to steady himself with his one good hand. Then the youth chuckled.

"What a way ta go." And then the rickety platform shook again. The smile vanished from the youth's lips and he spread out his good arm more, trying to gain some purchase in the soft earth.

"Hurry!" Hansum screamed again. Then the floor broke and Lincoln disappeared into the dark of the shaft. There was a splash, and then silence. "LINCOLN!" Silence. "Lincoln."

"He's dead, Signor," the officer said.

Hansum couldn't believe it. Lincoln's name was now added to the growing list of people he had seen die. In his previous life he had never known a corpse. Now he had lost count.

"At least we got one of 'em," a townsperson said. "We'll split the reward."

"There won't be much, split so many ways," said another.

"We'll share it at the *taverna*," a third added.

"You'll not touch this man," the officer ordered. "He is my prisoner."

The officer drew his sword. Several of the foot soldiers followed his lead. The officer looked down at Hansum.

"Signor, I cannot vouchsafe your person at the prison where I must take you," he said, "but I will get you away from here safely. If you will climb on my horse and promise not to interfere with me, I will believe you."

Hansum's stared at the officer, hardly able to think. Then he blinked slowly and nodded. Two soldiers gave him a boost onto the back of the large horse. The animal danced around for a second, getting its footing with the extra weight. Hansum briefly looked at the well into which Lincoln had disappeared. As his eyes met Bruno's, the tailor crossed himself.

"Never have I smelled a battlefield so fetid, Signor," the officer said over his shoulder to Hansum. "May God grant we never smell anything so putrid again."

# Chapter 19

It didn't take long for Hansum to smell something more foul than the human bonfire. He was taken to the Arena, which was being used as a makeshift prison. As the heavy iron door clanged shut behind him, Hansum breathed in its foulness. The open concourse under the stadium seats was being used as a large open cell. The high, dark arches of the Arena's under-structure, built with ancient cut stone and brick, entombed not only the prisoners, but the air. It was fetid with rotting corpses, both expired and still walking.

Hansum was told to go down the corridor to where people of means were. As he made his way, he had to step over countless bodies of dying and dead. Excrement and vomit were everywhere. Inmates milled around crying softly, wailing and praying. Some were tearing at their clothes, trying to relieve an incessant itch. Where clothes had finally given way, you could see the swollen buboes under their arms and between their legs. The buboes were followed by red splotches on the skin, which soon turned black.

When Hansum got to where the better class of prisoners were, he discovered it did not mean the conditions were any better. He found that he and these others were by a large barred door, where jailers stood on the other side. They were taking turns shaking down those prisoners who had coins or valuables to exchange for favors, small amounts of food or water.

Hansum found himself in the company of men and women picked up for looting. Some were fairly well dressed, and all had excuses. They cursed the soldiers who arrested them unfairly. The soldiers and guards only wanted to steal their purses. Guards came to the cell bars and held out wooden bowls with scraps of food or water. They held them just out of reach, smiling at those who had coins. Hansum paid for a few bowls of rotten food for a mother to feed her dying children. The more affluent prisoners scolded him for such stupidity. He walked away from them and found a quiet spot near a pile of dead. As bad as they were, he knew he couldn't catch the disease from them. He sat there, trying not to think, but images of the fire at the della Cappas' the night before would not leave him. He was staring into space when he saw a familiar form lying, almost hidden, in the shadows.

"Shamira!" She was on her side, limbs outstretched, mouth open, eyes closed. Several black splotches stained her face and arms. Hansum rushed to her side. He rolled her over and she grimaced in pain, but no sound came out. He turned her on her back, took off his hat and used it as a thin pillow for her head. Shamira looked up at him, her eyes infected and oozing pus. She moved her lips to speak, but no sound came out.

"Lie quiet. I'll get you some water." He ran back to the iron-barred door. He shouted at several guards, who ignored him for fun. He screamed again, cursing them and banging at the bars. One looked up and smiled. Hansum screamed for water and he just looked away. Hansum fumbled through his purse. He only had three silver soldi left, plus the gold coin Mastino had tempted him with. He took out two soldi.

"Here. Two. Two coins, you bastard," Hansum shouted. "Come on! Water!"

"Denarii?" the jailor asked from a distance.

"No, you vermin. Soldi!" Hansum screamed.

Several guards ran over to trade a cup of water for two whole soldi.

"It's my turn!" shouted one guard to the other.

"No, it's mine!" argued the other.

"I'll take them both," Hansum spit, reaching in his pouch for his last soldi. He took the water and said to one of the guards, "You better keep hold of those coins. By the looks of that spot on your face, you'll be on this side of the bars tomorrow."

When Hansum got back to Shamira, he sat down on the damp stone floor and lifted her head onto his lap. He gently cradled her head in his arms and spoke lovingly.

"Here, sweetheart. Here. Have a sip of water. Slowly now." She coughed a bit, but was soon able to get some of the filthy stuff down. Hansum then took a few sips from the other cup and kept the rest for later. He nursed Shamira the best he could, dabbing at her eyes and face with a small piece of rag. Shamira looked up at him, croaking out a word.

"Lincoln?"

"Dead," he whispered.

Shamira closed her eyes for a few seconds, then opened them. She stared at Hansum, and he back at her, both with nothing to say. Then Shamira's eyes slowly closed and her breathing became labored. She fell into a deep sleep.

Hours passed and Hansum sat there with Shamira in his arms. Dead bodies continued to accumulate around them. As night came, the air became cooler and the prison fell into silence.

The clanging of a large iron lock being turned echoed throughout the prison. The screeching of the rusted hinges and the flickering of torchlight followed. A deep voice called out through the still air.

"Make way for the death cart. Make way, move aside. The best man's here to claim the devil's bride."

Wailing and pleading among the prisoners began again, as three men pulling a large cart entered. Another, holding the torch, directed the others. The cart stopped at Hansum's feet and the man with the torch looked down at him.

"You're picking gravely poor friends, my son. I'd move to better climes if you don't want to become one."

"I'm caring for my friend."

"Oh, poor duck. She'll be dead and released soon, if she's any luck."

"Just go about your job," Hansum said. "I'll tend to mine."

"Well said, my boy. Well said. You take care of the living and I the dead. Just make way then, move aside. The best man's here for the devil's bride." He smiled and directed his helpers to start. They picked up bodies and heaved them onto the large cart, stacking them like limp cordwood. They ignored the inhumanity of their opened-eyed and gape-mouthed clients, giving no heed to their silent protests. Hansum already knew where their final resting place would be, the fire pit. He tried to expel the image from his thoughts and closed his eyes, burying his face into Shamira.

"What's taking so long?" a jail guard shouted gruffly to the head collector. He walked up and spoke harshly to him. "The live ones are getting hard to handle again. Be gone quickly."

"A few moments more, Signor," he said, smiling.

The guard didn't return the nicety. He just grunted. Then he looked down at Shamira.

"What about this one?"

"Your young signor is tending to his friend. Not to worry. I'll no doubt take her in the morning."

The guard had a staff that he used to touch the inmates. He poked at Shamira's foot. It wobbled, showing no force of its own against the stick.

"Take her now. I don't want her rotting corpse in here all night."

"She's not dead," Hansum protested.

"I said out with it!" retorted the guard.

"NO!" Hansum screamed, pulling Shamira closer to him. She was like a rag doll. The guard growled and turned away.

The dead collector leaned down and looked at Hansum with surprisingly compassionate eyes.

"I'll take good care of your familiar, my friend. I won't bury her until she's at an end."

"I don't want her buried in the pit. Not the pit. Will you do me a favor? I'll pay you."

"What favour would that be, my son?"

Hansum brought out his coin pouch. He fumbled through it and found his last coin.

"Here. I've got gold. I want you to bury her at a church. It will only be a few soldi. There'll be lots left for you."

Without taking it, the man said, "Phew. That's a lot of treasure for an old and never to be older collector of the dead. Enough to bribe your freedom from these kindly guards."

"It doesn't matter anymore. If I die, you can do the same for me."

"Si," the collector of the dead said. He smiled and took the coin from Hansum's fingers. "I'll come for you soon enough. Okay, give us the little dear. Help me, my fellows," he said to his assistants. "Be careful with the little pigeon. Place her gently upon her bed. It's lumpy enough. That's it. Place her down gently."

Hansum looked at Shamira lying on top of the twenty-odd bodies in the cart.

"Goodbye, sister," he said quietly to himself.

"I'll drop her by a priestly friend of mine who'll take good care of her. He'll make her shine in the Lord's eyes," the dead collector said.

"You'll really do this?" Hansum asked weakly.

"Oh, from the Father I won't be 'errin'," the man assured. "Okay, my boys. Let's move our freight," and the three other collectors pulled and pushed the cart back toward the jail's gate. The remaining inmates began to plead and wail again, begging to be released or praying for release.

Soon, in total darkness again, the quiet was punctuated by continuous moans and sobbing prayers. Hansum pulled his knees to his chest, all alone now. He had several years before his inoculation implant would run out, so all he could die from till then was starvation or murder. Both were imminent possibilities. Hansum finally fell asleep. The last thing he remembered of the prison was a sobbing woman asking a question to God.

"*Perche, Dio? Perche? Perche?*"

The light was bright. Even through Hansum's closed lids, it was so bright, it hurt. He could hear people laughing and birds chirping, like at a picnic. Hansum opened his eyes, but still he saw nothing.

"Give it a minute," a cheery feminine voice said. "Shade his eyes."

Someone lifted up their arms and a shadow fell over Hansum's face. Hansum looked up and could start to make out two faces smiling at him. One was a young man, the other a female. The man had his arms outstretched, causing a shadow much wider than his arms could make. What was it that was causing the shadow? Wings? Why would a person have wings?

"Hey, Hansum," the girl said familiarly.

"Welcome, old buddy," the young man added.

"Shamira? Lincoln?" Hansum said, his eyes starting to focus. "I'm in Heaven?"

# Chapter 20

When the time traveler went to secretly check on Podesta della Scalla, he found the noble sitting by himself in his planning room, planning nothing. Mastino just sat, bereft of inspiration and energy. Three days had passed and still Nicademo had not returned from retrieving the plans and Mastino's discs for the eyes.

"We were so close, cousin. So close," Mastino said to the air. "I would have created monuments to make men tremble for thousands of years," and then he himself shuddered.

The traveler watched Mastino from his out-of-phase perch, suspended in time. He made one last note on his pad, transcribing the nobleman's words, and then he touched a node on the side of his neck. Closing his eyes, he thought of his next destination. When he opened them, he was in the planning room of the Bella Flora Estate.

Nicademo lay dead with the rest of them, Grazzana and the lieutenants, Nicademo's mistress, their children, and even the children's dog. Almost half of the Bella Flora peasants were sick or dying. When the time traveler had been there several days earlier, he had see how Jacopo, the one who knew the most about the nitre beds, the saltpeter and black powder, was the first to die. He was therefore one of the few who got a Christian burial. Now bodies were left to rot and the living had taken to wandering from village to village.

Immune to the disease, the traveler stood over Nicademo. The stench of maggots was ripe in the air, but this did not deter him from his mission. He bent down and searched Nicademo's pockets till he found one of the things he was sent for. He removed Mastino's beautiful tortoiseshell spectacles from the dead Baron's breast pocket. The time-travel council did not want the bifocals to become a puzzling curiosity for some future archaeologist. Then he scooped up the papers on gunpowder, cannons and the other inventions brought to the past before their time. Satisfied that he had left no trace in the manor house, he touched his node and thought to go to the next place. In a blink, the traveler was at the abandoned barn. There the barrels of black powder sat, waiting for cannons that would never be built. He placed a device among the barrels and put the plans Shamira had drawn on top of them. Then he walked outside and took in the beautiful country surroundings. They were much like his home in the  thirty-first century. The day was so wonderful that he decided to walk the ten minutes it took to the shack that housed the saltpeter. Birds were singing and there was a warm, refreshing breeze. The only blemish on the day was the distant, slightly sour smell of rotting bodies, both human and animal. Now a safe distance from the barn, he thought the appropriate command. One second the barn was there, and then it wasn't. The black powder ignited into an explosion the size of which wouldn't be made for the better part of a century and a half. The plans and tools for making black powder vaporized. The saltpeter shack received a similar fate a few minutes later.

The plans at the late Master Calabreezi's estate had also been destroyed, as well as any trace of the advanced cannon making. The first cannon, ruined during the battle with the Gonzaga, had been brought back to Calabreezi's for re-smelting. The traveller used a pencil-sized laser to reduce it into an unrecognizable puddle, leaving no hint of its former use. The traveller knew that, in a few years, that same bronze would be used to make a beautiful bell, then a cannon, then another, and finally, a statue of a winsome girl, who millions have seen over the centuries. 'Yes, a much better use for the metal,' he thought.

He looked at his checklist of  fourteenth-century people who had learned future skills. He noted that three of the journeyman bell makers were dead. The fourth had fled on foot into the mountains toward Germany. He would bring a little knowledge to the cannon makers there, but not much. The unused plaster molds were already crumbling, but he broke them more with a handy sledge. The traveller also knew that, within a year, the saltpeter beds would collapse and become temporary mysterious mounds in an overgrown field. They would lie there, fallow, waiting for another generation of unknowing peasants to cultivate the ground around them. The soldiers who had manned the one cannon successfully were all dead. The rest, who had seen it used, were scattered among the thinning ranks of soldiers, all called back to protect the borders and ports from the unseen killer's entry. The time traveller also knew that Mastino would live another five years and never achieve his great ambitions. But he had to admit in his report that the noble had lived in interesting times, done many exciting things and left a host of enduring monuments.

His report followed all the major players of this tragedy. Ugilino survived. There was monumental proof showing that he had even reproduced. With a small stipend of the stolen gold, given to him by Father Lurenzano, he was able to prove his worth to the miller and marry Serindella. And Master della Cappa was right about Ugilino and Serindella's children being ugly. Ugilino's grandson, who looked just like him, was the inspiration and model for one of the Hunchbacks of the Altar by Gabriele Caliari. He inserted a picture of the newly finished sculpture, that he took in the fifteenth century, into his report. "If you want to see what Ugilino looked like," the time traveler wrote, "just visit Santa Anastasia. It's the hunchback with the curly hair and bulbous nose." Since there was no more need for lensmakers in Verona, Bembo moved back to Venice. He worked there for the rest of his life, marrying and having many children. The Satores survived. They made their garments, loved each other and thought of their good neighbors whenever they looked across the street at the burned-out lot.

# Chapter 21

"I'm in Heaven. There really is a Heaven," Hansum said. A familiar voice laughed.

"Heaven?" Yes, that was definitely Lincoln's voice. Hansum squinted as his eyes acclimatized to his new surroundings. There was Lincoln, his arms still spread wide to form a shadow.

"Are those wings?" Hansum asked.

Lincoln laughed even harder. He put down his arms and brought his face right over Hansum's. He smiled his old perfect smile. There was no gap where the tooth had been knocked out.

"Yeah, that's me. I'm an angel," Lincoln joked.

"Here. Let's help you sit up," Shamira said. "You'll still be pretty stiff from sitting on that damp floor in the Arena. Phew, I had almost forgotten the awful stink of the place."

Hansum looked into Shamira's clear eyes, onto her smooth, clean skin. She was well scrubbed and her hair was pulled back into a tight, short ponytail. She was neat and prim and healthy.

"Shamira? Shamira, it's you! Oh, I'm so glad there's a Heaven." Shamira looked at Hansum sweetly.

"No, no, Hansum. We're not in Heaven." Hansum looked shocked. "No, we're not there either," she added. "We're alive."

Shamira was sitting by him on a thick mattress. Lincoln was kneeling over him, dressed in strange clothes. To Hansum it didn't look like clothing from the fourteenth century, or their own, the twenty-fourth. Lincoln wore loose trousers and sandals made of a grass product. His top could be called a tunic. Hansum looked at Lincoln, who smiled, raising his arms to show what had made the wing effect. Lincoln was wearing a cape with the ends attached to his wrists. When he raised his arms, he looked like he had wings.

"It's just a style around here," Lincoln said. "I like it. I even helped spin the thread and weave the cloth." He twirled around to show off his attire. Then he fell to his knees and looked into Hansum's amazed eyes. "It's good to see you, brother," Lincoln said.

"I saw you fall down the well," Hansum said in quiet confusion. "And you." He looked at Shamira's wonderful complexion and thought back to her infected, pus-riddled face not too many hours ago. He reached out and touched it.

"Yeah, I was pretty much a mess," she agreed.

"And that water I fell into was cold," Lincoln added. "The part of me that could feel." Lincoln and Shamira both laughed.

"But, but you're both okay now?" Hansum asked.

"We're all okay now," Shamira said reassuringly.

"Ah, he's awake,"
a voice said from across the room.

"Arimus!" Hansum exclaimed. "You're alive! I thought . . ."

"I'm sorry for the deception.
It was to benefit your perception."

"Then it *was* a History Camp?"

"No, dear boy.
That place was not a toy."

"Where are we now?"

"In the thirty-first century.
At my home in the Kentucky hills.
You're here to recover, to debrief,
to understand, to prepare."

"Prepare? For what?"

"Come into the garden, my boy. Take a walk.
There we will sit, eat and we'll talk."

Shamira and Lincoln took Hansum by either arm.

"Here. We'll help you up," Lincoln said. "Man, it was weird watching you in the Arena. We could see you on what they call a Mists of Time viewer, what people here watch events from the past on. It was even weirder watching me."

"The Arena," Hansum repeated, confused. "Mists of Time?"

As they walked outside, the beautiful dark green hills of Kentucky filled Hansum's vision. The village where Arimus lived sat on a ridge overlooking a river and vast stretches of green. It was a beautiful, sun-drenched day. There were no roads coming or going. All the buildings in the village were low-rise affairs, one storey of either traditional log cabin design or hand-cut stone beehives, which seemed to sprout out of the earth. The windows and doorways had no glass or wood in them, but used energy fields, which allowed in fresh air and light when you wanted it, or kept insects — or whatever it was asked to — out. All around were food gardens, decorative plants and well-groomed paths. One path led to a central courtyard, where Hansum saw villagers congregating for communal meals and fellowship. There was a creek with an area dug out into a deeper pool, where people were bathing and playing. Hansum stared about at the simple, idyllic setting.

"I'm in the thirty-first century? For real?"

"Yes, my boy.
You're all here in the year 3012."

Hansum stood quietly thinking, putting all the information together.

"And you aren't dead. You made us think you were, so we'd believe we were trapped."

"Yes."

"And when Lincoln died, looked like he died, and Shamira . . ."

"Oh, I thought I was dead," Lincoln admitted. "That water was friggin' cold and I couldn't swim up to the surface. I thought I was a goner. But a second later, I found myself on the same mat you just did. And my back was broken. That was two months ago."

"Two . . ." Hansum's voice trailed off.

"It was the same for me," Shamira said. "The last thing I remember, sort of, was you giving me some water in the prison. Then Arimus apparently took me away. But he brought me here only a month ago, in my time."

"Only a month . . ." Hansum began, then, "Arimus? That was you? The collector?"

"Make way, move aside.
The best man's here for the devil's bride.
I believe this is yours."
Arimus handed Hansum back the gold florin.

"Giving up that coin to bury me was pretty impractical," Shamira said, smiling. "But it was nice. Thank you."

"Why did you do this to us?" Hansum asked weakly.

"Oh boy. Now that, you'll never guess," Lincoln said.

"All this to cure us from being hard cases?" Hansum asked, suddenly looking like he could become very angry, very quickly. "All we went through, just . . ."

"It was more than that," Shamira assured him, putting a calming hand on his arm. Then she turned to Arimus for him to explain.

"To hear of hard famines, of war and death,
It rings a lot truer with a witness's breath.
And we choose for these witnesses
those whose aptitude's strong,
To be History Camp counsellors,
helping others along."

"You put us through all that so we'd become History Camp counsellors?" Hansum asked curtly.

"Time-travelling History Camp counsellors," Lincoln added.

"And only if you wish it," Arimus said.
"The choice is for you.
It's an invaluable experience
we can give to but few.
And then we chronicle your experiences
for others to view."

"Others will watch what I — what we all — went through?" Hansum asked.

"It reinforces the lessons greatly.

But only if you agree. "

"But why such extremes?" Hansum asked.

"Because it works," Arimus said. "Because we can. It's the most resource-neutral way of completing the plan."

"Resource-neutral," Hansum repeated. He had heard that phrase many times growing up. Then he stood there, numb, and mumbled, "The plan?"

Arimus showed Hansum to a wooden lounge chair and bid him sit. Then he explained everything to him. Twenty years before Hansum was born, scientists of the twenty-fourth century had perfected time travel. That's when people from the future allowed themselves to make contact. They worked with the government and History Camps secretly at first. He asked Shamira to finish the explanation.

"In our era, time travel is just being made public. It was announced just after we left, actually. But over the past twenty years, select hard cases, like us, were chosen to go back and have experiences like we did, to bear witness and to be shown as holovision programs. We were chosen because our school testing showed we have the aptitude to be time-travelling History Camp counsellors."

"Yeah," Lincoln said. "We're to be at the core of the Time-Travelling Team for History Camps from our century, if we want to be."

Poor Hansum sat quietly, not reacting. He had only recently come to grips with the  fourteenth century and now he had to fathom this new reality. When the explanation was finished, he sat quietly, thinking, calculating. A hopeful look came to his face.

"Guilietta? Is she . . ." he began, but Arimus's look of practiced compassion gave him the answer.

"She was of the fourteenth century.
We could save her not.
We have tried, I have tried,
But you shall see
Blessed time just won't let it be."

Hansum couldn't respond. Arimus explained what a curious thing time was.

"We can go back to the same place in time
and have experiences diverse.
Some go better, others worse.
There's no predestination, free will still abounds,
for us and for them, and as strange as it sounds,
Time itself has a will of its own,
It pushes and pulls us, and sometimes we're thrown.
And when we are thwarted, and events just won't reverse,
We accept it as a mystery, of our great universe."

Hansum sat for a few seconds, staring at Arimus. Then he closed his eyes.

"Guil," is all he said.

Arimus leaned over and took both of Hansum's hands in his. He looked him in the eyes and spoke oh so softly.

"It will take you some months to find your new calm
And understand this new era to which you belong.
Perhaps permission will be given,
not too long in the distance
For you to go back and reverse time's resistance.
Till then, my son, give comfort to your tears.
Guilietta's been free, without pain,
for sixteen hundred years."

Hansum, his face still blackened from the soot of the mass graves and the dungeons of the Arena, looked up at Arimus.

"I've no place to mourn her." Tears welled in his eyes again. To his heart, his loss was not sixteen hundred years old, but barely two days old. Arimus came close to Hansum's ear and whispered.

"After the fire, they found the remains of the della Cappas.
Father Lurenzano, corrupt and in need to hide his foul deed,
Had them buried with some ceremony.
Their place of rest is known to me."

"Where?" Hansum asked, and Arimus told. Then Hansum wept in earnest. Arimus patted his arm, rose, and left Shamira and Lincoln to care for their friend. He saw him only briefly over the next few weeks. Aside from the physical wounds needing healing, Hansum needed time to heal emotionally as well. For where thirty-first-century advanced sciences allowed the youth's physical problems to mend quickly, no remedy had ever been found to heal a broken heart.

During the following month, as Hansum gained the ability to cry a little less each day, he became resolved to one thing: He would become a time-travelling History Camp counsellor and would try to save Guilietta.

# Chapter 22

Several months passed. Hansum, Lincoln and Shamira were back home in their twenty-fourth century when Hansum contacted the others.

"I'm going to Verona tomorrow. Will you meet me?"

The next day they all met in Signori Square. The palace and many of the surrounding buildings were still there. The square itself had been built up about a meter higher than in the fourteenth century. Several of the palace's arches had been bricked in. This made the buildings seem a little less grand. Where the captain of the guard had been stationed, in the middle of the square, there was now a large statue of Dante Alighieri. When they had last looked at Santa Maria Antica, there was only the one monumental sarcophagus of Cangrande della Scalla. Now there were three raised tombs. One held the remains of Mastino. Hansum looked at it and remembered this complex man, a man of his times. If Hansum couldn't forgive him yet, he was beginning to understand him. They toured the inside of the palace. The three walked around slowly, memories washing over them. Most of the furniture was different and many of the windows were larger than in the fourteenth century. The marble floors and stairs were exactly as they remembered, except that they were worn or chipped in places.

Taking in their surroundings, the three separated and walked about, immersed in their own thoughts. Hansum stood for a while in what had been Nicademo's office, remembering him sitting behind a desk. Then he found himself in Mastino's planning room. The big table was still there. He thought back to when, while facing Mastino, Pan had hopped around on the table behind the Podesta, trying to get Hansum to understand what he was miming. Hansum smiled as he remembered his friend, Pan. He thought of the time he spent over that same table with the Podesta, explaining things to the noble that Pan had just explained to him. Then his mind wandered to the others he met during his adventure. He thought about everybody, but mostly, he thought of Guilietta. 'As time goes by,' he wondered, 'will I truly remember her face?'

"Dead. They're all dead," he said quietly.

Lincoln came into the room, excited.

"Hansum, come here. You've got to see this." He took his arm and pulled him down the hall, into a sitting room. "Look," he said, pointing to the wall.

Hansum's breath left him and tears filled his eyes. Shamira came in and saw what he was staring at.

"Oh, you idiot," she said to Lincoln.

"Oh man, I'm sorry," Lincoln said.

"It's okay, pal," Hansum managed to say.

It was Shamira's drawing of Guilietta, the one which the Podesta had liked so much. It had survived the centuries and was now on display in this obscure room. And then Hansum did a strange thing for a person of the twenty-fourth century. He got down on his knees, like he had learned at the Church of San Zeno, crossed himself and said a prayer for his dead wife. The other two joined him. At the prayer's completion, Hansum looked at the image of the smiling girl, her beautiful eyes staring at him through the centuries.

"Let's go to where she's buried," he said. "To where they're all buried."

Soon they were at San Francesco al Corso, the Church where, so long ago, the boy known as Romero Monticelli married the girl he had fallen head over heels in love with, Guilietta della Cappa. Now, a millennium later, Hansum was making his first visit to where his wife was buried. He took out Arimus's sketch, to show him where the grave markers had been.

They were long gone, centuries ago, and Guilietta and her parents' bones had long turned to dust. The ground above their final resting place was now neatly-cut lawn. It surrounded a simple well with a wrought-iron top. Coincidentally, this same site has been worshipped by millions over the centuries as the burial place of another Guilietta.

Hansum got to his knees and took a note from his pocket. It was a page created from special crystals and written with a similar ink. It was indestructible, either by the elements or time. Only when the sun went nova, consuming the earth, would it perish. Hansum closed his eyes and said another prayer. He crossed himself, kissed the note and kneeled on the grass. With one hand, still strong from working on the lathes, he dug down into the earth. He rubbed a bit of the heavy humus through his fingers. Perhaps some atoms of what had been his beloved had migrated up over the centuries. Then he placed the note in the hole. The sun's rays glistened off the bright surface and Hansum read the words aloud.

"I love you, Guilietta. When I next see this note, we shall be together again."

Hansum covered up the hole, smoothed it down, rose and walked away. He didn't look back. Shamira and Lincoln walked abreast of their friend, each slipping an arm through his. Then they all walked out from the protection of the cloisters and into the world.

They walked along a path, right by Arimus, who hovered unseen, suspended in time. He watched them, a smile on his face. As they passed out of view, he looked down and spoke the final words of his report.

"And without a doubt,
this is what the journey
is all about."

So, what's next for Hansum, Shamira and Lincoln?

To find out, read the third and final installment of the Verona Trilogy, entitled

# The Loved and the Lost

In it Hansum, Shamira and Lincoln go back in time, over and over again, trying to save Guilietta. But Time turns out to have a personality of its own and fights back.

Now, being a time-travel saga, you'll get to revisit many of the characters you've either come to love or hate. You'll be able to see our three protagonists, as well as Guilietta, Agistino, the Signora and Pan, as well as Ugilino, Mastino, Beatrice and others.

Not even Lory knows whether the teens will be able to save all or any of them. You see, as of this writing (April 2011), *The Loved and the Lost* isn't finished yet.

To keep up to date on what's happening with the History Camp series, visit our website. On it is Lory's blog, links to interesting sites, comments from readers, and a link called Back Story. This is an ongoing essay with extra information about both the historical events and all the future world building in the novels.

To visit the History Camp website, go to:
## www.history-camp.com